First Light
Tales of the Vanguard: Rune Saga Book 1
Verity Rose

TALES OF THE VANGUARD: RUNE SAGA BOOK ONE

VERITY ROSE

This book is dedicated to my loving wife who has stood by me through everything. Every tear shed, and every smile gifted was one of the driving forces finally bringing my author's dreams to fruition.

To our darling son:

May this book remind you that you never let the realities of life stifle your creativity, imagination, or joy

Finally, to the earliest supporter of this story:

Leah Wells. Without your input, energy, and excitement, this project would never have seen the light of day, nor would any future creation.

Vendreya
To Borros
To Zent
Forest of Ruin
Hyra
Guldin Castle
Guldin
Nejera
Fort Black
Rosendale
Lake Hyra
Faradin Pass
Faradin
Port Monte
Lorn
Lake Fera
Selde
Jilt
Ternfeld
Locke
Morrovaan Ocean
Greatwood
Lakeside
Dorn
Corsa
Hilden
Uldera
Dena
Greatwood Lake
Tri-Spire
Jelmoore
Volar
Castle Nyer
N
W
E
S

Contents

Prologue

From nothing, Chaos began. From its oceans, beings embodying Order formed, becoming the gods. It was they who found a weakened world, one of many created and destroyed by the toiling of Chaos. It was they who isolated it, protected it. It was they who imparted their Order and blessings to its inhabitants.

- Excerpt from *Origins of All* compiled by the Archpriest Henner of the Crucidian Church

Rune

Surrounded by open fields, broken only by the occasional knoll, a group of six people stood at the ready for their hunt. A gentle spring wind whipped through their hair. Some kept their eyes trained on the tree line in the distance, while others maintained a careful watch over the skies above. Each carried a hunting bow in hand with a quiver full of arrows strapped to their backs. Simple iron short swords clung to their hips. Of the six, two of the people were shorter than the rest, appearing to be only twelve or thirteen at most. Simple leather armor covered their forearms, chests, legs, and feet.

One of the two children was a girl with blonde hair and brown eyes, while the other was a boy with hazel eyes and silver hair. Both of them exuded a nervous yet excited energy that was only barely contained, thanks to the occasional, stern glance of one adult with them, who had similar silver hair to the boy.

"Keep your eyes on both the sky and the forest canopy. The beasts move quick and if you aren't careful, you could end up with a few broken bones, or worse. Got it, Arkrune? Tara?" the silver-haired man barked.

"Yessir, Vickar, sir!" Tara giggled while giving a mock salute.

The only response the man had for her was to sigh before he glanced back at the trees. Arkrune stifled a small laugh, when the sound of screeching drew his attention to the treetops. Several brown blurs launched into the air in a loose, V-shaped formation. The objects initially soared straight into the sky above the trees but were clearly moving toward the hunting party.

Vickar brought two fingers to his mouth and let out a loud whistle. In an instant, the group scattered, breaking into pairs. Arkrune and Tara paired together, diving to the right of the formation while Vickar took the center. Arkrune clipped his bow to his back before drawing his sword. Today's hunt had him acting the part of the distraction, while Tara was to pick the birds off.

Bash Eagles were not strong beasts, but their aerial maneuverability made it difficult for all but the best marksmen to target them in flight. The best way to hit them was to catch them by surprise in their nests or by baiting them into initiating their diving attack. As their name suggested, they dove at their enemies with their hardened skulls. Once the diving attack started, they lost all of their previous agility for a devastatingly powerful attack. This state left them vulnerable to a practiced hunter.

It was a dangerous gamble because if the person acting as bait was hit, then the resulting impact could be rather deadly.

Culling the local population into small hunts like this was a tradition for their village of Locke. Neither Tara nor Arkrune had been on a prior hunt. Both of them had been training with Vickar for months and pestering him for a chance to put their practice to the test.

Being out in the field after so much begging sent Arkrune's heart into a wild beat. *This is what I wanted. A sense of adventure, action, excitement. Truly, this is...* The cries of screeching beasts drew his eyes back into the air and cleared his mind. There was no time for flights of fancy. As the bait, he needed to attract the Bash Eagle's attention and give Tara an opportunity to strike. By becoming a moving target and waving his sword around, he hoped to create an enticing opponent for at least one monster. His father had taught him a technique sure to draw attention, but now was not the time for it, as it could draw the attention of all the beasts present.

Two birds broke off from the pack, aiming directly for his position. Tara shouted something, but the roar of his heart in his ears drowned out almost everything else from Arkrune's perception. He knew what the plan was—what he was supposed to do—but being in the moment was different.

Both birds began their dive with a terrifying amount of speed. They seamlessly transitioned from a graceful glide into a nosedive with a single large flap of their massive wings. With them bearing down on his position, the boy found his body refusing commands. The panic froze him in place. No longer was he in the gravel training pit his father had made; now he was facing a true threat to his life, and it terrified him.

When the dull yellow eyes of the Bash Eagles became visible, Arkrune's brain started working once more. It was too late; there wasn't enough time for him to react. Moments before the first monster reached him, Tara's small frame appeared as a blur in the corner of his vision. With a loud, high-pitched scream, the girl rammed her shoulder into the belly of the monster. It squawked in surprise as the impact forced it to relax the powerful back muscles that kept its spine and skull straight. The Bash Eagle crashed into the ground, spraying up clods of dirt and grass. Debris pelted the side of Arkrune's face.

The second monster flapped its wings and quickly soared back into the sky. Now that its prey was obscured, it had retreated to the safety of the sky until it came into view once more. *That was incredibly close.* The boy swallowed what felt like his heart jumping into his throat.

"Chaos take me, Rune! You froze!" Tara shouted. She crouched protectively over his body after he sank to his knees from the shock. "I can't believe you right now. Get up. There's more to this fight."

Arkrune stood with the help of his best friend's outstretched hand. She had a silly grin on her face, clearly putting in a lot of effort to stop herself from making a sassy remark. Before she lost her self-control, Tara lightly shoved the boy's shoulder with her fist. They turned to look along the ground, where the Bash Eagle had landed. It was sprawled out with its head unnaturally folded into its back.

Tara was lucky that she managed to slam into a special pressure point near the stomach of the monster. Because of a hard enough impact at the right location, she had forced it to relax the strengthened muscles in its neck. Without that increased reinforcement, it had no longer been able to withstand the impact.

A loud screech yet again pulled their eyes to the sky to see the remaining monster gently flapping its wings with its furious gaze locked onto the corpse of its ally. Crying out in frustration, it dove once more. As they were both standing near one another, it was hard to tell which person it was aiming for. Before they could organize their thoughts, Arkrune and Tara bolted in opposite directions.

The monster stuck out one of its wings slightly and pitched itself towards Tara. Once he noticed the change, Arkrune planted a foot on the ground before twisting his body and redirecting the energy into his leg muscles. Using his own form like a spring, he darted in the exact opposite direction. It was like how the Bash Eagles themselves moved and was a staple in the primary fighting style his father had taught them in.

"Tara, watch out!"

Arkrune held his sword with both hands, grasping the hilt. The stitching in the leather bit into his palms from the force of his grip. Time slowed to a crawl as the visual information of the world around him seemed to flow into his mind at an ever-increasing pace. The boy's small body moved faster and faster, something the girl he was trying to protect seemed to notice.

With a sharp cry, Arkrune swung his sword upward toward the monster. Using the energy of its own dive in opposition to his swing, the boy tried to sever the bird's head from its body in one clean strike. At first, there was resistance, and his arms and bones ached. Just as he felt his grip loosen, he suddenly felt a warm sensation spread through his body. His strength increased. The two pieces of the monster's corpse rolled along the ground, splattering blood and gore over both of them. Tara's bright eyes turned as wide as saucers, stunned by the display. Shortly after, a massive grin spread across her face.

Arkrune panted from the exertion. Strangely, it felt that his breathing was from excitement more than anything. Not even a hint of exhaustion existed anywhere within his body. Every muscle burned with energy as if prepared to take on an army of beasts. The ache from earlier was simply a memory. *What is this? Is this battle-lust? Father told me of it, but it doesn't quite feel right.*

His thoughts were interrupted by Tara's body colliding with his own. "Rune! That was amazing! Thanks for the save!"

Both of their bodies fell into the grass as she tackled him to the ground. Tara's brilliant smile was unmarred by the blood painting her cheek. Peals of laughter escaped her lips as she clumsily released her hold on him. Arkrune noticed a hint of blush on her cheeks as she did so and was going to say something before an angry yell interrupted their celebratory hug.

They looked toward the source of the voice and both paled when they locked onto Vickar's enraged expression. The other hunters averted their gazes as they began working on breaking down the beasts for materials. "You damned brat! By Chaos, why did you freeze? You could have gotten yourself hurt or killed. Do you know what your mother would have done to me if I brought her son back crippled?"

A worried tone underlay Vickar's angry shouts. Arkrune's shoulders sank, prepared for a punitive strike. It never came. Instead, his father's larger form wrapped around him with a near choking embrace.

"You damn fool! You froze, but you recovered quickly. You even protected Tara. Good. I'm glad you're alright."

Arkrune looked beyond his father's shoulders to Tara who was standing beside them. She had a concerned look in her eyes.

"Live combat differs from training, I know. However, you must always be on your guard. A moment of delay can lead to devastating consequences. My son, you are far too young to walk into Death's embrace." Vickar continued as he pulled away from him and rested a calloused hand atop his head.

"I'm sorry, Father."

"Good." Vickar nodded. "I will be taking the next two months away from the forge. During that time, you and I will be training non-stop from sunrise to sunset. That will be your punishment."

Tara gave him a pitying glance before she slinked away, hoping to remain unnoticed by Vickar. Unfortunately, she was not so fortunate as the blacksmith's heavy hand took hold of the collar of her shirt. "Not so fast, lil' missy. You will be joining us. Get ready, both of you. Take the rest of today to rest. Training begins outside the forge tomorrow morning before the sun rises."

Vickar laughed evilly as he stood and walked away from them. Arkrune felt the beginning of a headache forming but was easily distracted from the pain by Tara placing her slender hand on his forearm. Each gave a solemn nod before standing and assisting with the harvesting of the Bash Eagles.

Rune

Back in the village of Locke, they sat under the shade of a tree. It grew atop a hill behind the church's graveyard. From there, a pleasant view of the ocean and small fishing piers greeted them. Ever since they had been allowed to venture about town without an adult, Tara and Arkrune had frequented this spot to play and relax.

Only a handful of hours ago, they had faced down their first life or death experience, and in less than twenty-four more they would be subjected to two months of torturous training as punishment for Arkrune's panic. Still, while they had this moment to relax, they enjoyed it to its fullest. As such, they rested side by side in the soft grass, letting the cool breeze blow over them. It was Spritendus, the second month of spring, so the gentle breeze brought with it the pleasant smell of flowers that grew along the base of the hill.

"You know, you don't have to work at the church when you grow up," Arkrune muttered, only barely audible to his friend.

Tara sighed but gently smiled while she turned to lay on her side and face him. She brushed her short, wavy hair behind her ear and away from her eyes. "I told you this already. It's something I want to do. If I don't work for the church, I will have to take over the shop for Dad. And I don't know if you knew this, but I'm not really merchant material." She laughed softly, joined by a small huff from Arkrune.

"You can always join the Vanguard with me, you know? You fight just as well as me. By Chaos, you are way better at the bow than I am, and you can keep up with me pretty well using the sword, too! Gods, you saved my ass earlier!"

"Rune, you know that's not the kind of life I want to live. It is good to know how to fight to protect yourself, but seeking out fights..." Tara sighed once more, though in a much sadder manner. "That just isn't something I want."

"Stop calling me Rune," the boy said. "My name is Arkrune, you know."

This time, his friend squinted her eyes at him with a teasing expression. She jabbed her finger into his cheek. "Ah yes, the boy from a small village with the name of a hero. My apologies, mi'lord. You are destined for greatness. Pity me, good sir, for making a mockery of your regal name."

"Stop that!"

They laughed together for a moment and wrestled each other for a few more. Years ago, the odds of winning had been much closer to even, but as they grew older, Arkrune had grown larger than Tara. Such an advantage led to his victory in their short bout, ending in them flopping back onto the grass once more.

"I think Rune suits you better. Besides, when you become an S-Ranked warrior, don't you want the people to sing your praises instead of mixing you in with the praises of some long-dead legend?" Tara whispered.

"I guess that makes sense." Arkrune nodded in agreement. He glanced between several leaves above their heads and contemplated her words before clenching his fist with renewed determination. "You're right, Tara. When I register for the Vanguard in a few years, I will do it under the name Rune! When I become S-Rank, I'll come back and we…"

He glanced at Tara, whose face suddenly felt much closer than before. A faint rosy hue colored her cheeks. "What will we do when you come back?" she whispered after his voice trailed off.

Arkrune gulped slightly. "Uh, we will…"

The sound of a bell interrupted him mid-sentence. Someone had rung the central bell outside the chief's house, which also served as the town hall. Before rising, they exchanged an unsure look. There was no scheduled meeting today, leaving them to wonder what was going on.

Chapter One

Rune – A Few Years Later

Rhythmic pounding of someone hammering metal pulled Rune from his slumber. Rubbing the sleep from his eyes and stretching his arms and legs before him, he deeply inhaled the fresh morning air. It tasted clean at first, but there was a subtle hint of soot flavoring it. A fact of life in the village of Locke. His door was slightly open and through the crack there was a feminine face peering at him with glowing purple eyes.

His precocious sister stuck out her tongue. She threw a wet rag at him with a laugh before she slammed the door and ran off. Their mother's voice could be heard from the hallway that seemed to chastise the girl. It was firm but, in a way, gentle.

Rune took a moment to adjust to being awake. Once he had done so, he remembered it was the twenty-fourth of Spritistus. His birthday had been two days prior, which meant today would be a big one for him; one he had been waiting on for a while.

"Arkrune, get up, please. I know Ulma already gave you the washcloth. Clean up and get ready for the day," the same voice called out.

"Yes, Mother!" he yelled back while using the cloth to wipe away any dirt that had accumulated from last night. "And remember Mom! I go by Rune now! Not Arkrune!"

His mother laughed out, "Yes, yes. I know sweetie. To me, you will always be my little Arkrune. Now, hurry! Your father wants you at the forge."

Rune performed his morning exercises by stretching his limbs and joints. Out of his eighteen years of life, the last decade had revolved around exercise and combat drills from his father. Because of that, he had developed a toned form and habits for staying both fit and limber. After all, pulling a muscle mid-battle was a pain. Literally and figuratively. Once finished, he hurriedly washed himself. Rune donned his simple shirt and leather pants before he rushed out the door to head to the forge near their home. Springtime sun, joined by a comforting breeze, refreshed him the rest of the way, truly preparing him for the day ahead.

At the anvil, just a few steps outside the home, Rune found his father. He was a tall man with a chiseled, muscular physique. Even now, Vickar's form felt massive to his son. In his hand was a short sword that was still glowing hot. The man frowned before he set the weapon back on the anvil. There was a slight flash of violet light as he swung the hammer. Rune watched in awe as a shining vein of copper-like metal seemed to grow and burrow itself deeper into the glowing steel of the blade. Vickar repeated his swing three more times, sending out showers of orange and purple sparks. With each strike, the off-color metal changed its shape and pattern. He inspected the weapon again, this time garnering a slight smirk from the smith.

Rune's father quickly quenched the blade and again, a slight flash of light came from the sword as the oil sizzled and popped from the heat. Vickar was one of several smiths in the town of Locke, though he was the only Wanderer and the only smith capable of smithing this expertly with a rare and delicate metal occasionally found in the village's iron and copper mines. Vickar removed a pair of goggles that guarded his eyes, revealing a raccoon-dog style band on his face, although inverted from the beast's black mask. He had silver hair like Rune. Vickar's eyes also glowed a faint purple color similar to Rune's younger sister, Ulma.

As his eyes glowed, so did the coppery veins of the sword. Even from this distance, Rune could feel the power dripping from the blade. It was yet another masterpiece by his father.

"Son! Come here. Test the feel of this sword. I haven't added a handle or guard yet, but I want to see what you think of it so far."

Rune stepped up and grabbed the sword from his father. The metal was still very warm, though not too uncomfortable. To Rune, the blade felt decent. It was off balance at the moment because of the lack of a guard, pommel, or handle. Its base was that of quality steel. On the tang, there were three dots of the same metal, alderite. Each was about the size of a silver piece and was connected to what he knew to be a complex matrix of the metal folded, and blended throughout the entire weapon.

Rune shook his head at his father's creation. Three contact points were a bit much for an altered short sword, but then again, Vickar had definitely woven a large amount of alderite throughout the steel that was not visible from the surface. He nodded in affirmation and handed the weapon back to his father.

"It's a good sword. Three contact points, though?" Rune questioned. "A bit much, don't you think? It's not like it's a longsword or an axe."

Vickar's face scowled. "Well, see if I go the extra mile for you anymore. I thought you would want your first sword to be special when you leave, but I guess I was wrong!"

Blood drained from his face before he apologized profusely to his father. It seemed to fall on deaf ears as Vickar turned his back on his son. While Rune showered his father with apologies, niceties and all manner of placations, his mother, a woman in her early middle years with dark brown hair, walked up with a mug of ale and a pitcher of tea. She laughed as she handed Vickar the ale and poured a cup of tea each for herself and Rune. Rune saw the massive smile on his father's face which revealed that Vickar was, in fact, teasing him.

She laughed along with her husband at Rune's expense before wiping tears from her hazel eyes. Rune did not inherit his father's special eyes from his people's bloodline, like Rune's sister had. Rune instead took after his mother in that respect. Like all those with active Volari blood, Vickar and Ulma had purple eyes that changed hues, depending on several factors. Rune also took after his mother's middling stature, leaving him on the smaller side of average for a boy his age.

Tears of laughter soon turned into light sobs. Even though they had long established today as the day of his journey, the woman still grieved for the reason her husband had made this sword. Rune was eighteen this year, which was the coming of age in the Faradin Kingdom. Normally, it was a time of one's life when they would look to get a job in town and start finding their own place in life and making their own family. Rune was not interested in that right now, though. Rather, his interests lay outside the borders of his home village. Rune wanted to join a caravan out-of-town, bound for Hilden, where he would finally take up membership with the Vanguard.

Vanguard warriors visited Locke frequently and brought with them tales of adventure and grandeur. All of which fascinated a boy such as Rune, who felt stuck in the small village. As for why they visited such a place so frequently? This place was important to them, as it possessed both an iron mine and a copper mine nearby. Both were metals whose ore veins sometimes contained impure alderite. Alderite was so similar in color to copper that it was often confused for it. At least, until someone tried imbuing it with Aura, something that could not be done with copper. That same rare, copper-colored metal was laced throughout the sword currently being given a pommel by Vickar.

Another factor in their frequent visits by the Vanguard was the fact that the southern territories of Faradin had a higher concentration of Organization members than the north. Southerners relied upon them to handle most of their monster and bandit problems. At least, those that the citizens themselves could not handle. Vickar also attracted many of their warriors to his home, as someone capable of using Aura to manipulate alderite and blend it carefully into any weapon he made. He was a highly skilled Wanderer who was unaffiliated with the Kingdom of Volar, where most smiths like him usually resided.

Of course, Vickar was just one man and the Vanguard's numbers were un-countable, so making a weapon for every warrior who asked for one just wasn't possible. Most of the warriors who showed up simply bought raw alderite to return to their own smiths or hunted in the Greatwood that bordered the village. While the Greatwood bordered many villages, Locke was at an intersection of the dangerous forest and the Wyverntooth Mountains, meaning that the monsters from both often fought each other for territory. This made it somewhat safer for some of the Vanguard to collect materials and venture a short distance into the Greatwood's depths.

Rune looked down at his feet for a moment, somewhat unsure about his future. He was concerned he might not be able to use the sword his father made. Only Awakened humans or people who inherited Volari blood—like his father and sister—could use the sword the way it was intended. It was unfortunate, but Rune had not inherited those abilities from his father's bloodline. His mother was a human and had no known Awakened relatives on her side, so Rune's chances did not look good.

"Father, the Goddess of Innovation blessed your work again, or maybe Lady Fate determined it was time to make such a masterpiece." Rune sniffled. Lydia looked at her son with caution and Vickar had a look of mock annoyance, which failed to hide the pride on his face. "I don't know by whose will you made such a blade. Though, I may not be able to use such a great gift, you know. I fear you might waste such a fantastic weapon on me."

Vickar huffed as he hammered in the final blow to seat the pommel. The sword was now complete. The handle was made from the trunk of a petrified tree and the cross guard was inlaid with Rune's name, written in the ancient tongue of the Volari, Vickar's people, before had become a Wanderer. The grip was leather and had three small circles of alderite peeking through; screws that reached to the alderite spots on the sword's tang.

"Arkrune," Vickar said calmly, gently putting his hand on his son's shoulder and shaking his head. "No. Rune. You are going to join the Vanguard and whether you find out you can use this sword on your own or not, I made this for you."

Vickar pointed the bottom of the pommel at Rune. The small spike at its base glinted orange in the morning light. Vickar continued, after seeing the knowing look on his son's face, "I made this for you to fulfill your goals. It comes equipped with a core. I have it surrounded in a small steel shell so no one can tell what's there, of course. I have also charged the core well beforehand. You can use this sword, whether it is with your own power, or borrowed."

"Father…"

"Rune, it took many hours to extract enough material to make a core this pure. It is my best work and this sword will serve you always. If you find that no one among the Vanguard will charge it for you, then…well, I guess you have an excuse to come see your mother and me now, don't you!" Vickar finished with a hearty laugh.

Lydia hugged her son tightly while Rune felt a powerful sense of pride and respect for his father rise to form into a lump in his throat. Rune grabbed the sword gingerly while his father set down his tools and handed Lydia a belt and sheath for the sword to hold temporarily. Ulma stumbled out of the family home with a set of light clothes, leather studded armor, and bracers in her grasp.

"Here, brother," Ulma mumbled with a slight glisten in the corners of her eyes. "Mother and I worked together to get you a nice change of clothes to use during your application exam. And some light armor. It's not much, but maybe you won't die with it on."

Lydia lightly smacked Ulma on the back of the head for her last statement before helping Rune put on the leather armor and bracers while Vickar tightened the sheath and equipment belt around Rune's waist. When they were finished, Vickar stepped back and appraised his son before turning around to dig behind the counter. He pulled out a small shield. It was diamond-shaped with a large, round metal stud in the center. Surrounding the central stud were several smaller ones. Vickar also pulled out a few leather straps and metal clips. Rune held out his left arm while his father attached the small buckler to Rune's bracer. It locked into place with a satisfying click before Vickar moved to clip the bracers to the sleeve of his son's armored shirt.

Rune stepped away after he was settled and looked down at himself. He fit the picture of a perfect newbie Vanguard warrior, perfectly primed for the next steps of his life. Looking at his sheath, he noticed that there was a second sheath, empty, right next to it. He looked up at his father, confused, when he saw his father holding a normal short sword. There was no inclusion of alderite. It was a simple sword.

"Remember, an altered sword is stronger and sharper than all others when it is charged during use, but if you use it or block with it while not charged, it'll snap. Alderite rarely binds well to other metals. Because of that, it weakens the integrity of the weapon. Also, the vibrations of battle when not charged might cause interior cracks to form, even if you don't see them on the outside. This will cause the transfer of power to be inefficient, weakening its overall effectiveness," Vickar reminded his son.

"Yes, Father. If not enhancing the altered sword, use a regular instead. Thank you," Rune affirmed, sheathing the second weapon.

Rune was slightly worried he would stand out too much, having an altered sword before he was even a beginner with the Vanguard. Few F-Rank members had the funds to afford one, but Rune did not care. A major part of being an alderite smith was being able to test your work, so his father was quite handy with the sword and had passed those skills on to his son and daughter. Rune figured he should be able to handle himself from anyone trying to take his stuff. Plus, if he didn't unsheathe it around others who weren't trustworthy, no one would know he even had it. At least, that was what he hoped. These cautionary steps were predicated on anyone actually caring, though.

Rune hugged his family once more, saying his last goodbyes for some time before he headed towards the town inn, where any caravans leaving town stopped before departure. Ulma walked after Rune before he was out of sight.

"Rune! Aren't you going to say goodbye to Tara before you go?"

Rune stopped and shook his head before he shouted back, "No, I spoke with her yesterday about my trip. If I go talk to her again, I'll have to avoid her parents. You know how they feel about me. I'll send letters when I get to Hilden. You can take them to Tara for me!"

Ulma rolled her eyes at her brother and clicked her tongue. Vickar laughed and shouted out in a dangerous tone, "Hold on a minute, boy!"

Rune stopped in his tracks before turning to face his father, who had a scary look on his face, sword in hand. Rune gulped. "I suppose I have time for one last lesson before I go…"

Vickar chuckled and motioned for his son to follow him to a sparring ring they had set up behind the forge. It was a simple dirt circle that they had dug out and lined with stones and filled with a bit of gravel. Rune felt the familiar crunching beneath his feet as he went to the center of the training ring his father had basically raised him in.

Despite being a blacksmith, Vickar was also a highly skilled warrior. He had trained both Rune and Tara on everything he knew about his preferred fighting style, as well as several others. Vickar was a master fighter with most weapons, but his specialty was the short sword with a buckler. This was the same style that Rune had taken a liking to as well, which made Vickar's life easier.

Rune had also received training in a few other things growing up, like the bow and daggers. These had proven rather useful in life since he and Tara spent a lot of time hunting near the woods for Bash Eagles and general game. Her skill in the bow outclassed his own by spades, but he knew enough to keep up at least.

"Alright boy, head out of the clouds," Vickar shouted. "Ready yourself. You attack first."

Rune brought his standard sword out and held it at the ready towards his father. He wanted desperately to use his newly gifted weapon, but this was a sparring match and he was not used to how it felt to wield a charged weapon in constant combat.

Once he felt ready, he stepped forward with an attack on his father's left side, which the man easily blocked. Rune followed up with a lunge towards Vickar's chest that was easily slapped away by his father's sword. Rune smiled as he followed the momentum and added to it by spinning and performing a leg sweep. Doing so allowed him to simultaneously duck under Vickar's slash towards the shoulder.

Vickar jumped back to avoid the sweep and gave a brief nod of approval before following up with an attack of his own. Vickar slashed down with an overhead strike. Instead of blocking it head-on, Rune stepped just slightly to the side and overlapped his blade with the edge of his shield just as the strike was going to land. Vickar's blade connected with Rune's and slid down the length of Rune's sword and shield, planting itself into the gravel. With his opponent's blade stuck in the ground, he kicked Vickar in the chest while smacking his wrist with the buckler. His father stumbled back and Rune followed up with a quick slash, leaving the point of his sword at his father's throat.

Vickar grinned widely at his son, clearly proud of his performance. "Great job, son! I can happily say you are ready to make your way into the world. I cannot believe you bested me. It was only a few years ago I took you to fight you and Tara to fight your first monsters. Now look at you."

Rune eyed his father with intense annoyance. "You held back so much that it would have been embarrassing if I lost. Thanks, Father. I will do my best to make you proud."

Rune sheathed his weapon and gave his father, mother, and sister one final hug. He noticed a slight hesitation from Ulma, but quickly dismissed it as her not really wanting to say goodbye to her brother. He did not know how long he would be away, after all. He glanced at his humble home and the forge Vickar had built set apart from it. His childhood was here, but his future lay elsewhere. Rune was destined for more than this, or at least, that was what he believed. Hilden awaited and, with it, his life of adventure.

Chapter Two

Rune

Rune rushed into town at a dead sprint. Excitement filled every fiber of his being. Near the gates to Locke was a carriage that would set him on a path to the rest of his life. People yelled to him to either slow down or shouted pleasant goodbyes. Vickar was a boon to the economy and ingratiated the family with most of the other merchant and trade families in town. Because of this, most people knew who he was on sight.

Rune slowed briefly as he passed the general store belonging to Tara's family. It, like the rest of Lock's buildings was a simple wood structure with a thatched roof. The rough-hewn log walls were larger than the neighboring buildings, indicative of the large shop space inside. Before he could stop himself completely, the door opened slightly as someone exited. The person who left the building was short with blonde hair, just like Tara. It was her mother and her eyes flitted around quickly before settling on Rune. The moment her eyes locked onto him, his look of nervousness faded and turned into anger.

"Leave. How many times have we told you, stay away from here, you damn brat!" the woman shouted, raising her fist.

The commotion attracted the attention of Tara's father, who also emerged. Before he could fully come out into the street, Rune rushed ahead faster. Less than a minute later, he was in sight of the inn. Out front was a caravan made up of four different wagons and carts preparing for travel.

The carts were meant for wares and were filled with ore, ingots and simple weapons and were covered with tarps. Those were being pulled by donkeys and mules. The covered wagons were meant for people and were attached to horses instead. The difference was likely so in the event of an attack, the wagons with people could rush away from danger. As a merchant, you could replace your cargo, but money was useless if you could not keep your head.

Surrounding the carts—aside from the merchants and porters transporting goods—were a set of warriors. Several men and women surrounded the goods while wearing all kinds of armor, but a few stood out. One warrior was stout with green hair. He wore full plate armor and had a great sword strapped to his back. There was also a tall yet lanky gentleman wearing leather armor lighter than even Rune's with a longbow draped over his shoulders along with a quiver. The lanky man also kept several daggers around his waist. The final warrior of note was a woman in her late forties, or maybe even early fifties. She was exceptionally fit, and by facial features alone, looked to be a kind woman. Though with her massive frame, she also looked like she was both able and willing to cleave someone in two with the two-handed axes hanging at her side.

Next to the three dangerous-looking ones, none of the other warriors appeared to be anything special. At least to Rune's eyes. He could not understand why, but something about the air they gave off felt powerful. A small voice in the back of his mind screamed at him to run if he ever pissed them off, or better yet, just stay on their good side in the first place.

"Hey, kid, slow your roll." the large woman stated while stepping forward with one hand raised. Her other rested casually on the head of one of her axes. "Don't get too close to the merchandise. What is it you want?"

Rune pulled a paper document from his hip pouch and handed it to her. It was a simple contract that caravans gave out to people who paid for passage. "Don't worry, I paid! I am supposed to be traveling along till Hilden!"

The archer stepped forward and examined the document and compared it to his own before nodding at the woman. "Aye, it checks."

"Sorry, kid. We just gotta do our jobs and make sure no one is try'na pull somethin'," the woman said as the archer passed the paper back.

"Oh! That's more than fine, ma'am!" Rune said, giving her an awkward salute.

The guards all gave Rune an odd look before sighing and returning to their duties. An embarrassed warmth spread to his cheeks. The scary woman shook her head and hiked her thumb towards the covered wagon, showing Rune where to get settled for the trip. For a moment, he thought she flashed a smile, but he dismissed the notion. The cart itself was nothing much and was most certainly not built for comfort. There were other things were inside of it aside from people. Much of the space was also filled with barrels and goods.

That makes sense, I guess, he thought. *Have to maximize profits by using all the space you've got.*

The other guards and members of the caravan moved about quickly, checking things off their lists and doing head counts of the passengers. After a few moments, Rune noticed someone had exited the inn; the owner. He seemed to argue something with the elderly merchant Rune had purchased passage from a few days prior. It was eventually resolved by the not-so-subtle change of coins from one hand to another. The innkeeper saw Rune and gave him a big smile, bidding the boy goodbye.

Another hour passed and Rune nodded off from boredom before some guards clambered into the wagon, startling him awake. His tired appearance solicited a few chuckles from the group, which caused a slight red blush to move across his cheeks. He had not even left town to begin his new journey before he had already embarrassed himself. Rune figured he would need to do better than to fall asleep from boredom if he wanted to make it into the Vanguard.

There would be times in the field when hunting monsters or bandits where he would have to pull all-nighters or spend several hours on watch. If he could not be trusted to do those simple things, what use would he be in a party? The simple answer was none, Rune decided. What he would be was a liability and he could not be the reason someone got hurt. He clenched his fist with a renewed determination. This behavior actually brought a small smile to the mouth of the 'scary woman' Rune had spoken with earlier as she watched over the boy.

"Go ahead and get some rest, kid," the woman said. "The excitement will pass faster when you sleep. Someone will get you in a few."

Rune sighed and closed his eyes once more. The vibrations of the cart in concert with the rhythmic clomping of the horses lulled him back to his slumber quickly. As his consciousness faded, the scent of fresh spring and the sounds of a gentle humming filled his senses. He suddenly felt a small tug at the back of his mind that told him he wasn't in the cart anymore.

A gentle voice whispered into his ear, "Not yet, my dear Rune. We will meet soon. For now, simply rest."

As quickly as the sensation of being elsewhere had arrived, it vanished, replaced with dreams of grandeur and hopes for a life of adventure.

Vickar

A few hours after Rune left home, Lydia was preparing lunch for the family. Vickar did not plan to continue his work at the forge today since he was distracted by his son's departure. He told his wife that it was bad luck to his people to work on a day someone left on an important journey. As the dedicated protector of the family, he could not risk spreading bad luck to his loved ones.

Lydia giggled to herself the entire time Vickar fumbled around before settling on that explanation. There were three things that Lydia obviously found wrong with his excuse. First, she knew Vickar was a Wanderer—a Volari who purposefully renounced both their homeland and their culture. Second, she knew her husband more than he knew himself and could easily see how sad Vickar was to see their eldest leave the nest. Of course, what father would not be worried about sending their child into the great unknown that was the world?

The last and final reason was not at all as important as the first two, but it still applied. It was that no such belief existed at all among any culture in the known world, let alone Vickar's homeland. Vickar knew Lydia like the back of his hand and appreciated that she did not call him on his bullshit. Regardless of how much she wished to do so, with the desire to tease him written plainly across her face.

Vickar watched his wife lovingly prepare their meal and listened to his daughter Ulma hum while finishing up the latest batch of clothing patches she and Lydia had agreed to do this week. Vickar always thought that he would have a child blessed with his eyes who could forge alderite with him and pass on his skills to the next generation. Rune had not been born with this trait, but Ulma had been. Vickar sighed at the twisted thread of fate that blessed him with a child who was interested in the forge but lacked the trait to excel, and also have a child who had the trait to excel and lacked the desire to forge.

Vickar still remembered the day that Rune and his friend had first told the family of his son's future dreams of joining the Vanguard. He wanted to become one of the famous wandering warriors who traveled the kingdoms of the world fighting monsters, saving villages, and become a legendary S-Ranker. His heart had dropped out of his chest when Rune shared his dream, knowing that his son could just as easily become a hero as digested in the belly of some swamp monster halfway across the world. It was as if Vickar had ordained his son's desire for adventure and action by virtue of his namesake. *Perhaps Fate herself is playing tricks on me. Would not be the first time.*

He had done everything he could to make Rune give up. Vickar ran his son through stricter drills and harsher training than even he experienced. All that effort to push him away through fear and exhaustion... Still, his son never stopped holding onto that dream. Nothing stood in his way as he trained in the sword every day with both Vickar and Tara. He had also learned how to wield a smith's hammer like his father, how to perform repairs, as well as how to recognize quality steel from junk polished to a shine.

While Vickar reminisced about the past, and renewed some of his worries, a petite hand rested on his shoulder. Vickar looked at his daughter, who stepped up behind him and locked eyes with him. There was a bright glow to them today that was not normally present. Vickar shook his head. He had known it would happen to her one day, like it had for him. Normally, a Volari had to meditate and practice in order to activate the special sight their eyes would give them. However, Vickar had a very strong bloodline for this special sight, so it was no wonder Ulma just naturally developed it with no effort—just as he had. Ulma had awakened her abilities long ago, but the sight had yet to come. At least, before today.

He reached out to gently pat her head with a warm smile. Ulma did not return the affection or smile, and Vickar shuddered slightly at her icy stare.

Ulma leaned in to whisper in Vickar's ear, "Why haven't you told Mother? Why didn't you tell Rune?"

Vickar instantly knew what it was that Ulma referred to. Vickar had been in the forge every day, from dusk till dawn, working on Rune's sword for a month. He did not know when it was that Ulma's eyes became able to see the Aura that surrounded and flowed through them all, but he already understood what she saw. He experienced the same feeling after seeing Arkrune at the moment of his birth.

"They don't need to know yet," was the only answer he felt he could give. This was a world with many dangerous places and monsters. Even more danger-ous people. He had done what he could to prepare his son, but there were some things that were better left found on his own. Rune's journey was his own and while it probably would have helped to teach him more, train him more, maybe even reach out to an old friend... that just wasn't the path Vickar had chosen.

Ulma was unimpressed by his answer. She huffed before she turned around and left the room. Vickar knew Lydia had seen their daughter's frustration with him, but just shrugged her shoulders before she set the table. Vickar continued to ponder the situation. He knew he made a dangerous gamble sending Rune on his way to join the Vanguard without knowing how to use his Awakened powers, but it felt just as dangerous to keep him here and train him alone. Struggle granted strength. When Rune arrived at Hilden, he would interact with an Awakening Crystal and would be able to fully understand what his class was. Everything would be fine. *Perhaps my friend will find him, anyway.*

Chapter Three

Rune

Rune woke for his watch just a few hours after leaving Dorn, a town south of Locke and halfway to Hilden. Sleep had nearly escaped him due to excitement, but exhaustion had taken hold in the end. It was to be his first watch with the guardsmen who promised that after they left Dorn, they would teach Rune the ropes. He also gleaned through listening to some conversations that some fighters were not simple caravan guards, but a few were actually hired Vanguard. They would be his future comrades, and he wanted to learn a thing or two from them if he could.

As far as Rune could tell, the archer who had examined his travel papers, the woman wielding two axes, and the armored warrior with a great sword and plate armor were all members of the Vanguard. He had yet to witness them do much in the way of fighting, but the way they carried themselves and the general air about them screamed veteran warriors that far outclassed your average guardsman. Even though they had only left Locke a couple of days ago, Rune could at least determine that much.

While Rune hopped out of the moving wagon for his turn on the watch, he noticed that one of his allies for his first round was the tall archer. After getting a better look at him, he noticed the man was wearing a thin green cloak that covered most of his armor. Surprisingly, he had a decent amount of leather fortifying his wiry frame that flashed from behind the cloak every few steps. What really drew the youth's attention though, was the bow slung over the man's shoulders. Occasionally, there was a small metallic gleam that would flash in the morning sun's light as it caught the front of the bow.

The man seemed to notice Rune's curious glances and smirked before taking the bow from his back. He held it out in front of him. He gestured for his partner to inspect it. With permission to have a closer visual, Rune carefully analyzed the bow from a few angles while the owner continued to hold it. Rune could tell by the firmness of his grip that the archer had no intention of letting it leave his grasp. This was a 'look but don't touch' situation, not that he cared.

At first, it appeared no different from a typical hunting bow. Nothing seemed unusual regarding the type of wood and the string. Once Rune's eyes settled on the front face of the weapon, though, they widened in moderate surprise. Running down the front length of the bow were a series of copper-colored rings. Each ring was connected to another by a thin line of the same metal that ran from tip to tip of the bow. It was inlaid deeply in the bow's wood. Any normal bow would be weakened by the process of inlaying metal that deeply into the wood. Not only did it present an extreme risk of the weapon snapping, it also could cause simple problems with the firing of an arrow if it affected the spring-rate of the wood itself. Fatigue from repeated use would also wear out the metal eventually, leaving behind cracks that broke the alderite circuit.

"Is that an altered bow? You actually got someone to inlay alderite into it? Not many people do that! It is so expensive and it…"

The archer smiled and returned the weapon to his back before responding, "Yes. I know down here my bow is a rare make. I hail from the north-western coast. Far flatter that way. Long-distance fighting is standard with the beasts there."

"Are you saying that you infuse the bow to increase the distance your arrows fly? That level of control must either be insane, or your Aura reserves must be massive to maintain it constantly."

The archer chuckled at Rune's childlike interest. He explained that he had easily pegged Rune for a potential applicant the moment he showed up for the trip. No one normally carried two swords of different makes. Of course, the man already knew one was altered, while the other was nothing special. He explained that only Vanguard or highly skilled knights did that. Rune was obviously neither of those, so he figured the young man was intending to become a part of the Vanguard. Rune was flabbergasted by the archer's astute evaluations.

"What do you know about Aura?"

"A decent amount," Rune answered honestly. "My father is a Wanderer, so he's taught me a bit."

The archer paused for a moment before leaning uncomfortably close to Rune's face. He scrutinized the boy for a few seconds before shrugging and saying, "You don't have the eyes. Might still be an Awakened. Rare, but possible."

Rune shifted uncomfortably, but said nothing. He could not bring himself to admit to a prospective comrade that while he clearly didn't have the Volari eyes, he also has shown no inclination or capacity to store Aura within him like an Awakened. There was one instance in his childhood that made Rune think he might have the capacity and was just a late bloomer, but nothing ever actually came of it other than a painful experience.

Vickar had also told him he was an Awakened human, but did not elaborate beyond that. Rune still had yet to exhibit any signs of showing his Awakened Class. Fortunately, the Vanguard still enthusiastically accepted normal humans who were not Volari or Awakened. This was especially true in the southern territories, where the populace relied heavily upon the organization's services to supplement their lack of regular soldier patrols.

Rising through the ranks without the ability to see, manipulate, or even use Aura could be difficult and expensive. Rune still had hope, since it was not uncommon for an Awakened human to be unable to learn their class or use class skills without help from an Awakening Crystal. Still, they could infuse Aura into altered weapons. Unfortunately, Rune could not do even that much.

Suddenly, Rune's companion made a strange whistling sound, like a bird call. A few of the people resting in the wagons glanced at him. The archer made a fist close to his chest with two fingers pointing up before waving it in a small, circular motion. The caravan continued at its pace, but the resting guards in the caravan started to wake and become alert without making much sound. The two others Rune suspected were Vanguard casually jumped from the cart with smiles on their faces, greeting the archer.

They fell in line and, while maintaining a relaxed disposition, whispering unintelligibly between themselves. Rune was confused before he felt a small chill down his spine. Something was watching them. Something was close. Movement amongst the trees and shrubs drew his eyes to them, but that did not feel right... The towns and roads in this area all bordered the Greatwood, a massive wooded region home to many beasts and monsters. Sometimes bandits would make camps short distances into the woods, but never more than a few hundred yards in.

Rune felt the shiver a second time and flinched, moving his head a few inches to the left. A dark purple streak flew past his face and impaled the bench of a wagon behind him. An arrow vibrated slightly in the wood, buried a few inches into it. A moment later, more arrows started buzzing past. Rune brought the buckler attached to his gauntlets in front of his face while pulling out his primary sword. It was too early to use his altered weapon, and it might only make him a bigger target. Rune rushed towards the direction the arrows flew to guard the merchants and distract the attackers.

Right as he stepped out into the field, he felt a tug at the back of his neck before being thrown backwards onto his rear end. He glanced up in anger at the large woman who had flung him to the ground like a doll. She smirked back at him before kicking Rune back into the dirt when he tried to scramble to his feet.

"Stay down, kid," she ordered; her hands drew the axes from her hips. "You'll get your chance to fight when you get to Hilden. For now, stay down. Stay alive."

The man with the great sword nodded in agreement at the woman's words as he turned around and planted his sword in the dirt. After clapping his hands together, a dull purple ball of light formed between them before it slowly expanded outward. The dull glow quickly became a bright light. The man cried out, "Shield: Area Barrier!" The light dimmed suddenly, then flashed brightly. A gigantic wall of purple light surrounded the entire caravan. Arrows continued to fly from between the trees, but none met their targets. They harmlessly bounced off the massive wall encircling them.

Rune noticed beads of sweat roll down the warrior's face; his knees shaking. "Any time now, boss. This ain't forever, ya know. Gods above, this sucks."

The woman smiled and ran toward the arrows, calling forth the other guards to follow. Her eyes blazed momentarily at Rune, a silent order for him to stay put. The other guards followed and as they reached the wall of light, Mr. Greatsword released his ability and finally fell to one knee, with the sweat from the exertion pouring off his brow. Though Rune was confused at first, he realized the man intended to rely upon his weapon to act as a support once he canceled his ability.

Mr. Archer stepped up and released several arrows into the woods. He had been monitoring the specific locations the attackers were targeting them from and intended to return the arrows. The front of his bow glowed a similar shade as the barrier as he drew his string back. At the moment of release, Rune could have sworn he saw a slight shockwave left behind by the arrows. Several more shots flew from the archer in rapid succession, each either finding their mark or flushing the enemies out of their positions.

Bandits shouted orders from the woods and surged forward. There appeared to only be about ten of them, but that might not have included all the ones who were shooting from behind cover. Their swords clashed, with the guard quickly overwhelming the bandits. The scary woman easily outclassed every bandit who dared approach her. Her twin axes each fended off a different enemy. Once the guard advanced with the help of the large woman, it took mere moments for the attackers to lie on the ground, defeated, with their blood soaking into the dirt.

Rune felt another chill from behind him. Danger. He swung his sword backward and felt his blade connect with metal. The new arrival held a dagger out and had barely blocked his sword in the crook where the blade met the guard. The dagger and its owner's arm shook beneath the pressure. Thankfully, Rune was stronger. He was not normally in positions where there was a direct competition of strength, so this was a toss-up.

The enemy jumped back quickly as they released the hold against Rune's blade. Unable to compensate for the lack of resistance, Rune fell forward. Taking advantage of the opening, his attacker rushed forward and slashed the weapon downward onto the back of Rune's neck. Just before the strike landed, blood sprayed into the air from the assailant's neck where an arrow had pierced their throat. Rune saw the person's eyes widen with fear and then fill with pain as they gurgled out incoherent words.

After the person collapsed, Rune noticed there was a subtle purple light coming from them before being replaced with white as they rolled into the back of their head. The attacker was Volari, likely a Wanderer, if they had stooped to banditry. They wore pure black clothes with no sign of armor or padding. Their intention was obvious: finish the fight quickly, in one strike and without having to deal with the risk of retaliation.

Damn, I froze. He groaned internally. *Just because it's a person doesn't mean I can stop like that. Father would have killed me himself had he seen that. No more. You're joining the Vanguard. Get it together, Rune.*

As he examined the would-be assassin with a shamed expression, the other guards and the three Vanguard warriors gathered the bodies of the fallen bandits. They collected the decent-looking weapons among them and then piled the bodies to burn. Leaving them untouched could cause disease or attract monsters from deeper in the woods. Either scenario would be terrible.

A few hours later, when the fires burned out, the group continued their trek to Hilden. Rune was told he could rest in the wagon again until they reached their destination. He thought about arguing, but after witnessing such a commotion, he decided against it and simply did as he was told.

The woman with the axes approached Rune and congratulated him on surviving his first encounter on his journey. "By the way, kid, the name's Mona. The archer is Lex and the pansy gasping for air still is Tabor. We're Vanguard based out of Jelmoore, but we spend a lot of time in Hilden and frequent the routes between them and Locke."

The man with the great sword, Tabor, looked at Mona with eyes full of indignation. "Woman, how many times I gotta tell you that this shit takes a lot out of me? Next time, why don't you do it? Oh wait, you can't! 'Cus, you ain't a Shielder like me! Best stop pestering me before I find another party that treats me better!"

Mona and Lex laughed, and Rune wore a big grin. It sounded like these three had worked together for a long time. Rune was glad they finally felt he was worthy to know their names. The friendly exchange also excited him. Rune hoped that one day he could join a party and be as close with them as these three clearly were.

"My name is Rune!" he answered excitedly.

Mona

A little while after the ambush, the party was still a day away from their destination. Lex continued to monitor their surroundings while Mona replaced Rune on the guard's rotation. Lex broke the silence after a few hours. "That Volari was a Shadow-Weaver. Scary stuff."

Mona nodded. "I figured. I am concerned why someone like that was spending time with bandits this far away from Volar. Could be a Wanderer, but still. Skills like that rarely lead one away from their home. Good thing you caught on to his presence in time."

Lex shook his head with a grim expression. "Wasn't me. Was the kid." Mona looked at Lex with a raised eyebrow, prompting him to continue. "Kid noticed them before me. Swung around to catch him, too. One or both of us would be dead if he didn't somehow notice him."

Mona nodded slowly and looked towards the wagon with a gaze of surprise and mild respect. She had not expected a country bumpkin and son of a smith to have beaten Lex in battlefield awareness, let alone a Shadow-Weaver.

"Dodged an arrow, too," Lex stated plainly.

Mona was even more impressed now. To her, it seemed the kid had talent. She wondered how well the kid would do on the entrance test and training. She also wondered if the kid had it in him to work with Hilden's resident problem child. The thought of Rune working with them made Mona chuckle to herself. *They would get along famously,* she thought sarcastically. *I'm gonna make sure that kid gets in. Awakened or not, that kind of innate awareness he has will keep him alive. And if it keeps him alive, it'll keep his party alive.*

Tayven

"A gain!" a commanding voice shouted, dripping with annoyance. "You'll practice swings till your arms fall off! After that, you'll run around the walls till your legs fall off!"

A young man currently undergoing cruel and unusual punishment gasped, desperately trying to draw in the air his lungs so desperately craved. He was tall, with deep blue hair, and fairly muscular. His arms had started trembling twenty minutes ago, and now he felt they might actually fall off. The young man did not know if this was some form of punishment for the mistakes of a past life, or if his instructor was simply a demon in disguise. It felt a bit much for what had actually happened...

"Alright! That's enough!" the trainer shouted. He watched as his victim collapsed in a sweaty heap on the ground. "Fine. Call it a day. You'll run tomorrow morning before lessons. I think you've had enough. Don't do it again." He turned around and left the training hall the two had been in all day.

Its wooden floors were covered in scuff marks, with some visible gouges that had yet to be repaired. The blue-haired trainee dropped his practice sword with a *thud* as he immediately sank to the ground. He massaged his wrists, making sure they were still useable after his torture.

"Lord Tayven, some water for you." A short butler walked into the room carrying a pitcher of water to refresh the noble's body. The young noble's brown eyes hungrily stared at the jug of life before him.

"Thank you very much," Tayven gasped between gulps of water. "I'm thinking that demon has it out for me."

The attendant chuckled. "Well, you wouldn't have to do these extra practice sessions if you just showed up on time to the normal ones. Here at the Vanguard Academy, even nobility is treated equal to the common folk, so no special treatment for you, Young Master. Besides, you are the one who elected to take these extra courses before formal registration."

Tayven nodded. He knew that attending the Academy would mean no special treatment by staff or peers. In truth, it was the main reason he came all the way to Jelmoore from his home in the trade city of Nefera. Most of his peers attended the Noble's Academy in the capital, but that was not what Tayven wanted. He was the fifth son of the lord of Nefera, so he was out of succession unless all four of his brothers died or gave up their succession rights. Not to mention he was a bastard with a different mother. With those facts in mind, he had decided to take a different path in life.

The butler gestured for the nobleman to exit the training hall and partake in dinner for the evening. Likely a bath too. Tayven nodded and began to stand and exit before he realized he could not move.

"Um…" he began. The butler chuckled again before coming to his lord's side and helping him walk towards the bathhouse.

"Young Master. To avoid such a scenario in the future, I would suggest you not show up late to the next training session."

Tayven nodded grimly at his servant's words. He again thought he was being punished for something else. Being late did not feel like an adequate reason to torture him so. After the two reached the bathhouse, Tayven could walk by himself once again. He stepped inside the baths and was welcomed by steam and the scent of herbs and oils. The natural hot springs beneath the Academy were a boon to the students who attended as the water, along with the herbs and oils infused in them, helped tortured muscles relax after long days of workouts and exercise.

Tayven sunk slowly into the hot waters and felt the tenderness of his muscles instantly vanish. A satisfied sigh escaped his lips as he sank up to his neck. Everything felt right in the world; so long as he didn't move his arms at all.

Almost an hour later, Tayven left the bathhouse with some water still dripping off his dark skin. He returned to his quarters, where a lukewarm meal awaited him on a small table next to his bed. It was simple slop compared to the meals he had grown up with. However, he knew it didn't need to taste good, since he was going to scarf it down before passing out, barely touching his tongue to the food. Tomorrow, the practice instructor would probably have him run laps around the walls of the academy just after dawn, and then he would have to attend afternoon classes. All he needed was the energy, not the flavor.

"What's on the menu tomorrow?" he asked no one in particular, while grabbing a notebook he used to track his weekly itinerary. Even though he was not a formal student yet, those who moved in early were required to participate in some base level activities. "Aura Theory...damn."

Tayven wasn't stupid by any means, and he wasn't annoyed at having to partake in an intellectual pursuit. He was simply tired of learning so much about Aura Theory without putting that theory into practice. In a few months, the Academy would host a delegation from Volar, and returning with them would be the Aura Arts instructor. She had taken a leave of absence to see family several months ago. Only when she was present could the school host the Awakening Ceremony, a ceremony where the students at the school would learn what kind of Awakened they were if they were one. This was assuming the student had not already learned of their Class.

Tayven knew he was one, but did not know what class he possessed yet. Realistically, there were only three options for him. He could end up as a Shielder, a Pulser, or an Enhancer. Others were possible, but not likely. Just like all young men with a passion for the sword and a dream of heroics, he hoped his Class was an Enhancer, able to strengthen his own body with the mythical powers of Aura. Only time would tell for him, of course.

Chapter Four

Ven

Dozens of thoughts ran through Ven's head at once. None of them were flattering or kind. She did not appreciate the newcomer in the Vanguard's Hall, and she certainly did not enjoy witnessing how chummy they seemed to be with Mona and Lex. Their party was only gone for a little over a week on a mission to Locke to fetch alderite and kill a few beasts coming from the Greatwood. Yet it seemed they found the time to pick up a stray and brought it home.

The silver-haired boy walked slowly through the building, looking at everything with doe-eyed innocence. It irked her, watching him investigate her home like it was some sort of carnival attraction. Seemingly able to feel her glare, the boy turned in Ven's direction and gave her a polite smile, accompanied by a small wave. In response, the young woman simply rolled her eyes before she returned to her grueling training.

She had been learning how to shoot from Lex ever since she had found out she did not have the aptitude to be an Enhancer. She knew she was Awakened, but the Vanguard Hall in Hilden was only in possession of a damaged Awakening Crystal. In its current state, it could only reveal someone as an Awakened and show their class if they were an Enhancer. Anything else, and it was simply a useless hunk of rock.

Before Lex left with Mona's group, he gave her an assignment to shoot from dawn until dusk. Alternatively, she could shoot until she hit the bullseye one hundred times in a row. Whichever came first would successfully complete the task. By this point, her skills with the bow outclassed people of her same rank, but that was not good enough. She had to get to Lex's level.

The young woman watched from the corner of her eye as Mona walked up to the Hall Master to discuss something she couldn't hear. Ven turned back to her target and counted the arrows in the center until she reached seventy. She sighed in defeat, still having not gotten to Lex's goal for her before dusk. She knew it was less about the number of perfect shots she made and more about muscle training, but she still wanted to surprise her teacher by doing both.

Lex walked up to his pupil, saying simply, "Good job. Seventy. Not bad."

"Yeah," Ven pouted. "But I really wanted to get to a hundred."

"Were these in a row, or did you miss a shot in between them?" Lex asked. He took her hand to examine the callouses on it. His fingers pressed on a few pressure points to relieve some aches in her hands.

"No misses...If I missed, then I cleared the target before shooting again."

"Then it's good enough for now," Lex finished as he put one hand on Ven's head. He lightly patted her raven-black hair before walking away. It was a simple gesture, but it meant the world to her. Her teacher was a man of few words and even fewer actions. She had always looked up to the man as she had grown up in the Hall, so she knew that this sign of affection meant a lot coming from him. At this point, he was basically her uncle...

"Venraya!"

"Master!" Ven snapped to attention and faced the leader of the Vanguard Hall, who also was her father. The man walked up to the girl and gave her a pat on the shoulder.

"At ease, kiddo. This here is Rune. He's gonna be joining up with us here, and I need you to show him the ropes as his senior." Ven's father, Jacob, instructed. "When we sign him up tomorrow, you'll also take him on his application quest. Don't let me down."

Ven's mouth tightened into a thin line as she nodded. She was not looking forward to acting as a babysitter for some starry-eyed newbie. Conflicting emotions welled up inside her though, since this was also the first responsibility her father had given her. Ven might have grown up in the Hall, but she had only actually become a member a year ago, only just recently completing the requisite ten jobs to move from F-Rank to her current E-Rank. She eventually decided that this was a net positive and gave her father a full smile and tapped her fist over her heart. "Got it, pops!"

Her mother walked up to the duo and wrapped the girl in a massive hug. She was much larger than Ven, which made her feel like a child yet again. Granted, she was only nineteen, just a year older than when most kids left the nest. Mona smiled as her daughter begrudgingly returned her motherly affections.

"Thanks, Ven. He's a good kid. Got a good feeling 'bout him, so be nice," Mona said while gently stroking her daughter's hair. She then gave a small nod to Jacob before walking off to submit proof of her team finishing the escort job at the reception desk.

The silver-haired young man rubbed the back of his neck awkwardly before addressing her directly. "Nice to meet you! The name's Rune. Thanks for having me!" He put on an unnecessarily charming smile as he extended a hand to her.

Ven took it half-heartedly and gave a single, droopy shake. "Right, same. Rooms are this way. Your exam will be tomorrow. Let's go." She led Rune up the stairs to the second floor, which was just next to the entry doors to the building. After leading her charge past several doors, she stopped by the last one at the end of the floor before another set of stairs went up again.

She opened the door and guided Rune inside, showing him the small amenities he was afforded as a newcomer. "Right. So, the first month's rent is free. After that, the standard rate is ten silver a week. If this place isn't good enough for you, the inn further down the road has bigger beds and better food for thirty silver a week."

Rune nodded at his guide. "Thanks, this will do just fine, since I don't need anything fancy. Closer to the training hall, after all!"

"Right. Well, that's assuming you pass your exam tomorrow. Meet me at the front desk after sunrise and we will head a bit out of town to hunt a Bash Eagle,"

Ven said quickly before turning around and leaving Rune in the closed room. For a moment, the newcomer perked up at the mention of the monster they hunted, but it vanished quickly.

Rune

Rune watched the door close and heard the latch click. He sat back on his bed and looked around the mostly empty room. It was furnished with a single bed, a small trunk at its foot, and a desk in the corner. He stepped over to the desk and found it was already stocked with a quill, some ink, and paper. A pocket-sized ledger book was also stashed in the drawer. Rune guessed it was a gift for keeping track of your coinage from quests and expenses.

The Vanguard assumed that most applicants could read and write. In fact, it was one requirement on joining to prove that you could understand the job notices you took and could read any specific orders you were given. Thankfully, Rune's father had taught him how to read and write from a young age, so that was not a problem for him.

He placed the ledger into the pouch on his belt for safekeeping after marking down his current funds. Rune then unhooked his twin sword sheaths from his belt and leaned them against the head of the bed against the wall, while placing his belt on the back of the desk chair. He sat down and began writing a set of letters home to tell his family and Tara that he had made it to Hilden and was about to take his entrance exam to finally become a member of the Vanguard like he always dreamed.

In his letters, he described the eventful trip where they ran across a large party of bandits and the Volari with the ability to manipulate the shadows. He also told them how after that, Mona and her party talked to him like he actually existed instead of basically ignoring him. Mona was extremely kind. Lex was very reserved, but still approachable...and Tabor was a loudmouth. Granted, he had had little time after the fight to actually talk to Tabor since his Area Barrier skill drained most of his stamina and he conked out for several hours afterwards. Remembering the man passed out in the wagon with his tongue hanging freely from his mouth brought a smile to Rune's face.

It turned out he and Lex were Shielders, or Awakened with the ability to crystalize Aura into defensive shields. Apparently, Tabor had been practicing on using the wide-ranging form of Barrier to help in buying time for allies to prepare for a counterattack. It was effective, but it also took up almost all of Tabor's Aura reserves to do it. After he ran dry, he would often collapse from exhaustion.

Mona teased him about it being the first time in a long time that he hadn't passed out after using the skill. This concerned Rune since Tabor could not maintain a barrier while passed out. He could have just as easily wasted his energy instead of giving his allies time to fight back. Of course, Tabor called Mona out on her bullshit and claimed he never once passed out and that the last time he had gone down, he was just 'resting his eyes.' Later, though, Rune overheard him complaining that something 'weird' had made it harder to activate his skill.

At first, Mona had dismissed him, until Lex also had stated that charging his altered bow seemed to draw more power than usual and was more difficult to maintain. Mona had taken their concerns seriously, but Rune had fallen asleep nursing a painful headache before he could hear them finish the discussion.

Rune loved seeing the true party dynamic between the three after they had kept themselves reserved with Rune in their presence. It seemed they had been feeling him out at first, but something about the bandit fight changed their minds and told them he was a 'good egg,' as Mona put it.

I really like them. Mona especially is a really kind woman on the inside, he thought. *Surprising Venraya is her daughter. They aren't a lot alike, and it feels like she doesn't like me very much. Or maybe she's just abrasive by nature.*

Rune left out the gory details to avoid worrying his mother too badly, but he was still excited to share what his first outing from home was like. He also declined to mention the freezing incident to keep his father's wrath at bay. After finishing up the letters, he folded them and put them in the same pocket as the ledger before starting to undress and lay down to rest. Tomorrow was going to be an exciting one for him, since he was going to go on his examination quest.

Just as he was removing his shirt, there was a knock at the door. Rune reflexively called for them to enter, as if he were still at home. The door opened to reveal Venraya had returned to tell him something.

"Hey, Mom—I mean Mona, wanted to invite you to dinner," she stated. They both froze as he stood there, half-naked, with his shirt pulled over his head and around his arms.

"You dumbass!" she shouted before slamming the door shut. "I'll meet you downstairs, you idiot!"

Rune paused for a moment, not quite registering what had just happened. He looked down at his chest before realizing what he'd done. *Great, I didn't stop to think about that...Maybe I should just avoid her for a little while.* He put his shirt back on before deciding to equip his swords as well. His father had taught him to always keep a weapon on hand, so Rune did just that. He left his armor off, opting to instead just wear normal clothes.

Rune quickly exited and locked his door, bringing with him his letters. At the Reception desk, there was a sign for outgoing mail. Two elderly women were currently manning the desk, and one stepped over to meet the new arrival.

"Hello there, young man! How can I help you?"

"Um, I don't really know how it works, but I need to send these letters to Locke."

"Oh, that's fine, sweetheart! I heard you are new to all this, so the first time is free. After that, it will cost two silver per letter or ten silver per package, if the package is small enough for the birds. If it's too big, you'll need to negotiate with someone heading that way, or submit a quest," the receptionist kindly explained. Rune happily turned over the letters and thanked the woman before turning around to exit the building. "Don't worry. We will get them sent by messenger hawk since it's a simple set of letters, so they will arrive in a day when we send the hawks out."

Just outside the door were Mona and the Hall Master, Jacob, as well as Lex, Tabor, and Venraya. Mona and Jacob appeared to be flirting with each other like teenagers in front of their annoyed child and Mona's party members. Venraya locked eyes momentarily with Rune and looked away quickly with a slight blush that Rune chose to 'miss'.

Mona, however, did not. With a slight grin, she asked, "What's that about, Ven? You already getting up to something with the newbie?"

"What? No!" she shouted angrily at her mother, giving her a punch to the shoulder.

"No, that's my bad," Rune explained on the young woman's behalf since he was the one at fault, after all. "She knocked, and I momentarily forgot I wasn't home when I told her to come in, so I was in a state of undress. Sorry about that Miss Venraya."

"Hmph."

Rune awkwardly laughed with a hand on the back of his neck. Mona and Jacob laughed out loud before gesturing for everyone to head towards the West Gate Inn. So named for the fact it sat next to the western gate of Hilden. Jacob suggested this place to grab dinner, since it was his favorite place to eat in town. For his part, Rune was simply excited to try some place new versus the food he had long gotten used to in Locke.

Dinner was lively and fun, with Tabor bragging about feats of bravery and strength and Mona knocking him down several pegs. Even the ever-serious Lex let out a few chuckles. Venraya loosened up a little as well, but Rune decided not to push his luck and talk to her. It was plain to see she was not his biggest fan. After a few hours of drinking, eating, and laughing at Mona's and Tabor's antics, everyone returned to the Hall. Rune headed towards his room and finally laid down to sleep. It did not come easily, thanks to the exciting prospect of finally taking the first steps toward fulfilling his dreams.

Rune

Rune awoke to a dull roar of voices beneath his feet. It was a mixture of angry shouting, laughter, and the white noise of general conversation. He got out of bed, dressed back up in his clothes and armor, and made a note that he would need to purchase additional outfits. Otherwise, he would be stuck in his skivvies while getting laundry done. The last thing he needed was for Venraya to walk in then. He picked up his swords when he realized he had yet to check for damage after his sword strike was blocked the other day. Thankfully, it seemed he had not rolled or chipped the blade.

Rune thanked his father silently for being able to make such high-quality weapons and returned the blade to its sheathe before he walked out of the room. He picked up the room key he had tossed onto the desk the night before, locking the door behind him before going down the stairs. While there was no immediate reason to distrust the Vanguard, neither was there reason to trust a building full of new people who had unknown motives. After all, the only thing that bound them was the shared goal of killing monsters and making money. Though Rune had grand ideas for how his life could go, he was not so delusional to think all members of the Vanguard were of a similar ideal.

The Vanguard Hall was situated right inside the northern gate; the same one they had entered upon arriving the day before. While the second floor was essentially a U-shaped hallway lined with rooms, the main floor was mostly a wide-open space. Just to the left of the stairs Rune came down, were the large double-doors leading outside. Directly in front of the stairs was the reception desk, tended by the two nice elderly women. Next to that was the job request board, which currently had several people in various styles of armor surrounding it.

To the right of the stairs was another set of doors that led to the training area, which held two small, rectangular fight pits and an archery range with moving targets. The targets were attached to a conveyer system powered by a windmill next to the building. A lever would engage or disengage the system to switch between moving and stationary targets. The doors had been held open yesterday, which was how he could catch Venraya practicing when he arrived.

Past the door to the training area, the rest of the first floor was an open space taken up by a massive bar. At first glance, it appeared to be the main source of the dull roar that had woken Rune up. However, when someone exited the training hall, the gap in the doorway revealed several people shouting excitedly at a couple of people fighting in the training pits.

"You're late. I said sunrise, not two hours after," a frustrated voice called out. Rune turned to see Venraya walking up with a very unamused expression. Rune bowed in apology.

"Right!" he shouted. "Sorry! I overslept after my trip. I think the road exhausted me more than I expected and the dinner party after did not help…"

"Hmph. I guess it's okay. My da… I mean, the Master hasn't left his office yet this morning, so we couldn't have left, anyway," the young woman explained in a flat tone. "Next time don't make me wait, 'cus he could have been here and then we would have wasted valuable time. Besides, I wanted to head out at first light. Good luck and all that, I guess."

Could have? But he wasn't…

The girl motioned for Rune to follow her to the Reception desk, where she explained some of the basics.

"Rune, this is Reception. They confirm the jobs after you take one from the board. They also pay you out on completion. Of course, that over there is the job board. Once you pass—if you pass—you can take Common-Level jobs on your own or F-Rank jobs with someone else."

Rune nodded in understanding as Venraya explained the rules. According to her, members of the Vanguard were ranked F through A and then S at the top. Every rank had a card. Each card was also printed in a separate color. In order from the lowest to highest rank, they were: Red, Orange, Green, Blue, Purple, Gold, and then Black. Members could take exams to rank up after completing a requisite number of jobs. F to E was ten jobs, E to D was fifteen, and so on. The only exceptions were that you had to complete special requirements to advance past C and that moving from A to S-Rank had even more special qualifications. Venraya was not sure about those special requirements, as it was quite rare for someone to progress that high. *Better find out some day. I'll be one, eventually.*

Rank determined what jobs someone could take. Any member could take a solo job one rank below theirs or take a group job equal to their rank. Group requirements simply required two members of the requisite rank or higher. All other members could be of any rank. This meant that an E-Rank could go on a C-Rank quest, so long as the party comprised of two C-Ranks. C and D-Ranks were the most common among the Vanguard because they could not handle the required amount of strength or declined to meet the additional requirements.

The Vanguard would pay out your rewards on completion minus a ten percent commission they kept. This meant that no one needed to pay dues to maintain membership. Besides the jobs, the Vanguard would also buy monster materials from its members. The value of materials depended on quality, monster rank, and current market trends; again, with the ten percent commission taken out before payment.

"That's a lot to take in," Rune expressed honestly, "but I think I get the gist of it. Thank you, Miss Venraya."

The girl raised an eyebrow. "Miss?" she questioned. "You know I'm only a year older than you, right? You did it yesterday too…Just drop the miss."

"But you're the Hall Master's daughter."

"Nope! Stop right there," Venraya interrupted. "He is my pops, but with Vanguard business, he's simply my Hall Master. Don't give me special treatment."

Rune looked the girl straight in the eyes for a few moments and was met with a resolute expression. "Got it, Venraya. Thanks for the information."

Just as Rune began asking another question, Master Jacob walked up with a white ball in his hands. Getting a good look at him, Rune saw that Jacob was shorter than Mona, but had short black hair just as dark as his daughter's and possessed the same green eyes. As for what was in his hands, it looked like a giant pearl that was easily a foot in diameter. It had a small crack around the circumference. Jacob cradled it and placed it on a small pillow on the Reception desk. He gestured for Rune to touch it.

"Alright, kid. This here is our Awakening Crystal. It tells us if you are an Awakened or not and it will normally tell us your class. Unfortunately, someone dropped it and it currently will only tell us if your class is Enhancer..." Jacob coughed uncomfortably while Venraya gave him a sideways glare. "Anyway, if you aren't an Enhancer, it won't do much else besides give us a 'yes or no' on if you are Awakened."

Rune grunted. "I'm starting to think I'm not. I still have to rely on alderite spheres to supply Aura to an altered weapon, but I'll give it a go, anyway." Rune reached out and touched the crystal gingerly, prepared for what he assumed would be no reaction.

After a few moments, nothing happened. Rune groaned quietly, having gotten his hopes up slightly. Just before he pulled his hand free, the ball let out a bright white glow. Happiness swelled within Rune's chest as he felt tears well up in his eyes.

"Well, would ya' look at that? Right there, kid, looks like..." Mona started from behind the group. She was interrupted by the sound of the orb beginning to crack, and the light quickly dissipated into nothing.

"I am so, so, so sorry!" Rune shouted as he pulled his hand back from the ball. "I didn't mean to break it! I can't possibly afford to pay for it right now, but if we can make a deal about a portion of my jobs..."

Jacob laughed and put up a hand to stop him. "I thought it would last longer, but the thing was on its last legs. So, you just got lucky that you were the one it broke on. Thing is older than me, anyway. We have one on order from House Mithra in the Kingdom of Volar. It should be here in a few months. Anyway, you aren't an Enhancer, otherwise it would have glowed purple and forced you to activate your powers, but it at least looks like you are an Awakened. One with quite the potential it seems. Say kid, who is this father of yours?"

"Vickar of Locke. He's an alderite smith and a Wanderer."

Jacob's eyes widened for just a moment but quickly changed to a more thoughtful expression. "Is that so...?"

Rune looked at the Master with relief written all over his face. He was ecstatic to hear he was not at fault for destroying what was clearly an expensive item. However, he was even more happy to hear that his father was right, and he was at least an Awakened. Mona had a large smile on her face as she clapped her hands down on both of Rune's shoulders. She squeezed tightly before letting go and leaving the boy with her husband and daughter. Mona had not known him for very long, but the admiration and understanding in her eyes showed Rune she knew how important this was to him.

Chapter Five

Rune

Jacob allowed Rune a moment to collect himself before he pulled out a paper and passed it over to Venraya. "Alright kid, Ven is going to act as your proctor for the exam. You are going to be hunting down a single Bash Eagle. It is an F-Rank monster, so I don't expect you to kill it on your own. Ven will assist you and grade you on your performance. All you gotta do is hold your own against one. Sound good?"

Excitement filled him. Bash Eagles being the target of the test worked out great in his favor. Since they were a pest around Locke, he had plenty of experience in taking on several.

"Good. Head out the western gates, then turn north towards the Greatwood. There's a nest of them just on the edge of the woods, as they hunt down field mice and rabbits between there and town. Dismissed."

Venraya silently nodded to her father and left the building so quickly Rune was forced to run after her. They passed through most of the town on the way to the gates. Since the Vanguard Hall was next to the north gates, the main street to get to the western ones took them through the heart of Hilden. Rune was in awe at his new environment.

Compared to Locke, Hilden was easily three or four times larger. Its walls towered over the town itself, unlike the small ones made of stacked rocks back home. Those were only waist to chest height, depending on the spot. The market in the center of town already had numerous people starting their morning shopping. There were so many people just out shopping and they already dwarfed the population of Locke by several times!

The market stalls were composed of various goods sold by an array of traders, artisans, and apothecaries. Some stalls were selling weapons that Rune wanted to check out. No doubt the ore to make them came from Locke. Some had probably come from home as well, but Hilden might have had at least one or two blacksmiths of their own. One stall looked to be selling crossbow bolts, a weapon Rune had heard of from his father but had never seen. A young man was excitedly accosting the poor trader. On top of that, the main roads were laid with stone. Unlike back home, just traveling through the main areas of town, there was no dodging of wagon ruts and muddy puddles with unknown depths.

"Hey," Rune asked Venraya, "how many smiths does Hilden have?"

"Um, two...I think." Venraya stopped walking to answer Rune's question and gave him an odd look. "One focuses more on weapons while the other is more of an armorer, but you can get any kind of work done at both."

"That's odd. I would think you all would just import weapons from Locke."

"Oh, I am sure we bring in a fair number, but as a town, we have to be self-sufficient in some capacity, you know? We can't just buy everything we need, like the northerners. Besides, most of the material we import from there are raw and refined ores, I believe. Look, I'm just parroting something my mom said. Go ask the actual smiths later. Let's go."

Venraya turned and hurried even faster toward the gates. Rune tried his best to sightsee at least a little. He noticed Hilden had a similar architectural style to Locke, with simple wooden homes that had few windows and stone chimneys. The only buildings that seemed to use stone as a primary construction material—beyond a simple chimney—were the church, with a bell tower peaking over the rooflines, and the Lord's home. It could be seen just off the market in the town's center and looked as though it could house five full families alone. With a stone foundation and corner supports, the wooden walls that made up the rest of the building made it a beautiful feature to the town. Most of the buildings near the lordly manor were also larger than any of the buildings back home.

Likely a noble district. Or something that passed for one this far away from the capital.

Such an interesting place! So many people in one spot... I can't even imagine what Jelmoore would look like... Suddenly realizing he was distracted by the sights, Rune had to rush to catch up to his senior once more. Unfortunately, there were a few times on the way to their destination that Venraya was forced to slow down for him. It was obvious the girl did not think highly of him, but he could not figure out why, for the life of him. Rune simply shrugged and wondered if it was like how Mona and her party had been reserved before the bandit ambush. Either way, there was no reason to let this get him down. He was still just as excited to finally fulfill his childhood dream of adventuring as a member of the Vanguard.

Once the pair finally reached the western gates, the size of them shocked him. They were a fair bit larger than the ones facing the road to Locke, but he figured it made sense since this road led to the large port city of Jelmoore and connected them to the rest of the kingdom. Guards at the gate waved at Venraya, easily recognizing her. They simply waved the duo past without checking papers or anything.

The perks of being known around here, I suppose, Rune mused, continuing to follow Venraya's lead to the hunting grounds.

Ven

About an hour away from the city gates, Ven finally heard the cawing of a flock of Bash Eagles. She was worried at first that her charge would pester her with questions, considering how entranced with the town he was. Against her expectations, he remained silent and only offered insight into potential creatures of interest they passed. Most of the area around Hilden was set up for farming, but the untamed grasses beyond that held a handful of smaller creatures such as horned rabbits and tunnel ferrets. She knew Rune was excited to join the ranks of the Vanguard, but she needed to be the one to make sure that he met the high standards of Hilden's Master. Or rather, her own high standards.

Ven heard more cries of Bash Eagles in the distance and finally eyed several black objects in the sky above the tree line. They had ventured much closer to the woods than they had expected, which made the mission a little riskier. Anywhere between one and three Bash Eagles was an F-Rank job, but if they went above three, it became an E-Rank mission. As an E-Rank herself, she would need at least one other Ranked member to join her. Rune did not count since this was his test. Maybe they could lure one away from the flock... No, it was probably best if they called it here.

Rune stopped just to her right and crouched down. He motioned for her to come closer. Doing as asked, she crept towards him. Each step grated on her soul, rustling grass and fallen leaves. Doing her best not to create too much more noise, she whispered, "What? Did you see something?"

Rune nodded his head with a finger over his lips. He pointed to their right. A few hundred feet away and circling in the sky was a trio of Bash Eagles. She had already noticed them, but he pointed to the ground beneath them where two more feasted on some other creature. They either did not notice the duo or were distracted by something they had just attacked. This was too dangerous. With five of them, it was officially a quest above their approved rank. There was no feasible way for one creature to be pulled from the rest with them all being so close to one another. The three above kept watch over those currently feasting. Most likely, when the others finished their meal, they would trade out spots. For birds like them, it was strange behavior, but indicative of their flock mentality.

Ven swallowed her anxiety. She turned to face the young man and advise him they would pull back. Either they would go out another day, or the Hall Master would give them a different quest. Rune had other plans, it seemed. Instead of concern, his eyes were full of confidence. Not with fresh-faced bravado, but with experience. She was no stranger to that look. Part of her hesitated, but ultimately readied her hunting bow. She notched an arrow while remaining crouched on one knee. Rune came closer and whispered quietly into Ven's ear.

"Count to ten, then take a shot. I'll distract them with a call. At least one of them should pause. That's the one to hit."

Before, his childish demeanor and innocent expressions had annoyed her. Now that they were about to enter battle, the young man changed. Ven found herself willing to listen to him, despite their difference in rank. It was like he had become the party leader and that frustrated her.

Ven nodded and counted to ten in her head. The moment she hit nine, she heard from just behind her the call of what sounded like a baby Bash Eagle. Suddenly, one of the three monsters in the air flapped its wings to stop its circling and change direction. At that exact moment, Ven released her notched arrow. It flew straight, landing solidly in the beast's neck and dropping it to the ground like a rock.

The other two monsters in the air beside it screeched angrily and dived straight towards the girl who had killed a member of their flock. The two on the ground looked up, confused, and had not yet spotted the source of the commotion. Ven felt herself become glued to the ground. She knew she had to move, otherwise the Bash Eagles would land a direct hit on her, and that would put her in a world of pain. It could even kill her. Something else, however, seemed to tell her that if she moved, her death was even more assured.

The first of the two diving birds had closed the gap and quickly appeared only a few feet from the girl. She saw a flash of light and a silver blur as Rune dashed in front of her. In one quick motion, he sliced off one of the creature's wings while he simultaneously deflected it to the ground with a simple smack of his shield. Not even a moment later, he propelled himself off the ground and landed the pommel of his sword into the side of the second monster, who was just inches behind the first.

Ven heard a sickening, wet crunch as the two Bash Eagles struck the ground at full speed and broke their necks. Red gore soaked into the dirt. She looked up at the silver-haired boy with surprise. Rune flicked some blood off his sword. Something was different, but it was hard to say what. The young man's movements seemed to blur together. His head snapped toward the feasting beasts.

What in Chaos's name was that?

By that point, the two on the ground had seen everything and launched into the air, sending out a small puff of dust. Ven pulled herself from her thoughts and loosed another arrow at them. Her target avoided a killing blow, but the arrow still struck its wing, forcing it to fall back to the ground. It flopped around in pain, helplessly flapping its wings in a vain effort to take to the sky.

The other one made it into the air and tried to retreat. Rune placed his buckler in front of him and started rhythmically smacking it with the flat of his blade while also dragging it across the metal studs. A painful screech of scraping metal rang in her ears. Ven could almost feel the rage building in the remaining beast. With a twitch of its head, it screeched a sort of war cry. Its feathers puffed out and it dove straight at the young man who taunted it. Instead of moving, Rune held his ground. The Bash Eagle picked up speed, faster than the other two. A few inches from hitting him, he stepped to the side and let the monster hit the ground. Thanks to its hard head and spine, the Bash Eagle simply created a small cloud of dust. By the time the dust cleared, the monster had already taken off again.

"Venraya! Quickly finish the one you disabled. Approach it from behind and put a blade right behind its skull, or just shoot an arrow into it if you don't want to get close. I'll handle this last one. Seems to be the head of the flock. Faster. Tougher," Rune ordered before chasing after the monster.

It took a moment for her to react to his words. The way he had sidestepped that beast...could she have done that? No. She wasn't fast enough. Ven did as she was told and moved to kill the one she had wounded earlier. It was simple enough to move into position while the creature squawked in defiance against its own fate. The noise hid her quiet steps. Bash Eagles were incredibly weak without their aerial advantage, so it was a simple task to overpower it. A single stroke of her blade was all it took as Ven planted one of her daggers into the base of its skull. She remembered to do it just to the side of the spinal cord and aim for the brain and not directly into the tough muscles that ran the length of its spine.

Ven turned around to catch Rune dodging a second dive, then a third. She contemplated helping him when the beast started a fourth dive, but held out as she realized that the boy's plan was to tire the monster out. The fourth and final dive was initiated at a lower altitude and was nowhere near as fast or powerful as the previous attacks. Had it made a mistake and attacked too quickly? As it approached, it was finally slow enough for Rune to sidestep and attack. He had dropped his short sword before the last dive, and pulled out a knife, which he plunged into the beast's belly, allowing it to gut itself with the momentum.

Innards splattered across the dirt and grass, some spraying on to Ven's leg. With a wide-eyed expression, she watched as Rune cleaned his blades before he grabbed the last kill, taking it over to the other two he had killed. He nudged them with a foot, testing to make sure they were dead. She watched him momentarily rub the side of his head with a look of discomfort. It quickly vanished when he turned around to face her.

"Nice team work!" the boy—no, young man—shouted as he gave her a thumbs up with that stupid grin he had worn earlier.

A strange pinch came from inside Ven's chest before she shook her head before she went to fetch the two Bash Eagles she felled and brought them back to where the other three lay. By the time she returned, Rune had already used the knife from the last kill to separate the armored skull plate that gave the beasts their names and remove their wings at the joints. The wings were not worth much other than the primary flight feathers. He also plucked the tail feathers and put them into a pouch.

"As a thank you, I figured you can take the feathers from these three, too? As long as I can keep the skull plates from the ones I killed? Of course, you can still keep the plates and feathers from your two!"

"Sure. Thanks." Ven stated. She continued to be pleasantly surprised by Rune.

She had not expected him to understand that the flight and tail feathers from the beasts made excellent arrows. As his proctor, she technically had rights to all the materials from the beasts, but seeing as he had killed three while she only killed two—one being with his help—she had no complaints about sharing the loot. Besides, she was his senior. She would do well to set a good example for the boy by letting him have some of the spoils.

Who are you? Ven opened and closed her mouth a few times, the words still trapped in her mind. Meanwhile, they worked together to collect the materials. She was honestly quite impressed at Rune's performance. If it had been her, she would have avoided the fight being only an E-Ranker herself. It was beyond her technical threat limit. Yet, the unranked newbie had confronted them without a moment of hesitation.

"Hey...so tell me a bit about yourself Rune," Ven mumbled finally.

"Really? Okay. Well, not a lot to tell, actually." Rune sighed. He looked relieved at her more muted tone. He understood this was an effort of hers to try treating him as something better than an annoyance. "I'm from Locke, born and raised. Mother is the daughter of the village head and my father is a blacksmith."

"A blacksmith from Locke? How'd you learn to fight then? Your movements are so... flowy and weird. I've seen a number of styles, but yours is just different." It was true. Most of the warriors she knew fought with solid stances. Rune almost stood in a haphazard one; like a simple shove could knock him out of it. Yet, he used that light stance to his benefit. Dodging with the slightest movements. When he actually fought the creatures, he relied less on his own strength, rather, using the monster's own power against them.

"Oh, my father taught me that since I could never do more than basic smithing, unlike him. He's a Wanderer and his specialty is alderite smithing. As for how he learned to fight, I don't really know. My father doesn't really talk about his life before the village."

Ven could barely contain her surprise. This newbie was just one shock after another. "Your father is a Wanderer? And you somehow were born Awakened?

Do you know how uncommon that is? If one parent has Volari blood, then most of the time you either get their bloodline abilities or nothing at all!"

Rune nodded in agreement. "Yea, I know. That's one reason I was shocked when I got that reaction from the Awakening Crystal. Honestly, I thought I was just a normal human. My father said I wasn't, but he said he couldn't really tell me much more than that. As far as I can remember, I haven't been able to manifest any Awakened abilities, so I never truly believed him."

Ven sighed, "Yea, I haven't either. You have to use an Awakening Crystal or like go through something really traumatic. Before that, the best you can do is funnel Aura into an altered weapon."

Rune shook his head solemnly and released a pained sigh. "No. I know that. I mean, I can't do that either. The only way I can use an alderite altered weapon is by using a charged alderite core. Just like a normal human does."

"I see," Ven said simply once she noticed Rune was closing off his body language. He was clearly done with this conversation. She shifted uncomfortably until that strange pinch returned, but it felt somewhat different. "Sorry, Rune, I didn't mean to upset you or pry. But, hey! You fight pretty well. My mom is just a normal human, and she does just fine!"

Rune nodded, clearly unconvinced, as the duo finished their gathering and prepared everything to set out on the return trip to the village. Ven was the one who kept the silence going this time. She had seen how excited Rune was to find out that he was Awakened, but he had been reminded that it was pointless if he could not actually use the Aura in his body. On top of that, he was the son of someone with a Volari bloodline who could manipulate the Aura in the environment. Ven wondered if it would be better or worse for Rune to have been born a normal human. *Dammit, Ven,* she cursed herself. *You just had to open your big mouth.*

Just before they left, Rune began processing the corpses by breaking them down into smaller pieces and scattering the remains in the field. Unlike with human bodies, scattering leftover monster pieces was standard practice. *They look a little malnourished. Did we get lucky?* As she was helping with the breakdown, she noticed most of the creatures looked a little on the thin side. Maybe that was a factor in how they could take them out so easily?

"Rune, I'm..." Ven started before she paused. A moment passed before she swallowed her pride. "I am sorry for how I acted before. Mom was right. You're alright."

"Oh. Thanks. I was worried that I had done something when I first arrived to upset you." Rune laughed awkwardly.

"No, you did nothing. I just don't really do well with people. Especially new people. I thought you were just some idiot with delusions of grandeur. A lot of people show up thinking they are going to be heroes and ignore what it actually takes to be Vanguard... A-anyway, the way you fight is really cool."

"Oh." Rune blushed a little. "Thanks!"

"Kinda looks more like dancing than fighting, though."

"Right."

Both of them maintained an awkward silence for the return trip to town. On top of that, Ven refused to look at the young man. After seeing him fight and how easy he made taking down a large group of Bash Eagles look, she could not help but think back to the day before, when she had walked into his room. The memory brought a warm feeling to her cheeks and a slight sense of either unease, shame, or something else. She could not decide.

When they finally arrived back at the gates, the evening sun painted the sky beautiful shades of orange. The gates would close soon, but the guards held them open for the pair, letting them inside without any checks. Upon entering, Ven caught wind of a commotion. Dozens of people were shouting outside of the West Gate Inn. Out of curiosity, they went to investigate the source.

In front of the building, there were about twenty people surrounding two different groups. One was a group of four people in white robes that normally adorned members of the Crucidian Church. The other group was a group of three people with purple eyes.

"You Volari are heathens! Damned raft rats. Just stay on your island if you don't want to follow the true gods," one man in white robes shouted. "You worship death and believe it a final destination. You deny the truth of the Goddess of Reincarnation! The beauty of life is without end! You doomsayers should return to your island or come to accept the truth!"

"Yeah, you filthy Volari! Reject your 'Path' like your Wanderer brethren. See the truth of the world lest the Goddess of Reincarnation make your next life that of an actual rat."

The three Volari simply stood and said nothing. Two of them appeared to be warriors of some kind, but the third wore fancier clothes. Ven suspected him to be some kind of noble or merchant. He did not appear to be a holy man, so the religious dispute was likely one-sided.

"What's happening here. Venraya?" Rune whispered to her.

"Hm, I guess missionaries don't really bother a place like Locke, huh? The guys in the robes are from the Crucidian Church. They replaced the elder priest who passed away a few months ago. Ever since they arrived here from the capital, they've been harassing any Volari that come to town."

"What about the ones that already live here?"

"Them too, or rather the ones that don't attend sermons. It's been a pain in the neck. The mayor of Hilden has made requests for them to be reassigned, but so far... no luck. Come on Rune, just ignore it. Let's get back to the Hall."

Most of the townspeople ignored the church members. However, one approached a Volari woman. She gasped as the clergy member's hand wrapped around her wrist. Vile words spewed from his mouth joined by his friends' calls for the woman to repent. That would not end well.

Just as Ven predicted, several townsfolk rushed to the scene. A couple of larger men abandoned wheelbarrows filled with debris, likely from a house they were working on. They rushed the assailant and shoved him into the dirt. Another person ushered the woman away gently with a few others, trying to make sure she was okay. The other woman comforting her cast angry glares at the priests.

"Not very pious of them to try to attack a woman in the street," Rune growled.

"No. No, it is not."

"Are things always like that?"

Ven sighed. "Lately it has been getting worse. The lord has his hands full constantly trying to manage the city and lands around it. He scarcely has time to play politics with the church. So, they get away with a lot. I hear it's worse in bigger cities like Jelmoore and Nefera."

"What about places like Rosendale or Hyra?"

Ven laughed, drawing a questioning look. "Sorry, sorry. You really don't know much outside your little town, do you? Well, I'm no expert, but Volari don't really venture into northern territories much. Hell, even our organization barely has any members there outside of Fort Black itself. Come on, the guards are on their way. They'll take care of it."

<u>Chapter Six</u>

Tayven

Tayven awoke to the sound of grunting in the corner of his room. He turned over, looked outside, and saw that while the sky was brightening, dawn still had not come. He groaned loudly at his roommate's antics and turned to face the obnoxious sounds. In the room's corner was a massive gorilla of a man doing squats with weights larger than Tayven's chest was wide. They probably each weighed about as much as he did, too.

The young man in question was Brick. He hailed from Borros, a continent to the west of Vendreya made up of a seemingly infinite number of mercantile city-states. As for Brick himself, he was an oddity among his fellow Borrosans, because of the focus he placed upon training his body and heart instead of his mind and guile. He stood well over six feet, with shoulders almost twice as wide as the average man. His skin was a healthy tan and his sand-colored hair paired well with his light-almond eyes. Despite what his bulk would suggest, he was only eighteen and was also a prospective enrollee at the Vanguard Academy, like Tayven.

Sweat poured down Brick's face as he did one last squat and set down his weights with a light *thud*. He wiped his face and chest with a wet rag before he grabbed a set of clothes and towel to head off to the baths. He had light brown hair and brown eyes, and despite his intimidating stature, always wore a warm, comforting smile.

"Lord Tayven! Good morning." He chuckled. "It appears that I have woken you again! Apologies!"

Tayven waved his hand dismissively at his roommate. "No, do not worry about it. I have to be up soon, anyway. Maybe this time I'll stay awake so I don't miss training again."

Brick laughed boisterously. "Yes, it would do well for you to not anger the martial instructor more. I'm afraid your punishments will lead you to an early grave!" Brick then left the room, locking the door behind him. Tayven knew that if he did not follow through with his words and get up soon, not only would he risk falling asleep and getting to training late, but he also would miss the rare opportunity to avoid the posse of female classmates attempting to ingratiate themselves to a young lord.

As a son of the Nefera family, Tayven held a lot of political sway in the kingdom. There were only a handful of large towns on the continent and, as such, very few lords were landed. Even fewer of them were in the south, as compared to the far wealthier and safer north. Many nobles were simply knight families that served the handful of major lords. Marrying into a landed family, let alone a major one like the Nefera family, was a rare and enticing offer for many young women. In addition to his family's political and financial weight, it helped that Tayven was quite the attractive young man.

Lord Erich Nefera—Tayven's father—held a lot of sway with the southern lords of the kingdom despite the Nefera family being northern nobility. The Nefera family estate frequently held dinners for the various noble families of the southern half of the continent. Tayven's father frequently collected their concerns and voiced them on their behalf to the palace since it was hard for any of the poorer families that made up most of the southern part of the nation to visit the capital themselves.

Tayven threw his training clothes on as quickly as he could, deciding not to care how they looked as long as he reached the training grounds early. Hope still existed that if he was early this morning, then the martial instructor would be lenient on the rest of his punishment and forget about the laps. The young man shivered at the thought of having to run the perimeter of the Academy, or worse yet, Jelmoore's city walls. Thankfully, when he arrived at the training grounds, the instructor just so was in a good mood. There was a small grin on his face and a faraway look in his eyes.

He simply motioned to the practice weapons and armor to have Tayven arm himself. They were weighted in tiers so that the trainees could gain experience with the real thing, but without the increased risk of live-weapon sparring. The school's clerics already had enough issues keeping up with student injuries as it was.

After he readied himself, Tayven looked at his instructor, who silently moved a finger in a circular motion before holding up two fingers, then making a zero. It seemed the boy would get off with twenty laps around the training hall instead of the academy walls.

He must have heard about the professor returning from Volar, Tayven thought as he began his exercise. *Fool is smitten with that woman even though he should know he doesn't have a chance in the Sea of Chaos. Then again, he's got such a thick skull, I bet an arrow has a better chance of piercing stone than him realizing she's not into him.*

The professor in question was Lady Lylah vas Mithra. She was from a branch of the ruling family of the city of Corsa; the largest of the three cities in Volar. While she was only from a branch family, there was no way she would partner with someone not of Volari heritage. Nobles of the Volari were strict regarding who their heirs could marry. Per their customs, only other Volari could marry their nobles. They were not so strict as to require nobles to marry nobles, as it was quite common for branch family members like the professor to marry commoners, but they were always other Volari and never humans. Awakened or not.

After a few laps around the room, some of the other early entrants to the Academy had trickled in. He was one of a few dozen students starting the next term. Said term would not start for a while yet, but the Academy allowed early applicants to partake in martial classes and use its facilities while waiting for the next term to start. Tayven finished his run before joining the rest of the class to pair up for practice sparring. Of course, they could not just freely use the facilities. They also needed to take a supplemental course to prepare for the incoming semester.

When he first arrived at the academy, the students had been practicing with swords, which they were still doing. After that, they would move on to other weapons like axes, hammers, hand-to-hand, and archery. Tayven was most proficient with the sword as he had been taught by his father and several hired instructors and knights, so when other people started training with other weapons, he would likely seek to continue developing his sword skills. He was not unwilling to learn other forms of combat. In fact, he even understood that learning the basics of other styles could help him come up with strategies to combat them, but for now, he wanted to better cement his knowledge in his preferred weapon.

The martial instructor ordered the students to pair up for sparring practice. Even though they were friends, Tayven purposefully avoided Brick so he would not be subjected to his roommate's heavy and unpredictable swings. Brick was primarily a hand-to-hand specialist, a dangerous form of fighting when dealing with monsters. However, with his size and strength, he had little to worry about. It was this same strength that made every impact hurt regardless of their equipment being made of wood or even blunted metal. Avoiding his friend caused Tayven to be stuck with one young lady that followed him around campus during his time off.

He had partnered with her before and cautiously avoided eye contact as much as possible while he practiced his parrying skills against her clumsy attacks. She had a build better suited to daggers or short swords, so it was a simple matter for Tayven to defend against her when using an unfamiliar weapon. Their difference in skill lessened the difficulty, allowing him the possibility of breezing through the session, even while not fully engaging his opponent. It was going to be a long day, but at least he had made it to class on time and would avoid further punishment.

Both Tayven and his opponent grabbed a simple shield. While it was great for him not to leave class with severe bruising or even a stretcher from tangling with Brick, he also could not go all out against his current opponent. It was not the fact that she was a girl, but that she was extremely inexperienced. Tayven had an unfair advantage over most people in his class. As a student at the Jelmoore Academy, he was naturally a member of the Vanguard. Currently, Tayven's skills put him at an E-Rank. The girl he sparred with was likely equal to an F-Rank, if that.

The girl nervously readied herself, but in a way that made Tayven sigh deeply. He guided her on the proper way to ready her shield instead of instantly cowering behind it before the fight began. To continue helping her out, he covered basic movements and started a step-by-step sparring session. She would swing, receive a correction from Tayven, and then he would start a swing of his own and allow her to block, dodge, or parry. Gradually, she became more confident in her movements and stance. Though she was not using equipment suited for her build, gaining the basics would help her fight against potential enemies that used these skills. Slowly but surely, their session sped up as she grew more confident.

"That's it. Strike firm. Use the weight of the weapon to assist in the swing. Don't fight it," he demanded, subconsciously mimicking the tone of his father. "Do not be afraid of the strike not landing true. Move to the next swing, lest the enemy take advantage of your hesitation."

"Yes, Lord Tayven," the young woman squeaked. A heavy blush was painted along her cheeks. Though it could have been from the physical exertion, Tayven highly doubted it.

This kind of training lasted the entire class period. Though instructing others could be rewarding in its own right, Tayven still hoped that the next round of student enrollments would happen soon. Everyone here had enrolled during the first semester, but they had a mid-semester enrollment coming up soon and it would hopefully bring in a batch of recruits who were a lot more competent.

After training was over, everyone put away their equipment and headed to the baths to wash off before classes. Waiting near the equipment rack was

Tayven's butler, who had been with him since he left home. He had a complicated look on his face and a letter in his hand. Upon handing it to the young noble, he bowed and left the room quietly with a strange sense of...finality?

Tayven, of course, opened the letter as quickly as he could and read the contents. It was a letter from his father, Lord Erich Nefera.

---Tayven,

I heard from your attendant that you are doing well at the academy. I hear that you have also been causing trouble for the martial instructor and that has resulted in extra punitive exercises.

Remember that while nobility grants you little in the ways of benefits at the Vanguard's Jelmoore Academy, you still carry my name, and as such, your actions reflect upon our house. Ensure that you endeavor to improve your behaviors.

Also, I have ordered any servants that I sent with you to return here upon delivery of this letter. Since you expressed your desire to separate yourself from our household and make a life that is yours alone, then it only makes sense for me to retract the unnecessary supports that I have provided you. I have thought long and hard about this decision and feel that by continuing to provide you with attendants that you will not truly experience this life you wish to build.

You do not need to worry about tuition or food. I have ensured that your tuition is covered until graduation, and as long as you dine at the food hall as a commoner does, then so shall you have food to eat. Beyond that, however, my financial support of you ends so you may live this life of independence you desire. For anything above the minimum provided to all students, you must figure out how to cover those expenses alone.

Erich Nefera---

Tayven folded the letter and returned it to the envelope with a heavy sigh. *Thanks, father. At least you didn't order me home,* he thought with a wry smile.

Brick gave him a light tap on the shoulder from behind. "Everything alright, my friend?"

Tayven nodded. "Yeah. My father just 'cut me off', as it were. Thankfully, I see this as a positive outcome. More so when considering I thought he'd demand I come back home instead. So, it's like I'm free!"

"That's amazing!" Brick smiled widely. "Shall we visit you-know-where, in town?"

Tayven gave his friend a wink. "Abso-fucking-lutely."

The two friends rushed out of the room, intending to cut the lecture class they had after. Of course they went where all young, red-blooded men wanted to go to celebrate after a long day of work...a bar.

Specifically, they were heading to their favorite restaurant and bar in town, the Shadetree. Normally, it was hard to get in without a reservation, but since it was in the middle of the day, there was little chance of a crowd. It took little effort to leave the grounds, since the guards at the academy walls did not care what the students were up to. They were present for security, not truancy.

Many people moved about in the streets of Jelmoore, performing their typical day-to-day tasks. Day laborers were mostly at their places of work, which in Jelmoore was primarily the port and the many warehouses. While the city of Nefera was the city of trade on the continent, being the crossroads for the north, south, east, and western cities, Jelmoore was the largest port. There were other port cities and towns, like Rosendale near the capital and Port Monte, but even with those two being the largest, their flow of goods was dwarfed by Jelmoore. The primary reason for this was that it was the only port in the Faradin Kingdom that the Volari Kingdom would do trade with. Of course, it was not just the fact that the distance between the island kingdom and Jelmoore was less than a day by boat; it was also thanks to a generations-long friendly relationship that the Jelmoore family had with the Volari nobility.

That positive relationship was also what built up the largest population of Volari and Wanderers in all the continent of Vendreya outside of its island of Volar. Shadetree was run by a Volari couple that had immigrated to Jelmoore and brought with them the sweet and spicy cuisine of their homeland.

"Brick, my friend, you are a genius," Tayven whispered as he took a deep whiff of his favorite dish, a sweet and spicy curry. Many cultural dishes from the Kingdom of Volar incorporated many spices that grew in abundance across the nation. They also served a lot of fish and chicken-based dishes. Tayven's dish came with chunks of crab.

"I told you, best place to celeb—" Brick was cut off by a commotion outside. The pair looked out their window and saw a large group of people wearing white robes with different colored under-clothes and sashes walking through the street. A handful of normal citizens following behind them. Curious, Tayven and Brick stepped out to see what was happening.

"Lord Jelmoore is a heretic!"

"He stands in the way of our righteous mission!"

"Southern lords like him stand in the way of the gods!"

Several men and women in white robes with golden trim paraded through the streets, shouting different variations of the same statements and leading the citizenry and their fellow clergy. They were met with mostly jeers from the local populace, but a handful of Crucidian adherents gave them their support. Brick was confused about the whole situation and turned to Tayven for an explanation. All he could offer his large friend was a simple shake of his head and a shrug. They simply returned to their lunch and hoped that the noise would die down.

Even Nefera—which boasted a large population of Volari itself—had struggled with these kinds of demonstrations. Since the Crucidian Church worshipped the Goddess of Reincarnation as the primary deity, it put them at direct odds with the Path of Volar. The Path was the faith of the Volari and in it, they worshipped Fate and Death, where death was a final destination. The Path also did not allow for the existence of the other gods in the Crucidian Pantheon, such as the gods of Change, Innovation, and Honor. They both had entities in their myths that represented Chaos, but that was not enough to find common ground between the faiths.

Most of the church representatives who put on these demonstrations were born in the northern cities, where they had time to exercise such freedoms because of the safety of their walls and roads. Southerners had no such luxury and struggled together to survive, regardless of faith or origin, leading to less time for religious participation. The demonstration was nothing more than a chest beating. In Jelmoore, at least. The people would not partner with northerners at the cost of betraying their Volari neighbors.

Tayven looked at the husband and wife behind the counter. Their faces were nervous, with the husband tightly holding onto his lover. When their eyes met, Tayven smiled. "Would be a shame to let good food be spoiled by unpleasant company. You know what, though; I think I'll try that dessert you've been hounding me for the last few weeks."

The man smiled. He looked out to the street for a moment, then answered. "Mango pudding coming right up, milord."

"Just Tayven is fine. And you know what? Let's add one of your homemade brews. You told me it goes well with sweets."

The owner chuckled and vanished into the back while his wife took a deep breath and poured a cup of the house wine. Tayven took a deep whiff of the fragrant drink the moment she set it on the table. Floral yet fruity aromas filled his nostrils. Shadetree truly was a gem.

Chapter Seven

Lylah

Salty ocean air whipped at the purple hair of a beautiful woman with deep purple eyes. A delicate braid framed the side of her face. Her eyes analyzed the surroundings, taking in the sights of home before she left it once more. Unlike the urban sprawl of human cities, the streets of her homeland were filled with flowers and trees. A stunning blend of civilization and nature. A part of her would miss it. Only part.

After several months of both work and personal business, the woman finally could return to the Jelmoore Academy and resume her passion: research. Teaching was a secondary responsibility to her compared to her research, but as long as she performed well, the Academy had no problem footing the bill. As one of the few Volari instructors at the Vanguard Academy, she did not have as much competition for research grants as the schools in Volar. The students she instructed were also her specimens, in a way. Vanguard Academy granted her access to all the questionnaires students filled out, which included their known ancestry. As a woman looking into the genetic link between bloodlines and Awakened or Volari abilities, it was invaluable data.

"Lady Lylah! Please, wait!" A short man with similar features to hers ran up to the woman while panting and holding a large, cube-shaped chest.

"What is it?" Lylah demanded in a frigid tone after the man stopped panting. Lylah had little patience for being interrupted while lost in thought and was doubly annoyed that the perpetrator was a cousin from an even smaller branch family of the Mithra than her own line.

"My Lady, please take this with you back to the Academy. The Vanguard ordered an Awakening Crystal from the Mithra family and we only just completed the work."

Lylah clicked her tongue and nodded for one of her attendants to take the package from her relative. Normally, she would have reprimanded him for requesting that she act as some sort of courier, but given that it was to fulfill a request on behalf of her benefactors—the Vanguard—Lylah had no other choice than to accept without complaint. Surely the Headmaster would dock her pay or even cancel some of her grants in retaliation if he found out she had delayed the delivery of such a valuable item.

A shout from the docks rang out, calling for passengers to Jelmoore. She gave a curt nod to her relative and turned to board with her attendants. She had been back in Volar for a few months to handle some family matters. Her father had wanted to marry Lylah off to a knight family based out of Uldera, Volar's capital city. Of course, this ran counter to her own plans to work at Jelmoore's Vanguard Academy until she was granted tenure at Tri-Spire, where she would no longer be required to teach students and could focus solely on her research. Tri-Spire also received copies of any data she could want, expanding her data pool beyond students at a school. Instead, her new research subjects would encompass nearly every member of the largest organization filled with Awakened and Volari anywhere in the world.

It was also possible for Lylah to take a shortcut and marry a researcher already working at Tri-Spire, but as far as she knew, they were mostly all human, save for a few elderly Volari. Most Volari researchers tended to be from merchant families or noble lines, and they all worked at bettering their own kingdom. However, only the Vanguard, a global organization, was publicly leading the charge on Aura research. Lylah would be stupid to assume that her own country was not also pursuing ground-breaking research, but it was almost certainly clandestine in nature, which did not suit her personal tastes. State secrets were not something she was keen on protecting.

Lylah returned from her thoughts and looked out at the ocean before her. She listened to the sounds of sailors rushing about the deck of the ship to complete the final preparations to disembark. Excitement bubbled up in her chest. The young woman felt a small *thump* in her chest, telling her that something exciting was in store this year. *Might Lady Fate be hinting at my future? What awaits me, I wonder.*

Ven

The receptionist at the Hilden Hall blinked slowly several times in a row. Her eyes flitted back and forth between the silver-haired newcomer and the familiar Vanguard Warrior who accompanied him. She also glanced back towards the bags with five Bash Eagle skull plates and a few bags of feathers. The elderly woman knew that Rune had been out on a test for his promotion, but it was more about surviving the encounter, not actually killing the beasts.

"Miss Venraya, you didn't happen to have killed these, right? You know it would void his test if you did all the work…" the receptionist mumbled. She was surprised that Ven could take out five F-Rank monsters even with the help of a non-ranked applicant. Ven was not eligible to take on such a job with just her and an unranked initiate.

"No. I only took out two, but really Rune here just used me as bait…" Ven grumbled as it really hit home that Rune had indeed used the her as bait for the three monsters he slayed. "Rune took care of three of the five on his own. I'm keeping all the feathers, but pay him out for three skull plates and two for me."

Mona and the Hall Master Jacob, saddled up beside their daughter with surprised looks on their faces. Lex was just behind them with the corner of his mouth upturned ever so slightly. "Well, son," Jacob said, "looks like you're in. Hey, wanna start out at E-Rank? If you can already take out three damnable bird monsters alone, you are without a doubt stronger than an F-Ranker. Maybe even an E-Ranker" He awkwardly avoided an angry glare from his daughter.

The receptionist stared at Rune with her mouth opening and closing like a fish out of water before she recovered and questioned her boss, "Master Jacob! Can we even do that? He hasn't completed the requisite number of F-Rank quests to qualify for the E-Rank test! Let alone actually taking that test! Also, he's not technically a member yet as—"

Mona waved her hand dismissively at the woman. "It's more than fine. Jacob can start him out at E-Rank. Just means his promotion up to the next rank would have to be held in another city under the watch of a different Hall Master, but I think it is worth it. Whaddya say kid? Wanna skip the line and join at E-Rank?"

Ven rolled her eyes, but could not really argue with the situation. She was there. Rune easily showed the requisite skill to be her equal. More than that, even. He was certainly capable enough to join her as one of the Hall's many E-Ranks. This did not mean she was not annoyed at him already becoming her equal. Especially without doing all the quests she had done, but she knew she would get over it...eventually.

Rune, on the other hand, had that familiar starry-eyed look on his face once he realized what was happening. He enthusiastically nodded in agreement and filled out the paperwork for his Ranking Card with reception.

"Um, miss Janice?" Rune prompted.

Janice, the woman who typically worked the mail and material evaluation, looked at the young man. "What is it, dear?"

"For name, do I have to put my birth name?"

Janice chuckled at Rune's statement, but Ven found herself oddly interested in the conversation. "No, you don't, but be warned that your Rank Card is unchangeable. So whatever name you put on that is basically your legal identity till the day you die."

"Okay."

Even though she was busy trying to eavesdrop on Rune's conversation, Mona and Jacob motioned for Ven to follow them and explain the specifics of what had happened. She quickly left Rune to his own devices and followed them to the Master's office on the third floor of the hall.

"So, Ven, how did he do it?" Mona asked before Jacob could open his mouth.

Ven explained to them what Rune had told her. According to him, he and a girl from his village had been taught swordsmanship by Rune's father, who was a Wanderer and blacksmith. Rune had also spent time hunting on the outskirts of Greatwood with the village's hunting party. It was there that he had learned that if you time your strikes right—and with enough damage—you can shock the creatures into relaxing their spines and back muscles. When in this state, they lacked the reinforcement and the ability to suddenly swoop back into the air. Their impact on the ground would then be enough to break their necks.

He had claimed it was easier to do when the monster was targeting someone and a second person performed the strike. Doing this prevented the creature from trying to disengage from the dive. This was why Rune had used Ven as bait. When Jacob heard the details, a range of emotions flashed across his face. On one side, he was impressed a fresh-faced eighteen-year-old could devise such a tactic. The amount of skill and speed required to do that to not just one, but two Bash Eagles at once was more than impressive. On the other hand, Rune had used Jacob's daughter as bait, and if he had not been able to follow through on the plan, she could have ended up very hurt or dead. From what Rune shared, the window of opportunity to perform the act was extremely small.

Ven noticed her father repeatedly clenching and unclenching his fist. She eyed her mother to help him calm down. Mona caught on quickly and placed a hand on her husband's shoulder. "Jacob. I haven't known Rune for very long, but I am sure that he wouldn't have done something to purposefully harm Ven."

"He only did that with two of the monsters, Dad. The third one, well, it was almost otherworldly. His movements were so fluid, and as the fight dragged on, he got..." Ven paused, trying to remember the fight more clearly. "Faster?"

This caught both Mona's and Jacob's attentions.

"He got faster?"

Ven nodded. "Yeah, the longer the fight went on, the faster and more agile Rune got. It was like the opposite of exhaustion. I thought it was just adrenaline, but that didn't really feel like what was going on. He would dodge dives from the pack leader at the last moment and with such speed that I couldn't believe my eyes. Not to mention, he did it with just a little maneuvering. I can easily say I haven't ever seen someone move like that."

"Anything else?"

She paused, wracking her brain to remember every minor detail. Her parents waited with bated breath until she thought of something she had not realized until now. "I couldn't tell with the others, but when he faced the leader, it tired out much quicker than I thought it would? I didn't think anything of it, but I guess I would have expected it to keep going for a lot longer. Now that I'm thinking of it, each of the monsters was a little... thinner than I expected? So maybe they were just hungry?"

"Hmm..." Jacob put a hand on his chin and thought silently for several moments.

The door to the office suddenly opened with a *thud*. Ven looked and saw Rune standing there with an apologetic look on his face. "Master Jacob!" Rune stated while giving a slight bow. "I apologize for putting Miss Venraya in trouble. If she were going to take a hit, I was willing to jump in front of the Bash Eagle's strike. However, I promise that she was in no real danger."

Rune paused for a moment to look up at Jacob. The 'bait' in question saw her father arching one eyebrow at Rune, while the young man continued. "These monsters are quite the pest in Locke. I have a lot of experience in hunting them in this manner, both as the attacker and as the bait. I apologize again for endangering both a comrade and your daughter."

Jacob sighed and waved his hand. "What's done is done. Clearly, Ven allowed this to happen, so it was not a big deal. At least, that's my opinion as Hall Master." Jacob paused before his tone dropped dangerously low. Purple sparks flashed between his fingers. "As her father though, if I hear of this again, then I will fill you full of holes. Understand, boy?"

"Yessir."

Before her dad made his threat, she was going to say that Rune had never actually told her his plan. Well, other than asking her to shoot an arrow and stay still. However, she kept her lips tightly sealed. *What Dad doesn't know won't hurt him...or Rune.*

Janice entered the room a few moments later, passing to the Hall Master a handful of documents. The ones that Rune had just completed with her at reception. Jacob thanked her as she bowed and took her leave.

"Alright, then. Rune, are you ready to take your oath to become a member of the Vanguard?"

"I am, sir."

"Do you, Rune, swear to abide by the tenets of the Vanguard? Do you swear to do no harm to the innocent or your fellows unless in self-defense or the defense of others, to neither steal, poach, trick, nor deceive the organization or its members, to always maintain an honorable and respectable position when negotiating with kings and countrymen and to hold these vows for so long as you live?"

"I do so swear on my honor, my life, and my soul."

"Congratulations. On the 8th of Spritendus, year 471 Foundation, I recognize Rune of Locke as an E-Rank member of the Vanguard. Do not disappoint me, boy." Jacob said with a smile. He stood and shook Rune's hand firmly.

After the conversation was over, Rune received a temporary Ranking Card from Jacob while they waited for a formal one to be issued. Ranking cards themselves were a technology developed by the Volari and had an intricate web of alderite weaved within them that somehow held information such as kills, quest completions, and general identity information. Every Vanguard Hall had equipment that could read and record this information and having new ones created took time and could only be done within Tri-Spire.

Ven waved to her parents and walked down to the main floor to collect the reward money before getting some food for the evening. She quickly caught up with the boy, who started pinching the bridge of his nose with both eyes closed. He could use an explanation of how the Rank Cards worked physically, so she wanted to provide him with one.

"You alright?"

"Yeah, I should be. It's just a headache. Second time in a few days, too. I think it is all the excitement of leaving home for the first time and the lack of quality sleep on the road here."

"Yeah, that'll do it," Ven said. "After collecting payment, wanna get a bite? I'm curious if you have any other handy tricks from your village."

Rune shook his head. "No, I think I will head to bed after getting some bread and nuts from the bar downstairs, write a few letters to home, and then see if I can't sleep off this headache."

That made sense, but she really wanted to make up for her behavior. Not only was she rude to him in the beginning for what turned out to be no reason, but she had also done something to unsettle him after the fight.

"Oh, come on, it was your first job and my first time as an exam proctor." Ven pleaded with her best attempt at a friendly smile.

"Oh fine, since you insist. I suppose I should celebrate my acceptance into the Vanguard with someone!"

"Exactly!" Ven jubilantly agreed before leading the way to Reception. "By the way, your treat!"

"What? Why my treat?"

"Because you used me as monster bait, and if you don't, then I'll go right back up there and tell my father you did not actually clue me in on your genius little plan like he thought. Fun fact: telling me to shoot a monster is not a fair warning that I would also act as bait."

Rune paled for a moment before he acquiesced. "Fair enough."

At the Reception desk, the second of the two ladies, Jenna, had already prepared for them their completion payments. She kept ten percent as the

Vanguard's cut, and the remaining amount was split evenly between Rune and Ven. They then went back over to her sister Janice and received the money for their skull plates. As planned, Ven kept the feathers to give to the fletcher and lower the cost of her next batch of arrows.

After their transaction was complete, Ven eagerly led Rune to the West Gate Inn for dinner. "Come on, slowpoke!" she said with a smile before rushing ahead.

It was likely her change in behavior would shock Rune, but something about him simply allowed her to loosen up a little now. Especially after seeing he would not be dead weight. *I may have misjudged him in the beginning. If we partner up in the future, I might take on some E-Rank quests finally, too.*

They arrived at the inn and took a few seats right at the bar. Their particular spot was on the farther end, away from the small stage that was set up for the bard's performance and while not perfect, it would be at least a little quieter.

"So, Rune, tell me," Ven started with a sly smile, "what 'cool' name did you choose to put on your Ranking Card? Should I call you 'Mortimer the Calamity' or something?" Ven could not hold her laughter at her own awful joke, which prompted Rune to join in.

After a few minutes of joking back and forth about the awful names he could have put, Rune finally answered the question. "No, I didn't put anything ridiculous. I just put my nickname on it."

"Oh? What's your nickname?"

"Oh! It's Rune. The name my parents gave me was Arkrune, but I just go by Rune, so I figured I could just put that on my card."

"Oh, that's a unique name."

"Says Venraya." Rune laughed.

"Okay, you got me, fair point." Ven laughed. "The name Arkrune, though, is a little unique. What does it mean?"

Rune sat for a moment, pondering something. A handsome smile spread across his lips, like he remembered something fondly. "Arkrune vys Volar. He was known as the hero king of the Island of Volar."

"Who the fuck is that?" Ven questioned with a genuinely confused expression. She was born and raised between Hilden and Jelmoore, but most of her formative years had been spent in Hilden, so stories about Volari heroes were not as prevalent. Also, she had grown up among the Vanguard, so the heroic stories she had heard blended together. Keeping different stories separate was hard when she was surrounded by the very people who had the potential and desires to create their own legends.

"Well, centuries ago, maybe longer, Arkrune vys Volar led a group of heroes on a quest to save his people. It was said that they made landfall on an 'island of death' and cleared it of all monsters in a single night."

Ven was unimpressed so far with the story. It had the standard makings of most legends, but she allowed the boy to continue.

"After defeating thousands of beasts on the land, in the sky, and in the sea, he and his party brought the remnants of his people to the island for it to serve as their haven from persecution. To honor him, his people took his name, created a kingdom, and placed his descendants on the throne."

"So then, how did he know the island was the place to go if it was filled with so many deadly monsters?"

"Allegedly, he received a divine revelation saying that he was fated to become a hero to his people and that he would find his true goal on the 'island of death'."

"Is that where the whole 'Path of Volar' thing comes from?"

"I think? I don't really know the religious side of it. My dad isn't really one for the Path, or even the Cruicidian gods, for that matter. Hence why he's a Wanderer now. He turned his back on their gods and their ways, though he still taught my sister and me the basics."

They continued to talk for a few hours together and enjoyed a healthy meal of meat, bread, and wine. Ven explained to him how the Rank Cards worked. Rune was impressed that the cards themselves were functional objects and not simply an identification card like merchants often carried. The Volari had created the cards to store information about the holder. Each Vanguard Hall was granted a special machine that could read and write information to it. Though home halls would keep periodic paper copies of said information and send that to a central repository at Castle Nyer, it was also fair to say that losing one's card could cause someone needing to start over from scratch. Thankfully, the periodic tracking meant just accessing those records, but that took weeks of time.

"So, you're saying that every quest I take is tracked on those things?" Rune asked, bewildered, while staring at the palm-sized rectangle in her hand.

"You got that right! All thanks to the Volari. Though they gave the technology and process to our organization. Nowadays, the Vanguard simply makes all of them at our research tower, Tri-Spire."

After turning Rune's world upside down, they returned to the Hall a little less sober than when they left. West Gate's food and drink were both cheap and tasty.

"Hey Rune, thanks for dealing with me," Ven muttered shyly. "I don't really do well with people. They aren't my thing; but you might be alright."

"Well thanks, Venraya."

"Um." She shifted uncomfortably for a moment. "Just 'Ven' for you."

"Thanks, Ven," Rune said with a smile.

"Hey, I leave in a while to go to the academy. Classes start on the 1st of Sumnistus. Do you want to group up for some missions in the meantime?"

Rune agreed happily before he bid Ven goodnight and returned to his room, leaving the girl to her thoughts. She was surprised at Rune's performance on the job, and while he had a long way to go in proper communication and teamwork, he certainly seemed able to hold his own. There was also the fact he remained kind to her, or at least cordial, despite her bad attitude towards him. *He's certainly interesting,* she thought. *I have to wonder what that 'friend' he keeps mentioning is like, though...*

Janice prepared several quest papers for the board, readying them for the next day. Now that she could take on E-Rank jobs, Ven felt excited for the first time in a while. So far, she had mostly stuck to training and operating solo. Now she was no longer stuck.

Lost in thought, Ven turned towards the bar and saw a familiar figure in a ratty, old cloak leaning against the wall. His eyes followed Rune's steps up the stairs. The figure nodded at her while she returned his gesture. She had not seen him in the Hall for a while, so she also smiled slightly at her only other friend before she also went to her own room to turn in for the night.

Chapter Eight

The God of Change is neither malevolent nor benevolent; he simply is. Many question whether he cares at all for humanity or if he remains indifferent to their desires and plights. However, whether for good or ill, change occurs always and is inevitable for man, regardless of status, wealth, or fame. Those who defy change, defy the order of things, and by extension, defy the gods themselves. Without change, the world stagnates and in stagnation, it will rot.

- Excerpt from *Words of Divinity* of the holy scripture of the Crucidian Church

Lestreus

Lestreus Faradin walked through the halls of the Faradin Knight Academy. Most people referred to it as the "Noble's Academy" since only those born to nobility and knightly families were allowed entrance, with a few exceptions made for truly spectacular individuals. The institution had been formally named after Lestreus' kingdom and family.

Lestreus was average in both build and height. He was not the most muscular or toned of his adult siblings or even his fellow students, but the mandatory training provided in his youth had kept him from being small. The young man was more of a scholar than a fighter, unlike his other siblings, choosing instead to learn of the history of his kingdom. As the fourteenth prince, he focused primarily on his studies in order to be of service as a minister to whichever of his siblings actively vying for the throne won the dispute. Should he choose to pursue it instead, a path to work for the Crucidian Church was also open to him given his specific circumstances.

Courtesy of his father, Lestreus was still very striking in his looks because of his scarlet hair. He received many suitors regularly, both for political and vanity purposes. His red hair and blue eyes were an uncommon trait in the kingdom, being a marker of the royal family. Today, like most days, he had a small entourage of students following behind him on his walk from class. Several of the young men and women would eye those who attempted to intrude on the prince's personal space before they themselves could do so.

Such behavior amused Lestreus greatly, so he allowed it to continue instead of putting a stop to it. The excessive attention helped to soothe his ego as well. Being the fourteenth prince meant most people in the royal court completely ignored him. His father had other children to attend to. His mother was but a simple concubine with other brats to care for. Being a student in the Faradin Knight Academy gave him the notoriety and attention he desired—or rather, deserved.

Even though he had many followers among the students, there was no one he would call a friend. His admirers' names vanished from his mind the moment they entered. Perhaps it was cruel for him to treat them the way he was treated, but what else did he know? As a prince, even one from an over-saturated line, he was within his rights.

The prince walked through the halls of the Knight's Academy towards the Divine Temple, the headquarters of the Cruicidian Church. It was linked to the Knight's Academy through a handful of designated hallways. These halls were used relatively frequently since many of the educators were also members of the church clergy. Only a small selection of students were permitted to traverse the halls connecting the school to the temple, with Lestreus being one of them. As he turned down one of these restricted passages, his gaggle of admirers quickly dispersed.

He continued down the long hallways, passing dozens of paintings of former and current priests on one side and excerpts of scripture from the Words of Divinity, the holy book of the church. Lestreus was receiving additional education from the upper echelons of the clergy at the benevolence of Archpriest Henner, the current head of the church. This was in addition to his studies at the Faradin Knight Academy.

Just as Lestreus was about to turn a corner into one of the many altar rooms, he bumped into a very tall man in gray robes. Lestreus contained himself from having an outburst, as he did not want to leave a bad impression on any member of the church.

"Ah, pardon me, young man. Prince Lestreus, if I remember correctly?" an almost disembodied voice stated. The prince could not see the person's face since an oversized hood covered it in its entirety. Only the man's mouth could be seen from the shadows. The gray robes appeared to flow well past the man's feet, making Lestreus wonder how the man could walk without tripping. Despite how much of the robe dragged on the ground, there did not seem to be any dirt or debris gathered on it. They were pristine.

"Apologies, your lordship." Lestreus bowed. "I was not paying attention to my surroundings before rounding the corner."

The man chuckled. It was low in pitch, much lower than his voice, and very quiet. Yet somehow, the prince seemed to hear it echo through the hallway, coming from multiple different directions into his ears. It was unnerving and caused Lestreus to subconsciously shudder.

"Do not apologize, young prince. Much like man cannot predict the future before it happens, neither can a man see past a corner before they round it. I am unoffended by these events," the man stated, a small smile appearing on his face. There was a moment of pause between the two before the man continued. "Pardon my impudence in questioning a member of the royal family, but please tell me, Prince Lestreus, as a learned youth, what do you think this kingdom needs? What future would you like to see for it? Many people wonder what the future holds. Surely, you do the same?"

The prince thought for a second. No one had asked him that before. There was no realistic claim to the throne, his only avenue for influence being a potential appointment by his siblings as a minister or advisor. His opinions on the laws and direction of the country were unimportant at best. All he knew was what he witnessed of his father and his family's histories. "It is the royal family's duty to shepherd the kingdom. Not to rule with an iron fist, but to guide it gently. Allow the people the freedom to govern their own and intervene only in times of strife and need." He parroted his family's ancient creed.

"Mmm," the man said as his head nodded slowly. "A textbook answer to be sure and one shared without confidence. Is that truly what you believe, or do you simply quote the words of men long dead? I shall ask you this question once more in the future. Perhaps then you will have an answer of your own rather than words from a dusty tome. Think on it, young prince, until then."

The priest walked past Lestreus with his robes simply dragging behind. Again, the prince wondered how the priest could move around without tripping over himself. After the man disappeared around the corner, Lestreus continued along his path towards the altar room. He opened the double doors to a large room filled with ornate wooden pews. Each had scenes from the Crucidian histories carved into their sides. A fine red velvet carpet lead from the door to a large, golden lectern. On the lectern sat a massive book, opened about three-quarters of the way through. In front of the lectern and turning the pages slowly while occasionally turning to a side table and writing something down was a short and chubby man who was bald on both his face and head.

Instead of the warm candlelight by which the halls and rest of the room were lit, the priest at the altar was washed with a sterile glow from a strange metallic implement. Veins of a copper-colored metal were inlaid into an iron cylinder with a white crystal at its head. It was from the crystal that the cold light emanated. *Is that some sort of Volari invention?*

"Lord Henner," Lestreus said while giving a deep bow.

The chubby archpriest huffed, and without looking up from his work, said simply, "Prince Lestreus. To what do I owe the pleasure of the fourteenth prince's visit?"

Lestreus winced at the additional weight that Lord Henner verbally placed on his place in succession. The prince had been granted permission by this very gentleman to enter the Divine Temple as he wished and agreed to provide additional education by other clergy members, but it was just politics. Henner simply wished to please the royal family by saying yes to a simple request. The trade-off was simple and worth it. He could let other priests handle an insignificant royal while he received respect for granting such a boon to the royal family by providing special care and attention to Lestreus' education.

"I simply came to receive instruction today on the words of the gods, as I usually do this time of day."

"Well, as you can see, your instructor is not here today, and I am rather busy making notations of my own from scripture. So, young prince, if you can find your way back to the Knight's Academy, that would be for the best."

Lestreus nodded. The archpriest clearly did not have a high opinion of him and his tone was far from warm. It was unnecessary for him to provide any form of pleasantries with the prince, aside from at least acknowledging him. As the Archpriest of the Crucidian Church, he was automatically part of the king's cabinet of ministers and every church on the continent followed his commands as if they were from the very gods themselves. Due to his position, one could say that the amount of power that Archpriest Henner commanded in the Faradin Kingdom was second only to the king himself. His only limitation was the fact he was not of the nobility.

Lestreus turned to leave the altar room as commanded by the archpriest. Just as he was opening the doors, he paused. This caused Archpriest Henner to look up and raise an eyebrow. He had to ask about what it was the gray-robed priest had said.

"Lord Henner."

"What is it?"

"Is there anything that the kingdom could do differently? Something we haven't done before? I met a priest in gray robes who asked me for my opinion. He seemed displeased with my answer."

"Is that so?" Archpriest Henner had fully abandoned his note taking and placed his quill to the side. The rotund man walked slowly towards the prince. Every step echoed off the high ceilings.

"And just what was your answer?"

"To follow in the footsteps of my father and his fathers. Passively guide the kingdom. Not rule it with an iron fist."

"I see." Henner responded. "A valid answer, I suppose. May I ask you a question in return?"

"Yes, your lordship. Of course," Lestreus answered.

"Are you perhaps aware of the rising tensions in the kingdom? Between the factions of nobility. Are you also aware of our tenuous relationship with the followers of the so-called 'Path'?"

"I am."

"Many kings before your father have... guided... the kingdom along. Though some others might say they simply watched. Sure, it is a wonderful thought, to allow people to govern themselves as they see fit, but look where it has brought us." Henner spread his arms wide. "Two sides of one kingdom at each other's throats and heathens forsaking the words of the gods... Would you not say it is time for something new? Something different?"

"But Lord Henner! The Faradin Kingdom has been strong for centuries thanks to the efforts of my forefathers. Why would I do anything different from what they have?"

"So, you say, but is the kingdom really strong?"

Lestreus winced at the implication. "I don't know. Not that I will ever become king. I suppose it was fruitless to even ask these questions. It is not as if I could do anything to change the direction of our nation."

The priest stopped walking towards the prince and appraised him a little closer. Lestreus felt an odd pressure as he was scrutinized by the man. Archpriest Henner had never once looked at Lestreus as anything more than a stray cat he was forced to care for. That was, at least, until Lestreus had asked these questions.

"Why couldn't you become king? Do you believe you lack influence? Knowledge? Power?"

"Your lordship?" he asked.

"Tell me, Prince Lestreus," Henner commanded with a smile, teasing the corner of his lips. He leaned in towards Lestreus before continuing, "You said you were aware of our kingdom's struggles. So, I must ask. What do you really know about the differences between this nation's two halves? About Volar."

Lestreus paused for a moment, surprised at the sudden turn of the conversation. He knew things had been tense lately, though he had avoided looking too deeply at the why and only focused on the fact it existed. Before now, he thought it beneath his notice since he would have no impact on such issues were he to involve himself.

"In truth, I know very little of the intricacies of such things beyond common rumor and discourse," he finally admitted with a sigh.

Henner nodded, coming ever closer. "Truth be told, what is occurring now has been building for decades. If not for centuries. The southerners lacking the ability to care for themselves; something my church has graciously offered assistance with. Instead, they rely upon the Vanguard. Squandering money away on brutes and barbarians loyal to none but themselves and coin.

"Then, in the same breath they used to spit in the face of our church's kindness, they sing the praises and break bread with a country—Volar—whose people forsake the words of the gods for their 'Path'. They would rather work alongside a foreign power that creates and secrets away its knowledge from both us and them. Things that can be used to help millions, yet they refuse... A direct blasphemy against the Goddess of Innovation herself."

Lestreus followed Henner's gaze to the strange, flame-less lamp. "I see."

Henner sighed, returning to face him. "Within you there is potential, Prince Lestreus. I feel a fool to have not noticed it before, but by simply asking these questions, you have piqued my curiosity to where I feel required to support your education more...directly."

"Truly?" Lestreus felt his heart soar. Someone as important as Henner was interested in him? Never had someone with such power or prestige gave him the time of day, yet here this man was, arguably the second most powerful man in the kingdom, expressed genuine interest in him.

Archpriest Henner continued leaning in closer, mere inches from Lestreus' ear. "Yes, truly. What you need is knowledge and experience; two necessities for power. All you need to do is a small favor for me."

"What kind of favor?"

"What do you think of the Vanguard Academy? Would you prance about with commoners for a chance to answer your question? A chance at gaining the things you lack?"

Lestreus thought for a moment. Already, the nobles within the Knight Academy felt beneath him. Far from the throne or not, he was a prince, and they were not. Commoners in the Vanguard Academy were even lower than that. Was cavorting with them worth it? "Yes. But why there?"

"I intend to help your father ease tensions, of course! As I am in charge of your education, I think we could hit two birds with one stone, as it were. Showing we *value* the southerners by having a member of the royal family attend their academy. On top of that, your connection to me will show my personal interest in the citizenry of Jelmoore and their neighbors.

"I am sure our faithful in the south will enjoy knowing that we truly support them, regardless of their place of birth. Perhaps it might subvert the pride in their nobles' hearts to accept the gifts and help we have offered. They will find it difficult to refuse our offers of help and security if their people demand it."

"I will do as you say, Lord Henner." Troublesome though it may be. If attending school with common folk was all Lord Henner required of him to grant him the things he was missing, then he would happily attend the Vanguard Academy. The question remained: how would he do this? The reasoning escaped Lestreus for now, but someone as powerful as Henner had to know what he was doing.

Rune

*R*une *lay on a green patch of grass, shaded by a large oak tree. When he sat up, confused as he realized this wasn't the room he fell asleep in.*

As he observed his surroundings, he noticed there was a nice, gentle breeze, and the sunlight danced along his legs as it filtered through the leaves of the tree. The sky above was a perfectly clear blue, with no clouds to be found.

Upon standing, he saw a simple cottage in the distance. Next to it was a large river, though something about it unsettled Rune to his core. He scanned the area again and realized that other than the tree behind him and the cottage and river in the distance, there was nothing else around him. The grass stretched beyond the horizon, with no other landmarks of any kind interrupting the sea of green.

It was at this moment that the boy realized that not only was the area devoid of other landmarks, there were also no sounds other than the gentle breeze and rustling leaves. The sky held no birds. The ground held no insects. Other than the tree, the cottage, the grass, and Rune, the area was devoid of life. Rune felt his heartbeat jump into his throat, and echo in his ears.

A tender melody danced along the wind toward him, breaking the deafening silence. It reminded him of the lullaby his mother would hum to him and his sister as children whenever they were sick or could not sleep. Rune slowly walked towards the cottage, following the comforting song. Once he reached the door, Rune knocked.

After a while, without an answer, he realized the musical voice was coming from behind the cottage, not inside it. Rune gulped, because that was where the strangely disturbing river was. His instincts screamed to stay away from the waters, but the only clue where he even was or how he had gotten there was that feminine voice and source of the alluring melody.

A woman was crouched beside the river with a basket of laundry beside her and a clothesline behind her, filled completely with white shirts. There was clearly no room on it for more clothing, yet the woman continued to hum and wash the dirty laundry using the water from the river.

The river was finally in view. Instead of clear, blue water, it was colored black with an eerie purple glow occasionally flashing within its waters in small, silent explosions of light. Rune found himself unable to focus on the river. Each time he would look at the water, his vision would blur and bring about a pain at the base of his skull. He quickly glanced to the cottage behind him and the tree beyond that without issue. He then attempted to look at the riverbank on the other side. Unfortunately, just like the river itself, Rune could not focus on the shore of the other side. It simultaneously seemed to exist and not exist, constantly vanishing and reappearing.

"Ah, welcome back. I am so glad we can finally converse. You were not ready before, but welcome to my domain once more. Ah, but first, tell me. What do you see?" a soothing voice asked. Without looking back at him, the woman continued to wash clothes in the pitch-black water. She wore white gloves on her hands, yet they somehow stayed dry despite being submerged in the murky depths.

"Death," Rune answered subconsciously.

His own voice and sudden answer surprised him. It was as if his subconscious mind knew that the water of this river held nothing for him other than his end.

The woman giggled. "I see," she said. "I've asked many people what they see when they look at the sea. Some have seen hope, others despair. Still others see chaos and destruction, while some have seen the fabric of creation. But death? So final, so resolute. It is interesting. There was once another who gave the same answer. But you are the only person since him. Is that all?"

Rune nodded his head but did not quite understand what was going on.

The woman ceased washing the laundry, stood up, and dusted off her knees. She turned around and looked at Rune with a sad, sympathetic smile. Or at least, that was what he felt she had done. Just like the river of death, he could not focus on her face. Her eyes, hair, and facial features seemed different every time he looked at her. Then, as soon as he pieced them together, they vanished from memory.

"It's unfortunate that all you see is death," she stated, still with that sad expression. "But you aren't wrong, not completely anyway. Neither are you right. It is no matter; I do not expect a mortal to grasp its entire nature. No matter how many times they gaze upon it."

"Wait, did you call it a 'sea' earlier? This looks like a river," Rune said, rubbing the bridge of his nose. A massive headache set in once more as he continued to glance between the water and the woman. Though he could not make out a shoreline on the other side, his subconscious knew it was not a sea.

The woman cocked her head inquisitively. "Very interesting. A singular path, maybe? No ocean of opportunity, but a river with a set destination..." she pondered aloud. "Well, regardless of what form it takes for you physically, you see it as death. The feeling that this water evokes tells a little about your past and future. For that, I am sorry." She sat back down and returned to doing the laundry.

"Um...who are you?"

"An excellent question! One I wish I could answer for you." The woman then rotated the clothesline, causing one shirt to vanish, before she hung another in its place. "Do me a favor, Rune."

"Um, okay," Rune nodded. His tone was one of caution. He did not remember giving the strange woman his name.

"Stay in Hilden. Do not leave until you have grown. D-Rank should work. Then follow the raven-haired girl. Venraya, I believe her name was." The woman pulled out a shirt from the basket that was almost black. She dipped it in the water and it came out pristine but filled with holes. With a sigh, she threw it into the water completely and watched as it disintegrated into nothing.

"Um, okay. Stay in Hilden until I hit D-Rank. Got it..."

"Ah! One more thing. You will soon make a choice. Stay hidden or confront. I suggest you remain hidden. It will be easier that way."

"What will I confront?"

The woman stood up and walked towards Rune. She took one of her hands and placed it gently against his cheek with a sad expression.

Chapter Nine

Rune

Adull, yet familiar roar flooded Rune's ears as he shot up in his bed. His surroundings once again were recognizable. Beneath him was the same bed he had fallen asleep on. All the furniture was where he remembered, and the smell of booze and sweat in the air was as he had grown accustomed to. None of the things from the strange grassland in his dream were anywhere to be found. *What was that about?* He wondered. *Who was that woman?*

While still trying to process the dream, Rune gathered his weapons and went downstairs to the main hall. At the bottom of the stairs, he watched Mona, Lex, and Tabor giving out their goodbyes to Jacob and a few other members of the Vanguard they were close to. Ven also doled out tearful hugs to them. She turned and noticed Rune had made his way into the main lobby.

"Hey there, Rune! Just in time."

"What's all this?"

Mona stepped forward with a sack slung over her back. She was dressed in her full armor and her twin axes dangled off her waist. "The group and I are heading back to Jelmoore. My main base of operations is out of there for now, so we have to head home, eventually. I'll be back in a few weeks, though, to pick up Ven."

"Oh? Why are you picking Ven up in a few weeks?" Rune wondered and looked at his...friend?

"How hungover are you? Don't you remember? I'm joining the Vanguard Academy! I have always wanted to, and you kinda have to if you wanna go past

C-Rank. Most people are fine with staying at C-Rank since those parties can take on most jobs, but I want more. You do too, Rune, so why don't you come with?" Ven explained excitedly.

"I don't have a problem with that," Rune began before he remembered his strange dream. A feeling rose inside him that suggested he should listen to the strange woman. "But I will only go to the academy once I hit D-Rank."

Jacob, Mona, Ven, and the rest of the group looked at Rune in shock. He had started as a newbie at a rank above normal, and he already seemed raring to go for the next rank up. Ven shook her head but had a small smile threatening to show itself. Jacob pinched the bridge of his nose. Mona and Tabor simply laughed while Lex stood there, emotionlessly.

"Kid... you heard me when I said your next rank exam would have to be held by a different Hall Master, right?"

"Sure, then I guess when I am ready for D-Rank, I will just head to Jelmoore and take my exam there... That should be soon enough."

"This fucking kid..." Jacob muttered while his wife continued to laugh.

"Never change, kid," She laughed, while rustling his hair. "Also, she lets you call her Ven now? How very interesting..."

Mona gave her daughter a sideways glance, which went unmet by the raven-haired girl. Suddenly, the corner of the room caught her attention, and no power existed capable of making her meet her mother's teasing gaze.

After a moment, Mona shrugged. "Well, that's that then. I'll see you in a few weeks, Ven! Rune! Don't get her or yourself killed in the meantime or I'll drag your asses back from the Goddess of Reincarnation herself to kill you again."

With that last threat and a bit more laughter, Mona and her party left the building. Jacob smiled after them and went back to his office. Rune was starving and asked Ven if she wanted to grab a bite from the bar in the hall before getting another quest, to which she eagerly agreed.

The food offered in the Vanguard Hall was simple at best and bland at worst, but it did the job and was easy on the coinpurse. The best part about it was the drinks were strong. However, Rune had no desire to start his day out drinking.

While they ate, he noticed more than a few pairs of eyes watching him now and then. Most of them seemed to be a passing curiosity, but there were a couple that kept taking multiple glances. One of them was a strange man in ragged-looking robes who sat in a chair near the job board. People seemed to avoid looking at him or sitting near him. Not out of fear, though. Respect. *Strange.* The other was a group of rough-looking guys a few tables away.

After several minutes of this uncomfortable staring, the rough guys came over to Rune's table. They shoved aside several chairs, creating a cacophony of uncomfortable squeals from the wooden floor. A person who was most likely the leader of their gang slammed one hand down on the table and put another around Rune's shoulder. He wore simple leather armor similar to Rune's own. It was slightly damaged in places, with some threads fraying. Clearly, it needed some work.

"Hey there, newbie. I heard you cut the line and went straight to E-Rank. Screwin' the boss' daughter to get ahead?" he sneered. His mocking tone was accompanied by the laughter of his cronies. Rune ignored them and return to his simple meal, but the hand on his shoulder tightened. It was at this point Rune noticed he was wearing studded gauntlets, which implied the man focused on hand-to-hand combat. The knuckles were reinforced with steel spikes, with additional metal bulging beneath the top layer of leather.

Few people in the world would risk fist fighting against people with weapons or dangerous monsters. Since he was one of those select few, it was likely that this thug was an Enhancer-class Awakened. Someone who could use the Aura crystalized inside his body to enhance his physical capabilities beyond normal human means.

"Shut it, Bordo," Ven growled. "For your information, Rune took down a group of three Bash Eagles single-handedly on his first run out. That means he beat an E-Rank threat on his own. Something that you would struggle to do even as D-Rank, I think. Everyone knows you bullshit your way to your rank."

The brawler, and potential Enhancer, known as Bordo tightened his grip again. "Is that right, girlie? Hey kid, she tellin' the truth?" Ven's comments about his lack of prowess either went unheard or he ignored them.

Rune nodded quietly. Despite Bordo's obvious attempts to the contrary, he was not intimidated by the man. In fact, he thought he could take him easily, but he wanted to avoid causing any trouble on his first day as a warrior in the Vanguard. Unfortunately for him, Bordo and his gang took this as a sign of weakness and laughed again.

"Right, this shrimp probably just—"

"Did you not hear me? I said, shut it, Bordo." Ven repeated coldly. The surrounding air felt like it had dropped a few degrees. "I won't pull the dad card, but I will pull the mom card. My mom, Tabor, and Lex all have a lot of high opinions of Rune. So, if you don't shut it and leave right now, I'll run out and catch her and have her teach you a few things. Maybe Lex will ask you to be a moving target the next time we train together. He won't be a problem, but I'm not as good of a shot as him. I might accidentally hit something vital."

Bordo paled instantly at the girl's statement and retracted his hand. Mona's party were all B-Rankers and much stronger than nearly everyone else in Hilden. They could be A-Ranks if they took the promotion exam, but they liked the freedom they still had as B-Rankers. He nodded to his group to leave, but not before shooting one last glare at the duo. Rune caught a smile on the face of the robed man, who watched the whole thing. He simply nodded and turned away when Rune's eyes met his.

"Dumbasses. Sorry about that, Rune. Bordo and his idiots like to rough up the new members. Unfortunately for them, you are my friend, so I won't let them bother you."

"Thanks, Ven!" Rune beamed. "Happy to have made my first friend outside of home."

Ven's cheeks took on a slight bit of color. "Anyway, I think our job today should be to take on this one I found this morning. It's asking for someone to take out a stray Shadow Wolf that has been harassing the animals of a few farmers outside of Dorn."

"Sounds like a plan!"

Ulma

"Damn it, Ulma," Vickar shouted. "I know you just started picking up the hammer, but come on. That's the second iron ingot you've ruined today. Hit it with purpose and quickly! If you don't hit it hard enough, then it'll cool before it gets to the shape you want, and if you let it cool too much before you hit it, you'll ruin the quality. Metal-weaving is a tool to assist you, not cover up for mistakes. You have to blend your abilities with your skill. Only when doing both will you achieve a quality result."

Ulma wiped the sweat from her stinging eyes. She had only just started learning how to work with her father yesterday and he already was expecting her to be good at it. Granted...she was. On her very first day, she had completed a sword and two small kitchen knives that were impressive enough for her father to admire. What had her messing up today was a distraction.

They had received a letter from Rune where he explained what had happened on his trip from Locke to Hilden. Ulma was not so stupid as to think that her brother would live a peaceful life. By Chaos, she knew that he specifically joined the Vanguard to search for fights either with beasts or bandits. Still, it worried her whenever she thought about how he could get hurt. She was also still unsettled by the new world she'd been seeing since her bloodline abilities had awakened.

Vickar did very little help to her in trying to understand how to use her natural gift because he was, to put it simply, a poor teacher. Ulma was struggling to figure out how in the world her brother and Tara had learned a single thing about fighting from the man. If someone did not do something right, he would explain it the same way, just louder. As if he thought that his volume was the problem for information not getting across.

Prior to the other day, Ulma had been content with helping her mother do seamstress work at home, but one night after Rune had left, she received a strange dream.

Ulma

*U*lma *found herself in some sort of cavern with a massive opening above her head. The air around her felt hot enough to boil her skin and turn the hair on her head to ash. Even with the oppressive heat, however, she felt fine. At first, everything was dead silent, like she was alone in this burning landscape.*

Ulma searched the area for a way out, since trying to pinch herself awake from the dream did nothing but hurt. A few minutes of exploration later, she heard cursing in between the sounds of clanging metal. With no other ideas on how to proceed, the girl simply followed the sounds. She hoped that whoever was shouting profanity was at least kind enough to help her find a way out.

When the girl located the source of the noise, she was amazed to see another actual person in this burning cave. They stood before a massive anvil next to a river of fire. The heat here was dozens of times more intense than the rest of the strange place, but instead of feeling uncomfortable, it soothed Ulma's heart. Instead of pain and oppression, she felt inspiration and hope.

The person before her was a woman who stood inhumanly tall, eight or nine feet. Her arms and legs rippled with muscles and her face, though very plain, was still extremely charming. Ulma could not exactly make out the woman's features. It was as if they were there and not at the same time. As though they forever changed.

The giant worked away at some sort of weapon, though it was so foreign to Ulma that she could not describe it or identify it. Truth be told, it could have been anything. Her curiosity heightened and excitement thrummed in her chest.

"Um, excuse me...what is that?"

The giant woman stopped and turned to face Ulma, who was easily dwarfed next to her. "And who in the Sea of Chaos are you?"

She gulped. Though she should have guessed the woman would have been gruff based on the cursing, her attitude was still jarring. "I'm Ulma, and I think I'm lost. I went to bed and...I think I'm dreaming. I mean, I have to be. Right?"

The giant woman put her hammer down and placed a hand on her chin, contemplating Ulma's claims. "That name sounds familiar. Oh, wait! You're...oh, what the fuck was his name? Vinny, Daniel, Carson, Jerod...no definitely a 'V' name... Kid, what's your dad's name?"

"Vickar."

"That's it! You're Vickar's brat. The one without the thing. Well, you have a different thing goin' on, I guess. What with the eyes and stuff. But not like your brother. Wow, didn't you get lucky?"

"What do you even know about Rune?" Ulma felt defensive. Regardless of who this entity was, even if she was a fragment of a dream, there was no way she would let someone get away with disrespecting her brother. Only she could do that.

"Hey, what do you think of this?" The strange woman cut Ulma off and gestured towards the strange-looking weapon. "It's a new farming implement! So, what do you think?"

As if compelled to give an answer, Ulma analyzed the object before her. It was made entirely of metal with large wheels. Somehow, it reminded her of an enclosed carriage, were that carriage equipped with massive metal spikes on its front and a strange metal tube reaching out from the top of it.

"The real one will be a bit bigger. Enough to fit a person. This is just a model. A proof of concept, as it were."

"Um, it looks well made, I guess. Farming? It looks like a weapon of war, not a tool for a field. What does it do?" Ulma asked. She wanted to circle back and

finish asking her own questions, but something about this person scared the living daylights out of her. That feeling of terror increased the moment she started feeling disrespected. Now, Ulma felt as if it would be best to follow along.

The woman frowned. "Damn, you can't tell? Supposed to be easy for you to understand... Welp, guess that's a failure. I'll look at the design again in a few centuries. Maybe by then, those Volari will start sharing. Either that or those damn humans will finally start catching up... well something, different. Some are trying, but I don't like their methods all that much." She quickly hid a look of disgust before she snatched up the model and tossed it into the lake of fire. In a fraction of a second, it melted away into nothingness.

"Anyway, brat, I ain't gonna tell you about your brother. I know you wanted to ask. What I will tell ya is to start workin' the forge! Ya got talent! And your dad's a good one. I like him."

Ulma nodded along. She had basically no interest in working on weapons, but again, she felt a strange sensation that told her disagreeing with this person was a terrible idea. "Father is a good smith. I'm sure I could learn a lot from him."

"You mean you will learn? You don't have a choice in the matter. Not if I have a say. The others claim I'm heavy handed, but a heavy hand makes for a heavy strike. When working the forge, that's what you need." The woman's aura changed into something incredibly dangerous. Ulma felt herself on the verge of losing consciousness. A moment later, it vanished, with the woman waving her hand dismissively. "Anyway, he's one of the best. Now piss off, I got work to do and you're distracting me."

Ulma

After the strange dream, Ulma had woken up like normal, and upon seeing him, had immediately asked her father to teach her his skills.

This shocked both him and her mother, but Vickar's shock was immediately overwhelmed by intense pride.

"Ulma! Come on, snap out of it! You are nothing like yesterday." Vickar's statement brought Ulma back to the present.

"Sorry, Father, I am just a little distracted is all."

"I can tell. You look like you haven't been sleeping well. How about you call it a day? Rest. We can resume training tomorrow. I know, why don't you go deliver Rune's letter to Tara?"

Ulma sighed and nodded in agreement. She definitely did not want to be a burden in the forge if she could help it. In fact, she oddly enjoyed the work. Even on the first day, she felt a strange satisfaction in her work that helping her mother never gave. *I guess I'll just listen to that woman from my dream. I'll keep training with father. Something just clicked for me, so maybe this was meant for me.*

"Sweetheart, is everything okay?" Her mother approached them with a look of concern. "I think it might be time to listen to your father and rest."

"I know, Mother. I was just about to head inside. Guess I'm still not used to Rune being gone. I've been having strange dreams." Ulma sighed. "Hey, pops?"

"What?" Vickar grunted. Her botched work was in his hands as he turned it over to see if there was a way to salvage anything from it.

"When will you teach me alderite-weaving?"

"My preferred answer would be never. But you and your brother are just as stubborn as each other. No doubt the more I try to scare you off from it, the more you'll run to it," Vickar sighed. He removed his goggles and placed them gently on the anvil. The twisted hunk of metal she had ruined was tossed into a pile of scrap with a loud *clang*. "When you can reliably make something without doing whatever that piss poor excuse at smithing was, then I will teach you."

Ulma nodded. She was dragging the conversation out. Her body was exhausted and the moment she rested, she would pass out and risk having another dream on that fiery mountain.

"Promise me," Vickar said quietly. His stern gaze was gone, replaced by worry. "When I teach you, just…stay here. In Locke. No matter who—or what—tries to pull you from this place, stay here."

Chapter Ten

Rune

Ven and Rune slowly approached the den of the beast they had been tracking for a few days. According to the locals, it had made a small hiding place amongst some thick bushes right off the edge of the Greatwood outside of Dorn's southern gates. The farmer who filed the request had already lost three of his cows, a few pigs, and a lamb to the monster. After all that, he was not too keen on losing more. He even offered to pay fifty percent over market value for the beast's pelt.

Normally, the hide of a Shadow Wolf was a desired item to collect from the monster, since it was well-suited for making high-quality fur cloaks and travel blankets, items valued by the Vanguard. However, the farmer's offer was too good to pass up. Neither of them needed or wanted to upgrade their equipment, either, so they readily agreed to the additional request.

Thankfully, the tracks Ven and Rune had found while scouting out the beast's territory and the farmer's fields showed their prey was a solo creature. If there had been one or two more, then it might have been too much to handle, bumping the quest into a D-Rank. Once they had found the nesting site, Ven set up a few hundred yards away from the entrance, while Rune was about half that distance. Every half hour, the silver-haired young man would change position to ensure that if the wolf was watching them back, that he at least would pull attention away from Ven and make it seem like Rune was a lone intruder.

Five hours into their stakeout, Ven noticed movement amongst the trees and gave the agreed upon signal, a simple bird call. Rune signaled back that he understood and acknowledged what she saw. The monster then emerged from between the trees. It was one and a half times larger than a normal wolf, and as the name suggested, it was covered in jet-black fur. The only splash of color on the beast was its golden irises, glowing in the evening light. Ven silently thanked the gods that they would not have to fight it at nighttime or in the woods themselves.

Tracking the monster's movements, Ven noticed as it slowed to a stop a few feet from the entrance to the nest it had built. It looked up and around while sniffing the ground and air. Ven tensed, anticipating the wolf monster's next move, and readied an arrow in her bow. She stayed low and out of sight for a few moments. At least, until the Shadow Wolf got into a crouched position and growled in the direction Rune was hiding. When that happened, Ven quickly stood up while finishing her draw. With only a single second to aim, she released the arrow at the creature. As if sensing the attack, the Shadow Wolf leaped to the side and dodged the projectile before it hit its mark.

Rune took advantage of the distraction and jumped out of his own hiding place to the creature's right. He drew his standard sword and slashed towards the creature's face. Ven released another two arrows in rapid succession to pin the beast down. Merely a distraction, but it would limit the beast's movements. They worked together to make the monster decide if it should dodge either her or Rune, but not give it the opportunity to avoid both.

Ven's arrows were the key part of the plan since a Shadow Wolf's pelt was rather resistant to slashing type weapons like swords. Using the penetrative power of her bow, they could pierce its tough hide. Alternatively, they could use Rune's alderite enhanced blade, but it would drain the core he had and could cause unnecessary damage to the pelt that would lower its value.

Eventually, the wolf decided the closer opponent was a bigger threat and took one of Ven's arrows to its hind leg, letting out a pained yelp. Blood spurted from the wound. *Must have hit something important!* Thankfully, the damage seemed to also slow the creature, making it easier for more shots to hit. After a few minutes of back and forth with Rune, the monster began to tire. Somehow, even after the hit to its leg and other areas of the body, it avoided future strikes to other vital locations. Not content to only serve as a distraction, Rune used his shield to smash the wolf's maw.

Ven noticed once again that as the fight dragged on, both she and the wolf were tiring out. Conversely, Rune seemed to get faster and stronger. His shield strikes, which the wolf was merely shrugging off in the beginning, now made it recoil with a yelp. Time between each hit also seemed to lessen as he appeared to move faster and faster.

What a monster, Ven mused. *Wonder if this has something to do with that fancy fighting style his father taught him.*

Gaining strength as a fight went on was an insane gift that most fighters would kill for. Ven was acutely aware of her own jealousy of his ability, especially since she was feeling her arms protest the repeated motions of drawing her bow.

"Ven, watch out! It's coming your way!"

Rune's warning was correct. The wolf broke away from Rune's increasingly painful strikes and rushed towards the weaker of the two opponents. Instinct told the wolf that it could no longer flee, so it resolved to take at least one attacker down with it. By the time Ven was ready for the creature's change in attack pattern, the wolf had already closed half the distance between them.

Ven took a deep breath and released three more arrows before stowing the bow. She then pulled out her backup weapons; a pair of daggers. The one in her right hand was designed for a reverse grip hold and the other was useful in either direction. Ven lacked the physical strength to go toe-to-toe with a creature as big and strong as this, so she ran diagonally from the monster to lead it back toward Rune's position.

The Shadow wolf leaped for her, exerting the remainder of its energy in going for her throat. Despite her disadvantage, she decided she could buy enough time for Rune to catch up. A huge mass of black fur descended on her position, ready to meet her blades. Right as the beast descended upon her, blocking out the sun with a large shadow, Rune closed the distance. From the corner of her eye, Ven saw a puff of dirt spray into the air from his feet. He jumped between the monster and his friend while smashing into its face with his shield. The impact caused the monster to howl and screech as it rolled several feet before skidding to a stop in the dirt, unmoving. There might have been something like the sound of cracking bones mixed in, but it was hard to tell.

"You good?"

"Yeah..." she breathed. "That was a close one."

"I thought you said you were done being bait. So why did you do it to yourself?" Rune's voice was higher pitched. Was he angry?

Ven shrugged before standing up and walking over to their prey. Her companion's frustrated glare followed her, but she ignored it. Still breathing, though shallow and ragged; the monster rolled its eyes to look at her. No fight was left in it. Death was its only future, and the wolf knew that. Ven eyed the monster's neck and sunk one of her daggers behind its ear, piercing the brain.

"That was fun." She smiled at Rune.

"If I'm not allowed to use you as bait, you can't do it either," Rune complained while patting her on the back. "Good idea on the direction you took. I think if you really tried for it, you could have gone for a single one right between the eyes instead of three as a distraction. In the mental state it was in and the amount of dedication in that last charge, I doubt it would have been able to dodge."

Ven shrugged nonchalantly. "Eh, maybe, but there was also the likelihood that I missed the target, or it could have held enough energy to pull off that dodge. Or...maybe this was going to be more fun."

Rune continued to grumble, eliciting several small laughs from her while they worked on the monster's corpse. They skinned it and collected its fangs as proof of a job well done before slicing up the rest of the body and scattering it about the entrance to the forest. Wolf meat was not good eating. Definitely a last-ditch food source and not for enjoyment.

They walked back to the farmer with their bounty and exchanged it for the promised money and a written letter showing they completed the job. Rune did most of the talking because Ven was—as she had admitted to him already—not good with people.

"Thank you, son. And the girl, too. Damned overgrown dog cost me a lot of money these last few weeks." The farmer sighed while looking at the animals in his pasture. "It'll be awhile before the cows start producin' again. I think the stress dried them up."

Rune laughed. "Well, I'm sure they'll come around. If you want, we can sell you the pelt at normal market value instead. Take that extra coin and get a few more dairy cows with it to get you back going while you wait for the other ones to calm down."

Ven's eyes snapped to him. She was not against the idea, but was surprised that the young man's kindness spread even to people he did not have to impress. It was looking like he was too good to be true. She had already gotten used to his respectful nature at the Hall, but she had been convinced it was to make a good impression on fellow members and the master. This farmer did not matter in the grand scheme of things. *Guess he's just a good guy.*

"You sure about that, son?"

"Well, I'd offer to give you the pelt free of charge, but I don't want to seem ungrateful for your offer to pay us more for it. If we kept it and sold it to the Vanguard, we'd lose out on about ten percent. So, we still make off better."

"Well, that is mighty kind of ya'." The farmer turned to Ven. "That's only if it's okay with the young lady?"

Once Ven nodded in agreement, Rune settled their negotiations and they began the trip back to Hilden. Rune remained silent while cradling his head. Ven had noticed that after fighting, he always seemed to get some sort of migraine. Asking about it seemed rude, so she remained silent. It was never a hinderance so there was not even a need to ask about it.

Remembering how he fought the wolf brought a blush to her face again. *I think I have a problem,* Ven thought. *I kinda wanted him to jump in to save me like that... He's kinda really cool.*

Lestreus

Lestreus sat before his father with a determined expression on his face. His father, King Leonidas Faradin, rubbed the sides of his head with both hands after listening to his son's request.

"So let me see if I understand this correctly..." he mumbled. "You want to transfer from the Knight Academy—away from the special educational opportunities I set up for you—to instead attend the Vanguard Academy in Jelmoore? Why?"

"I think it would be an excellent opportunity for multiple reasons."

Leonidas arched an eyebrow. "Those being?"

"For starters, it would provide me with worldly knowledge that none of my siblings have been granted. Even you and grandfather never ventured far from the capital. I think it is time that someone in our family learned more about the people."

Leonidas's expression openly portrayed how little he believed is son's words were his own. He did not know Lestreus very well—having basically ignored him for most of his life—but he knew his son had never been this motivated before. Sure, he was a bookworm, but he was also well known to look down upon others, and someone like that would not do well in an academy filled with commoners.

"Anything else?"

"Would it not be politically advantageous to send one of your children to stay in a southern city? It might go a long way toward settling some of the negative feelings right now."

"Sure, it could. Or it could cause more disruptions. I take it Lord Henner presented this offer to you? These words do not feel like your own," Leonidas asked dryly. "We should not do anything to be too disruptive in these times. Every action we take has the potential to affect the lives of millions. As royalty, we must be aware of this..."

Lestreus stayed silent, his face still determined.

"I see." Leonidas leaned back in his chair with a heavy sigh. "Listen well, my son. You are plainly aware of the dissonance between our nobles. What of the influence Volar has on our territories near it? Are you even aware, truly, of the frustrations that nation has with the Crucidian Church? It would be best to remain impartial to that which you have no experience."

"Father, why must we do nothing? We always sit here in our capital under the guise of impartiality. I... I'm not sure that's the right move anymore."

Leonidas sighed. "Lestreus, the south—Jelmoore in particular—and the royal family of Volar are very close. Sending my son, with well-known ties to the Crucidian Church mind you, to the only city that does trade with the Volari may cause people to assume I am supporting the church's behaviors. We must, again, remain impartial. It is how we have always ruled."

"Father, I don't think that's the way anymore. I fear our *guiding hand* has become something else. We let the nobles rule themselves and it has worked out for most. The northern territories are a veritable trove of wealth. Yet the southern cities are insignificant. Their populace toils away; struggling against monsters and bandits. Their only reprieve from such things is a third-party organization who thrives off violence.

"Their nobles do nothing of note other than cavort with foreign and private powers in spite of the freedoms they have been given. Gods above, Father, when has a southerner even attended your royal court? The furthest north I've heard of one of their lords traveling is Nefera."

"Son."

"The church sends their missionaries to spread the word of the gods, the very gods who blessed our family with rule over this nation. Through this, they have learned of the plights the southerners face. They have offered gifts and reprieve to the southern lords to ease the lives of their citizenry. Yet, they shoved those gifts aside!" Lestreus could feel the frustration rising, his voice increasing in volume.

"So, what if a foreign power believes we support the church? We should! They have offered to step in and improve the lives of our southern subjects, regardless of them deserving it, where you have not. We should be so lucky that people realize how important the church is to our nation! Look at how prosperous we are up north, where the words of the gods and the gifts of our faithful are graciously accepted!"

Leonidas sat in silence, allowing his son's words to simply wash over him.

"Father, I will go to the Vanguard Academy," Lestreus proclaimed. "Our nation needs to change. Our ways need to change. I don't have all the answers yet, but according to Lord Henner, this will help me. I have to do something different, even if that means spending time around brutes who masquerade as heroes. Heroes who would not be needed if their nobility accepted Henner's offer."

Lestreus left the room without a second look at his father. He knew these actions risked him losing financial support from the crown, but Archpriest Henner promised it would not be a problem. When he had first asked Lestreus what he thought about attending a commoner school like the Vanguard Academy, Lestreus was intensely offended. He had not let this offense show however, because Lord Henner was his benefactor.

The priest had explained to Lestreus that there were aspects of the world that he could only learn by witnessing them. He wanted to show the prince the 'evils' of the Path of Volar and the Volari people who refused to adapt to the ways of the church. He also needed to see the differences between the southern cities and those in the north himself.

Of course, the prince had another reason for going aside from the request of the portly priest. The mysterious man in gray robes was a larger reason for taking this step. His question of what the fourteenth prince would do differently than his ancestors plagued Lestreus nightly. Every moment was occupied by the obsessive desire to answer that strange man's question. For the life of him, the prince could not figure out why. Maybe that question was why he finally felt such resolve to stand against his father.

Chapter Eleven

Rune

In the weeks following the Shadow Wolf quest, Rune and Ven continued to take jobs around both Hilden and Dorn. They agreed to avoid any jobs that would take them to Locke or Jelmoore, at Rune's own request. Ven had no problem voicing her confusion about why he wanted to avoid these places so badly.

One night, she finally asked him directly what his reasoning was, so he answered her. Rune tried to explain how 'something' had told him he needed to avoid going to Jelmoore until he was a D-Ranker. For the life of her, Ven could not understand why he felt that way, but Rune silently refused to tell her how it had come to him in a dream, for fear of sounding insane. His reasoning for not returning to Locke was easier for him to explain, though.

"So, you need to feel you accomplished something before going home, huh?" Ven asked between sips of her drink. It was a watered-down mead that they had grown accustomed to drinking after returning from a job. The Hall served stiffer things, but they preferred lighter options. They were not the best tasting, but at least they were cheap. It also kept them from getting too drunk too quickly.

"Sure, I know I started out a rank above standard. That is usually considered impressive enough from what I've gathered, but I think I would like to wait until I figure out my Class," Rune shared while shyly scratching his cheek. "I, at least, know for sure I am Awakened, but I don't think I can face Tara without advancing past the basics, ya' know?"

Ven's face soured. "Right, Tara, your girlfriend."

"She's not my girlfriend. She's a childhood friend."

"I'll tell you something, Rune. No one talks that much about someone who is a 'friend'. So, take your bullshit elsewhere, will you?"

Ven snorted in frustration, cutting the conversation short. Rune could not find it in himself to keep it going either. Every time he brought up Tara, Ven's mood plummeted. He wasn't so blind as to not realize what was going on by this point, even though it had taken him longer than he liked to admit.

Ven was a charming and beautiful young woman; not in spite of her abrasiveness, but because of it. She was also someone he respected very much because of her open emotions and honest words. In time, they could have grown closer, but as things stood, he could not allow himself to move things forward with anyone else. Something like that did not feel right.

They continued to eat their meal in awkward silence before he broke it with a question of his own. "Ven, I've been meaning to ask you ever since you asked about my name. Why is your name so close to the name of the continent, Vendreya?"

Ven paused. Her face said she was still annoyed, but she graciously answered him. "It's a Zentus tradition. Our people are typically nomadic back home, and we place a lot of weight on exploration. So, when you have a child, you typically name them something similar to the place they were born."

"Oh, that's neat."

"Yeah. Mom's the same way. She's Mona 'cus she was born on a boat on the way here called the Monathis, I believe," Ven continued.

"Any other weird Zentus things I need to know?"

Ven took another swig, as if she needed bravery to help her answer him. She shifted uncomfortably before releasing a heavy sigh. "Yeah. I have two dads and another mom. Not my thing, but Mom's people tend to have multiple partners. Martin and Stella are my other parents."

Before Rune could make a comment on that, his focus was broken by a commotion at the door. They both looked up and saw a group of familiar faces.

The leader locked eyes with Rune and waved excitedly while heading towards the table.

"Rune! Ven! Good to see you both!"

Ven's eyes went wide. "Mom! Lex! Tabor! I didn't know you were getting back today!"

"Ha! Of course not. I wanted to surprise you, sweetie. I just got back from making a delivery to the Hall and spoke with Jacob. He said you two have been doing pretty well for yourselves!"

"Yeah, we've been working together, I'd say. We've done what...ten jobs together?" Rune stated.

"That sounds about right. We actually just got back from one tracking down an Echo Bear nest. We didn't fight any, but it was a well-paying scouting job, so we took it." Ven nodded before downing the rest of her drink in a single gulp. She stood up and gave her mother a heavy embrace.

"Missed you too, kiddo. Hey, I packed your stuff already. You ready to go?" Mona said while hugging her daughter. It was a strange sight, watching a powerful warrior like Mona play the part of a doting mother. Yet it was the most natural thing in the world.

"You aren't going to stick around?" he asked. His heart fell a little, realizing what was coming.

"Yeah, that's right, kiddo. Time to get back to Jelmoore. We just had to drop off a delivery and pick up Ven. Of course, you know I also had to see Jacob before heading back. Besides, I have to get back to Martin, or he will get lonely!"

The laughter of the situation died down. Rune could tell everyone was prolonging this on his behalf. It was kind, but also kind of hurt. Thankfully, Ven seemed to notice.

"Well," she coughed, "Mom is going back to Jelmoore and I'm going to enroll at the Vanguard Academy there. If you wanna break into the upper ranks of the Vanguard, get a degree there." Ven shifted, clearly uncomfortable with the somber mood that was setting in. "Hey, you sure you don't wanna come, too?"

Rune felt the sudden, intense urge to pack his bags, when he recalled his strangely realistic and terrifying dream once more. He shook his head. "No, I'm gonna stick around here for a while. I could use some more time getting used to life outside of Locke before I head to the big city. Plus, I have to get D-Rank first!"

Jacob who had walked into the building and positioned himself behind Mona, nodded with approval, and put a hand on the boy's shoulder. He gave him a solid thumbs up. The group then finished their goodbyes before Mona and her group finally left, on their way to Jelmoore. Surprisingly, Ven gave quite the enthusiastic handshake to Rune before leaving. He had figured she would be as sad as he was that they were separating, but maybe she was just looking forward to the future. She already knew of his dream to break into the S-Rank, so he would have to join her there, eventually.

Ven then shocked Rune by giving him a sudden hug. Contradicting the firm handshake, there was a momentary tremble in her arms, which faded quickly. "Look, you better hurry and get D-Rank. If you don't get in this semester somehow, I'll drag your ass to Jelmoore myself before the next school year. Also, I will absolutely bully you as your senior."

Rune could only respond with resigned laughter because he knew she was telling the truth. Mona seemed to give a sly smile to the pair of friends, but she quickly hid it before her daughter turned around to see it. Mona shot Rune a knowing glance, leaving Rune to only slightly shake his head. Mona frowned at his silent denial of her insinuations.

After a prolonged goodbye, Rune returned to the Hall alongside Jacob. The Hall Master informed him that now that he was on his own, he should look for a new party before he started taking jobs. At E-Rank, he could take F-Rank jobs on his own, but to take an E-Rank job, he needed at least one other member with him. While the young man stood in front of the job board, he noticed a few requests for Bash Eagle plates and feathers. There were also a few requests to hunt down some wolves and boars of various species.

"Hey, newbie!" a voice called out from behind Rune. "Saw that the boss' daughter ditched you here in town. Feelin' lonely now that your girlfriend is gone?"

Rune turned around to see a plain man surrounded by a group of his friends. They were all chuckling at their friend's attempt at a joke. Choosing to ignore the fool, he turned back to the quest board. Now that Ven was gone, it was a sure thing Bordo and his gang would bother him. Though, it was surprising that it had happened this quickly. It was likely because he was spending so much time around Ven and her family that he avoided it until now.

Bordo's group did not appreciate the idea of a newbie ignoring them. Their prey had escaped once thanks to the protection of another, but now he was alone. Ripe for torment. Bordo's hand clamped tightly onto Rune's shoulder, daring him to turn away a second time. The man's veins glowed slightly and his muscles bulged almost unnaturally.

He locked eyes with Rune and growled, "Listen here, twerp. I was talking to you. You're gonna learn to respect your betters."

Can't I have a moment to process my friend leaving town before this idiot comes to mess with me? Rune whined internally.

A familiar pain shot through Rune's skull. At the same time, the pressure of Bordo's grip seemed to lessen. "Okay, and how do I go about doing that? I don't really have it in me today to deal with some newbie-busting."

The aggression is his tone surprised him. Never had Rune spoken that way to someone, even if they were rude. It was a habit he had picked up from Tara and her parents when he would spend time in their general store. Well, before they started maturing and her father hated his guts.

"Watch your tone, kid. You are ten years too green to get sassy with me. You know what? How 'bout I show you why you need to respect me and my crew?" the man continued to grumble at Rune. His cronies surrounded the young man and shoved him towards the training area. Their sudden actions and his pounding headache kept him from making the right decision, which would have been to resist or even call out to someone.

The next thing Rune knew, he was in a fighting ring surrounded by dozens of other Vanguard members. People had passed money between each other, taking bets on how many minutes Rune would last. Bordo was already in the ring with him and hyping up the crowd. They responded to his posturing with cries of excitement. Bordo's friends were shouting praise behind him, egging him on and telling him to turn Rune's face into a paste. Bordo shot him a sneer while fitting a set of spiked knuckles over his gauntlets.

Out of the corner of his eye, Rune saw a group of people about his age looking on with concern. Two of them were young men with pitying gazes. They tried to leave, but someone in a worn-out robe blocked their path. Rune suspected the group was about to fetch Jacob, but the robed man did not want that to happen. The group of three younger members were then redirected to a space next to the ring. Once they found a spot amongst the crowd, the robed man flashed Rune a teasing smile. *I never got around to asking Ven who that guy is.*

"No enhanced weapons, kid. So best you remove the one on your belt. You can keep the normal one. Don't worry, I ain't gonna make you fight with your fists." Bordo instructed with a dark chuckle. Rune hesitantly complied, removing his twin sword sheathe and handing it—with only his altered sword in it—to the robed man, who had already approached the ring. He had the group of young Vanguard with him as well.

Rune shook his head. The headache that had been plaguing seemed to get worse by the minute. Taking a good, deep breath, he tightened his grip on his unenhanced sword. He was ready for the fight. Bordo opened and closed his fists a few times before getting into a fighting stance. The two locked eyes for a few seconds that seemed to stretch into minutes. Suddenly, the sound of a bell rang throughout the room, causing the pugilist to launch towards Rune. "Enhance: Leap!" he shouted. For a fraction of a second his face lit up in confusion.

A small flash of purple light erupted from the soles of the man's feet as he lunged directly at Rune with inhuman speed. Rune was an expert at reacting to the diving techniques of the Bash Eagles and could jump to the side just enough for his opponent to glide past him. Unfortunately for Rune, the pugilist was a human fighter, not a bird monster. This opponent could plan instead of just diving with reckless abandon. As Rune had forgotten to take this into account, one of the man's fists glanced off Rune's cheek.

Blood splattered out of Rune's mouth onto the dirt. Suddenly Rune's headache vanished. Replaced instead by a dull throb on the side of his face. His vision cleared while a subtle heat settled into his chest. Silent anger flooded his mind. The crowd fell into a hushed silence, expecting the fight to have been finished in the first strike. Several people grumbled, knowing their bets were already lost, with the young man surviving even a glancing blow.

Rune took advantage of his opponent's surprise and rushed towards him with a quick swing to the man's right shoulder.

"Enhance: Grip!" the man shouted as his left hand shot at the blade of the sword, intending to catch it. Once again there was a moment of confusion before the man refocused on the fight. Rune expected this and had already prepared to shift the energy of his strike into a kick.

With Bordo grabbing onto the blade, Rune let go of the sword in the same moment, not allowing the abrupt halting of his weapon to stop his physical momentum. Rune lifted one foot, using the other one as a pivot point, sending the energy behind the strike into a spinning kick. His foot landed with a solid *thud* in his opponent's side, forcing all of the air out of Bordo's lungs. This was the key to his 'strange fighting style'—as Ven called it—that his father taught him. Deflect and redirect. Every movement in a fight should connect to another. Never disrupt the flow of your body, simply shift it into the next move...and when you can, add your opponent's own energy to your own.

While his opponent kept his hold on Rune's weapon, he brought his left hand into a fist and punched the man's opposite side. After taking two powerful blows to his core, the pugilist could not help but drop the weapon and jump back to catch his breath. He recovered with deep, ragged breaths, anger pouring out of every part of his body. Rune simply picked his sword up and returned to a fighting stance. He motioned for the fight to continue.

A second later, Bordo leaped forward without an enhancement. After closing the gap, he shouted out another skill. "Enhance: Power Strike!" A dull purple light flashed from every vein in his left arm, starting at the shoulder. As soon as it appeared, some of the light faded. Rune knew that if the punch connected, it would shatter every bone around the impact point. As the young man ducked, it felt as if the world moved much slower. Bordo's arm came at him even slower than his initial attacks, despite being further enhanced.

Using the strange dilation of his perception to his advantage, he brought his arm back and did the only thing he could think to do in the time he had. He stabbed the sword through his opponent's foot. With a sickening squish and crunch, the sword found its home between bone and muscle, piercing even the ground beneath its target.

The pugilist roared in pain, pulling his fist away and grabbing the sword in response. Rune took that opportunity to bring his left hand up and bash his buckler across the man's face, knocking him unconscious using some of the remaining forward motion of Bordo's powered strike. After the other fighter crumpled to the ground like a sack of potatoes, Rune removed his sword from his foot, and wiped it off with his fallen enemy's cloak.

The silence was shattered by a roar of complaints, boos, and cheers erupting from around the ring. The man with the ratty cloak smiled as he collected a not-so-insignificant amount of gold from the person hosting the betting. He then stepped toward Rune with the young Vanguard that were with him and handed Rune his sword back. Rune nodded and reattached the double sheath to his belt to stow his remaining sword alongside his father's gift. The headache that had vanished earlier returned with a vengeance. Searing pain assaulted him, but he did his best to hide it from showing on his face. As well as refuse the bile that threatened to release itself from his stomach.

"Nice fight kid. Where'd ya learn moves like that?"

"My father taught me. Fighting him is a hundred times tougher than fighting that idiot lying on the ground," Rune stated matter-of-factly.

The man chuckled, clearly able to see that Rune was not simply bragging. "I'd like to meet your father someday. Seems like a man worth meeting. Anyway, the name's Karl. Veteran Vanguard of the Hall here in Hilden. Though I do little other than waste space at the bar these days. Well, that and I mix herbs on the side, but that doesn't matter that much."

"Nice to meet you, Karl. Thanks for holding onto my sword for me. Who are these people? The ones you stopped from getting help," Rune asked with plainly visible annoyance. He eyed Karl and the other three people with a sharp, critical eye. His headache was coming back, and his cheek had started swelling pretty badly. In this condition, he was ill-prepared for another fight.

"This group here is a fresh group of E-Rankers straight out of Jelmoore. They headed this way hoping to get some experience on the outskirts of the Greatwood, and you, Rune, are going to be joining them!" Karl proclaimed with a large smile. His rambunctious personality did not match his disheveled appearance. He had long gray hair, unshaven stubble, and a torn-up travel cloak covering a plain outfit that had also seen better days. If someone told Rune this man was homeless, he would have believed them in an instant.

"Um. I guess this is happening..." one of the three party members grunted. He had the air of a party leader. He had short brown hair and brown eyes and wore red, half-plate armor. "The name's Jeruul. I'm the leader of our group. We call ourselves The Pact. I use sword and shield, and I'm an Enhancer."

Rune nodded at him, while the second of the three stepped forward. He also had short brown hair and brown eyes. The two looked scarily similar. "Nice to meet ya!" he shouted enthusiastically. "The name's Dannon! Jeruul's my twin! Pulser! I dual-wield daggers, but I can also use a crossbow!"

The third person stepped forward. She was about the same height as Ven but had blonde hair and deep purple eyes. "Teryn vas Dena."

"Volari? What are you doing so far from Dena, ma'am?" Rune asked, shocked. "What's your specialty?"

"Wait! Rune! How did you know where Teryn is from?" Dannon shouted in surprise.

Rune looked at Teryn incredulously. She shrugged with a slightly defeated look. Her expression seemed to show she had attempted to educate her party member on more than one occasion, but had given up. Rune figured he would give it a shot.

"Well…" Rune stated while shifting his attention back to the excited boy. "Her introduction. Volari introduce themselves with their given name. Vas tells me she's a woman. By the fact her last name is that of a city, I know she's a commoner from that city. Only nobles have family names, and those names are always different from cities. A bit different from how Faradin does it."

Teryn nodded with approval and slight surprise at Rune's knowledge. Karl then interjected, "Yes, young Dannon. There's a saying… Oh, how did it go… 'If you can't find a Volari's name on a map, you're dealing with a noble brat'. You ever become a High-Ranker one day, then you'd do well to learn about other cultures, young man!"

"Crude, but true. Anyway…" Teryn continued, trying to bring the conversation back on track. "I manipulate the Aura in plants and use a single-handed saber. Most would call me a Plant-Weaver."

The three of them and Karl looked at Rune expectedly, awaiting his introduction. He smiled and sighed, "Rune. I'm from Locke, just north of here. Father is a Wanderer. I'm Awakened, but classless at the moment."

Teryn suddenly looked surprised. "Wait, wait, wait… your father is a Wanderer? And you are Awakened? Do you know how rare that is? How are you fighting like that without using Aura? That's insane!"

"Wanderer?" Jeruul asked. He was mostly quiet and seemed unsurprised at the information exchange. He was definitely the more educated and reserved of the brothers.

Teryn answered on Rune's behalf. "They're a Volari who disposed of their name and has rejected the culture. They become a Wanderer until they die, or decide to return to the fold and retake their name."

"Oh! So, if your dad is a Volari…then you are, too!" Dannon proclaimed, thinking he had pieced together a complex puzzle.

Teryn's face flashed with discontent and offense, so Rune hurried to continue educating Dannon and prevent her from snapping at the poor young man. Though something told him it would have been a normal occurrence. "No. I'm not. My sister is a Wanderer and so is my father, but my eyes don't meet the standard. Since I did not inherit the bloodline traits, I can never be considered a Volari, even if my father was no longer a Wanderer."

Dannon nodded his head in agreement, but it didn't feel like the information connected in his mind. Teryn's eyes glowed purple while she scanned Rune up and down. He recognized what she was doing and stood still. A moment later, a look of confusion crossed her face.

"You're Awakened alright...but you have such little Aura stored inside you. I'd think you were suffering from Aura Deprivation."

Karl stepped forward and waved his hands in front of Teryn to get her attention, then cleared his throat to get everyone else's. "Well then, you've met, introduced yourselves, and quizzed each other to your heart's content. Whaddya say? Wanna go take a job together?"

Everyone looked around at each other and gave shrug and nod in agreement. Except for Dannon who was enthusiastically nodding his head. If he were a raccoon-dog, Rune suspected his tail would wag just as much. The party, known as The Pact, stepped out of the training room to go take an E-Ranked job alongside their new recruit. Jeruul already had one in mind for them this time around. Apparently, the group's first quest together in the E-Rank would be, conveniently, to hunt down a pack of Bash Eagles.

I almost feel like I'm back in Locke with how many times I have to fight those damnable birds...

Chapter Twelve

1. Man shall hold no faith in death, only in the cycle of reincarnation

2. Man shall always move forward and better his neighbor as he betters himself

3. Man shall always face their foes and stand amongst the righteous to defend the weak

4. Man shall reject stagnation and strive for growth

5. Man shall not blindly accept choices made for him and seek out his own truth

- The Five Holy Tenants of the Crucidian Church

Ven

A massive set of metal gates stood strong at the entrance into the Vanguard Academy. In front of Ven was a line leading towards those same gates, with everyone filling out paperwork, with dozens of academy staff lining the pathway while seated behind a series of desks. Each table had one person handling paperwork, while an assistant gave directions to keep the lines moving smoothly. A few additional workers also passed among those waiting for a slot, reminding them of what they needed to have prepared before approaching a staff member to make sure everything would keep running smoothly.

Hanging over the entry gates was the symbol of the Vanguard. The symbol itself was a shield with three spires standing before a stone wall. The shield represented the stalwart leadership in Castle Nyer. The wall represented the impenetrable barrier that was Fort Black, while the spires were the characterization of the research branch of the Vanguard at Tri-Spire. While the Vanguard was a global organization with a major presence on every inch of inhabited land, their primary place of power was on Vendreya and Volar.

It had been a few weeks since Ven left Hilden before she finally made it to the academy. She traveled with her mother's party for the entire trip and even now, they remained by her side. Mona had insisted that she help her daughter sign up for classes. No amount of pleading or convincing would change Mona's mind about this either, so Ven simply stood there with a hint of embarrassment. Thankfully, it was not too bad since it appeared several other applicants also had family with them.

After a few hours, she was finally called to an empty desk. Sitting at it was a purple-haired woman with purple eyes who appeared to be very unhappy to be there.

"Name and place of birth."

"Venraya. I'm from Hilden. That's also where I received my Ranking Card."

"Noted." The woman stopped taking notes, then locked eyes with Ven before sighing and looking back at the documents. "You are not Volari or a Wanderer. So, human or Awakened human?"

"Awakened, but classless currently. Our Hall's crystal was damaged, so I could not use it."

"That is fine. You will be required to take my class. In it we will examine our Awakened students. You figure out your class then." The woman sighed. "I am

Lylah vas Mithra. Professor of Aura Development, Theory, and History. You start classes tomorrow. Welcome to the Vanguard Academy."

The professor handed her a stack of papers and a student identification card before she waved her off. Another woman next to the table shouted, "Next!" loudly, finalizing the sign-up process. Mona excitedly pushed her daughter through the gates of the academy, followed quickly by her party members, Lex and Tabor, who had looks of exasperation painted all over their faces. They had unluckily been wrapped up in the ordeal by her mother and were made to carry satchels of Ven's belongings. Mona completely ignored her friends as she excitedly pulled her daughter along, trying to find the dorms.

Dozens of students, who she assumed to be upperclassmen were patrolling the grounds for the express purpose of guiding new students to their destinations. One particularly handsome young man with blue hair, dark skin, and brown eyes was standing and arguing with another student. It appeared to be a friendly enough disagreement, but she was impressed by the blue-haired young man's ability to argue so confidently with his compatriot. This was because the other member of the disagreement was a towering human who was large in every sense of the word. He easily dwarfed Ven by several heads, and his shoulders felt about as wide as she was tall.

They sounded like they were arguing about training. It also seemed like they were roommates and the big one kept waking the smaller one up with his morning exercises. The bigger one kept repeating the argument of 'No pain, no gain' and 'early risers make great gains.' The smaller of the two kept insisting that neither of those made sense in the context of their disagreement.

Mona showed no concern for the massive student and walked right up to the pair. "Excuse me, we are looking for my daughter's lodgings. She will be an on-campus resident for her first semester."

The blue-haired boy gave a side-eye to his friend and then cleared his throat. "Sorry, ma'am, you had to witness our disagreement. Seems like my friend here doesn't respect other people's desire to rest." The large one huffed and crossed his arms before his friend continued. "My name is Tayven. This here is Brick."

Brick nodded with a grunt towards Mona. "Ma'am."

"Nice to meet you, Tayven and...Brick." Mona said, with a hint of sympathy at Brick's name. "Can you direct me to Ven's dormitory?"

Tayven looked at the paperwork that Ven handed to him at her mother's request. His eyes darted to Ven and her mother repeatedly. "Looks like she's in the mixed dorm. E-Rank Vanguard share a large mixed-gender dormitory. Miss Venraya, it looks like we will be neighbors. Follow me."

Mona clenched her fist and locked her jaw out of frustration. Her mother was not super pleased about the shared gender dormitory. However, since it was a long-standing rule for the academy, run by the Vanguard itself, there was nothing that Mona could do. She did not really have a house in Jelmoore that she could have Ven commute from since Mona's second husband, Martin, was given a single bedroom apartment as part of his tenure as a professor.

Of course, Ven could sleep in the common area of the apartment, but she had no desire to intrude upon her mother's love-nest. Nor did she wish to be subjected to the horrors of thin walls. She would absolutely take her chances in the academy's dorms. *Besides, it is not as though the rooms are mixed.* Ven thought, *If Rune were here, though, it might be fine...*

Tayven led the group through the crowds of new students and their families before arriving at a circular fountain with three branching paths. Each path led to the door of a different building. The one to the left had a large letter C while the one to the right was emblazoned with a D over the doorway. The one straight ahead was the largest of the three and had a large letter E over the doorway.

Tayven led the group inside. The door immediately opened into a large common area with multiple chairs, couches, and tables, most of which were occupied by students and their families. It seemed the dorm was also serving refreshments to the newcomers. Brick took the lead after Tayven was suddenly accosted by several new female students. He led Ven's group up to the third floor and showed them to a mostly empty room.

It was furnished with two beds, two dressers, two bookshelves, and two armoires. The room was completely symmetrical, and neither side appeared to be occupied. Brick gave a nod to Mona and turned back to either rescue or torment Tayven, who had become pre-occupied downstairs. Mona threw the bag she had shouldered on to one bed before turning to face away from her daughter.

Lex and Tabor nodded at one another and quietly stepped out of the room, dropping their loads onto the ground gently before closing the door behind them. Ven heard a quiet sniffle and saw the back of her mother's shoulders quivering.

"Mom...?"

"What?" Mona questioned. "Am I not allowed to be proud of my only child moving on with her life?"

"I'm nineteen, going on twenty now, mom. I've been 'moving on' for a while. Almost two years into adulthood." Ven tried to explain, but the logic of her words did not seem to do much to help her mother's emotional state.

Mona let out a small, shaky sigh. "I know that, but this has more of a sense of finality to it. By coming here, you really cemented your life as an adult. You aren't my little girl anymore..." Mona sobbed a little louder this time.

Ven looked at her mother sympathetically before giving her a small hug from behind. Mona took the rare opportunity of affection from her child and spun around with lightning speed, wrapping her daughter up in a massive embrace. The two stood silently for several minutes before Ven lightly tapped her mother on the shoulder.

"Thanks Mom, Would you like to help me unpack before you leave?"

Mona nodded in affirmation and placed a gentle hand on her daughter's cheek.

Jeruul

Jeruul and Dannon had been together their entire lives. Such was the obvious fate of twins. Growing up, they both had dealt with situations far beyond what young boys should have to deal with. Their mother died when they were young and their father was a married minor noble in Jelmoore. Though he had an estate and the title of knight, he was the definition of someone being a noble by name, but not in spirit.

He did nothing to help their mother when she carried his sons in her womb, nor did he do anything when she passed on and left two six-year-old children to fend for themselves. The only fortune the two had been they were born in Jelmoore, where the city's lord ran an orphanage to help children like them.

It was an institution run in concert with the Vanguard, and many of the children grew up to become warriors within the organization's ranks. Others became soldiers, while others still took on jobs as city officials. Such an agreement helped build a veritable army of people who were loyal to the city of Jelmoore, the lord who ruled it, and the Vanguard itself.

When Jeruul was young, he often fancied the life of a soldier; something simple and honorable. His brother was not built for such a thing. Dannon hid his pain and trauma behind a mask of sarcasm and humor. Eventually, that mask transformed into a permanent fixture upon his brother's personality. Such a person was not suitable for the rigors of a soldier's life. As such, Jeruul decided he would join Dannon as a member of the Vanguard.

For years, they practiced together, Dannon with daggers and the bow and himself with a sword and shield. When they came of age, they joined the Vanguard together and fought their first beasts. It was exhilarating, terrifying, and above all...fun. The feeling of freedom beyond Jelmoore's towering walls and the rushing of adrenaline as they fought for their lives was a sensation beyond compare.

Nearly a year later, their party of two gained a young Volari woman that Dannon had almost dragged into the hall. She quickly fell into their group dynamic, becoming somewhat of a face for their group. Dannon was far too aggressive in his social interactions, and Jeruul knew himself to be far too withdrawn. Teryn quickly became their filter and thus, their party was formed.

Now, after some time, they had a new face added to the party. A kindly young man named Rune. His odd hair, hazel eyes, and friendly demeanor created a unique presence that did not quite blend with his combat ability. When Rune had fought against a D-Ranker and won with what appeared to be relative ease, Jeruul's mind was blown.

One did not expect such a performance from someone like Rune, who by all accounts, had been a member of the Vanguard for only two months. When they went on their first quest together, the young man easily handled the Bash Eagles, taking out four of them on his own. When the battle was done, he apologized for taking care of most of the work alone, but claimed he had thought it was a test of his skills.

Had he not shown his skills against Bordo, then they might have thought of testing him. However, Dannon quickly informed Rune they had no such requirements for their group and that they already trusted his abilities. Given how much of the job was handled by Rune's skill alone, they tried to give him the lion's share of the reward and harvests, but he quickly denied them, asking only for an equal cut.

A few weeks had passed since then and their new friend had finally blended in with the group. Rune stopped overwhelming enemies and acted as a front-line fighter, protecting Teryn and Dannon, who acted as the middle guard and ranged attacker, respectively. There was only one thing that was odd.

"Hey, Teryn!" Dannon casually called out. "Why are you always staring at the new guy?"

Right, that...

Teryn glanced away from the young man in question, who was walking a few hundred feet away between various stalls at the city market. He was in charge of this week's supply gathering, something they each took turns at to share the responsibilities. Since the group had a party fund, they each took turns using those funds for party needs. Secretly, they all wanted to make the new member do it every time. He had a way of charming the vendors into better prices with his sincerity.

"I'm not always staring at him."

"Okay, then why are you *usually* staring at him?" Dannon pressed.

"I'm not."

"You actually do look at him quite a lot," Jeruul interjected. Teryn was definitely hiding something. The look in her eyes was an odd blend of intrigue and suspicion. Jeruul was worried it would eventually become a problem. If they could not trust each other, how could they work properly as a party?

"There's just something in the way he fights. It's odd. I can't really describe it."

The woman had a point. Many times, they had discussed the strange fighting style and abilities their friend had. He was far more skilled than he appeared and fought unlike anything that Jeruul had seen. Rune's movements flowed like water, always gaining in momentum, never wasting energy. Each attack smoothly flowed into the next one, sometimes incorporating his enemy's own strikes and defensive movements into the flow, turning every fight into a macabre dance of death. And other times...

"Odd though it may be, it is supremely helpful. I have no complaints," Jeruul finally said with a shrug.

"I think it's really neat!" Dannon agreed in between bites of a smoked leg of meat he had picked up from a nearby food stall.

Teryn shrugged. "Okay—a fair point—but what about the headaches? He gets them all the time. Should he even be allowed in the field?"

"They only happen after the fight is over. Since it doesn't really hinder us, I don't see a problem with it either. Besides, he says he's managing them. If it becomes a problem, we can talk about it again later," Jeruul continued. "We all have things we keep to ourselves. If he wants to share information on where he learned to fight, where his headaches come from, or anything else... that's on him. Just stop creepily staring at him all the time."

Teryn nodded once more, but pursed her lips in frustration. Silence settled into the surrounding air, broken only by the loud chewing sounds coming from Dannon and his meal. A few moments later, the woman excused herself politely. The twins followed her movements with their eyes. Her target appeared to be their friend. Teryn stepped up to Rune's side, and they began discussing something before walking to another set of stalls together.

Jeruul sighed once more. *It is only a matter of time. We will fall in step with one another off the battlefield, eventually. For now, working together on jobs is good enough. Maybe we can truly become a party at some point. I know Dannon would love that.*

Chapter Thirteen

Lylah

Lylah sighed to herself, standing in front of a class full of new students. It was yet again the start of a new term. Another year of being assigned to instruct the introductory class on Aura History and Development. This year's batch of students was about average in size and so far, no one seemed to stand out as exceptional. Lylah also noticed that there were no Volari nor even Wanderer students this year, which also bothered her.

The murmurs of conversation came to a slow stop once Lylah put up a hand and addressed her new students. "My name is Lylah vas Mithra. I am your professor this year. I teach Aura Development, Aura Theory, and History. Welcome to your introductory course in Development and Theory. I don't have a lot of patience or care for formalities, so let us get to it. Who can tell me what Aura is?"

Lylah looked over the faces before her. The room was set up as a large lecture hall with several levels of desks, each spot filled with questioning and confused faces. After several moments of silence, a hand rose near the front. "It's the source of life that flows through the world."

Lylah shook her head. "No. Anyone else?"

The class confusedly talked amongst themselves again at their professor's denial. She knew she would have to break their misconceptions. *Humans.* A minute passed before she finally answered on her students' behalf. "Aura is, for lack of a better term, everything. It is matter, energy, the essence of reality itself, and even something quantifiable: life."

She paused before continuing, "Many believe it simply is the source of life because of how frequently one is exposed to Volari who manipulate the Aura in living things such as plants. Plant-Weaving, as such a skill is called, is the most common skill among Volari. Our eyes can also see the concentration of Aura within people and the surroundings. This thought process is understandable, as Aura has higher concentrations inside of living creatures and things. Such a fact is especially true for the Awakened. However, Aura exists in non-living things as well."

The students were visibly confused, so Lylah provided a demonstration. She took a simple stone out of her pocket. "See this stone? There is nothing special about it. I picked it up on my walk here this morning. Now observe."

Lylah's eyes glowed as she clasped the rock in both hands. She collapsed her hands flat, as though there was nothing in them. A small disc then flew out of her hands and spun lazily in circles in the surrounding air.

"As I would hope you all know, a rock contains no life. Yet there are Volari such as myself, a Stone-Weaver, that can manipulate the form of the earth itself."

There was a collective gasp from the audience. Several of the more studious members were furiously writing down these new revelations. The stone disc maintained its orbit around the woman while she continued. "Even Awakened do not manipulate life...usually. Rather, they slowly accumulate Aura from their environment inside special 'wells' in their bodies and can release the con-centrated energy in bursts. This takes several forms, like the barriers, bolts of pure energy, and the strengthening of one's body."

A blue-haired student raised a hand. "Usually, professor?"

Light flashed from within her eyes as Lylah scanned the class. In this view, the world was simply shades of purples, violets, and blacks. While all Volari could see Aura like this, she was more adept and able to see the concentration of Aura within a person, and the channels in their bodies through which it flowed. Seeing this could allow her to determine if someone was Awakened or human.

It also allowed her to see if someone was Volari without being able to see their eyes. In some specific scenarios, she could detect a person's class.

Satisfied with what she saw among her students—or rather did not see—she finally answered the student who she identified as Tayven Nefera. "That lecture is beyond the scope of this coursework. It can be further discussed should you continue into higher-level courses in Aura History and Theory, Mister Nefera."

The boy put his hand down, mildly annoyed he had not gotten his answer immediately. At least he understood he would receive one, eventually. Questions such as that continued for another hour before Lylah finally cut the conversation off.

"Alright!" She clapped her hands. The stone hovering around her shattered apart, spraying dust across the class. "That is quite enough for day one. Next class will begin with a lecture. For those of you who are Awakened and are also still classless, please follow me to the training fields. Normal humans and Awakened who have already determined their Class are dismissed. Unless you would like to observe. Since our number lacks any Volari... well, no instruction for that."

The professor did not wait for anyone to raise their hands or gather their things; she simply left the room. Dozens of students rushed after her since many of them had just started and would get lost if they did not follow her closely. After a few minutes of navigating the halls of the academy, the group noticed several of the upperclassmen leaned against the stone walls, whispering to each other while they watched the procession. Silent murmurs bounced off stonework, creating a dull roar despite each person's individual volume being hushed.

It was commonplace for the older students to gather and watch Awakened students finally learn about their classes. It was a good way to know who to ingratiate themselves to, who to party with, and who to ignore. While the academy did not boast extra-curricular activities like some schools in other parts of the world, it allowed some of its students to form parties and complete jobs for the Vanguard. Since most students were members of the organization, it only made sense for such allowances to be made. Sometimes someone would be stuck with whatever party they could find, if their abilities appeared to be lacking. It was useful for those who possessed power to be approached by the strong. The established groups benefited from knowing who would be useful and who would be fodder.

Tayven and his larger friend both appeared to be well aware of this, having been at the academy for some months already while they waited for the second term to begin. Unlike them, most of the other students were shifting uncomfortably under the analytical gazes of their betters. These proceedings always amused Lylah and were anyone to pay attention to her, they would notice the faintest hint of a smile teasing her lips.

Soon, the group arrived at their destined location. Waiting for them was a circular table with a perfectly cuboidal box. On either side of the table were two strange-looking individuals. Their face coverings and glimpses of metal beneath their cloaks hinted at their dangerous nature. There was an air of confidence exuding from them that could only be seen by the most veteran of warriors. Something, Lylah noticed, did not escape Tayven Nefera's attention. *Seems a noble's upbringing has done much to benefit his perception.*

Lylah approached the box while giving a slight nod to its protectors. She opened it and reached inside, pulling out a large, white sphere. "Anyone know why we use these crystals on Awakened?"

She was met with silence before a raven-haired girl spoke up. "It's the only way to complete your Awakening."

Lylah sighed once more. "Incorrect. An Awakened can learn their class without this, though it is usually triggered by a stressful event. This crystal, however, bypasses that stress trigger and forcibly pushes Aura into your bodies. This causes your body to expel the excess Aura in a way that aligns with your class abilities and activates the pathways your abilities use. With those pathways being forced open, the recipient of the Awakening Crystal's power will utilize their pathways without additional assistance."

The same girl locked her jaw momentarily before asking a follow-up question. "If all it does is shove extra Aura into our bodies, what causes a crystal to only complete the Awakening of a specific class? Hilden's Hall possesses a crystal that can only assist with awakening Enhancers."

"Good question," Lylah stated with surprise. "Each class uses Aura at a specific frequency. Those inner pathways only allow Aura to either enter or exit using that same frequency. If you don't know what the word 'frequency' means, consider that an assignment. It will be on your next test. And yes, I do require tests in my class. Anyway, sometimes a crystal will break or degrade and be incapable of forcing Aura of the correct frequency into someone's body. This effectively prevents it from helping anyone who is not in a specific class. If it cannot attune the Aura directed through it to the necessary frequency, it's no different from trying to pour water into a canteen without removing the lid."

She stared at the group once more and motioned for the girl with the questions to come forward. "You first. Please point your dominant hand towards the targets and place your non-dominant hand on the crystal."

The girl did as was requested of her. For a moment, nothing happened, before suddenly, the crystal glowed. The glow faded and seemed to focus itself near where her hand touched the object. The glow then seemed to enter the girl's hand. She briefly winced before a purple flash erupted from her right palm and exited as a bolt of purple energy at the targets. It was far larger than Lylah had expected. The entire center of the target was completely missing, with the edges of the new hole sizzling.

"Congratulations, girl, you are a Pulser. With decent potential, if I do say so."

"Venraya is my name; not girl."

"Sure. Next!"

The girl huffed and walked away, barely hiding the excitement in her face while she flexed her hands. The next up was a very large student, one that always seemed to be near Tayven Nefera. He also placed one hand on the crystal and another in the air, pointed at the targets. The same glow began again, just like with the first student. This time, however, the purple flash did not create a bolt of energy. Instead, the veins in the student's entire arm flashed with purple light.

"Enhancer. Congrats, it seems to fit your...aesthetic. Honestly looking at you, anything else would have been a cruel trick by the gods."

Next up was Tayven Nefera. He turned out to be an Enhancer as well, which Lylah figured was something he was happy about, given his whooping and shouting. The process repeated a few dozen times, resulting in several Pulsers, Enhancers, and Shielders.

Not everyone was happy with the results. Some students seemed confused about how to implement their class abilities into their already developed fighting styles. Of course, this was also part of their coursework while at the academy. They could either adapt the power to their fighting style, learn a new style, or completely ignore their class abilities and only focus only on using enhanced weapons. Many would fail, and as a result, die in the field. But this was the Vanguard Academy, not a daycare.

This is going to be a long year unless something interesting happens, Lylah thought. *Though with this batch of students, I doubt that. So much for that exciting feeling I had before the boat ride. Seems my hunch was wrong.*

Everyone eventually trickled back into the building, leaving the training field empty. Lylah looked back for a moment, seeing someone standing off in the distance. No else one seemed to notice a man in an oversized gray cloak standing by the targets. The sheer volume of fabric suggested he would trip the moment he took a step, and his face was completely hidden by its hood. The figure gave her a slight wave before he noiselessly walked away from the field. Lylah rubbed her eyes, thinking she had been seeing things and when her vision returned, the figure was gone.

Odd.

Unknown

Two people clad in black robes stood in a dark room, separated from one another by several paces. The tension in the air was so heavy, one could scarcely breathe under its weight. They locked eyes for several minutes before one finally broke the silence.

"The white-feathered raven flies north..."

For a few moments, only silence passed, time itself feeling still. The one who had spoken first slowly reached for a weapon on his hip.

"...towards its inevitable end in the Forest of Ruin," the second person answered finally. Her voice was soft and sweet, hiding underneath it a threat of death. She was clearly not one to be trifled with. The first of the two sighed with relief, removing his hand from the sword on his hip.

"Took you long enough," the man mumbled. "I've been waiting here in this cursed place for months and you just show up now, without warning. Do you know how hard it is to sneak away from the damn watchmen here?"

The woman laughed. Purple light flashed in her eyes. "You're foolish to be wary of the men inside and not the beasts outside." The woman paused for a moment, as if pondering the validity of her own statement, before she shrugged. "Regardless, I am here now. Pass along a message for me."

"Alright. What is it and where is it going?"

"Let our mutual friends in Nefera be made aware that the Church is working on moving assets to the south. It seems they are not content to leave things as they were. Additionally, I expect things around here to get a little more exciting. Pressed for time and all that..."

"That's it? Do you have any specifics?" The man sighed, knowing that their 'friends' would not take kindly to vague information. Unfortunately, the woman simply smiled before she vanished into the shadows. Her presence remained, no doubt ensuring that the man would not act in an untoward manner.

Nearly an hour passed as he waited in the dark tower sitting atop the center of Fort Black. Outside the windows, a full moon bathed a silent forest in its awe-inspiring rays. Many of the trees were dead or dying, most of them losing their lives because of the warring beasts within.

Finally, the man felt as though the danger had passed and quickly left the dark tower being used as a storage room. His footsteps echoed through the empty stone halls. Many of the fort's inhabitants were asleep at this time of night, save for the night watchmen. In truth, Fort Black never truly slept. Each soldier was among the strongest and most ruthless of the Vanguard and trained both day and night in keeping the horrors of the forest beyond from creeping into the kingdom. The only thing more fearsome than those beasts was the commander in charge of such a place.

"Going somewhere?" A voice as cold as ice and sharp as a dagger cut through the air, stopping the man in his tracks. "Come with me."

The man waited for the voice's owner to pass him by. Once the woman stepped past him, he fell in step. Her short, purple hair swished with each step and contrasted heavily with the pitch-black cloak that hung off her shoulders. She was the commander of Fort Black and one of the three commanders of the Vanguard. Her power was said to be a force of nature and her temperament as calm as a raging storm.

After several minutes of silence, the duo walked into the commander's office. She sat at her desk and gestured for the man to do the same. He hesitantly agreed to her request. Upon his settling down, the commander cleared her throat.

"What have you learned?"

"They wish for me to send word to my contacts in Nefera that 'assets are being moved south' and that things around here are going to get busier. She declined to provide any other information or clarifications. I am sorry, Commander. I have failed you."

The woman waved her hand dismissively. "No. It's likely they are being purposefully vague. No doubt my kinsmen are up to no good. Their underbelly prepares for war. It's wise. However, it is only so effective when the country's surface remains blissfully ignorant of the truth beneath their noses."

The woman paused and squeezed the bridge of her nose. "I will find out what it is they are doing beyond my walls and how they are bypassing my guard. Whatever it is, has started agitating the beasts. Assaults increase each month and our scouts report troubles on a nearly daily basis…" She sighed again, her purple eyes flashing in the dimly lit chamber. "Continue as you were, then. If you receive any other contact, report to me the moment it is safe. Make sure you pass along any information you receive as you promised… the other party. Though your life is at stake, I appreciate what you offer us. Dismissed."

The man stood and saluted before hastily exiting the room. He was thankful she was in a good mood today. Though he hated her unpredictability, at least the things the commander did were for the good of the people. The Vanguard did not care about one's national loyalties or place of origin. It stood for the common people, and even the commander abided by that. These other people… the same could not be said of them.

Chapter Fourteen

Rune

Four individuals dressed in different armor slowly crawled their way over a small hill overlooking a flat plain. The largest of them clinked a little as his apparel was heavier, with more metal components, than the rest. A few hundred yards away from their position was the ever-present tree line of the Greatwood. Between the group and that barrier stood a pack of five Razortusks. The monsters were boar-like in appearance, but they were about twice as large with tusks as sharp as a sword. They also had thick hair covering their bodies, hiding painful quills to protect from attacks from behind.

Tusks fetched a good price with apothecaries and clerics since, when ground, the powder made from them made an excellent coagulant for wound closure. Fletchers would take the monster's quills to hollow out and use as paralyzing or poisoned bolts and arrows. Their meat was also much more tender than a normal boar since their natural defenses allowed them to laze about in the wild without fear of predators and build fat.

Dannon had prepped a crossbow bolt made from a Razortusk's quill filled with a paralytic poison. They were a little expensive, but the group had purchased a set of ten of these bolts for the job, anyway. They would get more than the ten out of this attack if all went to plan. Thankfully, the poison was both fast acting and quick to decay. By the time the creature was butchered, the meat would be left edible. It was expected that only one or two would be needed for the pack leader to go down, leaving the other four without a leader.

Teryn's eyes glowed as she prepared herself to assist in the pending charge. Rune looked at the other three who all nodded in affirmation that they were ready. Everyone locked their eyes on the largest of the group. It was enjoying the hot summer sun beating down on its thick fur. As the pack leader, it seemed to enjoy a moment of laziness while its lackeys kept their eyes out for attackers, albeit poorly.

Dannon breathed in deeply, closing his eyes. During his exhale, his eyes shot open and he loosed the first bolt before rapidly reloading a second and letting it fly as well. His crossbow was built for rapid firing and as such was not as powerful as a standard crossbow, but as a piercing weapon, it would have no issue finding purchase within the monster's flesh.

Both bolts sunk into the side of the pack leader in rapid succession. The beast roared in agony with bloodshot eyes, jumping around rapidly, trying to search for its attackers. Knowing they would be discovered in the next moment anyway, the party stood up to make themselves as visible as possible. Teryn, Jeruul, and Rune then charged forward, indicating to their quarry that they were the culprits behind the surprise attack, which earned the Razortusks' ire. The leader roared and charged at the group upon standing. The other members of the pack roared in concert before they joined the leader. Twigs and rocks scattered about vibrated as the charge shook the ground from the beasts bearing down on their position.

With the excess movement, Dannon's poison quickly rushed through the leader's bloodstream, slowing him. His pack-mates quickly overtook him in the assault. He then collapsed a few seconds later, unable to move from the paralysis effect. The other four monsters failed to notice and continued on. Immediately after seeing the leader fall, Dannon launched two more bolts at another of the pack.

Teryn's eyes flashed brighter as she stopped momentarily and waved her hand toward yet another of the Razortusks, her confident expression faltering for only a moment with a slight frown. Such an expression was quickly hidden as the targeted monster stumbled and fell to the ground, skidding a few feet from the momentum. Rune noticed that the grass beneath it had wrapped around its feet, preventing it from standing once more. It continued to struggle against the writhing tendrils, but every time a foot broke free, more plant material would rise to restrain it. Sweat glistened on Teryn's forehead, either from the heat or the exertion. She quietly whispered a frustrated curse.

Jeruul met one of the remaining two and side-stepped at the last second, shouting out, "Enhance: Full Body!" Purple light highlighted every visible vein in his body as each muscle pulsed with inhuman might. Because of the side-step in combination with the beasts' lack of agility, the Razortusk only barely missed the young man. Jeruul thrust out his sword and with the help of the enhancement keeping him from being knocked to the ground, used the force of the beast's own charge to leave a massive slash down the side of its body.

"See that, Rune? Jeruul can do it, too!" Dannon laughed out.

"Not the same thing!" Teryn responded. "Shut your trap and focus on the fight, dipshit!"

The beast roared in pain and anger as it wheeled around a second time for a follow-up attack. Jeruul was visibly sweating from the effort of expending so much Aura to enact the enhancement over his whole body. However, he still had more left to fight with and turned to face the enemy. He held up his shield with his sword once again at the ready. Now that his prey was weakened from the large slash and no longer could achieve a full charge, Jeruul appeared confident in his ability to confront the creature in a one-on-one melee.

Teryn and Dannon quickly ran up to the incapacitated Razortusks and finished them off before they could recover. Only Rune was left with his own target. Individually, Razortusks were no more threatening than a standard F-Rank monster. It was the fact that they would only fight in groups of five or more that elevated them to an E-Rank threat, similar to Bash Eagles. As long as one fought smart, it was easy to take advantage of the monsters' slow movement, lack of agility, and relatively low stamina. Because of this, Rune was far from worried about himself or Jeruul. Avoid the quills on their backsides and their initial charge, and the creatures were pitiful opponents.

Rune had decided this job provided him with a good opportunity to finally use his father's altered sword. In order to activate it without Aura manipulation of his own, he had to rely on the alderite core that his father had installed as the pommel. There was no way to control the release of Aura when the core contacted the rest of the alderite matrix in the weapon, so in order to activate it Rune had to tighten the pommel by a quarter turn.

The core and the alderite matrix inside the weapon made full contact; the entire blade began to hum and give off a purple glow. With his activated weapon in hand, he met the Razortusk's charge. To slow the beast down, he ducked to the left and slashed where its leg met its rotund body. Rune was surprised to find next to no resistance as the blade cut through a sickening combination of flesh, muscle, and bone. The monster howled in pain and impacted the ground with a wet *thud*. Though wracked with pain, it stood once again. Its leg had been cleanly separated at the joint, lying next to him leaking blood into the dirt.

Rune felt a strange sensation after he too turned around to face his target a second time. The world became clearer, his vision sharper. He could see the individual quills and fur bristle along the Razortusk's back in slow motion. *What is this?* Strength and power surged through his arms and legs like a tidal wave. Every ounce of blood, every nerve, every fiber of muscle; all of his being felt under his control. Taking advantage of the sudden burst of power, which he attributed to adrenaline, Rune leaped towards the monster. It attempted to meet his attack by lowering its head and aiming the tusks that gave its kind their name straight toward the boy.

Weak. A strange thought formed in his head, accompanied by a sensation of superiority and something else...

Just before meeting his prey, Rune lowered his sword and used his increased strength to strike the outside of one of the monster's tusks with his shield. *In a contest of strength, I will win, beast.* Its head was thrown in the opposite direction with a high-pitched squeal, both from surprise and from the sheer force of the blow. Rune used this opening to quickly sink his sword right behind the Razortusk's ear, sinking the blade up to the hilt and piercing its brain. Bone and sinew gave way to the weapon with zero resistance. The monster's eyes turned glassy, and it collapsed on the ground, its own weight pulling Rune's sword free, bringing with it a smattering of blood and brain matter.

Rune exhaled. The strange feeling from a moment ago faded away as if it never existed.

Dannon began clapping excitedly, whooping and hollering after watching the show. Jeruul wiped his blade clean and stared at Rune. Teryn was also staring before she asked, "What the fuck was that?"

"Um, it's an enhanced sword. My father made it," Rune stated plainly while gesturing at his sword. The blade was no longer glowing, meaning he had used up the entire charge of the core. He was surprised. It should have lasted a couple of fights, but perhaps even his father could make mistakes and produce a faulty core.

"Not the sword, you half-wit," Teryn huffed in annoyance. "That movement. You don't normally move like that. Every time we fight, you become like another person. You move faster, hit harder... This time, something else changed. You just tossed that Razortusk around like a doll instead of dancing and dodging. I just don't get you."

Rune scratched his head in confusion. Whatever answer she was looking for, he did not have it. Not at the moment. With the sensation from earlier fading, so too did his focus. *Why did I do that? Father would scold me for sure for confronting something so directly.* The twins looked between themselves and simply shrugged before they all started collecting the resources from their kills. They quickly gathered ten tusks and hundreds of quills. The skins of the monsters were rather useless and only the belly meat was actually desirable, so they did not have to worry about leaving good materials behind in order to get home.

They secured the collected meats in a special wrap coated in a food-safe potion that staved off rot. It would not last long term in the summer months out in the open, but it would keep the meat good long enough to hand in it to the client. The job request had been jointly filed by a butcher and the town apothecary for the meat and tusks, but the quills were fair game.

At Dannon's own suggestion, they decided to simply sell them all to the Vanguard for ease of transaction rather than trying to sell them alone at the market or try to craft their own ammunition for the crossbow. The Vanguard would take a cut of the coinage, but they agreed such a loss was fine. It wasn't as though they hurt for money.

After a short trek back to Hilden, the party found themselves back home just in time for the sun to set. The reception desk was mostly deserted, with any other parties having already turned in or accepted their jobs for the day. Thankfully, one of the two old ladies, Jenna, was still present. Jeruul was the leader of the party, so he and Dannon went to handle the paperwork while Rune and Teryn went to reserve a table at the nearest inn for a celebratory dinner.

Teryn turned to Rune after they found a good table, and with a teasing tone, commented about his recent change in behavior. "You know, this is only the second time you've joined us for a post-job meal. The only other time was after our first job hunting that pack of Bash Eagles, when you first joined up. Normally you go to your room and write letters to gods know who." She was in a much better mood than earlier in the afternoon.

Probably best not to mention it.

"Yeah, normally I struggle with these pounding headaches, but today, it's nowhere to be seen. Because of that, I figured why not?" Rune answered with a smile. "I can write letters later, so why not enjoy a meal with friends now?"

Teryn giggled. "Friends, are we?"

"I would hope so," Rune answered with an expression of mock pain. "We've done more than a few jobs together at this point and have been together for several weeks. Besides, you can't get much closer to someone than bleeding together in a fight."

Teryn nodded absentmindedly. "Alright. Friends it is. Anyway, who is it you are writing all those letters to? You do it like every day."

"My family and friends back home." Rune told her about his home while they sipped on ales and waited for the twins. She listened patiently while he described his father's job and strict training regimen, his mother's kindness and cooking ability, and his sister's penchant for trouble. He also regaled her with stories of hunting in the woods with Tara and the trouble they had gotten into growing up.

Teryn's eyes glowed with glee at the mention of Tara. "Oh, ho, ho...and this 'friend' is also getting these letters of yours?"

Rune smiled with a little blush and sadness. "Yeah. She's my best friend, so of course I would tell her stories of my adventures! Not like she's here with me, so I have to tell her somehow."

Teryn poked his cheeks teasingly, mocking him for writing so-called 'love letters' on a daily basis. "Why didn't she just join the Vanguard with you? If she can fight like you can, then you would have no reason to join a bunch of chumps like us," Teryn questioned.

"A life of fighting wasn't for her. She wanted to work at the small church in town. Her parents run a general store and she claimed merchant life wasn't for her either."

"I can understand that." Teryn responded, her tone becoming slightly sadder. It was clear the conversation was taking a more somber tone, so Rune quickly changed the subject to something else.

Shortly after they had downed a second set of drinks, the twins finally showed. Jeruul placed two bags of coins and a receipt for their payment in front of the two inebriated friends. He chuckled at the pair and ordered another round for the whole table.

The party really started to liven up when Dannon finally faded away from sobriety. "And another thing, Rune. How, in Chaos's name, do you move like that?"

Rune tried to focus on his friend, but could not really seem to decide which of the two he was supposed to look at.

"You sure you're classless? Moves like that...you sure you ain't an Enhancer like my brother?"

"Yup," Rune stated with an exaggerated pop. "Never been able to manifest Aura except this one incident when I was a kid. Bandits tried to raid the village. I saw a flash of purple light erupt from my hands during the attack and passed out. When I woke up, I was back in my room, nary a clue of what happened."

"Well, that's helpful," Teryn complained. "A flash of purple light from your hand? That could be anything. A Pulser, Shielder, whatever. At least we know your dad's Volari blood isn't doin' shit." It was hard to make out what she was saying, but everyone, even Jeruul, seemed to get the gist, especially when Teryn was pointing in the general position of her own eyes. Rune, even in his own stupor, felt bad for Jeruul. Poor soul was the only one of the four who could hold his liquor.

While the group continued to party and enjoy a hearty meal, an acquaintance of theirs approached. Karl had a big smile on his face and a mug full of ale. Despite always dressing as though he was homeless, with his tattered cloak and disheveled clothes, he was clearly drinking one of the finer offerings in the place.

Rune eventually learned that while he might not look it, Karl was likely the wealthiest man in Hilden, thanks to the riches he had earned when he was still active within the Vanguard. Karl was simply a unique individual who rarely spent money on himself unless it was liquor for imbibing or food for choking down.

"Well, well, well, my young friends! It looks like my hunch was right! You make a great team! Thanks for getting those tusks for me, by the way." Karl laughed while gesturing with his cup, causing its contents to splash about the table. "Rune, my boy, how's the headache treating you?"

Rune had been seeing Karl after every job and any days that his headache plagued him. Since Ven had left, Rune had been struck by regular migraines and dizzy spells. Jacob suggested he visit Karl since the church's cleric could not figure out what the problem was. Of course, the church worker could have just lied about not being able to help. Crucidian acolytes rarely interacted positively with the rest of the town, but they were especially abrasive to the Vanguard.

When Rune had finally visited Karl, he was shocked to learn the man not only practiced minimalism to an excessive degree, but he also used his spare time to learn about medicinal herbs and had settled in as the town apothecary. One thing was for sure: the man knew his stuff. Every visit to him left Rune without a headache for at least a day or sometimes two. It would always return, but any amount of relief was welcome, and it was a lot better than the nothing that would happen when he tried visiting the church.

"Not too bad!" Rune answered happily. "No headache for the last three days! Though I suspect I will have a pretty big one tomorrow!"

The party laughed together and joined the rest of the patrons in singing along to the drinking song that had begun. Rune thought he caught a flash of worry cross Karl's face, but it vanished faster than it appeared, leaving him to wonder if he saw anything at all.

In truth, Rune hated his condition. There were times he thought he should give up on being a Vanguard warrior. Having a debilitating headache after every other mission made him feel inferior and like a dead weight to the party. This was despite his party-mates claiming otherwise. Even during the lightened atmosphere, these thoughts resurfaced. His face seemed to show what he was thinking because Teryn moved from her spot across from him to his side. She stumbled awkwardly, trying to drunkenly maneuver a chair around the table, but she made it.

She threw one arm around his neck and smiled broadly. "Don't look like that! If I know you, you're still worried about holding us back. Let me just say: you aren't, and you won't. So, drink up, relax, and have fun." She brought her mug to his. "To friends!"

Rune felt his face warm. He returned her smile. "To friends."

They both drank down what remained in their cups before asking for refills. *Huh, she's actually kind of nice...*

Jacob

"So why is it you don't want me to use the Awakening Crystal?" Jacob asked his old friend. "Mona took the delivery quest to bring it all the way here so we can finally have a working one. I'm sure that Rune would be ecstatic to use it and solve his personal mystery."

Karl chuckled. "He doesn't need to use the crystal for us to know. I already know what he is. However, it is too soon for him to find out. He's strong, but he needs time to mature."

Jacob pinched the bridge of his nose. It was unbelievable to him that Karl would ask him to not use the Awakening Crystal, not just on Rune, but on anyone, until Rune was ready to move on to Jelmoore. No one knew how long it would take for that to happen, which frustrated him. It almost crippled his recruitment efforts since a lot of classless Awakened would move on to Jelmoore for the sole purposes of using their Awakening Crystal. After seeing all the city offered, very few of them came back to Hilden.

"You owe me for this, Karl," Jacob growled. "Can you at least tell me his Class? After hearing the stories of how he fights and the strange things that happen around him, I am dying to know. He and his friends are doing great work, but the rumors are spreading by the hour. You should know, since you basically live here in the Hall's bar or other taverns."

Karl thought for a moment with a hand stroking his gray beard. "Listening to everyone's stories is quite entertaining, to be honest. So, no, I don't think I will tell you."

"Right, 'cause, why would you make this easy on me?"

Jacob glared at Karl, but ultimately knew he could not force his hand. Karl was possibly the Vanguard's highest ranked warrior on this side of the Wyverntooth Mountain range, which translated to him having a free pass to do almost anything he wanted. Of course, Jacob could call in a few of the many, many favors that Karl owed him to extract the information. For the sake of their relationship, though, he let his old friend keep his secrets.

"Have you heard anything from Vincent?" Karl asked, changing the subject.

"Not much of anything, really. Things in the kingdom are rough, politically speaking. Our commanders are keeping quiet right now. Well, all except for one. Not a peep from any of the Council either."

The robed man let out a sharp laugh. "Of course, she wouldn't shut her trap. Neither does it surprise me that those other bastards want to stay quiet till the last minute. Same for the damnable Council. I'm sure they aren't resting on their laurels, though. Nyer is a veritable den of vipers. The moment they stop scheming is the moment the Sea of Chaos consumes the world once more."

"What do you expect them to do? The Vanguard holds loyalty to no nation," Jacob reminded. Karl, as a high-ranker, was held under higher levels of restriction by the organization as it related to operating within his kingdom of residence. Once a Vanguard busted through the upper ranks, they basically served a global military organization and were bound by its laws. Granted, that military focused on the control over the monster population. At least, on the surface.

Karl laughed sarcastically before he finally answered. "I don't know...but something."

Chapter Fifteen

Brick

As the days turned to weeks, the training and education given by the Vanguard Academy provided Brick with ample opportunities for growth. Finally able to use his abilities as an Enhancer increased his drive for improvement. Prior to this point, he had focused on training his body and fists to be as prepared as possible for any of the classes. Were he a Shielder or a Pulser, it would have been harder to incorporate into his current style, but not impossible.

One of his primary focuses of late had been to limit his enhancements. At his current level, the activation of his abilities maximized the part of his body he was trying to strengthen. This resulted in much harder punches, higher jumps, and faster sprints. However, if he always maximized those activations, then it would drain his reserves quickly and leave him helpless in a longer fight.

People who were prepared to end fights quickly with overwhelming power had every right to train that way. Brick, on the other hand, wanted to be ever-prepared for fighting battles, where that was not an option. Being the size he was, his enemies would often assume that was how he fought, but if he proved he could perform just as well or better in drawn out fights, then many enemies would struggle to adapt. Monsters seldom had such advanced thoughts, but Brick was not so simple as to believe he would only ever have to fight monsters. Sometimes the dangers that the Vanguard confronted in the field were caused by people.

Once again, Brick closed his eyes and took a deep breath. He looked within himself and felt the Aura wells within his body. Aura seemed to roil like an angry sea begging for release, held back only by his will. A single thought was all that was needed to allow that energy to run rampant throughout his body, strengthening his bone and muscle. Though difficult, Brick slowly opened the gates, trying to allow only a trickle of the chaotic energy to leak out.

Highly trained warriors could exercise control such as this after several minutes of preparation. Having to spend such a large amount of time to achieve such a result only showed the young man how much further he had to go. *Gods, how do they do this?* Sweat beaded along his brow, neck, and back. Suddenly, a torrent of Aura burst through his control, throwing open the 'gates' Brick had visualized. Before the energy could fill his pathways, Brick closed it off. He was just in time to hear a familiar situation develop.

"What the fuck did you just say to me?" a shrill voice screeched out.

Brick felt a wry smile tease the corner of his mouth. Such incidents had become commonplace as of late. Two students would always end up at odds in the training room, the halls, the classroom… anywhere, really. The perpetrators of such fights were none other than Tayven Nefera and Venraya of Hilden. Those two could not seem to find common ground, no matter what.

"I said that your focus on the bow has weakened your swordplay. While your abilities with the blade are not the worst I have seen, they present a weakness in your fighting style," Tayven responded. His tone was measured and plain, as if he was trying to provide guidance as a teacher would to a student. Unfortunately, this only increased Venraya's frustration.

"Asshole, you always have something smart to say to me, don't you?" Venraya shouted back. Her green eyes were wide with rage while her face reddened. "Since you want to talk about swordplay so much, my friend back home would trounce you in a second. Don't come talk to me like you're some sort of sagely sword instructor."

"While I cannot claim to know the skill of your 'friend', I do know that my own skills are not lacking. My father provided me the best…"

Oh, not the response I would have chosen, Tayven, Brick thought, while starting his walk over to them.

"Of course, your father gave you... blah, blah, blah. You nobles and having everything granted to you. I had to teach myself while asking for the occasional tips from local hunters and Vanguard warriors who felt kind enough to give advice or instruction. Not everyone had their skills handed to them in exchange for a few coins. Even the person who taught me refused until I proved myself. I earned my skills, at least."

The young woman was prone to outbursts when she felt as though she had been wronged. Brick had noticed she had a hard time fitting in. Many other students had avoided her because of her frequent arguments with Tayven. As the young noble had been at the academy prior to the term starting, he had established a presence and position of respect among their peers. To them, Venraya was the one in the wrong in any disagreement between them, even if that was not always the case.

Before Tayven could retort, the woman threw her practice swords onto the weapon rack while storming out of the room. Several dozen eyes silently followed her retreat, brought out of their collective stupor by the slamming of a door. A few moments later, the sounds of weapons smacking shields returned, accompanied by a tired sigh from Tayven.

Brick turned towards his friend with a comforting smile. "Can't help yourself, can you?"

"She's impossible."

"So are you."

Tayven glanced at him. "What in the names of the gods are you talking about?"

"Tayven, it is not always what you are saying that is the problem, but sometimes it is the delivery that is insulting." He groaned. "I understand—because I know you—that you were simply trying to educate Miss Venraya on swordsmanship. We all know that her skill with a bow is the best in our class, and I know you are concerned it has created a gap that can be exploited.

"It is true that being a more rounded individual can save one's life, but there are better ways to say it. Also, falling victim to her frustrations regarding your background was another mistake on your part. Everyone knows you are of nobility. While you did not intend it to come off that way, using your nobility as a weight to the conversation backfired and made you come off as—to be frank—a pompous ass."

Brick let his words sink in for several moments. Tayven's eyes drifted around the room as he mulled over the information. Slowly but surely, realization dawned on the young noble. Once he had fully realized the truth behind Brick's words, Tayven smacked his forehead with the palm of his hand. "I've been an idiot, haven't I?"

"A little," Brick replied. "There's also your physical demeanor. Though it is hard, maybe tone down the noble posture. It makes it seem like you look down your nose at people, regardless of your intentions."

"Noted. Thank you, Brick."

Lestreus

"Prince Lestreus, what is your answer?" a balding man asked the red-headed prince.

"Hm? I'm sorry, Father Stephen. I was distracted." Lestreus bowed as deeply as he could from his seated position behind his desk. The argument with his father a week ago kept playing in his mind on repeat. He had never once been so forceful with anyone, let alone his own father, the king.

"I had asked about the tenants of the church, young prince. I know you are to attend that commoner academy soon and it would do much to settle my nerves to know that you would not be tempted by their relaxed views." Father Stephen sighed with resignation. "That city is rife with faithless and those that deny the gods to follow their 'Path'."

"Yes, um... Man shall strive to move forward and better both himself and his neighbor."

"That is correct, Prince Lestreus. A holy commandment handed down to us by the Goddess of Innovation. Another was shared by her brother, the God of Honor. That is?"

"I believe it is to face your foes and stand amongst the righteous to defend the weak?"

"That is correct," Father Stephen confirmed.

Prince Lestreus had spent the majority of his time since his conversation with Archpriest Henner and with his father in the temple attached to the Faradin Knight Academy. His teachers within the church had been hammering into him religious theory and history as if it were the end of days. Of course, he knew that this was at the request of his benefactor, Lord Henner, so Lestreus knew better than to fight against the requisite learning.

A knock at the door appreciatively interrupted Father Stephen's prelude to the next set of lectures. While the prince understood the importance of it, even he was tiring. Though as studious as one could be, a human only had so much patience. The person who entered was none other than Lord Henner himself. Upon seeing the portly Archpriest, both the prince and Father Stephen stood at attention, each giving a slight bow.

The man chuckled and put up a single hand to motion them to relax. "Father Stephen, I thank you for your time spent with the young prince, but I believe it is time we allow him at least a brief reprieve. Even an impressively intelligent young man like him deserves a break every now and again, yes?"

Father Stephen nodded and bowed before leaving the room quietly. Lestreus turned to the Archpriest and asked, "What brings you here today, sir?"

"I have selected someone to join you on your journey to Jelmoore. I needed a replacement for the head priest of the church there. With that in mind, I figured why not have you two travel together?"

"Of course, Lord Henner. Who will my traveling companion be?" Lestreus found himself extremely curious as to the identity of his new companion. He was also unaware that the clergy in Jelmoore was due for a change. Seeing as that was the case, then Lord Henner was in the right that it only made sense to kill two birds with one stone.

Henner motioned for someone to come into the room. Behind him was a tall, skinny man with a large, bushy black beard and mustache. His head was completely bald and his green eyes glinted with dangerous intelligence. A shiver ran up Lestreus's spine. "Prince Lestreus, allow me to introduce you to Father Gelroy. He is a loyal member of my inner circle and previously served at the temple in Rosendale. He has a long history of faithfully serving the church."

"Prince Lestreus, it is an honor to meet you." The man's frame and his deep, gravelly voice did not match up in Lestreus's mind, and something about his presence created a feeling of unease within the prince's stomach. Henner seemed to be completely unfazed by the situation, but Gelroy noticed the prince's discomfort and smiled. While the action was innocent, the way his grin failed to reach his eyes only deepened Lestreus' concern. The shiver from earlier turned into a shudder.

"Regardless," Henner continued, "Father Gelroy will take post in Jelmoore at the same time you transfer to the Vanguard Academy. They have already passed the period for their mid-term enrollments, but as a prince, your transfer will be accepted automatically. Father Gelroy will also take over your education, both here and while you are in the Vanguard Academy. This will ensure that the church's promise to your father of educating you is kept. He is a very devout man, so I am sure you two will get along famously!"

At that, the rotund priest dismissed himself from the room and left Gelroy and the young prince alone. Gelroy's presence instilled a fear in Lestreus that he simply could not shake. Gelroy's only response to the situation was to continue giving Lestreus a strange, hollow smile. The man then dropped a massive pile of books onto the desk with a resounding *thud*. "Shall we begin?"

Each of the tomes was nearly three or four fingers thick. The one that Gelroy opened crackled in protest as though it had been left unread for decades. Lestreus could almost see a cloud of dust spray into the air from between the sheets of paper. "As you say, Father Gelroy," he mumbled.

"You only have so much time before we leave for Jelmoore. When we leave Nefera, we will have to hire Vanguard warriors as an escort. Southern roads after Jilt become unsafe," Gelroy informed him.

Lestreus nodded. Henner had told him of such things already. The church and local guards worked together to keep the roads in the northern territories safe from monsters and bandits through regular patrols. Unfortunately, those patrols ceased just south of Nefera. By the time people got to Jilt, they were forced to suffer dirt roads, potential highwaymen and monster attacks.

"Can we not use church guards or even royal guards as an escort? I may only be the fourteenth prince, but I am still royalty. Surely—"

"No, young prince," Gelroy cut him off quickly. "Marching through southern nobles' territories with too large an escort will not be seen in a positive light. Besides, if you are to attend the Vanguard Academy, then we should arrive with Vanguard warriors. Though we may not feel their importance, appearances do matter. As I am sure you are aware."

"Understood," he said finally. *All of this could have been avoided if the southern nobles just partnered with the Crucidian Church, but in their stubborn pride, they refused such help. Nonsense.*

Chapter Sixteen

Rune

Intense pulses of pain bounced around Rune's head so intensely that it felt as if his brain was being blended inside of his skull. A part of him almost wished it would be so he could find relief from the sensation. The usual roar of conversation from the bar below felt louder than usual and only increased his discomfort. He thought back to the night before, where he was once again celebrating with his party of friends. Ever since the fight with the Razortusks, he had taken part in almost every celebratory dinner with the party. Last night, like most nights, they had drunk until Jeruul had had enough of his brother's shenanigans.

After the more responsible twin had carted his brother back to their rooms in the Hall, Teryn and Rune had completed their new ritual of drinking water and eating stale bread to sober up just enough to prevent a hangover. Unfortunately, they had been particularly excited after a much larger payout than planned, so it was impossible to pinpoint when they had actually done that last and very important part of their drinking ritual. If they had even remembered to do so.

Their job had had them confronting a swarm of Aura Bats that had taken to roosting in the barns of an unfortunate farmer north of Hilden. Aura Bats were pests most of the time, but when they gathered in large numbers, they could cause a lot of damage. For such small creatures, they held a large concentration of Aura in their bodies. Once they felt their swarms were large enough to take down larger creatures, they would attack almost anything that moved with Aura-enhanced teeth and claws.

Eventually, he realized he was on the floor and leaning against the bed instead of laying on it. He reached up to use the bed as a brace to help him stand, but his hand landed on something that felt vastly different from a blanket or mattress. Rune slowly looked over and saw a dainty hand move out from under the blanket, and a light moan and rustling came from the bed. A moment later, Teryn's visage appeared.

"Morning, Rune," she said with a yawn.

Rune's face drained of all its color. "I am so sorry, I don't..."

Teryn looked at her friend with an expression of visible confusion. Her eyes glanced about the room. They latched briefly onto Rune, then moved to the bed she was laying in before finally glancing at Rune's letters on the writing desk that were not yet sent. A look of realization came to her face as she finally understood this was neither her bedroom, nor a campsite out in the field.

"Well..." she said slowly before a smirk formed on her face, "How was I?"

Rune broke into a fit of coughs, choking on spit as he accidentally inhaled from shock. "Wait! So, we... did we really...? I didn't... I don't..." he stammered.

The young woman broke out in laughter at the poor friend she was teasing. "Don't worry, Rune. Nothing happened. Unlike you, I sobered up well before we returned to the Hall. You, on the other hand, fell a few times on the way home. I was worried you'd drown in your own vomit if no one was here to watch you."

Rune sighed. "Thank the gods..."

Not that I'm opposed. She is quite beautiful...

Teryn's jovial disposition quickly faded, replaced by offense and annoyance. "Thank the gods for what, you little shit?" she growled. "I'll have you know I am a catch, and you'd be lucky to have spent a night with me."

She once again sat there while Rune fumbled over his own words, attempting to find an apology to not make things worse or awkward. Once again, the Volari woman laughed at his predicament. She bid her goodbyes and turned to leave the room. Rune stood to walk her down since they were both already dressed, having passed out in their armor. Just as he reached the door, the world spun. The pain in his head surged in intensity. Rune's vision blurred before going completely black, and he felt himself fall. The last thing he heard before his consciousness left him was Teryn shouting his name.

Teryn

Her wounded screams brought a wave of people up the stairs. The ever-present rumble of conversation from the crowds below instantly ceased, casting an uncomfortable silence unfamiliar to the Hall. The first to enter the room were Jeruul and Master Jacob. Teryn was on her knees, cradling Rune in her lap. She held two fingers under his nose to make sure he was breathing.

His breaths were so shallow and quick that the rise in his chest was nearly imperceptible. She then placed two fingers on his neck to check for his pulse. It was there, but it was also erratic and weak. A crowd of people had quickly gathered outside the room with Jeruul and Dannon rushing to the front to keep them back. Jacob broke through the crowd while he shouted for someone to fetch Karl.

"Girl, what happened?"

"I don't know. We woke up and were about to leave to meet our party and take another job. He followed me to the door and suddenly collapsed like this."

Dannon raised his eyebrows at the 'we woke up' part, but said nothing. Teryn realized that while he was a loudmouth, he seemed to understand the time and place for whatever comments in his head was not that moment. Jacob shouted out once again, yelling for someone to get Karl in the room. Several excruciating minutes later, the disheveled man finally stepped into the room.

"Damn fools don't know how to move out of a man's way," he grumbled. "What's going on?"

Teryn quickly explained to him what had happened. She backtracked all the way to their last fight against some Shadow Wolves that had been pestering Dorn and finished with the moment Rune fell. Karl was observing him before whispering something to Jacob. Jacob nodded and shouted at everyone to leave and head downstairs, Jeruul and Dannon included. He allowed Teryn to stay, much to her surprise.

She was about to ask what was happening when Karl closed his eyes and ran his hand over Rune's chest. He did not actually touch Rune, rather he hovered about an inch or two away from the boy. A faint glow then emanate from Karl's palm.

"What is..." Teryn asked. She had seen Karl's eyes, so she knew he was not a Volari, yet he seemed to manipulate Aura like one would.

"I am not doing what you think I am doing. I am very much not a Volari," Karl stated. His eyes were still closed, but he seemed to feel Teryn's intense gaze and easily guessed her thoughts. "What you are about to witness, you will tell no one. Including Rune. If you do, you will put him, yourself, and your other friends in danger."

Teryn nodded slowly. Normally, she would not agree to such a vague request, but for her friend's safety, she had no other choice. Karl accepted her response. He quickly glanced at Jacob and nodded. Jacob responded in kind and pulled out a dagger, holding it in Karl's general direction. Seizing the unconscious boy by the neck, Karl whispered the activation of a skill. "Drain." His voice was gravelly and dark; a far cry from his normal upbeat tone. The act of him grabbing Rune's throat made Teryn twitch, but she held her trust in the man who had brought them together.

Teryn pushed power through her eyes and witnessed a massive amount of Aura leave Rune's body and flow into Karl. It had been some time since she had actually looked at Rune through her Volari Aura Sight. The last time had been when they first met and he seemed so devoid of Aura she thought he was suffering from Aura Deprevation. Now, there seemed to be so much in him that it nearly blinded her. Such a sight shocked her out of her concentration, returning her vision to normal. Somehow, though, she still could see a light purple and pink mist shed from Karl's body. Whatever the mist was, it spilled out of his every pore.

Jacob lightly tapped the man on the shoulder with the blade of his weapon. He looked on edge and was ready to pounce. Karl grunted and let go of Rune's neck. The strange mist was still falling off him while he sweat profusely. Karl's breath turned ragged.

"Jacob, I need to go let out some steam after this. Have the Vanguard stay away from the woods for a day or so. I'll be back," Karl choked out. Each word sounded painful, but the man quickly left the room. Teryn was left alone with Jacob in a confused silence, with her friend unconscious in her lap. Rune's breathing stabilized, though, and she felt her muscles relax.

Teryn slowly ran a hand through Rune's hair while brushing it away from his forehead. She felt that his fever was gone and saw his face was no longer contorted in pain. Her eyes met Hall Master Jacob, questioning him. He simply shook his head while rubbing his temples, clearly at a loss on how to explain to the girl what she had just witnessed.

"Karl is..." Jacob began slowly. He swallowed before he continued, "Unique. I think that's the best way to put it. What you saw is something you should never share with anyone in the Hall. Rune also needs to be kept in the dark about what happened."

Teryn's eyes widened in sudden panic. Her grip tightened around the young man in her arms. In contrast to his normal strength, he seemed so fragile at that moment. "But what if it happens again? What if he needs Karl to help again?"

"Don't worry. He can be told that Karl helped him. You can also tell him to continue to go to Karl for any help, just like he has been doing. Nothing needs to change. Simply leave out some details."

Teryn visibly relaxed once she confirmed that her friend's health would not be in danger in the future. A few seconds of silence passed while she watched the gentle rise and fall of Rune's chest. "Master, is Karl a Reaver?"

The temperature in the room seemed to drop several degrees. The young Volari did not dare to look up at the Hall Master. She knew if she did, what she saw would strip her of any drive to continue her questioning. She felt the intensity of Jacob's stare, but she needed to confirm what she had seen. Karl was definitely not a Volari. What the man had done was extract Aura directly from Rune's body; an impossible feat, even if he was Volari, as they could not remove Aura from an object, only manipulate it. This was how Volari clerics would do their work. They would move the Aura within someone's body to force the energy to focus on supporting the body's natural healing processes in the local area of injury. No, she knew Karl was doing something different. He was capable of something shared as myths, legends...campfire stories at best. It didn't seem real.

"Yes," Jacob answered, his voice dripping with frustration. "Karl is a Reaver."

Based on the tone and the look on the master's face, she knew that the threat from Karl earlier had been true. If she did not keep silent about what she learned, then she and her friends would be in a lot of danger. Master Jacob appeared so resolute in keeping this information a secret that it was likely the dagger he concealed would find itself in Teryn's heart if she blabbed. Teryn locked eyes with her Hall Master before she nodded in solemn understanding.

Brick

Tayven stood in the training ring of one of the academy's many practice rooms under the mirthful and watchful eyes of his much larger friend. The young noble's opponent was a small, raven-haired girl with piercing green eyes. She held two wooden daggers, while Tayven held his wooden longsword and a practice shield. The two of them had sparred a few times already. Each match was almost exclusively started in response to them getting into an argument.

Tayven could not keep himself from making small comments that seemed innocuous to him, but in reality, came off rudely. This continued despite Brick's earlier warnings. The girl, Venraya, was rather quick to anger and was still yet to get along with anyone else in class. In fact, the only person she seemed to do okay with was the professors. Though Brick had to admit, he had no particularly negative interactions with her himself.

"Look, Miss Venraya, I'm sure I don't understand why you are so pissed off at me this time, but this fight will end, like all the others, in your defeat." Tayven sighed.

"Really? You snot-nosed punk! I don't know how your breakfast tasted on that silver spoon you shoved up your ass, but maybe if you spent a little less time acting so high and mighty and a little more time learning tact, then you might actually make another friend aside from Brick."

"Ouch," Brick mumbled. Tayven shot him a look, which Brick returned with an apologetic shrug. *I tried to warn you. Thought you listened; yet here we are.* Brick only smiled and kept his thoughts to himself.

While Tayven was distracted, Venraya attempted to take advantage of the situation and charged towards the blue-haired noble. It worked for the first attack, as her dagger contacted the outside part of his shield arm and ripped the young man's sleeve, but the second was easily parried by Tayven's sword. Tayven stepped forward to make a swing, but missed when Venraya quickly moved out of his striking range.

She's improving.

This earned a small huff from the male combatant. In every fight, Tayven would take at least a few hits and though he tried to play it off as an allowance, Brick knew it showed Venraya's skill. Brick remembered his friend complaining not too long ago that he could find no one to fight 'for real' with, but now that he had a worthy opponent, he was not enjoying what that meant. Brick was highly amused by the sight of his friend taking a few hits. He could always strike Tayven, but after a handful of matches, Tayven had quit sparring with Brick altogether.

Tayven grunted in pain again as Venraya landed a second hit on him. This time, she had baited a swing from her opponent before ducking beneath the blade and swiping at Tayven's leg.

"Oh! That's gonna bruise!"

"Shut up, you are not helping, asshole!" Tayven shouted.

"I'm not supposed to help!" Brick laughed.

"You are not supposed to distract me, either!"

Their fight continued for another few minutes before Tayven began to sweat from the exertion. Venraya was taking some shaky breaths too, but was still in a lot better shape than her opponent. This surprised both men since Venraya had been moving around easily two or three times as much as Tayven had during the fight.

"You ready to eat dirt, asshole?" Venraya said as she began a last lunge. About halfway into it, she threw her primary dagger straight at Tayven's face. He instinctively brought his shield up to block. This blocked his line of sight of Venraya, who had dropped low to the ground. She quickly swept his legs as she slid past him, sending Tayven flat on his face. Faster than he could blink, she was on his back with her dagger pressed to the side of his neck.

"I yield, Miss Venraya, and for whatever it is worth, I apologize."

"Good," she said while rising from the ground. She glanced at Tayven's outstretched hand before leaving the room without assisting him up from the ground.

Brick followed her and waited till out of earshot of Tayven. "I wanted to let you in on a little bit of information. While Tayven may occasionally say things in a way that appears rude or tone-deaf, he certainly does not mean it. It is hard to combat one's upbringing. I assure you, his tone and his intentions do not always coincide. Also, I think you should know that he earned his way here. His father cut him off financially, so if he cannot perform adequately, he's out."

His word seemed to make Venraya to pause for a moment before she turned and faced him. "I didn't know that. I just assumed he was using daddy's money to buy his way through the ranks."

"Actually, he's only an E-Rank like us. He earned it himself after signing up in his hometown and doing his first ranking exam in Tennfeld to avoid any preferential treatment," Brick informed her. He watched her closely and noticed that there was a blend of annoyance, guilt, and understanding flashing through her eyes in rapid succession, each replacing the other.

"I'll keep that in mind. He's pretty good with the sword at least. He can't fake that, I suppose."

"No, he cannot."

By this point, Tayven had dusted himself off and stowed the practice equipment away. He had easily caught up to them and obviously overheard a portion of their conversation.

"Miss Venraya, I thank you for the compliment to my sword skills. Moving forward, I will endeavor to better understand how my words can impact others, even when unintentional." Tayven bowed towards Venraya and then extended a hand. "Friends?"

Venraya paused for a moment and looked back and forth between the two young men. "Acquaintances first, at least. Maybe friends later, if you teach me how to wield a sword a little better. I may have won this time, but going one-for-five is not something I'm proud of."

"You have got yourself a deal, Miss Venraya."

"Drop the 'miss' please. It makes me uncomfortable."

Brick smiled at the two. Something whispered in his mind that the girl's rough exterior was most likely her being awkward with people, just different from Tayven. He had not known how bad it was when he first met her, but after spending a few weeks with her in classes, Brick could tell that it was quite the interesting personality quirk. Almost everyone in class was fair game for snide remarks or being downright ignored. Tayven and Brick were the only ones who even continued to make attempts at interacting with her, at this point.

Brick was sure that Venraya appreciated this in some small way, otherwise she would not have asked for sword lessons from Tayven. *It is still strange to me that someone so small could pack such a large amount of anger and frustration in their body.*

Chapter Seventeen

Jeruul

Finally, Rune's breathing stabilized. His head was still in Teryn's lap, her eyes wet from concern. She gently ran her fingers through his hair. Every few minutes, she seemed to test his breathing with a finger under his nose like an anxious mother over her child. The party had spent quite some time together by this point and had gotten decently close. *Fighting side-by-side will do that, I suppose. Or maybe...*

Dannon and Jeruul had known Teryn for the better part of a year. Though they had formed up together for the first time in Jelmoore, none of them had joined the academy. Opting instead to simply work their way into E-Rank before heading eastwards towards Hilden. The southeastern portion of the continent where they were now located was well-known for its beautiful weather and rather steady work.

Most monster hunting jobs were solidly within the E- and D-Ranks with only a handful of high-ranking quests needing to be done. Though, this was ignoring the fact that higher-level monsters in the depths of the Greatwood could decide to leave their domain for easy prey. All the locals knew that there were two places you did not venture. First was the Greatwood, as anything deeper than a few yards into the tree line was basically a death sentence. The second place to avoid were the peaks of the Wyverntooth Mountains.

Jeruul had talked a bit with Rune about why, since his village was at the base of them. Locke's rich mineral resources were thanks to the many mines they maintained that dug into the mountain range's depths. Rune had explained that the danger of the place resided within the peaks. The entrances of the mines Locke maintained never went higher than a thousand feet above the village. Any higher than that and they risked coming into contact with many dangerous mountain-dwelling beasts. The largest concern being the namesake for the place, Wyverns.

Wyverns were terrifying monsters, but rarely interacted with people since they lived on mountain peaks and fed mostly on Shatterhorns and other monsters and animals that made those places their home.

"Hey, brother," Dannon whispered. "Just got done speaking with Master Jacob. He said that Karl gave Rune approval to continue work tomorrow if he wants. Says that he should be fine to fight again soon, as long as he rests up today."

So soon?

"If they think he should be fine, then he should be fine. I trust Master Jacob and Karl," Teryn stated. Jeruul was about to say something, but let their friend continue. "We've come to rely on each other as a team, and I would hate for us to mess with the plans we've created together. I won't fight without him."

Jeruul nodded. "Of course. I wouldn't dream of leaving him behind now. Our next job was supposed to be a scouting mission just west of here. According to the quest documents, there have been some strange movements by local bandit gangs and they wanted us to check out some abandoned campsites."

"Oh, that sounds cool. Wonder if we will find anything neat." Dannon chimed in.

"Finding things is the point of...whatever. Anyway, need any help, Teryn?" Jeruul asked, still giving his brother a sideways glare. Teryn nodded and asked for assistance, putting Rune back on the bed. She probably could have handled it herself, but it was easier on their friend if they worked together to make the transition gentler.

"So," Dannon asked Teryn, "you gonna spend the night with him again?"

"If that's what's needed."

Dannon let out a whistle before Jeruul planted an elbow in his gut. "Shut it, idiot. Clearly not the time for your antics. Teryn, do you need anything before we go?"

"Yes, can you grab me something to eat and drink? And bring some bread and water for me to have on hand in case he wakes up."

Jeruul nodded and left the room. He grabbed his twin by the collar and dragged him along. They headed down the stairs to the bar to just grab something quick and easy. The food was not the greatest, but quality was unnecessary. It just needed to work. Good food could come after their friend was conscious again.

Jeruul had noticed that Bordo was harassing another set of newbies at the job board. At first, he was planning to ignore the obnoxious dickhead, but Dannon decided they needed to step in.

"Hey, Bordo, picking on someone again? Forgot what getting your ass kicked by Rune felt like already?" Dannon taunted.

"You got a problem with the boss?" one of Bordo's lackies piped in. "'Cause, if you do, then you got a problem with us."

"Brave to bring that shithead up. Heard the brat couldn't hold his liquor and was nursing a headache so bad he needed to cry for the Hall Master. Maybe act tough when your wimp of a savior can actually help you out, eh?" another hissed.

"Yeah, everyone knows the runt got lucky anyway!" the first one continued.

Dannon squared his shoulders up with the lackey while Jeruul slowly readied his fists for any outburst that might start. The newbies that were being picked on had taken the opportunity to run. Silence filled the air as onlookers from the quest board, Reception, and the bar all stopped to look at the group. Their conversations had yet to develop into anything deep since many of them had just returned from checking out Teryn's scream. A few tables of people put their hands on their weapons in the event something happened. Suddenly, the air seemed to shift, and a strange pressure weighed down on them.

"Bordo," a dangerous voice grumbled. "How many times do I have to tell you to stop messing with the newbies? I am especially not in the mood today."

"Well boss, maybe if you didn't let a waste of space like that Rune kid in then maybe you wouldn't—" Bordo began.

Jacob, who had stepped into Jeruul's line of sight, held a terrifying expression, promising certain death to the recipient. "Do you want to try that sentence again, Bordo?"

The man's voice caught in his throat before he could respond. Purple energy crackled between Jacob's fingers, threatening to arc forward and strike the cowering man. Jacob was a renowned Pulser, known best for his rapid firing technique. Not only had he developed the ability to fire off nearly twice as many bolts as a normal Pulser using that ability, he was also scarily accurate. Jeruul had heard the rumors that he had 'calmed down' a bit after Venraya was born, but seeing how threatening his presence seemed, it was likely those rumors were exaggerated.

Bordo and his crew stood with their eyes locked on Master Jacob. All sounds and movement in the hall ceased as the entire building became eager to witness a slaughter. Finally, the ruffians grumbled something under their breath before slinking out of the building. Jacob put his hand over his eyes and sighed.

Rune

Rune groggily opened his eyes to a curtain of blonde hair and a pair of deep purple eyes that appeared to be glowing. The cheeks of the woman above him took on a slightly red hue as she jumped back in shock and emitted a small yelp. This made the young man smile in amusement as he began to slowly sit up.

"Ugh, I feel like I'm going to barf..." he grumbled as he fought back the urge for his stomach to turn itself inside out.

"How's your head? You had a fever earlier, so that's what I was checking when you woke up," Teryn informed him. "Dannon and Jeruul brought up some water and bread from the bar downstairs a few hours ago."

"Hours?"

"Yeah, it's the afternoon now. You passed out and Karl came to help you. He came back after a... trip and said he would be back in a few days. He recommended that you take it a little easy."

"Damn, so I guess we won't be able to do our job."

"No, it was just a scouting job. There will be no issue in delaying it by a day. Karl said you should be good to go tomorrow. Just try to leave most of the fighting to us. Dannon will take the close range while you can hang back with me for support. You can use a crossbow, right?"

"Yeah, I know my way around them. Dannon's willing to let me use his, right?" he asked. "'Cause, I don't exactly have one of my own."

Teryn motioned to the corner of the room, where their friend's repeating crossbow—affectionately named Gerty, as Rune had found out—was leaning against the wall. Rune could not help but smile at it because he knew it was Dannon's most prized possession. Repeating crossbows like that were very hard to find, as they were an exclusive product of Volar. Many people had attempted to make them, but the small internal components essentially required a Volari Metal-Weaver to be involved in the construction.

"Since you are cooped up here tonight, mind if I stick around and keep you company?" Teryn asked, not quite meeting his gaze.

"Absolutely. I am completely exhausted, physically, so I don't really think I will move from here. But mentally, I am fully awake. So please, spare me from boredom," Rune begged.

Teryn could not help but giggle at her pleading friend. "I can always invite Dannon to keep you company, you know. I am sure he would love to chat with you. All. Night. Long."

"Please, no…"

Both of them laughed together at Dannon's expense. He was a really good person and was extraordinarily friendly. Even then, sometimes he could be a bit much. After a time, the conversation shifted to how Teryn had come to meet the other members of their party.

"Well, as you already know, I am from Dena. I'm the middle child of ten and all my older siblings have already moved on with their lives, and I felt like I needed to do something different," Teryn explained.

Rune listened as she explained her story to him. As the middle child of ten, there were a lot of times when she was ignored, though since there were so many children, basically every one of them had experienced it to some degree. Her family was the head of a small trading company that specialized in exporting goods to Jelmoore and also had dealings with a few ships out of Borros, so they never wanted for much.

That kind of life had satisfied her for a time, but eventually, as many children experienced, she felt a little bit of wanderlust. Sure, she enjoyed spending time with her siblings and friends, but the stories she heard from her parents' trading partners stirred something within her. After seeing her older siblings get married and join the family business, she decided she wanted to pursue something different. Apparently, this did not go over positively with her father who had envisioned all of his children joining his company and becoming representatives with trading partners all over the world. He figured that having such a large family would let his business break into the realm of the larger players. Teryn shook her head as she explained his dream of owning fleets of trading ships sporting his name and finally being given a noble title.

She reminds me of Tara. They would get along well.

"Your father sounds…delightful," Rune commented.

"You have no idea," Teryn replied. "I love him dearly, but a long story made short: my wants and his didn't align, and it left a sour taste in his mouth. He eventually relented and told me 'Do whatever you want' before I left, so I did. At least I didn't have to sneak off."

"After that, you left for Jelmoore and that's where you met the guys, right? How did that happen?"

The girl laughed at the memory as she explained how she had joined up with the twins. Dannon was the one she had met first. After she had arrived on the mainland, she wandered around the docks for a few hours like a lost child. Luckily for her, Jelmoore had a significant population of Volari and Wanderers and they recognized her as a new face immediately. According to Teryn, they could have helped her out immediately, but a new face getting lost in town was some kind of informal rite of passage amongst the immigrants.

Eventually, someone pointed her toward the one place that she absolutely wanted to be. The Vanguard Academy. In Jelmoore, the Vanguard Academy also housed the Vanguard Hall. Second-year and up students could take missions from the Hall as part of their coursework, so it only made sense for such a setup. Even with a general knowledge of where to go, though, Teryn had gotten lost a second time.

Unlike on the docks, Teryn did not see any Volari who could help her and so she was forced to have her first proper conversation with a human. That human was a boy with brown hair, brown eyes, and a loudmouth. He had been talking to a street vender and asking if they had seen someone who looked like him. Teryn's initial plan was to talk to the same vendor, since they seemed okay with helping the obnoxious boy, but when she approached, the boy switched gears and began talking to her instead. The vendor, who had apparently been stuck in a conversational trap for the better part of an hour, took his mobile cart with him and escaped from Dannon. Once he had a new conversational victim, Dannon was eager to change targets.

"I see, so he's always been so friendly." Rune chuckled.

"Yeah, according to Jeruul, Dannon got all the charisma and social skills, while Jeruul took all the logic and sense." Teryn laughed. "Anyway, the guys are born-and-raised natives to Jelmoore and Dannon explained he was a newer member of the Vanguard himself, so he escorted me all the way to the Hall at the Academy. He had been looking for his brother because they got separated when

Dannon was distracted, but Jeruul was already at the Hall. I guess he figured his brother would show up, eventually. Not too long after that, I took the test to join up, and the twins asked me immediately to join their party."

Rune and Teryn continued to share stories of their childhoods and adventures. Rune noticed a slight decrease in conversational tone when he talked about his time with Tara and Ven, but decided not to mention anything. Several hours and a good meal later, Rune finally felt tired. Teryn noticed this and bid him goodnight, advising that they were planning to head out first thing in the morning.

"Remember, if you don't feel up to it, just tell us. It's better to be down one person than that person to become a liability," she warned.

"You got it." Rune shifted his feet nervously. "Thanks for taking care of me."

"For you? Anytime!" Teryn beamed.

Tayven

"I think we should just form one ourselves at this point," Tayven proclaimed suddenly.

He, Brick and Ven were in the middle of eating dinner in the dining hall when he interrupted the silence. After the first fight Ven won, the pair had finally gotten on good terms with one another. Brick was never someone she had taken issue with, so it was only natural that he grew closer with her as well.

Nowadays, their sparring sessions were friendly and educational. Tayven taught her basic sword forms, while Ven gave him experience fighting opponents that would not just stand still to trade blows. It was a mutually beneficial relationship. Ven was still a little rough around the edges when interacting with other students, but she had calmed down a smidge. On top of that, her Pulser skills were seriously impressive.

Tayven and Brick had only recently learned that her father was Hall Master Jacob, a man whose intensity in battle coupled with his rapid firing techniques had inspired a generation of Vanguard hopefuls. Ven appeared to share some of his innate skills, though hers were far from refined. Despite this, her performance in Aura Development class with Professor Lylah was enough for many of the students to ignore her personality quirk and attempt to recruit her into their parties.

By this point, she had even received offers from parties with second-years in them, which would allow her to partake in jobs for school credits. Ven, of course, had zero interest in partying up with people she neither knew nor respected. However, the increased frequency and tenacity of these offers put the fear of the gods into Tayven that his friend would be poached.

"What are you on about?" Brick asked between slurps of soup.

"We should just form a party of our own. We won't be able to take missions until next year, but at least we will have an established party," Tayven explained.

"And why would I join a party that won't let me go on jobs?" Ven inquired.

Tayven gave her a sly smile. "A fair question, but at least if we formally register one with the Academy, then people finally stop pestering you," he countered.

Ven stopped drinking her ale for a moment and pondered the offer. Brick tried and failed to contain a wide grin. He knew that Tayven's original idea was enough on its own to get the girl to agree, but even if it did not, the chance at stopping people from bothering her absolutely sealed the deal.

"You make a good point. Let's do it," she agreed. "One condition though."

"Alright, I'm listening."

"We will not just rest on our laurels and wait till next year. I want us to seriously try and find someone we can add that will let us take jobs this year if possible." Ven stated. Her tone and demeanor begged no chance of countering. "I know it may not happen, but I want us to try."

Tayven and Brick looked at each other before simultaneously agreeing. "Deal."

With that, they returned to eating and enjoying some light conversation before they had to move to their next class. Once they finished and went to the lecture hall, they all sat together at the front of the room. Other students slowly trickled in before class started, the professor entering last.

"Alright, class, let us begin. Today, we will have a discussion on the naming convention behind Volari specialties. Normally, Professor Lylah vas Mithra would hold this class, however, she had asked me to fill in today," the man said before giving a slight nod and smile to Ven. "Nice to meet you all. I am Professor Martin and I normally instruct second- and third-years regarding Vendreyan History, Mathematics, and Vanguard Ethics."

Everyone in class stood and gave the professor a respectful bow. Afterwards, he motioned for the class to be seated before continuing with his lecture. "Who can tell me what almost all Volari specialists are called?"

A small male student raised his hand in the back of the class. "Each specialty uses the suffix of '-weaver', sir."

"That is mostly correct. Anyone know why?"

This time, no one raised their hands. The lack of response resulted in Professor Martin releasing a resigned sigh. "It is because Volari 'weave' the Aura in the environment to suit their purposes. Awakened use the Crystallization of Aura that builds up in their bodies to release or use as pure energy, but Volari manipulate that which flows naturally through the environment."

"So, when Lylah says she is a Stone-Weaver, that means she manipulates the Aura within rocks and stones?" another student asked.

"I would be careful how you address the professor, but you are essentially correct. I would also caution the use of the word 'within' in this context. Organic entities can contain excess Aura within internal wells as energy. However, in general, Aura simply exists as it is both within and is environment itself. There is a flow of sorts through objects as well.

"It is important to remember that Aura is what we've identified as a piece of the fabric of reality itself. It makes up matter, energy, everything. Volari are born with an innate understanding of the frequencies that Aura exists within. Some are tuned to the frequency that constructs rocks, some plants, and others are attuned to metal. There are types of weaving specialties that do not have to deal with matter at all. Anyone know of one?"

Ven raised her hand. As someone who had grown up in the Vanguard, Tayven figured that she knew of pretty famous example of a non-matter related weaver. "Sound-Weaver. They can amplify or negate sound. Some can even manipulate the pitch and tone of sounds to make them or someone else sound completely different. Lady Kyndra of the Vanguard is one of those."

"That is correct, Ven. Another well-known example is a Shadow-Weaver. These frightening specialists can bend the very essence of light and dark to make themselves invisible to the naked eye. As the name suggests, these types of specialists are usually known for infiltration and assassination," Martin affirmed.

"Professor Martin, if I may," a student asked. "Why do we refer to Volari who specialize in healing as clerics and not Flesh-Weavers or Blood-Weavers or something?"

Professor Martin's face darkened, as if remembering something extremely unpleasant. "Flesh-Weavers exist. As do Blood-Weavers. Though Volari clerics use many of the same techniques that those others do, the difference in the name has to do with how they choose to use their abilities. Clerics reject the abhorrent possibilities that their abilities present, while flesh and Blood-Weavers relish in it. When you get into upper-level coursework, we will discuss that topic in greater detail. For now, I hope you don't run into someone willingly using those titles."

After that, class continued as normal, though Professor Martin's demeanor was a lot colder after the student's question. It was clear to Tayven that it was more than just the knowledge of what Flesh-Weavers could do. Professor Martin must have directly seen it. *Honestly sounds terrifying. Maybe I should stay on the clerics' good sides. How about I deliver them a bottle of wine as a thank you?* He decided that being friends with their medical staff was suddenly a fantastic idea.

Chapter Eighteen

Dannon

"Aw, come on, Dannon! I just want a little more target practice!" Rune whined. Dannon was having none of it. His precious baby Gerty had been injured in combat almost a month ago by the absolute heathen named Rune. The day after his big 'incident' they had gone out to do a scouting mission in some areas where bandits had suddenly abandoned their encampments.

Since Rune had been recovering, and there was still a risk of relapse, Dannon had lent him his most prized possession in the world so he could take it easy. Everything went well until the sinner slid down an embankment and dropped Gerty!

"Absolutely not!" Dannon shouted. "You hurt her. Look. See this scratch here? It is all because of you! It didn't 'buff out' like you said it would. Take responsibility for your actions, you devil in human skin!"

Teryn and Jeruul could not help but laugh at their friend's antics. To them, it was a big joke, but Dannon was serious about not letting Rune have his weapon again. He was not actually mad at him, but he definitely did not want a repeat of what had happened. It had taken a lot of effort to get that old Volari trader to let go of a repeating crossbow. They were very hard to find outside of the island nation and nothing like it could be replicated in the Faradin Kingdom. A seemingly innocuous tumble could cause the sensitive inner-workings becoming jumbled. If that happened, Gerty would become a glorified paperweight.

"Don't worry, Dannon," Rune said calmly. "If something happens to it, I'll take it to Locke. I am sure my father could fix it. He is a Wanderer and probably the best blacksmith in the kingdom."

"Alright, but you are buying me more polish!" Dannon growled.

The group was spending time in a small town called Lakeside. Traveling by land only would have had the group go past Jelmoore, but thankfully, there was a boat that would take travelers to the town from across the lake. This cut the trip by half. Their reason for being in this small fishing village was yet another scouting mission.

Bandit attacks on merchant caravans and travelers had dropped in the area lately and no one could figure out why. It was not as though hundreds of bandits had suddenly changed their ways and returned to normal lives in local villages.

This scouting mission was the fifth one that Dannon and his friends had gone on since the first one a few weeks before. At every site, it looked like the Bandits had purposefully packed up and left. They were not in a hurry, either. Nothing valuable was left behind, the only signs of habitation being firepits, abandoned junk, and the latrines they had dug.

It was great that attacks and ambushes were down, but it was also concerning that there seemed to be a mass exodus of some kind occurring. There were less bandit hunting jobs available, too. So, it was not the result of any Vanguard group, nor was it the result of any collaboration between noble families and the military.

"I really just don't like this," Teryn mumbled while sifting through another pile of garbage, hoping to find some clue. "Just the amount of people that have up and vanished is strange. I know they aren't stupid enough to try to enter the Greatwood. So, where in Chaos's name did they go?"

"I don't know," Jeruul answered. "Our job is only to look for clues and share any information we find."

Jeruul's statement was cut off by an arrow whistling past his head. It sank into the ground behind him, having just barely grazed his cheek. The assailant was a rough-looking man in the tree line holding a worn-out looking hunting bow.

"Bandits! Looks like we caught these guys before they could leave!" Dannon shouted, bringing Gerty to a ready position.

Teryn and Rune jumped into a ready position with Rune standing between her and the trees with his shield at the ready. Jeruul also quickly jumped to his feet, held up his shield, and stood between the trees and Dannon. Dannon trained his sights on the archer and fired off three bolts in rapid succession. One sank into the trunk of a tree while another found purchase on the man's shoulder and then neck. Blood sprayed wildly from the wound, having ripped open a major artery.

"Well, we won't be taking that one alive," Rune mumbled. Dannon realized by the look on his face that Rune had probably not killed a person before. Killing people was never easy. Though their party had fought and killed bandits in the past, it was not really something someone got used to. *He'll have to get over it.*

Several cries rang out as six additional men charged out of the woods at the group. Dannon quickly fired additional arrows, but two of the bandits appeared to be Shielders. They shouted "Barrier!" in unison. Two glowing walls of light formed in front of them and their comrades as they charged.

Teryn's eyes glowed, and she waved her hand. Blades of grass started to grow and wrap around the enemy's feet, but nothing really stood up to the charge. "By Chaos! Again? What is it with my weaving lately?"

As the Bandits moved closer and closer, their barriers flickered before they suddenly shattered, as if made of glass. The surprised look on one Shielder's face told him they had not expected their defenses to fail. Dannon tried to ready one of his Pulser attacks, but felt the Aura gathering in his hands dissipate while it formed. Before he could call out a warning to the others, the attackers had already reached them.

Three men rushed Dannon and Jeruul with wild swings. Since the twins were well trained, the first attacks were easy to deflect. Jeruul took two of the men, while Dannon took the third. Dannon stepped to the left side of his brother and lunged forward with one of his daggers, drawing the third man's attention.

From the corner of his eye, Dannon spotted his friends similarly dividing the workload. Teryn had taken one, while Rune took the other two.

Even though Dannon was facing off against his own foe, he could not help but be distracted by seeing Rune fight. In between the clashing of steel, he watched as his friend seemed to dance across the battlefield. It was entrancing; unlike any fighting he had witnessed. Every battle seemed different, as if Rune's specialty had no specific movements. The young man adapted to his opponent's every step. Since the Razortusk fight, he rarely provoked attacks, preferring to respond and adapt as he had done every time before.

Dannon continued to clash with his enemy as they desperately probed each other's defenses. Eventually, he found a small opening that provided him with a small window to disengage and stab one of his brother's opponents in the back of the neck. Unfortunately, the blade was caught in the spinal cord, so Dannon had to release his hold on the weapon in order to recover in time to dodge his own opponent's next attack. He jumped to the left in time to narrowly avoid a deadly swing. As he sidestepped the blade, it slashed down the back of the bandit with a knife in his neck instead of Dannon.

"Sorry 'bout 'ya, bud!" Dannon laughed as he danced away, hiding the fact that he had gulped from the close call. Now he was down to only one dagger, which put him at a slight disadvantage compared to his enemy's longsword. Jeruul bashed the person in front of him with his shield, then pierced his belly.

After doing so, he rushed up behind the man facing Dannon and roared a battle cry. The bandit spun around to face the oncoming young man, but before he could bring his sword up to block, Dannon rushed up and slammed the hilt of his weapon into the bandit's temple. Once Dannon drew back, the bandit collapsed to the ground like a sack of potatoes.

"Good one, brother," Dannon managed between gasps. He glanced over to their comrades who had already dispatched their three.

"How in the fucking hell do you do that, Rune?" Teryn asked. She was once again referencing the strangest thing about the boy. That the longer a fight lasted, the stronger and faster he seemed to get.

"Yeah, I agree. I don't know what in the gods' names your father taught you, but I want to learn it if it's going to do that for me," Jeruul commented. Teryn had a conflicted expression on her face, but Dannon let it be.

"Ha! As if, brother!" Dannon laughed. "Clearly, I am more suited to the combat style. Your massive sword and shield are too clunky for moving around like that." Teryn nodded in agreement, but was also looking at her own equipment, as if silently wondering if she could pull it off herself.

"You guys are crazy. It's just adrenaline," Rune muttered quietly. His face was pale and eyes wide. Blood painted the front of his armor and dripped down his blade. Not an unfamiliar sight, but definitely an unfamiliar source. Dannon pat him on the back gently. First kills were never easy, something he had learned some time ago.

"All of us have adrenaline pumping through us right now, but you... You know what, never mind. How many times have we had this argument? Let's just tie up the survivor here and ready him for questioning," Jeruul mumbled. Even with his infinite grace, he was tiring of Rune's humility.

A few hours after the battle, the party of four sat around a small fire with their prisoner slowly coming back to consciousness. With the other bandits dead and their corpses burned, all that was left was to interrogate the lone survivor. Hopefully, he was someone who might finally give them the answers they had been looking for. At first, the man struggled against his bindings, but quickly learned that there was no means of escape.

"What d'ya want from me, eh? Bunch'a fancy Vanguard brats..." he finally shouted out.

"We want to know what all of you brigands have been up to lately. Known encampments have been left abandoned all around, and while normally, we would be happy to see you lot vanish, something isn't quite adding up," Jeruul questioned. His tone came off rather dangerous, and the constant tightening of his grip on his sword's hilt helped get across that he was not playing games.

"What's it matter, anyway? You're gonna kill me either way," the man groaned.

"Well. If you share what you know, it will be quick. If not, then…" Jeruul trailed off while Teryn stepped forward with her eyes glowing. Dannon watched as the prisoner slowly turned his head after feeling something soft brush against his cheek. A single blade of grass had grown from the ground and rubbed itself on his face before slowly lowering itself and wrapping around his neck. Additional strands of plant material swirled around the first, twisting into a sickly green tendril.

Sweat dripped down the man's brow and his breath became ragged as the plant wrapped itself around his throat once, then twice. Additional ropes of foliage tugged at his fingers, pulling them towards the back of his hand until the skin became taught; a less than subtle threat. He shouted, "Alright! Alright, I'll tell you. Just make it quick. I don't know much. The last boss was the one who did all the dealing."

"Dealing with who?"

"I don't know. Some scary woman. She threw the boss a bag of money and asked us to gather up and meet somewhere. I don't know where, though. My mates and I, we killed the boss in his sleep and took the money for ourselves."

"Where's the money?"

"I don't know! The night after we took out the boss, we heard this weird laugh, and the bag vanished right in front of our eyes. That was a few days ago," the man explained.

He relaxed slightly when the plant shrank back into the ground. Teryn was flexing her fist and looking strangely at the ground. Every once in a while, she would glance at Rune, who had been glaring icily at the prisoner without a word. No trace of the shock remained on his friend's face. His expression shifted to a cold, calculating gaze, similar to the one he'd worn while fighting Bordo or brutalizing the Razortusk. Looking once more at Teryn, Dannon could have sworn that she was blushing, if only slightly. *Interesting…* Dannon thought, amused.

"We hid just inside the woods the last few days because we didn't know if the woman would come back and collect our heads along with the money," the bandit explained.

"Well, she won't have to now, will she?" Jeruul stated plainly. With a flash of metal, his sword was no longer in its sheathe and instead glinted in the sunlight, the tip on the opposite side of the bandit's neck. The prisoner's eyes widened and his mouth moved slightly before his head smacked the ground with a wet thud.

"Damn, brother, that was brutal...but hey!" Dannon changed his expression to a joyful smile and gave a thumbs up to the group. "At least we are one mission closer to our Rank-up job!"

Vincent

A man with a massive frame and bulging arms sat in a luxurious suede chair, sipping tea. He wore a fine suit that only barely contained his form. He squinted his eyes mischievously at the woman in the room as he read through a notice on his desk. After gently placing the cup on a plate, he passed the letter to Anna and then picked up another document.

The gentle, lukewarm air of early fall filled the room, courtesy of an open window. Sumnuthras was over and with it, so too was the summer weather. This new season's chillier air and changing leaves meant winter was fast approaching. With only a scant amount of time until the cold season arrived, the already hard to locate answers they searched for would become even harder to come by.

"What do you make of this, Anna?" the man asked.

"Master Vincent, I do not know." Anna replied. She stood tall, proud, and confident, with a single longsword on her hip. Green hair hung in a tight braid over her shoulder. "The mobilization of these...people, is concerning. We have the Vanguard Halls of Tennfeld, Jilt, Jelmoore, and Hilden posting jobs to find all the information we can. Since most of them are simply scouting offers and not hunting jobs, we have reported difficulty in getting them completed."

"Ah, yes, I imagine the other Halls are struggling. Most people who will take these things are newer groups trying to bust into the D-Rank by simply fulfilling their quota for a ranking test. Veterans are too proud to take them and those already in D-Rank are too eager to prove themselves in combat," Vincent complained. "Though I heard that a few months ago, a small party captured a bandit alive and got some information. Other than that singular incident, no new information came about regarding who seems to hire groups of ruffians or why?"

"With all that in mind, sir," Anna stated, "we should probably think about canceling your trip to Hilden. I know you promised to meet with Master Jacob and Karl, but…"

"Ah, nonsense!" Vincent laughed. "I'm sure it'll be just fine!"

"I wouldn't tempt Fate like that," Anna mumbled.

"Hey, I knew you had been hanging out with that Volari worker at the cafe down the street, but I didn't know you were converting to the Path for him!" Vincent chuckled. "Handsome fellow, though. Kind, too. I'm sure he will treat you right."

Anna's face turned red and before she could stop herself, she slapped Vincent upside the head. "Shut up, Vincent! It was just a figure of speech!"

Vincent could not help but continue to laugh while he rubbed the sore spot developing. He was almost certain he felt his brain rattle. The man's glint vanished the moment he went back to reading additional reports. The source of his shock was a letter notifying him that the fourteenth prince, Lestreus Faradin, was going to be transferring to the Vanguard Academy. Vincent was the Hall Master of the Jelmoore Vanguard Hall and by extension, the Headmaster of the Vanguard Academy. It intrigued him that no one had informed him of this change before now, but figured that it was simply because of external involvement. Probably by the chubby priest, Lord Henner.

So that's what we can expect this year, huh? Strange, the prince is not coming with any sort of entourage to the academy but he's being accompanied by a... Vincent paused because he thought he misread the document.

"Anna?" he asked with a measured tone. "Please tell me the name you see on this form."

"Prince Lestreus Faradin, then a few random priests. Then—" she said aloud while reading. The last name on the list gave her pause. "Sir. Is this correct?"

"I think so," Vincent answered, his measured tone wavering. "Father Gelroy, formerly of Rosendale."

"Sir?"

"Get me a courier at once. I have to send a letter to Lord Jelmoore's estate. He needs to know immediately."

Anna placed the papers she had been holding onto the desk before snapping to attention. "Sir!" She then left to go fetch a courier while Vincent penned a letter to the old man.

The headmaster recalled memories of Father Gelroy, formerly Inquisitor Gelroy. Inquisitors were a loosely kept secret of the church. They held no standing army, but they provided intensive training to people they claimed to be guards. These 'guards' would protect the church's assets and pilgrims. The truth of the matter was the church used these guards to find exceptional individuals whom they granted the rank of Inquisitor. Gelroy, in particular, was a nasty specimen among these intensely religious warriors.

Rumors held he was the reason that Guldin Castle had lost its noble household after the Lord publicly denounced the Cruicidian Church. Once it fell, both the castle and Guldin Village, a day's ride from the castle, had become a religious haven of sorts for the most ardent worshipers. Gelroy's fanaticism knew no bounds, and this fact made Vincent suffer from a cold sweat. The city was barely holding together beneath the surface as it was. Demonstrations by followers of the Crucidian faith marched through the city on almost a weekly basis and incidents of missionaries stowing away on ships to Volar had increased to almost a daily occurrence. Vincent had even received a report of a fanatic who made landfall on the island nation and caused a public incident by spouting off nonsense about "heresy" and "abandoning the Path" right as he got off the boat.

Volar was a self-isolating country, politically and religiously speaking. This was because their people's Path of Volar and the Crucidian Church's faiths were diametrically opposed when it came to the afterlife. At least, that was what it was like on the surface and in the public eye.

In reality, the leaders of the church were power hungry bastards who did not like that there was a large group of people they could not bring to heel. The same could be said for the southern nobility. However, this was also what had led to the animosity between the southern and northern halves of the continent. Volar was not much better, as the pride most of its nobility had in their people's bloodline caused much friction with outsiders.

"Sir, I have brought the courier," Anna announced when she returned.

"Excellent. Girl, take this to Lord Jelmoore's estate. He is most likely on a hunt, so leave it with his steward. I have stamped the letter with my seal, but inform the guards that this delivery is on my behalf. They will direct you to the steward without incident."

"Y-yes, sir."

"Go. Here's ten gold for your trouble. Keep the change," Vincent added with a wave. "Anna, get preparations started on our trip to Hilden to meet Jacob and Karl. Add to the guard detail...let's say, we double it. Trouble is brewing. I feel it in my bones. We will leave in two weeks' time."

"By your command, sir."

Chapter Nineteen

Teryn

Teryn was used to being alone growing up. Despite being surrounded by family at nearly all times, she still faded into the background. So many people in their home coupled with her father's business needing so much attention, it was rather easy for anyone to be forgotten.

After joining the Vanguard and spending time with the twins, those feelings had waned slightly. Unlike her family, they paid attention to her, valued her opinion, and did everything they could to include her in nearly every activity. However, they still had a connection with each other that she would never be a part of. There was still something that made her feel left out once again. Was it probably just in her head? Sure, but that did not change how she felt.

Things changed once again when Rune joined the group. He was a party member, just like the twins, but he came with no pre-existing relationships within the group. His family and friends were far away, and despite them being much closer than her own family, she felt like he could understand her situation. The fact he was a genuinely kind person who cared about the feelings and opinions of his friends also helped.

In truth, it was no wonder that Teryn got along well with him. After several missions together, she had grown ever closer to him. He was kind, smart, and talented, yet he let none of that go to his head. Most of all, though, he made her feel important. Whenever they talked, he paid attention to only her. Teryn felt like the only girl in the world that mattered. On more than one occasion, their talks lasted until sunrise. Nothing felt forced.

Teryn sighed. She knew he was unlikely to reciprocate or even notice her budding feelings. At least, there was no way he would while he still had Tara back home. For now, being friends was enough. Then, a terrifying thought occurred to her: if she wasn't careful, then Rune might make her feel left out again.

"Teryn," the man in question knocked lightly at the door to her room. "Are you ready to head out?"

It was first thing in the morning, and she had not even bothered to get dressed yet, wearing only a thin set of pajamas slightly worn out from use. Normally, she was on top of such things and would be the one who woke Rune up for the day, but this was not one of those days. Instead of complaining, she quickly donned her armor before opening the door to let her friend inside. She gestured for him to sit while she completed putting belongings in her bag.

"Um, Teryn?" Rune said without entering, "Why are you dressed in your armor? We don't have any plans to go on any jobs today."

Teryn froze in place for a moment. Distracted by her early morning thoughts, she had prepared herself for a quest instead. Rune stood in the doorway with his two swords sheathed on his hip while he wore normal, everyday clothing. A plain shirt clung to his form. It had been a gift from her. When she had realized he only had a couple of shirts and pants from home, she felt the need to expand his options, if only slightly.

Today's plans mostly included them running around town and doing some shopping for the party and taking some time to enjoy themselves. A lot of the missions they had taken lately were scouting jobs requested out of Jelmoore. This meant they spent a lot of their time lately fighting against and tracking down humans.

As members of the Vanguard, fighting against people was not a rare occurrence. However, a majority of their efforts were put towards keeping people safe from monsters. Fighting off bandits and criminals was within the purview of guards and the kingdom's military, but that was up north, where they could dedicate the resources to it. Down here, the Vanguard picked up the slack.

After their frequent conflicts with bandits, everyone agreed to take a day or two of rest. There was a mutual agreement amongst the party that rest was something they desperately needed. Teryn had not been sleeping well lately because of the blood-filled jobs and from what she could gather from conversations with Rune, he was not resting well either. Fighting was still a fairly recent addition to her life, all things considered. Spilling the blood of others gave her poor dreams, many of which left her in a puddle of sweat upon waking.

She sighed deeply before slowly removing her armor. Rune turned his back to her. Since she had on normal clothing underneath now, it was not a big deal if he watched. However, for appearances, it was better that he did that. *Not that he has to...*

Such behavior was typical of the charming young man. He always tried his best to keep her best interests in mind even through the simplest actions. Were he to really try for it, Teryn knew that Rune could have been quite the ladies' man. She had already heard that he somehow broke through the tough shell that was Venraya. Though she had never really spoken with the girl, everyone had heard about Master Jacob's daughter and her abrasive personality. Yet Rune had conquered that, too...

"Alright, I should be ready now," Teryn said finally while she secured her saber to her side. Keeping a weapon with you at all times was good practice. Even inside of a settlement, one could never know when danger would strike. While wearing armor or a shield could be unwieldy in such situations, a weapon did not suffer such a fate. Besides, a weapon on her hip often kept the missionaries and church acolytes away from her.

Rune nodded simply and smiled before he jokingly offered his arm to her. Not wanting to miss a prime opportunity to gain some closeness, Teryn called his bluff and linked arms with the young man. Rune's eyes opened wide in slight panic before he cleared his throat.

"Let's go then, I suppose." He coughed. "Where to first?"

"The market!" Teryn giggled. She was thankful that Rune had turned his face away from her because from that angle, he could not see the reddish hues that her cheeks took on.

The hall was experiencing its normal hustle and bustle of the day. No one gave the pair of them a second glance either as they stepped off the stairs and headed out to the town. A few hundred feet from the door to the hall was the first of several stalls that made up the market, but the ones they were interested in were in the market proper.

This did not stop the venders of these smaller stalls from trying to seduce them into browsing their wares. Because they had just left the Vanguard Hall, however, not a lot of effort was put into trying to make customers out of the pair. Vanguard members were used to their position and tactics. By this point, they were just trying for the sake of trying, but had no heart in it. Many of them preyed upon newer members or guests.

Teryn could not help but imagine that they looked like a proper couple to everyone they passed. Such thoughts made her rather happy, even when she knew it was not something that could happen. Still, she enjoyed what time she could have in such a scenario.

In fact, it was her idea that they spend their day off together. Dannon and Jeruul had shared they would spend the day alone. Everyone knew that at some point the twins would end up together again because of their shared interests, but it left things open for Teryn and Rune. With Dannon out of the picture, she wondered how much time she could get with Rune with none of the annoying interruptions or mocking statements from their friend.

Rune had been open to the idea from the start, even smiling upon her recommendation of spending quality time together. Teryn felt something warm form in the pit of her stomach that she could not describe, and it made her curse herself for almost forgetting about it when he had woken her up that morning.

Walking only a few minutes further into town exposed them to the actual marketplace. Merchants of all kinds were completing their setup or were in the process of starting it. Many of the food vendors had long completed their preparations, sending smells of every sort into the air. Several inns had also conveniently aired out their dining halls in the morning, which would send the aroma of fresh breakfast and breads into the streets. Each scent was a temptation to Teryn's senses, each assaulting her sanity. Before long, her stomach betrayed her inner desires.

Rune laughed at her for a moment and made her realize he had been looking at her. "I take it you are hungry?"

"No, I promise that I—" Teryn tried to object, but a loud gurgle once more coming from her belly defeated any chance she had to disagree. The blush that had faded from her face returned with great fervor.

Rune continued to chuckle as he playfully nudged her shoulder. "Come on, let's get something to eat. I could go for a coffee too, I think. Master Jacob introduced me to it a few weeks ago and there is a place in the market that serves a sweet version of it. The way they make the bitterness of the coffee play with the sweetness of whatever it is they add in is remarkable."

He eagerly dragged her through the stalls before they stopped at a small tent with steam rising from a makeshift chimney poking through the roof. A warm and delightful odor wafted through the flaps of the tent. Teryn was not a fan of the drink itself, but that did not prevent her from enjoying the aroma. Attempting to impress the young man she was with, she ordered the same drink as he did. When Rune separated from her to retrieve the items they ordered, Teryn frowned. Her arms suddenly feeling empty.

The coffee was served to her inside of a cup made of cow horn. Instead of the normal black color that she was familiar with, this drink had a much lighter hue. Sitting atop it was a small layer of foam with sprinkles of crumbled pastry. A bright, beaming smile plastered on his face portrayed how happy he was that she was enjoying his favorite drink with him. The tent also sold simple pastries that the two of them happily enjoyed. They were likely the same ones crumbled atop the coffee foam and paired together excellently.

"Time to check out the rest of the market," Rune stated with a satisfied sigh once they returned their cups to the vendor's dishwasher.

Teryn nodded excitedly as they exited the tent to return to the main thoroughfare of the market. Once more, she clamped onto his arm, not waiting for him to offer it on his own. Most of the stalls had finished their set up by the time the duo had left the coffee tent. Dozens of vendors had rows of different types of jewelry and various knick-knacks. Most of the other stalls were filled with produce from the different farms around the outside of the city.

Many of the products were also from Dorn and Locke with caravans stopping to join in on Hilden's daily market before moving on to Jelmoore, where the larger trade would occur. Similarly, any groups traveling to the mining town of Locke from Jelmoore would do what they could to offload excess product to ensure they had less to carry on a return trip.

According to Rune, Locke did not want for much. The population there were simple folk who usually were only interested in food goods. Any of the extra things, like jewelry, were not something that interested them. As a town of miners and smiths, they were a hardworking group of people. Rune also laughed and mentioned that many of the smiths in town would panic if their partners brought home jewelry. It was a mark of pride in their own skill that they did not want someone else's craftsmanship decorating their home or family members.

Teryn smiled along with the joke, but did not really agree with the sentiment. Smithing a weapon was a vastly different skill than crafting décor and necklaces. As a merchant's daughter, she had seen several 'artistic' pieces made by weapon and armor smiths, who thought they could perform the delicate craft of a jeweler, and none of them were pretty. Weapons and armor required a different set of skills than artisan goods. Both required great skill, just of a different kind.

Their day together was full of laughter and joy. Many of the farmers who were selling the produce had heard their names circulating through the rumor mill by this point. Each conversation was pleasant and entertaining, helping ease much of the burden on Teryn's mind. It felt nice to slow down for the simple joys. Being a Vanguard warrior was everything she thought it was, but there were still moments that she wanted to slow down.

Karl had also stressed to them during several of Rune's treatments that Vanguard warriors needed to de-stress and find time to "smell the roses," as he put it. He cautioned them that if they did not, then it was possible one or all of them would end up like Karl one day. Dannon questioned how that was possible if they all stuck together. In his mind, as long as they remained a party, then none of them would let the others fall into a semi-permanent drunken state like Karl.

Jeruul failed to shut his brother up before the comment escaped his lips, but instead of getting frustrated, Karl simply gave them a sad smile. He warned them, "Not everything in life is permanent and someday those close to you won't be anymore."

Those words echoed in Teryn's head repeatedly as she watched Rune joke back and forth with an elderly man selling cabbages. His silver hair stood out against the surrounding people. While he spoke, she found herself mesmerized by his well-defined jawline and nearly perfect lips. To claim he was the most handsome man that she had ever seen would be a lie, however he was certainly on the upper end of the spectrum. His face was soft and noble in a way that drew people's attention. Of course, the fact he had such a kind heart only added to the charm. That was what had won her over. Had it won over Tara, too? Venraya?

Teryn slowly reached out toward him, trying to catch his attention. She wanted him to focus on her, not some farmer or merchant, but her. Having him around was important and the fear that one day he would not be terrified her. Just as her fingertips brushed his sleeve, a voice shouted from down the road, excited and full of energy.

"Hey, you two!" Dannon shouted while waving excitedly. "I split up with Jeruul a few minutes ago. He's off reserving us a table! Let's get some dinner at that fancy place near the mayor's home. I heard the food there is great! Why not splurge a little today?"

Many of the patrons of the nearby stalls stopped to stare at the young man who was shouting like an idiot. Teryn felt an urge to strike him well up from within her, but a deep breath and mental reminder that she was still next to

Rune kept her in check. Instead, she glared at Dannon with a gaze cold enough to freeze him in place.

"I feel like I interrupted something I shouldn't have?" Dannon whispered cautiously while cowering from her dangerous glare. He nearly started backing away when Rune held up a hand.

"Don't worry about it! We were just finishing up here. Teryn and I had a good time enjoying each other's' company, as friends do."

Rune's final words struck a painful chord in her heart, but she simply gave him a gentle smile. She knew already that this was not a date like she wanted, so it should not have been a surprise to her when he made such a comment. Despite that, the words hurt all the same. She silently cursed a faceless girl in Locke.

The cool fall air was already chilly enough, but a sudden gust of wind blew her hair back and sent a shiver through her body. Rune removed the jacket he was wearing and draped it around her shoulders. *Please don't. Stop it...*

"Here, you seem cold. Fall is certainly here, so maybe wear a jacket," the young man said. His stupid smile painted his face.

"Thanks," she muttered.

After paying for a few more necessities for the group, they dropped off the party supplies back in the Hall. They then joined Dannon and Jeruul at the restaurant that had reserved a table for them called Wulf's Den. It was owned by a former Vanguard warrior named Wulf, who had retired to open a restaurant. Supposedly, the man had tried opening it in the capital, where he was born, but he was chased out by polite society, who thought his past as a Vanguard warrior was too rough for their fair city.

No one knew if the rumors had any truth to them, but it did not matter when it came to the quality of the food. When Teryn observed the meals served to the other guests, she wondered if they could afford to splurge on such a fine meal. Not only did the food look fantastic, but it was also served on fired dinnerware. Normally, food was served on wooden plates, but Wulf's Den opted for the much more expensive pottery.

As the night went on, the four of them enjoyed the company with friends. Even though Teryn wished such a meal could have been shared with Rune alone, she knew it was not meant to be. However, she also made a silent vow in her heart that she was not ready to give up so easily, even if her competition had many years of advantage on her. Teryn clutched the jacket still draped around her. She refused to let go of it, even in the warm interior of the restaurant. *Tara, Venraya, a princess... I don't care. This isn't over yet.*

<u>Chapter Twenty</u>

Lord Death, take us. Guide our souls to the shores of the Sea of Chaos so that we may return to that from which everything came. Fate gifted us a life worth living, a journey worth traveling, and memories worth cherishing. All things that begin must one day end, and it is in your embrace that our stories come to a close.

- Traditional Volari funeral prayer

Ven

"Gods dammit, Tayven!" Ven cried out in pain. School's first term was swiftly coming to a close, and the weather was gradually getting colder. Of all that time, she had spent a majority with the blue-haired noble and his oversized roommate.

Ven knew Tayven had extensive training in swordsmanship and so, she had eventually started asking him for lessons. Much to her chagrin, he was not a gentle teacher. More often than not, Tayven would leave her with multiple bruises on her arms and hands. He would also hound her on any mistakes after almost every session. Though Ven was thankful for the education, a part of her wished he would take it a little easier. With Brick's help, at least Tayven's demeanor impacted her less and less over time.

Ven had been taught by Lex. As such, there was nothing that anyone among the academy's staff could teach her. However, this did not mean she neglected her practice. She still practiced the drills Lex taught her every day. Now, her basic routine consisted of archery practice every morning before dawn, then classes, followed by training with Tayven, and ending with reading and homework.

Most of the academy's professors did not assign work after classes ended, but students interested in better class performance often took additional notes on the discussion topics by utilizing the academy's extensive library. While the academy's collection was not near as grand as the Faradin Knight Academy in the capital, it possessed material the national institution did not. Since the Vanguard Academy was built by the Vanguard themselves, it boasted not only historical accounts but also maintained a selection of modern ones. As the global organization grew and learned more, so did the academy's library. The Vanguard knew that historical texts were important, but they also understood that all history had once been modern knowledge, so it was important to learn both.

"You're leaving yourself too open!" Tayven yelled. She quickly pulled her sword to parry a strike coming in from her right side. Her reaction was slow, but she kept the strike from hitting her shoulder. Unfortunately, in the process, she inadvertently directed the strike toward her face. It struck her across the cheek instead of her shoulder. Something wet and warm soon flowed freely down the side of her face, and Ven dropped to the ground.

Her sparring partner quickly ran over with a towel, helping the girl staunch the bleeding. Tayven looked at her with concern while inspecting the damage. Brick, who had been observing the bout, also rushed into the arena and smacked the young noble on the back of the head.

"You dumbass!" he shouted. "The sparring rules are to keep the blades below the shoulder, you dimwitted son of a bitch!"

"I did!" Tayven shouted back to salvage a small portion of his reputation. The commotion had drawn a crowd, and it would be best to prevent confusion about the incident. Lest the situation put a negative mark on his father's name. Breaching dueling etiquette was not something people took well.

"Brick, it's fine," Ven said with a slight wince. "He aimed for my shoulder and I pushed the strike upwards in a panic. Besides, the school's clerics will have this patched up in no time. I doubt it will even scar."

She had become rather close to the two young men. While she mostly spent time with Tayven for training, she did genuinely enjoy his company. Brick had also turned out to be a very nice person. Because of the latter one's stature, she had originally assumed him to be a muscle-headed idiot, but that was far from the truth. He was a gentle soul and while not an academic genius, he was not stupid. Where he really shined was in his understanding of people. Brick seemed to have a sixth sense about someone's needs and emotional state and could respond accordingly.

Ven's statement seemed to calm Brick down slightly as he huffed and mumbled something under his breath about Tayven still needing to be careful. Tayven nervously chuckled in response and grabbed another towel for himself to drape around his neck and wipe away sweat, carefully avoiding too much eye contact with the larger one. With an apologetic look on his face, he also passed Ven another towel, this one wetted with water and a disinfecting potion, to both help clean her face and refresh the old, bloody towel.

"Sorry Ven. From now on, I'll tone it down," her friend said. "Just know that I only have been pushing you as hard as I have been because you've been doing well."

"It's alright. You don't need to apologize. This is training, after all, and besides, an enemy will not hold back just 'cause I'm less experienced than them. So please, continue as you were."

Her words soothed Tayven's look of concern and replaced it with one of pride. Of course, he was a conventionally attractive person, so the smile spreading his lips garnered a few sighs from the female onlookers gathered around. Ven giggled to herself at her friend's admirers before she collected herself and headed to the medical office for a quick patching up. Cuts to the head and face often bled worse than the wound actually called for. For that reason, she was handed another towel to replace the rapidly reddening one in her hands.

On the route, she passed several teachers and students who had been released from evening classes. Almost all the evening courses were occupied by older students and any newer students that were already scouted to join some of the school-sponsored Vanguard parties. Ven, Brick, and Tayven had all received invites to several of these parties, but they had no intention of joining them.

Given Tayven's status, many parties were simply looking for ways to worm their way into his family's good graces. Brick's invites were obvious, and Ven's were, too. She had been noticed as an Awakened with quite the potential for her Pulser class, like her father. This naturally garnered a massive amount of attention from established parties, especially when her connection to Hall Master Jacob had been discovered.

In response to the deluge of invites each person had received, the three had formed their own party with Tayven as leader. They could not accept jobs without their leader being at least a second year at the academy, but that did not bother them since they would be considered as such in seven months. Though their delay in starting work early was unfortunate, it did not hinder their efforts to grow. All three were very dedicated to self-improvement, and they always had their eyes out for any potential newcomers.

Suddenly, Ven remembered something that one of her professors had advised them of a week ago. The academy was having another set of students enroll; three, to be exact. Normally, there were two enrollment periods. Tayven and Brick had been part of the first period, which was at the tail-end of a semester. Ven had joined the second, which was just before the beginning of a semester. It was quite rare for the academy to admit anyone outside of these two times. As a group, they agreed to keep a close eye on these applicants, since special enrollments were usually quite rare. Ven held a small amount of hope that an old friend would be among them. It had been some time since she had seen him and it had been a while since she had received a letter from him. *Idiot...*

A short walk later, Ven entered the medical center. Some students were lying on cots with different injuries from training or even missions they had returned from. The air smelled sterile. Mostly from cleaning agents and disinfectant, like the potion soaking her towel. There were a handful of caretakers moving throughout the room. A majority of them were people with glowing purple eyes. One of the Volari workers came up to Ven and looked her over quickly.

"Just the cut on your cheek?"

"Yeah."

"Not too deep, so it shouldn't scar. Here, I'll get you taken care of. The bruises on your arms you can keep. It'll remind you to improve."

The worker sat Ven down on a chair and placed her hand over the girl's cheek. There was a warm, fuzzy sensation accompanied by a dull glow at the periphery of her vision. The girl felt her skin slowly stitch itself back together. When the worker was done, she gave Ven a mirror, which showed no cut and no scar.

"How do you do that?"

"Those of us who specialize in healing use the Aura within your own body to accelerate regrowth. Basically, we just make your body do what it already would have, but better and faster. Anything short of a lost limb we can take care of. Even that, we can fix. If you keep the limb and are willing to spend several months being prodded by a Volari cleric, that is. Oh, don't forget to eat. We simply accelerated natural healing. As such, your body used up a lot of energy at once. Replenish it," the cleric answered, while checking her work. She nodded with satisfaction and waved her patient on their way.

"Thank you very much!"

"Huh? Oh right, you're welcome. May Fate's hand guide you and may Death pass you by."

Ven was confused for a moment and was about to ask what the cleric meant, but they had already moved on to another patient. She turned around and started walking towards her dormitory. Thoughts and memories of her last few days in Hilden flooded her mind. Chief among them were memories of the silver-haired boy who used had her as monster bait just before she came to Jelmoore.

Thinking back on it, he was probably on the same level as Tayven in the looks department. Ven giggled to herself as she imagined the naïve boy trying to fend off admirers at the academy. However, her stomach twisted itself in knots thinking about it. While caught up in her thoughts, she failed to notice that Brick and Tayven had caught up to her. Brick gently placed a hand on her shoulder, causing the girl to nearly jump out of her own skin.

"Woah there, Ven. Just us. You up to something? That why you're so jumpy?" Tayven cooed in a teasing tone.

"No, you jerk. I was just lost in thought."

"Again?" Brick asked, slightly concerned. "You've been stuck in your own head a lot today. Surprising that a smack to the head didn't teach you any better. Something on your mind?"

"Not really anything particular. Just a friend I haven't seen in a while." Ven shook her head. "Heading back, too?"

Brick and Tayven glanced at each other with knowing smiles. They had heard about this 'friend' before, but neither mentioned what they were probably thinking to her. Both of them preferred keeping themselves from getting hurt outside the practice ring.

"Yes, we are. Also, trying to pay our respects to the academy's new transfers! Apparently, they are moving in right now. They're moving into the C-Rank dorms!" Tayven exclaimed. His eyes brimmed with excitement at the thought of having a C-Rank join their party. All of them were only E-Ranked Vanguard. C was the highest rank someone could achieve without attending the academy.

Of course, there were plenty of C-Rank students living and attending the school, but these new students would be the only first-years with that particular rank at the school right now since the others were all basically third-years.

With a single glance between them, the excited trio sprinted to the dorms. Once they reached the circular fountain in between the three dorms, they noticed that yet again, another crowd had formed, this time outside the C-Rank building. Ven huffed in annoyance, wondering what the student body did in its free time for so many students to constantly be flocking together around anything remotely interesting. Ven caught a flash of a person with red hair who waved nonchalantly at the organized crowd. A smirk was plastered on his face.

After he disappeared into the building, another person followed behind. Ven's view was blocked by the shuffling of the crowd. By the time she could see the dorm again, the C-Rankers had vanished inside. She still glimpsed the back of someone's neck, which was covered in some sort of black webbed tattoo. Something about this person radiated danger. Everyone else in the crowd also reacted to his presence. Several students subconsciously backed away, and others seemed to sweat under the terrifying air surrounding the man.

After a few moments, the person finally entered the building, allowing for the crowd to take a collective breath. Brick turned to his friends. "Chaos! What. Was. That?"

Tayven's eyes were locked on the door to the C-Rank dormitory. "I don't know for sure, but I have an idea."

Brick cocked his head sideways while Ven verbalized their shared question. "Well, what is it?"

Tayven shook his head and smiled at his friends. "It is only a hunch. I'd rather not start rumors, and I'm sure we will find out for sure soon." He gestured around them and pointed to a significant amount of their peers listening intently to their conversation. Ven could only shrug in agreement. She knew her friend was right. Spreading rumors would be bad.

Ven still had hopes of recruiting whoever that was, so she could only go along with Tayven. If that person were to find out they were the source of unsavory rumors, they could kiss their chance at a powerful ally goodbye.

Rune

Rune groggily opened his eyes, blinking several times in rapid succession to clear out the blurriness that set in. He stretched out his arms and legs and felt several pops in his joints. The surrounding room was dark, lit only by two candles in the room's corner. There were no open windows at the moment. In fact, they seemed to have been purposefully covered by thick furs.

It took him a moment, but he finally remembered he was in Karl's home. After a recent quest, another migraine attack had happened, and Karl was his only option for reprieve. They had been clearing out quests like crazy lately and Rune was feeling the wear and tear. Karl was quick to help him as always, though his methods were strange to Rune. Every time he came for treatment, Karl would make him lie flat on a table, face down, with a towel draped over the back of his head. Unfortunately for him, this was after being forced to drink some strange concoction of herbs that tasted like a wet raccoon dog smelled.

Whatever Karl mashed together in that foul-smelling potion was the only thing that seemed to work for his headaches. It also knocked him out cold every time. Nothing else could ease the annoying spells, which now occasionally sparked fevers, dizziness, and nausea. The more intense symptoms had started around the time he passed out in a room with Teryn. He was thankful they had been drunk enough to agree to stay the night together because otherwise, Rune might have died.

He did not remember what exactly had happened, but Teryn had filled him in after. Apparently, he collapsed and was struggling to breathe. She yelled for help, which attracted Jacob, who quickly got Karl's help. Ever since then, Rune visited Karl after every mission just to be safe. His beautiful Volari companion had been stuck to him like glue since then as well. *Not that there's anything to complain about regarding that.* He smirked.

"Hey, sleepy-head, did that last job really tire you out that much? You passed out on Karl's table about an hour ago. And why are you smiling like a weirdo?"

Rune turned his head towards the sound of the voice and saw Teryn looking at him with eyes full of mischief.

"No reason. Hey, why are you smiling? What'd you do?" Rune growled.

"Oh, nothing at all. I am innocence incarnate," she pleaded with wide eyes. Those same eyes flicked between his own and his forehead.

Rune put a hand on his brow and when he pulled it back, there was a black smudge. "Oh, Teryn. I am so going to get you for this. I don't know what you drew, but oh, you are gonna get it next time we camp out!"

He grabbed the towel that had fallen off his head and wiped at his forehead before rubbing the towel in the face of his laughing friend, leaving a large smudge across her cheek. Her shock gave him just enough time to pull his shirt back on and run out the door. She chased after him, yelling and laughing. Their antics attracted the attention of the townspeople, many of whom smiled and laughed. The Pact had worked together to make a decent name for themselves in Hilden after all this time.

E-Rank jobs had been pretty slow the last few months, so most jobs were only F-Ranked or Common, which did not count towards their promotion quota. Many low-ranked quests included simple jobs around town or pest removal, which led to them doing a lot of work for the various townsfolk. By this point, everyone was aware of the two friends' behavior. Though it was a lot worse when Dannon was around.

Today, though, they had actually finished the last of the required number of jobs that would allow them to do a rank promotion exam. About ten minutes after running out of Karl's home, the duo stopped outside the Vanguard Hall, where Dannon and Jeruul were waiting. Jeruul had his arms crossed, acting disappointed, though a smile threatened to break across his face. Dannon, however, was looking dejected after realizing he must have missed out on the fun.

"You two back from Karl's place?" Jeruul asked while shaking his head. He had long given up on his friends. To him, they were as lost a cause as his own brother.

"Yep!" Teryn answered with a grin. The smudge on her face was still plainly visible.

"All patched up, boss!" Rune shouted with a mocking salute. "If you wanna talk to the master about our rank promotion, I am good with whatever you choose. But first, I have to—"

"Write letters to home!" the other three interrupted Rune at the same time.

"Yes, we know, gotta tell your parents and your girlfriend about what you did today," Teryn muttered as the twins laughed in the background.

"Oh, hush up you," Rune grumbled. "She isn't my girlfriend."

The twins chuckled as Rune left for his room. There had been a lot of moving around of the Hall's residents, but Rune's room was in the same place as it always was. However, he had a new neighbor in the form of Teryn. After his fainting spell, she had insisted on being given a key to his room and managed to 'convince' the former resident of the room next door to find a room 'more suited to their needs'.

Waiting for Rune inside was a package that had been placed on his desk. He rushed to open it. Previously protected within the paper wrapping were a handful of letters and a small box. Inside the box was a small copper colored ball and a folded letter from his father.

Rune,

I have included for you another alderite core. After what you told me about that fight against Razortusks, I'm worried the one I made you had a flaw I didn't recognize, so I made you another one to be safe. Hopefully, this lasts longer. If not, you can keep them both charged and swap them out between fights, I guess. Just remember, my son, that these cores are highly sought after, so be careful who knows about them.

Rune visibly winced. The fight with the Razortusks was the first of several battles that he had relied on his father's sword for. The lid was already off about his secret weapon. Thankfully, no one in Hilden actually cared all that much, their caution all those months ago all for naught. Rune silently apologized to his father before he continued reading.

Make sure you are careful around that Volari friend of yours. She may not be nobility, but most Volari have an intense dislike for Wanderers like myself, as well as their children. Since you failed to inherent my bloodline traits, you will be doubly disliked by most. I hope your friend is not like that and my words of caution are meaningless, but as your father, I cannot help worrying.

On to more pleasant news; your sister is also doing well. She was still refusing to join me in the forge until we got your letter about that expedition from home and having to fight those bandits. We were also impressed to hear of your fight with the Shadow Wolf in Dorn. I think the realization had set in with her you have chosen a path in life. Not to be outdone by her brother, she is finally choosing hers. Great for her, but not actually great for me. As it turns out, she's a natural. Of course, she is though; she is my daughter after all! I thought I would have loved to have her interested in her father's work, but...her talent is giving her a big head already... I'm hopeful she will have settled down by the time you visit home. If she is anything like you, though, perhaps those hopes are useless.

I love you so much, son. We are infinitely proud of the man you have become. Please stay safe.

—Vickar

Rune smiled after reading the letter from his father. Wet droplets peppered the papers in his hands. Similar letters from his mother and sister were also in the pile. His mother shared sentiments about how much she missed her son and shared the local news in the village. It also seemed like her seamstress business was doing well and they had quite a delightful bonus in income. Ulma's letter showed how good she was doing still at home and how she recently had gotten into a fight with their cousin about their dreams for the future. Ulma's desire to work the forge annoyed their cousin because it was not a 'girly' thing to do. A long time ago, she would have agreed, but after working alongside father for a few months, it turned out she was pretty good at it. Soon enough, she had found her spare time away from the forge was being taken up by ideas to try the next workday.

After reading all the letters, Rune sighed quietly. More tears fell down his cheek. He quickly pocketed the gift from his father and filed the letters away in the desk. A few moments later, he left the room to return to his friends. Since it had been a short while, it was likely they had already gathered the details on their next job. Jeruul was always efficient like that.

At the bottom of the steps, Teryn and Dannon waited side by side, having a discussion about where to enjoy a celebratory dinner. Teryn wanted to try the high-end butcher and restaurant in the main square, having developed a taste for fine cuisine after Wulf's Den. Dannon wanted to celebrate at the confectionary. Jeruul eventually came up and lightly tapped his brother upside the head and reminded him that dessert was not dinner, even in celebration.

"Well, Rune, already done writing your memoirs?"

He rolled his eyes. "They are just letters, and no, I will write some after the job. I just read a few that I got in the mail from home."

Dannon and Teryn jerked to attention. "Oh?" they asked simultaneously. Dannon continued the attack, wiggling his eyebrows. "Well, well, well, lover-boy. Did you get anything particularly lovely from your girlfriend? Perhaps something spicier in nature?"

Out of nowhere, Dannon yelped as Teryn's elbow found purchase in his diaphragm. Rune and Jeruul stood slightly wide-eyed at the act. Teryn normally joined in on teasing their friend, but at the moment, her demeanor was simply one of frustration.

"Right..." Jeruul stated, still confused, and ignored his twin's whimpers. "The promotion job is simple enough. We are to follow the road east out of Hilden. We have two things to accomplish. First, we need to defeat a mating pair of Echo Bears that have been harassing travelers. Second, we have to meet up with a group of people on their way here from Jelmoore."

In the past, Rune was told he would need to do his Rank-up examination at another hall. However, Jacob had informed him this would not be an issue in this instance. Though, he had declined to explain further why. They had already prepped for their next job while Rune was passed out at Karl's house, so they did not need to make any stops on the way out. Dannon continued to grumble about his stomach and cursed Teryn's ancestors for her sharp, boney elbow. Despite how uncomfortable he was, he was ecstatic about discovering what seemed to be a new way to pester not just one, but two of his friends at once.

Jeruul's tired expression told him he was also aware of whatever Dannon was thinking. Though he did nothing to stop any plans for future antics. While he was serious on the outside, there was a secret part of him that also loved the pranks and teasing that the others were so keen on perpetuating. Rune watched Dannon and Jeruul's silent contemplation as they walked towards the gates. He was terrified of whatever Dannon was planning, but he was excited to finally rank up to D-Rank.

Rune pulled out his Ranking Card. It was only for E-Rank, but the tiny metallic object represented the fact that he was finally on his path to the future he wanted to build. He was on the path to fulfilling his childhood promise to Tara. So far, he was experiencing everything he wanted. Rune had found friends, adventure, and fun. Soon, he would go to the Vanguard Academy just like he promised Ven and rejoin another of those friends, though it might mean leaving some more behind.

Chapter Twenty-One

Teryn

Hours after exiting the gates of Hilden, the group of E-Rankers set up camp. Their travels had led them close to the edge of the Greatwood after they came across what appeared to be bear tracks. Normally ranking tests were done individually, but because of special circumstances, they were tasked with hunting down a mating pair of Echo Bears, D-Rank monsters. They had another task to do after as well. Some sort of escort mission.

Teryn wondered why they had been tasked with hunting down two D-Rank monsters as a group when normally someone would have to prove they could solo-hunt an E-Rank monster. Someone behind her sneezed loudly while he was unrolling the tents. Rune looked up after realizing his friend was staring at him and gave her a short wave.

Right. I forgot. We have this powerhouse with us. Teryn released a deep, resigned sigh. *Love having him with us, but it might just be biting us in the ass right now... Love...*

She leaned down for a moment, hiding her face in her hands. After taking a few moments to breathe and clear her head, she continued helping the others set up the campsite.

Echo Bears were ambush hunters, but strangely preferred attacking in the daytime. Their own vision was rather poor, so they relied on their innate ability to mimic the sounds of various animal screams and calls to attract prey into their traps. This included human screams as well. Luckily, they could only mimic screaming and could not mimic true speech. With this in mind, it was much better for them to camp through the night before starting the hunt in the morning.

"Alright, watch order: Teryn, Rune, Dannon, then me," Jeruul said with a clap.

The campsite was ready for them and the group sat down to rest while Teryn prepared a small fire. It was mostly for getting some hot coals going for heat and not actually to start a blaze. Early fall was settling in, but the weather was still warm enough to not need additional layers during the day. The extra warmth of the fire was still welcome as the air chilled further with the sun's descent.

Various chirps and growls filled the space between the trees while insects buzzed in the night. To the Volari girl, nothing sounded either close or concerning, so she left it alone but kept an eye glued to the tree line. The open fields behind them and the road passing by were less concerning, but Teryn scanned them occasionally, too. Leaving any spots unchecked could cause them to be at a disadvantage if attacked.

As the hours passed, she thought back to the adventures she had had with her friends. Doing jobs with the twins was fun, but it had become infinitely more so when Rune joined. They had been fortunate to be dragged into watching his fight against one of the seedier members of the Vanguard.

No one had ever told Rune that the person he fought against had also picked a fight with the twins in the past, handily knocking both of them out in a two-on-one fight. It was an unpleasant memory for them as the twins had had no chance. Though rumors had spread about him being the weakest of his peers, Bordo was still a D-Rank. Much stronger than a pair of E-Ranks.

At first, the trio were going to simply ignore the fight, not wanting to see the same thing happen to another. However, while they were leaving, Karl had blocked the door and brought them to the front of the crowd to expressly observe. What they saw had astounded them. No one had expected that the new kid would not only hold his own against the infamous hazer, but he had made it look like child's play.

It threw everyone even more after the kid continued to duck, dodge, and counter-attack Aura Enhancements. Everyone assumed Rune could use silent skill activation, something that graduates of the academy and Vanguard veterans could easily do. To her surprise, Teryn noticed Rune activated no Aura skills. There was something odd, though. She had witnessed the hazing ritual several times after the twins' loss. Yet something about this fight was different. Bordo's activation of Enhancements were weaker than normal. It was like the Aura seemed to disperse slightly on activation, decreasing the effectiveness of his attacks.

Teryn continued to notice this phenomenon any time Rune fought against monsters or when even their allies used Aura near him. Nothing was concrete, but it just seemed like the flow of Aura was harder to maintain whenever Rune was around. Not only that, but there were small flashes of Aura through his body that just looked foreign to her. Something completely different from when the twins used their abilities.

Rustling blankets pulled Teryn out of her thoughts while her friend got up for his shift and approached the dying fire with a blanket draped over his shoulders. His eyes glowed slightly from the light of the coals and the tiny flames flickerng weakly in front of her. She noticed for the first time that his hazel eyes were actually flecked with spots of purple. *Those weren't there before, were they?* His eyes watched the fire for a moment in silence.

"Rune."

"Mmm?"

"What are you?" Teryn quickly covered her mouth. She had surprised herself with the tone she used. It sounded curious, but colored with a bit of fear. Rune turned his head to face her better, and the view caught her breath for a second. The moonlight and fire seemed to work together to highlight the boy's features, giving his silver hair a glow that rivaled the moon. The purple flecks in his eyes sparkled like stars made of Aura itself.

"I'm the son of a Wanderer," he answered with a sad smile, approaching her slowly. "My father taught me how to use the sword and shield. He taught me to remain fluid in my movements and whenever possible, use my opponent's strength against them. I'm supposedly an Awakened, but have been unable to determine my class. And I am your friend. Not sure what else you want to know about me. Or what else I really have to tell."

"Yeah..." Teryn whispered. She turned to face him more directly. "Don't give up on your class. Most people can't determine it without those Awakening Crystal things, right?"

Rune shook his head and placed his blanket around her shoulders. "Not just that. But I also can't infuse Aura into an enhanced sword. I have to rely on a core to power it for me."

Teryn nodded slowly, pulling the blanket tighter around herself. *It smells like him*. She knew he used an alderite core with his enhanced sword, since she had also helped infuse it for him between jobs. "Your father...who was he before he abandoned his name? The fighting style you use...I've seen it before. Once. When I was very little."

He laughed, which made Teryn's heart flutter a little. "I have wondered that, too. The way my father always answered whenever I asked about his past was: 'A fool. And eventually a fool in love'. But honestly? I don't know. He doesn't talk about life before my mom. The only thing I know is he was born and raised in Volar. He's a Metal-Weaver. He specializes in weaving alderite and he uses that ability to make extremely high-quality, enhanced swords."

Teryn choked on her own spit for a second. If the man who Rune called his father was an alderite specialist, he had to have been a very important person to Volar at some point. Volari able to weave the Aura of inorganic materials were common, but specializing in weaving alderite was extremely rare. Its exceptional conductivity of Aura often made it difficult to manipulate, even among the best of Metal-Weavers.

Teryn was about to follow-up with another set of questions, but she realized that her friend's posture was closing off. Seeing the change in behavior, she smiled at him before she bid him goodnight. The group only had three single-person tents. Since someone was always on watch, they just traded with the person who took over. This meant that tonight, Teryn would take the tent that Rune was just sleeping in. Before she crawled into it, she glanced back at him and watched how focused he was on their surroundings.

Teryn hesitated for a moment with her hand on the tent flap. She shot another, more furtive glance back at Rune. In her eyes, she did her best to send him a silent message. It was unlikely he understood, but it was a fun thought for her. Ignoring the heat in her cheeks, the young woman settled into the bedroll and pulled the blanket tightly over her head. Sleep was scarce, and she thought she heard sounds outside of her tent. Eventually, the comfort of smelling Rune around her lulled her into a pleasant dream.

When Teryn finally woke up hours later, the sun had already risen. Rune was the one who had shaken her awake. A group of people were approaching, and she needed to quickly arm herself. Off in the distance, said group of people were heading in their direction. Ten of them, to be precise. The person in front was extremely large and wore a nice suit. Behind him was a gorgeous woman wearing padded leather armor. Her hair was tied up in a ponytail to keep it out of her face. Everyone else in the group did not really stick out much. Each looked to be standard fighters.

Once they saw the man was wearing a suit, they realized the likelihood of him being a bandit was extremely low. Still, all of them kept their guards up, but they made no moves to act aggressively towards their new guests.

"Well met! We are from the great city of Jelmoore! Might we rest momentarily at your camp?" the man in the suit shouted. His group rapidly followed behind him after they saw there was no negative reaction from the camp they had approached. Once they came closer, it became apparent several of their new guests were bleeding or limping. Almost everyone was nursing some kind of wound. Even the man in the suit, despite his positive demeanor, appeared to have a slight limp, and his clothes were torn in several places.

"Is everything alright?" Jeruul asked. His hand was lightly placed on the handle of his sword, unsure of how things were going to go. This behavior did not escape the notice of the man in the suit or the gorgeous yet stern woman behind him. In response, she moved her hand to her own weapons.

"Good. Good. Caution will keep you alive," the man said with a slight chuckle while giving the woman a placating gesture. "But worry not! We do not mean harm. What we are is a delegation from Jelmoore to Hilden. In fact, I am the master of the Jelmoore Vanguard Hall and the illustrious Vanguard Academy. My name is Vincent."

Jeruul tightened his hand around the hilt of his sword and eyed the group suspiciously. "You are several days ahead of schedule. We were to finish up this hunt then head towards the intersection of the road that would lead towards Castle Nyer."

The woman stepped forward with a scowl. Her green hair had been previously braided nicely to frame her face, but those braids were now loose and messy. "You should know your place, pup. Lest you find yourself neutered before you grow." Her hand also tightened around the hilt of her own blade. Teryn did not know what to make of the situation. Both sides eyed each other with suspicion and silence.

Suddenly, Vincent interrupted the space. "Alright, calm down, everyone. You are correct, young man; we are ahead of schedule. However, a large bandit group cut us off on the road to Castle Nyer, and a second party headed off the path back to Jelmoore. Our only solution was to quickly make our way to Hilden for safety. We only just saw you and hoped that we—"

Vincent's words were cut off as Rune rushed forward and shoved both him and the woman to the side. An arrow whizzed past the three of them, narrowly missing Vincent and his comrade. Unfortunately, there were also several sickening, wet thuds as other arrows found purchase in some others in Vincent's party. At least three of the ten people fell from arrows, piercing their necks, chests, or heads.

"That's an enhanced bow! They have an Awakened archer! Everyone into the Greatwood! The trees will block some shots!" Rune shouted out as he rushed towards the woods. He quickly grabbed Teryn by the wrist and shoulder-checked Dannon to snap him to reality. Normally, running into the Great-wood was a death sentence. No one traveled into their depths on purpose if it could be avoided. As long as you kept sight of the tree line, it was fine, but when fleeing pursuers, your safety could not be assured, regardless.

For a moment, no one listened to the crazy command, until they finally caught sight of where the arrows had originated from. There was a massive gathering of people, at least a hundred strong, rushing towards them, easily dwarfing the now eleven people at the campsite. In a moment of panic, they listened to the eccentric individual who suggested they run into one of the continent's three most dangerous places.

Vincent

The Greatwood. Truly, they were really rushing into the infamous woods unprepared. It was that or they would have to fight off an unfair number of bandits, something that was hard enough, but they also had an Awakened archer. If they had one, then it was likely they had others with similar equipment or abilities. Especially considering the size of their force. Bandit groups this large were not common in the least. Most groups larger than fifteen would fall apart because of disagreements in leadership. Something important must have kept this massive group together.

Money.

The Master's first thought—and most likely the correct answer—was that someone had orchestrated this to kill him. Money was a fantastic motivator, after all. Vincent was not the most popular leader in the southern half of the continent. He and Lord Jelmoore had worked together to prevent too many proselytizers from the Crucidian Church from sailing to Volar. Vincent would personally assign missions to the Vanguard warriors under him for patrols to advise any members of the clergy to avoid confrontation with the Volari.

If he were to guess, this was payback for such behavior. With Lord Jelmoore himself being nigh untouchable, the Master of Jelmoore's Vanguard Hall was the next best target. This was to be expected, eventually. Something that was completely unexpected, however, was running into an alleged E-Ranker who would save his life. Neither Vincent nor his guardian could detect the arrows that had nearly ended one of their lives. Yet, this boy, who looked to be barely over the age of adulthood, could both detect and react to the attack in time to save them

Vincent chuckled quietly and thought, *I would like to see how far this kid goes. Though, we have to survive the forest and these bandits first.*

Not once in recent memory had the Greatwood been subjected to such an incursion. Eleven people rushed in, doing their best to stay together, and chasing them were dozens of men and women shouting for blood. The best solution would normally be to separate so that not everyone could be found at once, but in these woods, that was just as much a death sentence as standing and facing the veritable army at their backs. With everyone distracted by either fleeing or chasing, neither the bandits nor their prey noticed the chill that set into their surroundings. They did their best to ignore the hungry growls perforating the air, as any number of monsters could be hungrily watching them from the shadows. It was Vincent's hope they would snack on any bandits following them instead of their own group.

Bandit Chief

"**S**plit up into groups of ten or more!" a gruff voice ordered. "Half of you will set up camp just inside the tree line while the other half pushes deeper into the woods. Remember, the big man in the suit stays alive. The others...do with them what you want."

The man was in charge of the makeshift army. It comprised several groups, who had all agreed to work together thanks to the massive reward. He thought back to a few weeks prior when some shady woman had appeared inside his tent, sounding no alarm. She dropped a coin purse on the floor in front of him before presenting her offer. "Three thousand gold to each member who survives hunting down Vincent of the Vanguard. This contains a down payment of two hundred coins each to show we are serious. Meet at the intersection of the road to Castle Nyer and wait with the other clans we hired."

The strange woman did not wait for a response from the bandit chief before she vanished quickly and quietly, just as she had appeared. Of course, the man quickly picked up the bag of coins she left behind and could confirm that there was indeed enough money to give two hundred coins to each one of his men. If there were another few thousand coming for each of them, then the job was worth it. He knew little about the leader of the Jelmoore Vanguard, but for tens of thousands of gold, he did not care if it was attacking the king. They would do it. Upon mission completion, they'd have enough to buy a ship to Borros for all of them and then buy a city once they got there!

Looking back on it now, the man was unsure if he would have made the same decision if he had seen how many other bandits were hired for the same job. Their ambush was partially successful, but the man known as Vincent was a monster on the battlefield and the woman following him was no slouch, either. They tore through the battlefield like animals. All the while their blades slicing the flesh of their enemies with practiced ease. Blood painted their blades and faces and would likely haunt his nightmares for the rest of his days.

Even then, they were nothing compared to the mysterious woman who had hired them. Her entire presence reeked of death. It was as if something primal within his body reacted to her. With her every movement, his body screamed at him to escape. He knew such an effort was futile. It would only result in one outcome. Death.

The bandit chief shuddered at the memory of their employer. After the initial battle, they had taken out at least half of Vincent's entourage, which had forced him to flee. Knowing they could not let him escape, the remaining attackers had followed. Now they chased their prey into the Greatwood. If they killed Vincent, or simply found his corpse chewed on by a beast, they would lose out on some bonus pay that asked for him to remain alive. Regardless, the chief and his people would get their payday.

Chapter Twenty-Two

Dannon and Jeruul sat on a log, leaning against each other for additional support. They had been running for hours and had long since lost sight of the entrance to the forest. Those that had joined them in the camp were also suffering from exhaustion. No one dared to speak, the silence of the forest only violated by ragged breaths. Rune and Teryn were also panting and sitting together next to a tree. The only person among the group that seemed fine was the woman guarding Vincent. Her disheveled hair belied her condition, even if her face and eyes showed no signs of exhaustion or discomfort.

Jeruul did not fail to notice Rune was panting a little harder than normal. A slightly concerning flush tinged his cheeks and forehead. He made eye contact with Teryn, who had appointed herself as a guardian of sorts. Jeruul nodded towards Rune and after following his gesture, her eyes suddenly widened. She quickly grabbed the young man and pulled his head into her lap. Rune flinched in surprise while she poured a waterskin over his silver hair.

This was an awful time for his strange condition to act up, but everyone knew it was not a situation he was in by choice. Karl had been helping him manage it; however, they were out in the woods and would have to figure this out without him. Vincent caught sight of what was happening and quickly walked over to them and squatted down.

"What is going on? Is he ill?"

Teryn's eyes darted between Dannon and Jeruul, who both nodded in confirmation. "We don't know. When he exerts himself while fighting sometimes, he gets these headaches. The last time he got this bad, Karl had to help him." Teryn flashed the man, Vincent, a strangely meaningful look.

Vincent blinked, seemingly trying to process what he had heard. "Karl, huh?"

"Yes. None of the other healers in town can help him, but Karl has a unique method that seems to work."

Vincent stayed silent for a moment before nodding. The green-hared woman also seemed to point her attention momentarily towards the boy on the ground and the girl holding him, Vincent and Teryn's conversation drawing her notice. A snarl began to form on her lips before she snapped her attention back towards the woods. Jeruul followed her gaze after they heard a low growl from between the trunks of the trees. A large beast slowly stepped into the small clearing they were resting in. Its mouth dripped with blood and its claws held what remained of a corpse. Judging by the armor, it was one of their pursuers who had gotten caught by the monster. Jeruul immediately recognized the creature as a Lycanfang. It was a B-Rank monster that could evolve from various other wolf-like monsters.

Like others of its species, it had gained the ability to stand on its hind legs. Its upper body became more human-like above the waist, giving it an appearance similar to a bodybuilder covered in dark gray fur. These creatures were the source of the stories about werewolves, a half-human, half-wolf monster that appeared on the night of a full moon. Werewolves were simply stories, but Lycanfangs were very real and extremely dangerous.

The beast's pale, yellow eyes moved among the group and rested on the weakest member, the boy lying on the ground. It then made eye contact with Vincent's guardian, who it identified as the biggest threat, her posture being the only one presenting a challenge to the creature. Silence pressed down onto the clearing as no one made a move. The Lycanfang's claws glowed a faint purple, forcing Jeruul to choke on his own spit while Vincent scowled. Jeruul had forgotten that Lycanfangs could use Aura to strengthen their claws.

It was fairly common for monsters above C-Rank to use the Aura in their bodies to boost their strength or even attack similar to the Awakened. Monsters themselves were sometimes born from normal beasts who had an excessive amount of Aura in their bodies at birth. This excess power mutated its body over time. The Lycanfang was likely born a simple wolf before becoming an evolved species and eventually becoming the creature currently accosting them. A low growl resumed as the monster tensed the muscles in its lower body. It was preparing to strike. The only question was who it would go for first.

"Anna," Vincent calmly ordered his guardian. "kill it."

Anna nodded and lunged at the beast, keeping it from advancing any closer to their group. She drew the sword at her side, which also glowed with a similar light to the monster's claws. Jeruul, Dannon, and the other members of the group moved together to protect each other while Anna leaped into action to fight off the monster.

At first, the two appeared to be in a stalemate. Sparks and flashes of purple light illuminated the dark forest. Each burst centered where claw met sword. Anxiety threatened to overwhelm Jeruul. His heartbeat roared in his chest and his breathing became more rapid. Dannon's shaky hand settled on his shoulder, providing no small amount of comfort that his brother was still there. His brother was always there.

The commotion of battle had likely revealed their location to any who still pursued them. Though the beast had likely saved them some time by fighting off bandits on its own, no doubt more would follow. They had a fervent desire for everyone's heads and if they were willing to trail them this far into the Greatwood, a single Lycanfang would do little to stop their efforts.

After several minutes, Anna's movements slowed. All the while, the Lycanfang gained confidence and took ground against the woman. Her exhaustion was overwhelmed by the added strength of adrenaline. It was a matter of time before she was completely defeated. All it would take was a single mis-step on her part and the fight was over. Jeruul nervously glanced over at Teryn and Rune again. Rune's condition seemed to be about the same, but he saw what appeared to be a flash of realization in Teryn's eyes.

"Miss Anna! Jump back! Fight closer to us. Trust me!" Teryn shouted.

Vincent shot a judgmental look at the girl at the same Jeruul eyed her in shock. *What in the gods' names are you thinking, woman? Are you trying to get us killed?* Though his mind said one thing, his mouth refused to follow.

"Anna. Do it," Vincent calmly agreed.

Without a word, Anna purposefully gave ground to the Lycanfang, letting herself be pushed back. Slowly but surely, they came closer and closer to the group. No one knew what the girl's reason was, but she sounded absolutely confident in whatever she was planning. For several seconds, nothing happened, but then the most experienced of the group noticed something strange. The Lycanfang's attacks were slower and weaker. It was not much, but it was enough to bring the fight back to equal standing with Anna's exhausted state.

About a minute later, the glow in the monster's claws flickered. Its bestial eyes widened in panic, not understanding what was happening. Jeruul and Dannon looked at each other—just as confused as the creature for the sudden change—before looking back at the fight. Anna gained the upper hand. She swung the sword with a double-handed strike aimed directly at the Lycanfang's claws, shattering the now weakened weapons.

"Put everything you have into it!" Teryn shouted. "More than you think you need!"

Anna took advantage of the opening and closed the gap, placing her palm on the creature's chest before shouting out, "Pulse: Scattershot." A warrior of her caliber would almost never need to verbalize her skills. However, the amount of stamina and mental fortitude she had expended likely required her to bypass silent activation out of concern that she could mess up. Such a skill required concentration. Something she could not afford to rely on in this moment.

A bright light flashed from her palm, cast by a large orb forming between it and the monster's stomach. It rapidly expanded before launching into its core. The Lycanfang howled in pain and several small orbs flew out the back of the beast before an explosion of viscera erupted from its back. A dozen smaller motes of light pierced the trees behind it. The monster coughed up blood before collapsing in a heap after one last attempt at a weak swipe. Anna fell to one knee, and though beyond exhausted, she easily nudged the limp claws away from her.

"What's wrong, Anna?" Vincent teased after taking a few minutes to make sure they were not still in danger of any other creatures. "Tired already? Normally, you can fire off dozens of Pulses before running out your reserves."

The woman eyed her boss evilly. "You try doing that after fighting a fucking B-Rank monster for damn near thirty minutes and see how you feel...but you're right. That still took too much effort." Her demeanor grew cautious as her eyes fell upon the young woman who had instructed her about how to handle the fight in the end.

Coughing interrupted the conversation, and Jeruul shifted his eyes to Rune. He was sweating profusely, leaving a veritable pool around his body. The red tint to his face now encompassed every inch of his skin. His breathing was ragged, quick, and so shallow that Jeruul almost could not see the rise and fall of his chest. Anna walked closer to the group, when Rune's eyes shot open. No one could react as he quickly sat up and threw a dagger into the woods. Jeruul found himself shocked at the speed and unable to believe his own eyes. Rune was fast, but he had never once moved that quickly; that precisely. Before that moment, Jeruul had been unaware that Rune even carried any other weapons aside from his swords and the knife he used for resource harvesting.

The dagger had clearly found purchase in something, since a garbled yelp followed shortly after it vanished into the trees. Nearly four dozen people stepped into the clearing. Some had sneers and smiles, while a few were painted with unrestrained anger.

Rune continued to stand up. Every muscle in his body seemed to tremble from the effort. Despite that, his breathing changed from imperceptible to something that was surprisingly steady. Jeruul and Dannon stared at him, while Teryn was trying to pull him back down to the ground. Her efforts proved fruitless, regardless of his quaking form.

"Rune, stop! You can't fight like this."

Rune looked down at the girl, exposing unfocused and blurry eyes like that of an unconscious man. Stranger than that, they had developed a dull purple ring, glowing around the outside of his hazel irises.

Vincent muttered, "Shit," after a faint purple mist cascaded from Rune's body, evaporating the sweat covering him.

Anna stepped protectively in front of Vincent. She seemed unable to decide if she should point her sword at Rune or the bandits that had caught up to them. To make matters worse, she was in no position to accomplish either feat. "Sir, we need to leave. Now."

Anna pushed Aura into her sword and it glowed in response. It was only in that moment that Jeruul saw a copper-colored vein running down the length of her sword. *Like Rune's? Altered with alderite.* A second later, it flickered before the glow stopped. Vincent tried the same with his own weapon, the same happening to him. The few dozen bandits were also looking at each other. Though only a couple were Awakened, they seemed to notice something else strange.

Dannon

Dannon felt as if his entire world had turned inside out. Just yesterday evening, he was joking with his friends around a campfire. They were each excited to advance to D-Rank. Rune had constantly mentioned his leave for Jelmoore after achieving the new rank. At first, the party's separation seemed so far away, but now that Rune's D-Rank goal was so close... well it was a matter of time until he left.

The three of them had talked away from their powerful friend and came to an agreement that they would go to the academy as well. While Dannon and

Jeruul had no desire to join the school itself, they could still do missions out of Jelmoore and, as a result, continue their band of friends. It was going to be a surprise for Rune, but then all of this had happened.

Right now, that friend stood, weakened, shaking from the effort. Despite that, he appeared stronger than Dannon had ever seen him. His shivering body stood resolute against their pursuers now that they had nowhere else to go. No one was in any condition to run. Everyone was injured, tired, and mentally broken. There was nothing left for them. Dannon was the same... at least, until he saw this.

Dammit, Rune... you just had to rile me up. Dannon smiled, pulling his trusty partner—Gerty—to arms. Just before he could fire a bolt, he was interrupted. Teryn stood from the log she was sitting on and slapped Rune across the face. The sound sent some bandits into an uproarious laughter.

"See! Even she understands, boy. Roll over and submit," someone shouted.

Dannon's mouth moved wordlessly, unable to believe that Teryn would choose now of all times to initiate a one-sided lover's spat. Regardless of its intended purpose, the distraction allowed the other members of their party to stand at the ready without sending the bandits into a frenzy.

Rune's gaze stayed locked onto the trees. Strangely, it was not the humans that had his undivided—albeit hazy—attention. Dannon slowly approached his friends, Jeruul following him slowly. Following the direction of Rune's stare, they saw only darkness. Light scarcely permeated the thick canopy above, save for small clearings such as theirs.

By this point, his strange behavior had garnered looks of confusion from the bandits. They looked at each other briefly. Their leader had yet to call the attack. Some of the ones further back had frozen, their eyes wide. The source was unknown, but after a moment, Dannon felt it. There was a chill unlike any other gently settling down upon them. It was unnoticeable at first, but it progressively became more pronounced, until suddenly, it was omnipresent.

Dannon glanced over to Rune and noticed the strange glow subside. The odd mist pouring off his body trickled to a stop. He was still looking out into the darkness, but the blank look from before was now replaced with one of pure terror. Rune pointed towards whatever it was that he had seen or sensed. Following his finger, Dannon witnessed something that caused the chill in the air to reach into his chest and grip his heart.

A shambling creature—humanoid in shape—stepped into the clearing. It was less like walking and more like the creature fell onto each foot, shaking its form. Black rags hung off its miniscule frame. It looked like someone who had died of starvation, with pale skin exposing the shape of nearly every bone beneath it, as if stretched to its limit.

As they observed the creature, Dannon noticed that the skin on its feet, hands, and nose was all but gone, the only thing keeping its skeletal digits attached being desiccated ligaments. In place of its missing eyes were two purple, glowing orbs. A dry, raspy laugh escaped the creature's non-existent lips, sourced from rotten vocal cords.

Death.

"Wraith..." Vincent muttered.

"Wait? That's a Wraith?" Dannon asked. His teeth chattered as he spoke. Such a terrifying monster actually stood before them? Wraiths were often believed to be legends told by campfires to scare new members of the Vanguard. However, what was before them was no myth and no legend.

"S-Rank monster," Anna choked out. She was by far the strongest fighter in the group, but after everything, she had not had sufficient time to recover. Even if she had, it was obvious from her demeanor she could not fight off a creature like this.

The bandits also finally realized the danger. Some shook the fear that kept them rooted in place and fled. Others were still frozen, not even sparing the energy to exhale. It was a special ability of the Wraith. People with low mental fortitude would find themselves unable to move within a small distance of the creature. While Dannon came to grips with the reality of the situation, a field of purple light burst forward from the Wraith's chest. A solid ring of light erupted around it. The trees within the ring withered at a rapid pace.

As the ring continued outward, it encompassed several bandits. One by one, they began to cough and spit up blood. Their faces grew gaunt while the skin on their bodies tightened around their frames, their muscle mass rapidly shrinking to oblivion. Dozens of victims fell to the ground as human husks. The Wraith clapped its boney hands together, dispersing the ring of death. The other bandits who had been held in place by the creature's fear field suddenly found their will to run and left the clearing behind. Whatever payday they had been promised was not worth such a horrifying fate.

Dannon watched the scene before them with abject horror. He too had heard tales of Wraiths. He had also known they were real—despite many thinking them just story-time villains—but they were exceedingly rare creatures often found in the Forest of Ruin. Never in his life had he thought he would be confronted by one.

Dannon looked at his friends. Teryn's hands and legs shook uncontrollably. She looked towards Rune, who was frozen in place, barely breathing, with his unblinking eyes locked on the Wraith. Dannon figured he was under the effect of the Wraith's fear ability. Teryn took a deep breath, coming up with a plan to help everyone escape. Dannon stood and watched as the young woman steeled her resolve and initiated her Plant-Weaving abilities. The blades of grass beneath the creature began to grow and tangle themselves around its feet. There were no living trees nearby anymore, so she likely could not use any of those as a weapon. It surprised him that the ground remained untouched by the previous attack.

"Run! I have it pinned, even if for a second. So, run!" Teryn shouted.

Vincent, Anna, and the rest of their group quickly turned and rushed back towards the exit of the forest. Teryn stayed behind. Dannon was shocked to action and grabbed his brother by the arm. He and Jeruul moved to follow Vincent's group, but noticed that Rune remained still. His eyes were locked on the corpses scattered around the Wraith. *There's something else in his eyes aside from fear... Realization, maybe? Why is that?*

Teryn's own thoughts were easier to read: If Rune would not move on his own, then she would just move him. So, she shoved Rune into a set of bushes.

Dannon and Jeruul also retreated, trying to break the line of sight between the creature and them. She set her eyes back on the Wraith who stood with its feet tied to the ground by hundreds of thousands of blades of grass. It cocked its head at its captor before taking a step forward. A light appeared around its ankles and turned its plant-based bindings black before they disintegrated into a fine dust. The dark laughter continued as it stepped slowly towards the Volari woman. Every step turned the ground barren.

Dannon and Jeruul finally got to a safe distance, where they felt the creature could no longer see them. Teryn did not notice that they still stayed within a short range. Neither twin was willing to truly leave their friends behind. Rune was still out of the Wraith's sight. The creature had an amused look on its face—as much as a corpse could look amused, anyway—and was focused solely on her. Dannon, could see a resolute expression on Rune's own face. Now that the corpses were out of his line of sight, he could clear his mind. He made a decision.

Within seconds, the Wraith had come within striking distance of Teryn, who lunged at it and continued holding it off, even if for only a moment. The Wraith's skeletal hand shot forward faster than the girl could see or react. Just before it touched her, she was flung to the ground by Rune tackling her from the side. The skeletal hand grasped the space where she once stood.

Rune's involvement was a call to action which sparked Jeruul and Dannon to join the fight. *Damn these two!* Dannon rushed back into the clearing with their friends to help hold the monster off. Dannon shot bolt after bolt from his crossbow, not fully willing to engage in close quarters. Jeruul charged straight towards the monster and struck it with his shield, forcing it to take several steps back. The Wraith deflected the next several strikes with mere flicks of its hand. Bolts from Dannon continued to pepper it, but it showed no signs of taking damage, simply letting itself become a pincushion.

Jeruul's assault continued as Rune pulled Teryn to her feet. He shoved her behind him and readied his own sword, opting to use the enhanced one from his father. Rune then jumped into battle, activating the alderite core at the same time. His weapon hummed to life, brimming with power. With every strike, he slowly chipped away at the bones of the Wraith as it blocked hits, aiming for its vital spots. Both swordsmen were thrown back with a mighty roar followed by a quick shove. Before Jeruul was thrown too far, it lunged toward him and grabbed him by the throat.

"Jeruul!" Dannon screamed. "Let go of him!"

"Corruption..." the Wraith whispered.

The clearing instantly turned still. Despite the whispered voice, everyone heard the word clearly. A sizzling sound emanated from where the Wraith's hand connected with Jeruul's neck and a black mist erupted from his mouth. They watched in horror as Jeruul screamed and violently twitched. Dannon was frozen in place as his brother helplessly kicked, punched, bit, and bashed at the Wraith. Jeruul's movements slowed until he finally went limp. Black ichor dripped from his mouth and nose. The whites of his eyes turned red. His skin became a pasty white like that of a sheet, while the veins in his body turned jet black.

"You fucking monster!" Dannon shouted as he threw the crossbow down and ran toward his brother with his two daggers drawn. *You can't have him! I won't let you have him!* Tears fell from his face as he rapidly closed the distance. "Pulse: Scattershot! Pulse: Overcharge! Pulse: Rapid fire!"

Dannon's anger pushed his Aura skills well beyond his capabilities. He had never used power like this. His body protested the strain of forcing out so much energy, the wells within his being screaming in defiance. A scattering of small orbs of Aura the size of a human fist, followed by one massive orb the size of a head materialized at once. With a painful scream, Dannon willed them to attack the Wraith who still held his brother within its grasp. He roared once more and five medium-sized orbs stuck somewhere in between the others surged forward.

Jeruul's unmoving body was placed between itself and him. Dannon knew. He knew Jeruul was gone. Nothing would bring him back. Despite that, his heart was torn to shreds to see his attacks eviscerate his brother's corpse. The

Wraith threw Jeruul's body to the ground, now peppered with holes of various sizes. The Pulses that missed shattered the dead trees behind the Wraith.

Dannon used the gap created by the discarding of Jeruul to rush closer to the Wraith. Unfortunately, it caught both of Dannon's hands, holding him in place. "You monster. I'll kill you. I'll kill you! If it's the last thing I do, I will kill you! I will tear you apart. I'll scatter your bones across the continent. Your time in this world will end, you disgusting sack of bones!" Dannon screamed. Rune joined the attack, rushing the creature as well, trying to keep what had happened to Jeruul from happening again.

"No! Rune! Get back!" Teryn shouted. Rune paused momentarily and leaped backwards. Just as he did, a white blur lunged in between them. Jeruul had jumped off the ground and landed on Dannon's back. The Wraith tossed them to the side. Jeruul was thrown free from him as they tumbled through the dirt.

He glanced at his brother's twitching form. They stood together. Where he would once see his brother's calm, brown eyes, Dannon saw only enraged, red orbs. Jeruul's healthy skin tone replaced by a near transparent white. "Brother."

Jeruul's head twitched to the side, noticing Dannon's position. The shambling form of his brother slowly approached with a calm expression.

"Brother, are you in there? Please, Jeruul. I need you to answer me. Please." Dannon's tears returned, blinding his peripheral vision. "Jeruul. Come on, answer me."

Hoping that his pleas reached Jeruul, Dannon reached his hand out, grasping the side of his cheek. Faster than he could blink, one of Jeruul's hands dug into Dannon's side. Pain consumed him as what was left of his brother sank his teeth into Dannon's neck. Jeruul's fingers had morphed into claws, slowly sinking into his flesh. Dannon felt pain as Jeruul's hands ripped into his body. An uncomfortable warmth covered his chest. The world faded slowly. Darkness consumed him. "Brother. Please." Dannon gurgled. "Stop."

Chapter Twenty-Three

Teryn

"**G**houl! Kill it! Kill it now!" Teryn's legs had long since lost their strength.

She fell to the ground, surrounded by a warm puddle. Rune had already vomited from the horror they witnessed. Dannon hung limply in Jeruul's clawed hands. His entrails dangled from two gaping wounds in his side. A veritable fountain of blood escaped from the bite wound in his neck, quickly fizzling out as the young man's body stopped functioning.

Jeruul, now apparently a Ghoul, wheeled around and tossed Dannon's body to the side. It clicked its jaw a few times, releasing an odd, garbled noise that was a mix between a shout and groan. Rune readied his weapon and buckler for its impending strike. The Wraith seemed content to stand and watch its new thrall attack its former friends, making no moves to attack the remaining party members directly. It exhibited a cruelty and intelligence that one would not normally expect from a monster.

Jeruul's strength seemed to have multiplied two times over from his transformation. After having regular sparring sessions with him, Teryn could tell that this was not the same person anymore. From how Rune struggled to respond to its attacks, she could tell it moved faster and hit harder. Multiple holes littered its body, but none of them inhibited his movement.

"Teryn, how do I kill it? I don't know what it means for Jeruul to turn into a ghoul. Tell me! Quick!"

"The head! Take out the h-head!" Teryn shouted back, sobbing.

She knew her words were almost unintelligible. Thankfully, Rune nodded in understanding and shifted his positioning slightly to make counterattacks to the head easier. Claw and sword clashed, but despite his attempts, none of Rune's attacks could make it through Jeruul's defenses, even with the altered sword. She didn't know when it was that Rune had activated his father's weapon, but thankfully, he had. If not, he might not have lasted this long.

Teryn flashed her eyes and raised her hand. She influenced a patch of grass to catch Jeruul's foot off guard. She lacked stamina or time to truly bind him, but it was just enough to trip him up, creating a small opportunity for Rune to bash Jeruul in the face with his shield. Jeruul reeled backward with his jaw pointed toward the sky. Before he could recover, Rune slashed his sword towards his neck, severing it cleanly.

The Wraith jumped forward and tore through Jeruul's headless corpse, having used it as a distraction to keep Rune from seeing its attack. The mist around Rune returned, but with it came increased strength. Rune's reaction time improved, his strange constitution took effect once more. Where his strikes against the Wraith had barely garnered a reaction before, now with each swing, the creature shook from the impact. Even though it had a face that previously seemed capable only of creepy smirks and sneers, the Wraith now had one that resembled a hint of frustration.

Rune was supposed to have fallen by this point, yet his stubborn desire to live and to protect kept him alive. One of Rune's strikes was parried, and he was forced to step further away from Teryn in order to dodge a reactionary slash to his abdomen. The Wraith rushed her with an outstretched hand.

"No! Not her!" Rune screamed. Teryn felt an impact against her chest, accompanied by shooting pain. She was suddenly sent sprawling onto the forest floor, unable to move. Fear and anxiety turned her blood to ice and her body to stone.

Time around Teryn seemed to slow to a crawl while she watched the Wraith's skeletal fingers close around Rune's neck. "Corruption"

Tayven

"Spar with me, sir," Tayven demanded, while facing the newcomer of the academy. The man had stepped out of the clinic when the nobleman caught him unawares. His eyes looked empty and unfocused, despite having been issued a challenge.

"Why?"

"Because I want to test your strength. You are one of a few C-Rankers at the academy, and one of three new first-years."

The man said nothing, looking at Tayven with those unsettling, vacant eyes. His posture was completely relaxed, as if there was nothing to fear being confronted with an offer to battle. Nothing happened as silence passed between the two for half a minute. Other students rushed past the two men who awkwardly locked eyes in the hallway.

"Fine. Let's go."

Tayven hurriedly followed his opponent to the practice fields outside, now excited for the bout. He had no delusions of victory, but Tayven figured that, win or lose, he would still learn from the experience. The brisk winter air assaulted his skin, but the heat rising from the expectation of an exciting fight quickly pushed it away.

Walking behind the strange person, Tayven noticed he was not wearing a sword or any other weapon on his waist. When he thought back to it, never once was the C-Ranker seen with a weapon on his person. He had already been at the academy for a few weeks and did not seem to carry weapons with him. While the students were not permitted to use real weapons in sparring matches, they usually still carried them on their person. Rumors ran through the students like wildfire regarding his preferred weapon, his abilities, those web-like marks on his neck... everything.

"Weapon?"

Tayven was pulled from his thoughts by his opponent's voice. Pointing at him was the handle of a wooden longsword being offered.

"I've noticed you use a sword and shield. We fight using the same weapon, so we start on even footing," the man continued.

Tayven could not help but laugh at the suggestion that he could stand on even footing with a C-Ranker. At first, he thought he was being made fun of, but there was no sign of mockery in the man's eyes. Somehow, this warrior meant it. Such a thing shocked him because most Vanguard had low opinions of those below their skill levels. It was a fairly typical mindset, as the competition this behavior bred was good for motivation. After all, why would someone not be proud of their success and efforts to become strong?

He grabbed the hilt with a grateful nod and looked around. The field filled with students as word spread about finally seeing the mysterious C-Ranker fight. Even with the temperature rapidly approaching freezing, students flooded their surroundings. *Of course, they would come watch.* Out of the three new C-Rankers, this man was the most mysterious of his strange presence and odd tattoo on his neck. Of the two that had been seen, one was the person in the ring with Tayven, and the other was the fourteenth prince of the Faradin Kingdom. The third person was completely unknown.

The prince had taken part in a few classes already and it had been clear his rank was purchased, not earned. However, no one had seen this man fight, nor observed the third person at all. There were rumors, but nothing confirmed.

"Alright, let's make a deal," Tayven offered with a grin. "If I land a hit on you, then you join my party."

"How many are in your party?"

"Including me? Three."

"Fine, but I get to bring someone with me."

"Who is it?"

"My...friend. She came here with me."

Tayven took note of the odd pause, but chose to ignore it. "Deal!"

Tayven had no reason to think that the C-Ranker would agree to his bet when he offered, but he not only readily agreed, he also wanted to choose someone else to bring with him. Tayven grinned, readying himself for his opponent. He used the standard stance taught to children of noble houses with his legs spread even with his shoulders and sword pointing upward, ready to strike or defend.

The C-Ranker showed off a haphazard stance. At a glance, one could see a multitude of openings. Several other nobles around the ring frowned. For someone to become a C-Ranker but show such sloppy swordsmanship was usually an indicator that the person had either purchased their rank or relied solely on their strength. While it was not bad to lean on pure power sometimes, it would always stunt one's growth if they could not use the proper techniques to extend that strength further. Usually, warriors like this would cap out when their power stopped increasing.

Tayven did not let these same thoughts impact him. Even if his opponent was someone who would 'cap out' in the future or had already, he was still a C-Ranker. Having him join his friends in a party would still be useful. Not only that, but the presence he gave off already proved that he had bought his way up the chain. His presence was less terrifying than when he had first arrived, but Tayven had grown up around powerful warriors, being the son of a noble, and this man gave off the same feeling.

The C-Ranker stood still and unblinking. His eyes were still zoned out, as if his mind was everywhere else but on the fight. Tayven stepped toward him to test if his stance was simply bait, but drew no reaction. He continued to step towards his attacker with his guard up. Finally, Tayven moved into striking range and swung towards his opponent's free arm. In the blink of an eye, the warrior's sword parried his own.

Tayven pressed the attack, alternating targets between the sword arm and the free arm of the man, trying to disable his opponent. Despite every single strike being skillfully smacked away, leaving Tayven open for a counter, the warrior did not take advantage of any opportunities. *Is he actually messing with me? Am I being used as an example? Is he telling everyone that he can take control at any time?*

Tayven's frustrations grew with every crossing of their blades, the temptation to use his Aura grew along with them. They had never stated the rules of the match, so nothing kept him from doing so. However, Tayven worried that if he was the first to use Aura abilities, then his opponent would take the chance to do the same. If Tayven could not beat him now, then what chance would he stand by adding Aura into the mix?

All he had to do was land a hit, so it was now or never. Tayven remembered his lessons and although he could trigger his abilities silently, shouting them out in battle was like a trigger that queued the visualization in his mind. His rapidly rising annoyance and frustration threatened his concentration of silent activation. *No choice. It's now or never.*

"Enhance: Full Body!" Every vein in his body glowed purple as the enhancement took effect. His muscles tensed and pain racked every part of his body. He could only maintain this state for a few seconds before he ran out of power, broke a bone, or tore a muscle. "Enhance: Leap."

Dirt and gravel sprayed into the air, showering the onlookers with debris. His body turned into a violet-tinged blur as he lunged at the C-Ranker. Tayven's smeared form took on a deadlier shape as he swung his practice sword in an overhead diagonal slash. The opponent brought his sword up, but the speed was too much for him to parry the blow. His only option was to commit to a direct block. With the combination of Tayven's Aura-enhanced strike and the fact their weapons were simply made of wood, Tayven's weapon sliced through the opponent's. The blade struck the man across the cheek. Before anyone could react, the man spun with the strike. He lifted his rooted foot and spun around in the air before bringing it around and planting it into Tayven's side.

No one could react to the scene, barely able to process what had just happened. Tayven's body was thrown across the arena and continued into a slide on the ground before coming to a stop. All the force behind his strike had been redirected into the kick the man used on him. For a moment, he thought he had made an impact against the C-Ranker, but there had been a strange lack of resistance. Almost immediately after, he bounced across the dirt.

Brick had just arrived to watch the match. He scanned the arena quickly before locating his friend on the ground. "Tayven! Are you alright?"

Tayven took a deep, ragged breath. Every second was painful, and he also felt a few pops. "Yes, I may have broken a rib...or two."

Brick quickly lifted his friend's shirt and examined him for any signs of internal damage or bleeding, but saw nothing too concerning, which allowed him to breathe a sigh of relief.

"You lucky bastard," Brick laughed, "I cannot believe you tried to fight a C-Ranker!" Tayven chuckled along with his friend, but winced from the pain. A visit to the Volari clerics was certainly in order.

"Good win."

The C-Ranker nodded at Tayven, again with no signs of sarcasm or disdain. If anything, his zoned-out eyes came into focus just enough for him to provide respectful acknowledgement of Tayven's performance. Red blood trailed down the man's cheek, sourced from a small cut along his cheek. *I did it.* The C-Ranker turned and left the area, passing the students and some professors who had also gathered out of curiosity. What struck Tayven as odd was that Professor Lylah vas Mithra was glaring at him. To the untrained eye, it appeared as though she was angry with him injuring her student. When her gaze shifted to the boy on the ground, her eyes did not change. She kept that angry, disdainful look.

For a moment, I could have sworn she was angry on behalf of her student. Then again, it is Professor Lylah. Tayven sighed quietly. Brick grabbed his hand to help pull him back to his feet. His friend then kindly offered himself as a support to guide the injured boy to the clinic. On their way, they walked past Ven.

"What happened? What'd you do?" she shouted, rushing toward them. She was wearing a thicker jacket and had a flushed expression. Wherever she had been before, she had run all the way to them. "I heard something ridiculous and headed this way immediately. I take it the rumor about you fighting that new student is true, then?"

"Yep," Brick answered for his friend.

"I fought him and won."

Ven's eyes opened wide. "You won? You are strong, but you aren't C-Rank strong."

Tayven grimaced as he laughed out loud. "You are right. I got my ass kicked, hands down. But the bet was for me to land a strike, and I grazed his cheek!" The blue-haired boy was pumping his fist in satisfaction, as if scratching someone's cheek was a grand task. *It is, isn't it?*

"Bet?"

"Yeah, if I could hit him just once, he would join our party." Tayven grinned. "And, of course, I won the bet. That's all that matters. Even if I had to pull out Full-Body and Leap enhancements."

Ven whistled after she saw Brick's nod of acknowledgement, clearly impressed by her friend's performance. No doubt she was also elated they had added a powerhouse to their team. Not only that, but one that would let them go on missions while first-years. "So, what kind of Aura skills does he use?"

"I don't know. Didn't ask..." Tayven muttered.

"Did you not pay attention when he used his in the fight, dumbass? We need to know that to plan our strategies on jobs!" Ven growled.

Tayven coughed awkwardly as a faint redness creeped into his cheeks. It was feeling less and less like a win... "Actually, he kicked my ass without using Aura."

Ven's eyes went wide. "Did he use a short sword? And maybe a small buckler on his forearm?"

"Um, no? We used longswords. Single-handed combat with no shields. I'd be surprised if he fought well with a shield at all. The way he moved it seemed like his specialty was single-blade combat. Anything else in his hands would probably slow him down. Couple that with the fact that it took everything I had just to glance a blow on his face as it was..." Brick eyed his friend with pity.

The longer the conversation went on, the quicker Tayven's pride left him. Ven nodded along before cutting the conversation there and joined them on the trip to the clinic. Based on the look in her eyes, Ven, too realized he was becoming less and less satisfied with the effort his duel had required to get such a tiny result.

Chapter Twenty-Four

Teryn

"No!" Teryn's scream ripped through the air, echoing through a seemingly lifeless space filled with gnarled husks of trees and the desiccated corpses of fallen bandits. The only response was a cruel, dry chuckle from the Wraith.

Black mist rose from Rune's neck. The smell of burning flesh assaulted Teryn's senses. *No, no, no, no! Not like them...* Teryn's thoughts were consumed by saving her only remaining friend. It blocked out any sense of self-preservation as she helplessly assailed the monster with her sword. The creature barely reacted to her attacks at first, but then it released its grip on the boy.

Teryn feared the worst, refusing to look to where Rune fell. Tears filled her eyes; rage overwhelmed her heart. For a fraction of a second, she thought she sensed something else behind her. A powerful tug yanked her backward, forcing her to cough as her armor constricted her neck. The horrifically ugly visage of the Wraith in her vision was replaced with the branches overhead as she went from vertical to horizontal. For a moment, she saw a flash of graying hair. Before she could process anything, her back slammed into the ground, expelling the air from her lungs.

Lying next to her was the gasping form of Rune. His eyes were tightly shut with his hands protectively covering his neck. Standing between them and their demise was the familiar form of a disheveled man. His messy hair and unkempt beard were a welcome and surprising sight.

"Karl," Teryn whimpered. "Thank you, but you have to run!"

The Wraith stood stark still. It did not leave or advance, choosing instead to stare down the new entity before it. Was it gauging who to consume first? Was it afraid? Karl laughed without breaking eye contact with the creature. "No, I don't think I will, little lady. Don't worry, everything will be alright. You just watch the boy. Once he's stable, maybe take some notes."

"Notes?"

Karl continued to laugh. There was no hint of fear or concern contained within. "Not every day you get to see someone kick a Wraith's boney ass."

With that, the Wraith hissed. It dropped low with its hands stretched outward, like a two-legged beast ready to leap. Karl responded in kind with a similar stance. It was at that moment Teryn realized that the old man lacked any weapons. His tattered overcoat swayed with his movements, revealing that he lacked anything on his hips either.

What is he...

A flash of purple light formed in Karl's hands, thrown like a ball directly at the Wraith's head. It deftly ducked and propelled itself toward him. Karl snapped his fingers, resulting in a barrier of purple light forming directly in between them. A pained grunt erupted from the creature as it slammed into the wall of light. Using the precious seconds that had bought him, Karl moved to a still-living tree. His arms glowed, each vein was highlighted with purple light.

"Enhancement...Barriers... Pulses..." Rune whispered. "What is this?"

His voice was gravelly and pained. Teryn quickly pulled him into her lap. There was no way he could move in his current condition. She looked into his eyes and across his body, examining everything she could. Rune's skin was the same shade as before. His eyes were still that alluring hazel with purple flecks and that new purple ring.

"Beautiful..." she whispered despite herself. When he coughed, she redoubled her efforts in her panicked examination. The sounds of battle continued in the background. Waves of Aura washed over them, but right now. the only thing on her mind was making sure Rune was okay. Thankfully, there was no clear sign of a Ghoul transformation occurring.

Rune's gaze moved from Karl's fight to the bodies of their friends. Jeruul's headless form remained where it had dropped. The torso was torn to shreds and barely recognizable. Teryn followed his gaze and felt her stomach lurch. She looked over to check on Dannon, but noticed that his body was gone. The hair on her neck stood on end. A hot, damp breath brushed against her ear.

A garbled groan confirmed her fear: Dannon had been turned. She felt Rune twitch in her lap and heard a metallic scrape from behind her head. Somehow, he had gathered the strength to block Dannon's clawed hands from descending onto them. Rune's arms trembled. Dannon was attacking from above, using his body weight to press down on them. In the meantime, Rune lay awkwardly, his arms around Teryn, and his sword held firmly in both hands. Teryn could not turn, lest she risk impeding Rune's efforts. She closed her eyes and reached out with her senses. Something had to give in this or they would die here. Karl had given them a real chance at survival. She had to help.

Despite never having done it before, Teryn sensed a weak connection to a tree behind them. Until now, she had only ever manipulated the Aura of things like vines, grass, or flowers, each of them was already pliable. She had never really practiced on something as sturdy as a tree. On top of that, most of the plant life in the vicinity had long since perished from the Wraith or the various Aura skills that had assaulted them. Thankfully, one still stood, only barely clinging on to life. Whatever it was that the Wraith had done had not only drained the energy from the surrounding forest, but the scant amount left behind was outside of her ability to manipulate or was corrupted and decayed.

Dannon's garbled groans pressed ever closer. Rune's arms trembled even greater. Finally gaining control over something, she watched as a nearby branch reached forward and wrapped around Dannon, yanking him away from them. Teryn collapsed from the effort, the stress of manipulating a tree turned out to be dozens of times more difficult than grass or vines. Rune rolled out from beneath her to take on a ready position.

Wood creaked and groaned in protest as Dannon's clawed hands pried at the branches restraining him by the neck. With a loud *crack*, he broke free and rushed them once more. Splinters and chunks of decaying wood peppered them. Rune prepared to react to the strike, but something rushed past them, impaling the Ghoul against the same tree that had previously trapped it. Anna, the green-haired protector of Vincent, wiggled her large sword, pushing it deeper into the creature and into the wood behind it. After a moment of twitching, Dannon ceased moving and hung limply from her weapon.

Anna had returned and pierced the Ghoul through its heart. Knowing that this was not enough, she drew a secondary weapon, a large dagger, and sliced through Dannon's neck. Its head rolled free and hit the ground with a wet thud.

"Good job," Vincent's familiar voice called out to them as he approached. None of the other members of their group were with them, but he had seen fit to return to their side with Anna. "I found Karl on the way out of the woods. We came to help."

A grim expression was plastered over his face as he glanced around the clearing. Dozens of bodies littered the forest. The man's eyes, however, were glued to the ghoulified bodies of the twins. Vincent hung his head in silent prayer for a moment. His eyes opened and settled back on Karl.

Teryn quickly followed, having forgotten about the Wraith in the excitement of defending their lives from Dannon for a few moments. Flashes of light illuminated the forest. Both Karl and the Wraith slashed at each other. Surprising was the fact that the Wraith seemed capable of using Aura abilities as well. Like Karl, it threw up Barriers and shot out Pulses. She could not tell if it was using Enhancements because of the lack of muscles. As a monster, it already possessed terrifying physical strength.

Karl's speed and reaction time put Rune to shame, even at his best performance. Their strikes appearing as little more than blurs of light, skin, and bone. Anna stepped beside them, cleaning her weapon of blood. Her hair was still a mess, but she looked to be in much better condition than before they had fled.

Karl cursed. Teryn noticed the Wraith wave its hand. A second later, one of Karl's Barriers flickered before shattering. The Pulse he prepped in his hand fizzled out. He quickly backed off from his assault, pressing his hand calmly on another, still living tree. "Drain." the tree groaned and cracked. It was as if its life was slowly siphoned from it, the bark turning gray then black, leaving behind massive cracks along the trunk. The leaves above curled in on themselves, turning brown then crumbling to dust.

With renewed vigor, Karl jumped back into the fight. He threw up another Barrier that also flickered. He roared in defiance, the purple light highlighting his veins flaring up even brighter than before. The flickering stopped and the thickness of the Barrier nearly tripled. In response, the Wraith leaped back, hissing violently. Another lull in the fight had started.

The Wraith's gaze darted between Karl, then the group of people gathered together. With a loud scream, it leaped into the air, pulling a black mist around itself. Karl quickly launched a barrage of Pulses into the mist, scattering it. When it had cleared, the Wraith was gone. Everyone stood still as time seemed to stop. No one wanted to risk saying anything for fear of jinxing themselves.

Vincent sighed a few moments later. "It's gone. Good job, Karl."

Karl nodded, the purple light fading slowly from his body. Teryn noticed he grimaced with each step. Clearly, he had exerted himself beyond what his body could normally handle. A human, Awakened or not, could only handle so much strenuous activity. At Karl's advanced age, his threshold was most likely much lower for such aggressive fighting.

They worked together to quietly gather any personal effects. Teryn and Rune brought what remained of the twins' bodies together and constructed a small pyre. Vincent spat on one of the bandits' bodies before suggesting they simply leave them to the forest. With them being so far into the Greatwood, the normal risks did not apply anymore. Teryn gently cradled Gerty while Rune rested his hand on her shoulder.

By this point, she had thought all the tears she had were already gone. But somehow, she had more. Teryn's quiet sobs were the only thing everyone could hear aside from the crackling of the fire. Rune gingerly spun her around and pulled her into his embrace. They were similar in height, allowing her to rest her face in the crook of his neck. She knew that her tears and mucus pooled on his shoulder as she cried, but he did not seem to mind. Instead, he placed a soft hand tentatively on the small of her back.

Vincent quietly approached them. "You two fought well. Thank you for buying us time to get everyone out. Your friends... they died well and fought bravely."

"Died well? What does that matter? They're still dead," Rune responded. The normal kindness in his voice was gone. Devoid of all emotion. Teryn shivered. It scared her.

"That's right," Vincent answered, unbothered by the tone. "This is what it is really like to be in the Vanguard. You fight monsters. You fight people. You venture into fantastic and sometimes dangerous places. And, of course, sometimes you die."

No one said anything for a bit longer. Vincent continued, "I am the Hall Master of Jelmoore and Headmaster of the Vanguard Academy. Jacob was going to have me promote your group to D-Rank, since he lacked the authority to approve Rune's advancement. But I'm not going to do that."

Teryn was about to protest, frustration welling up inside, but a firm squeeze from Rune kept her quiet.

"I hereby promote Rune of Locke and Teryn vas Dena to C-Rank. Dannon and Jeruul of Jelmoore will also be recognized within our records as brave C-Rank heroes. Fighting back against a Wraith is no small task. Not to mention, those who put their lives on the line for the sake of not only friends but also strangers, deserve nothing less."

Lestreus

Three days after the fight between the two first-year students, rumors started flying around about the mysterious C-Ranker with an even greater fervor. Since the man had not been seen around campus after that, speculation of his life traveled like wildfire.

Some thought that he was a foreign assassin sent to kill the prince. Others thought he was a guard from a secret order of knights dedicated to protecting the royal family. Still, some others thought he was an S-Rank fighter who was punished by the Vanguard for breaking the rules on a mission and had been forcefully de-ranked and told to start at the academy from scratch.

These different stories made Lestreus laugh out loud. He knew the C-Ranker was strong of body, but he was weak of mind. Since moving into the C-Rank dorms with him, the man never dined, slept, or even moved about without the help of his companion. It was like the companion was the brain and the stronger one, the body. He was also a commoner, and no commoner would ever be chosen to guard a prince of the kingdom. Even if that prince was only fourteenth in line for the throne.

Really. Guard me? Ha! Maybe if he begged me for a job I would let him wash my boots. Lestreus laughed internally while he sat in a chair in the common area of the dormitory. The fire was going and the red-haired boy was enjoying the warmth while sipping wine. He read some documents forwarded to him by Lord Henner. *Things down here are much worse than I thought. The roads are simply dirt tracks. Monsters and highwaymen roam trading routes between towns...not only that, but Jelmoore seems to be the only city with stone walls protecting it out of all the southern cities. I cannot fathom why their idiot nobles ignore Lord Henner's offer of assistance.*

According to Lord Henner, not only do they continually deny his kindness, but the southerners also fail to attend royal court. If they would not take the church's offer, then they could ask the royal family to help. Instead, they break bread at the table of Lord Erich Nefera, refusing to present their issues to the actual lord of the land. They only offer complaints, and his father simply lets them.

All that Lestreus had seen of the southern territories was squalor and simplicity. The northern cities were full of trade, wealth, and strength. It was those cities that showed how strong their country was. His father was just as much at fault for the disparity as the pride of the southerners. If he had just taken them by the hand and forced them to change their ways, then the entire country could be stronger for it!

Since coming to Jelmoore, he had also spent every afternoon in the church further into the city, working with Father Gelroy. He had been teaching Lestreus many things regarding religious history and morality, as well as the important roles the church played in the kingdom's historical events. As he learned, there had been nobles causing a fuss several years ago in the north as well. The church helped locate the traitors who weakened the nation and rallied together the forces necessary to save the country from them.

This was the first that Lestreus had heard of such a thing. That the church had saved the country from one potential uprising already only further cemented in his mind that they had the best interest of the nation at heart.

Gelroy had also led additional demonstrations down at the docks and submitted numerous petitions to Lord Jelmoore to allow his people passage to the Kingdom of Volar. The stubborn lord of the city continued to refuse these righteous requests however, showing that he was more loyal to the heretical Volari than the church who had supported their kingdom since its founding. Even when adding his own name to the requests, they continued to be ignored by the old fool. Lord Jelmoore had yet to even invite Lestreus into his manor, something that was expected of a noble when royalty visited their territory.

"It seems you are expanding your knowledge of the world outside the castle and your old academy," a voice called from the dark hallway to the left of the fireplace. A man in an oversized gray robe stepped into the light. "It is always good to understand how the world around you works before you insert yourself into events. Though be careful that the information does not overwhelm you and prevent you from making a move. Sometimes it is nice to just take a leap of faith."

"Your lordship, I did not know you made your way to Jelmoore!" Lestreus quickly gathered himself and stood before bowing in front of the priest he had met before he transferred away from the Faradin Knight Academy.

The priest chuckled. "Do not be so formal, young prince. Have you thought about my question? Do you know what it is you will do differently than your father and forefathers?"

"I don't have the answer for you your lordship. Yet, I feel I have an idea," Lestreus answered. Truth be told, he was almost certain what needed to be done, but he needed a time to steel his resolve.

"Hmm. I see," the priest said. Though the words would normally portray disappointment, his tone sounded amused. "You have formed a close relationship with Father Gelroy and Archpriest Henner, have you not?"

"It is as you say, your lordship," Lestreus said with another bow.

"Such a respectful young man," the priest said again with a chuckle. "Lord Henner and Father Gelroy are staunch protectors of what they perceive to be the kingdom's true strength. They seem to only want what is best for the kingdom... for you."

Lestreus agreed. They had given him much. Henner made promises of power and knowledge. Looking at the stacks of documents and remembering the intensive lessons with Father Gelroy... that was the only logical conclusion to be drawn.

"I will check in again after some time. I feel you are much closer to a decision than you admit. But perhaps it isn't that you don't know, but maybe you aren't ready to admit it? Either way, do not shy away from opportunities and be ever mindful that sometimes opportunity is hidden behind adversity." The priest then returned to the hallway, disappearing from view. Shortly after, the sound of the front entrance closing echoed through the building.

Lestreus returned to his seat and continued to sip his wine. He set down his reports and mulled over the conversation he had just had. About half a second later, the caretaker of the nameless C-Ranker stepped through the door.

"Caretaker. Your patient has been up to no good lately. Imagine my surprise when I learned he might actually have the ability to think on his own. Rumors of his fight against the bastard of the Nefera family have spread across the academy." The prince laughed. "And it seems I either have a fantastic guard under my command, or have to sleep with a dagger beneath my head!"

"I have a name, you know," the caretaker stated flatly, "and one should always sleep with a weapon within reach. You never know when your life will come under threat."

The prince glared at the caretaker's back with annoyance. "Raft rat..." he muttered. The caretaker stopped momentarily, which caused the prince to smile, knowing his insult had been both heard and effective. He watched as they clenched and unclenched their fist a few times before continuing to their room.

One thing that Lestreus was good at was finding the weaknesses in his opponents' mental armor. It was a skill developed by being born into the most competitive of noble courts, the royal family. Every landed noble in the kingdom, as well as all the non-landed nobility within the capital city, were members of the royal court. As such, Lestreus partook of and observed the petty squabbles amongst them. While not the most caring and supportive of environments, it definitely bred mental fortitude and helped in the construction of a clever mind.

The prince sighed and retired to his room after having finished his wine. He had also committed to memory some notes that were hidden among the material. Lord Henner and Father Gelroy had taken time to circle him in on some delicate information. Another thing for him to be grateful for. They trusted him. Though he had had no delusions of pathways to the throne before, maybe—with their help, of course—it was actually something that could be realized.

Chapter Twenty-Five

Teryn

Teryn rushed upstairs to her room, hopeful that Rune was still in a more lucid state. Ever since investigating the bodies and aftermath of the fight with the Wraith, he had acted strangely. At first, he would simply zone out in conversation while they ate or talked. His answers were short and emotionless.

Seeing him in such a state hurt. Every second tore at Teryn's heart. Largely because there was nothing she felt she could do. Once, she offered to take him home to see his family and Tara, but he simply responded with a hollow, "No."

Such a response was understandable. No doubt he did not want them to see him in such a state. Being perceived as weak by those who loved him would have been a nightmare... or at least by others who loved him. In the time since the Greatwood incident, Teryn had finally accepted how she felt. With every day, she did her best to show it by caring for the person she had fallen in love with.

"Rune, I'm back," she quietly called into the room they now shared at the academy. As per usual, he sat in the bay window, staring at the campus. Were he in a normal state, maybe they would excitedly wander around Jelmoore taking in the sights. There was an abundance of places that served food from her homeland. Would he enjoy them with her? Would he enjoy peering across the ocean from the docks and talking with her about what Volar was like?

Jelmoore was much larger than any city he had ever been to before. In fact, she recalled he had only ever been to four different towns in his life. What she would give to see the look of wonder in his eyes. The reality of being in the Vanguard crashed down upon him. His dream had become a nightmare in the span of a few hours.

"Do you want to go visit the city? There's a restaurant with my homeland's cooking I can show you," Teryn continued, gently brushing the back of his hair. As usual, he provided no response. "We will wait for a day when you are a little more responsive. But hey, I noticed your neck markings from the wraith are gone today."

Rune let her guide him from the window to the bed. They shared a room with two beds, but mostly, they shared just the one. For Teryn's part, she had terrible nightmares whenever she tried to sleep, so seeing his sleeping face when she awoke in a fit of terror quickly calmed her. Rune was in no state to mind, especially as of late.

Once they arrived in Jelmoore, his pauses became longer and sometimes lasted days on end. He would sit or stand emotionlessly, acting only on basic instinct. He had moments of clarity, likely leading to his rumored fight earlier, and Teryn took advantage of those moments to enjoy some time with her friend. The last one she had left. Her eyes fell upon Gerty, Dannon's beloved crossbow. It had been damaged when he threw it away in the Greatwood. They would need to fix it someday.

She rested her head on his shoulder, hiding the pain in her voice as she spoke softly to him. "I'll be here waiting for you to come back. Whenever you feel you can talk to me, I am here for you."

Ven

Ven sat down at her preferred desk in the lecture hall. Today's class period was with Professor Lylah vas Mithra. The woman was a menace to have as a professor and did not provide any form of support to students who failed to immediately grasp the material. At first, Ven had gained her favor with her capability to absorb the information quickly and without excessive repetition, but this favor was immediately lost when Ven accidentally called her 'Lylah' and left off her title.

For a moment, she had forgotten how proud Volari nobility were to have their titles properly included. After that incident, the professor seemed to have it out for her. Tayven and Brick reveled in the situation, of course. They had spent a few extra months exposed to the professor before she took a short leave. Those months she was gone were apparently some of their favorites at the academy. When they saw Ven had somehow curried favor with her, they told her they could not wait for the other shoe to drop because, inevitably, she would piss the professor off. Brick and Tayven had a field day when their prediction proved correct.

"Hey, Ven," Brick said as he sat next to her.

Tayven followed shortly. He still sat down carefully, his injuries still on the mend. The Volari clerics always healed the important things, but left some of the minor things behind so students would not purposefully push themselves, thinking they would always fix anything. For Tayven, they left the bruising and soreness even though they completely mended his ribs.

"Class, we are going to the practice fields. Let's go." The infamous professor popped her head into the door before she issued the instructions. As she left, she put a quick sign on the door for any students who had yet to arrive.

Ven groaned and packed up her things before leaving with her friends to follow the professor. *I thought next week was practical studies. This week was supposed to be the last section on Aura Theory and class abilities...and it is so fucking cold!* Ven silently wondered what the reason for the change was while keeping her complaints to herself. Tayven and Brick were just as curious about what was happening, but they all had no choice but to comply with the whims of Professor Lylah vas Mithra.

After the class gathered in the chilled winter air, they noticed that the red-headed resident of the C-Rank dorm was standing at a podium next to Professor Lylah, along with an Awakening Crystal. The prince had long since made his presence known at the academy and had no shortage of followers already trailing him between classes throughout the institution. He had also exhibited his lack of sword skills in the training arena only barely being passable. At first, everyone assumed he was useless as a prince and warrior, but then he really showed his capabilities within the classrooms. Everyone realized he purchased his rank from an unscrupulous Hall Master, but he possessed a large amount of knowledge and his performance within tactical coursework was second to none at the academy. Put simply, he was a scholar, not a fighter.

"Well, it seems some of our class will be late, but that's fine," the professor mumbled as she began. "Today, class will occur outside, since we also have to perform an Awakening ceremony for a few of your classmates. We will also go ahead and have you all participate in some practical exercises while we continue our education on the classes of the Awakened. Prince Lestreus, please place your hands on the crystal."

The prince did as he was asked, and put his dominant hand on the crystal, while pointing his non-dominant hand towards the target range. The crystal glowed for a few seconds before the light was absorbed into the arm of the prince. Not even a moment later, a pale wall of light formed in front of his hand.

"Shielder. Congratulations," the professor stated without fanfare. "As the other student Awakening today is not yet here, for now, please form groups. Pulsers to the target range, Enhancers partner with a Shielder. And before anyone complains, yes, I know it is cold. If you put in effort into your practice, you can rectify that problem."

The students quickly divvied themselves up into the groups requested and began practicing using their abilities. Most partnered with their usual training companions. Ven, of course, was a Pulser, so she was at the target range. There were a handful of other Pulsers in class, but both of her friends were Enhancers, so they were a few dozen feet away trading blows with Shielders who were practicing blocking their blows. Prince Lestreus partnered with one of his followers who was clearly holding back, afraid of possible recourse if they broke the prince's Barrier.

"As you all know, there are three Common classes of the Awakened. The Shielder, Pulser, and Enhancer," the professor announced, starting the lecture. "What some of you may not know is that other classes exist. Uncommon, Rare, and, in theory, something else beyond that."

"What are those classes, Professor?"

"I was getting to that. Uncommon classes comprise what we know as Variants. Variant Pulsers lack the ability to shoot quickly or make larger shots. Instead, they take longer to form, and the projectile is rarely larger than a piece of chalk. However, their distance is increased by up to three times. Some cases show a maximum range of almost seven hundred yards.

"Variant Shielders lack the ability to make large barriers, or place them too far away from their body. In exchange, the shields they create are thicker and harder to shatter. Finally, Variant Enhancers can double the maximum strength output of a standard Enhancer. This is at the cost of double the energy required. That power is also restricted to their feet and hands, preventing them from enhancing any other part of their body."

By the time the professor had finished her explanation on Variants, the students were panting from exhaustion. They were all still relatively freshly Awakened and did not have the stamina to continuously use their abilities for more than a handful of minutes. No one seemed to feel the biting chill anymore. Right as Ven wiped away the sweat raining off her brow, a familiar face appeared behind the professor.

"Sorry I am late, professor. I was in the clinic and lost my way to the practice fields,"

Is that... it is! It's him! It's really him... He looks stronger somehow... Ven could barely believe her eyes. She also found herself thankful the flush of exercise hid the blush quickly spreading across her cheeks. The person who interrupted the professor was none other than the boy she had helped examine back in Hilden. His silver hair and hazel eyes were unmistakable. His smile was also there, but it seemed a little more forced than usual. Something about him was different, and it made her heart ache.

"Rune!" Ven shouted. "I can't believe you are here! Did you get a late transfer? Did my father approve it?"

The silver-haired boy smiled at his friend and shrugged before turning back to the professor. *That's it? What happened to him?* Professor Lylah had an extremely irritated look on her face. "Rune, huh? That wouldn't have anything to do with Arkrune vys Volar, would it?"

Rune's eyebrow raised in shock while asking, "How did you know that, professor? My birth name is Arkrune. I was sure I registered with the Vanguard and the Academy under just Rune."

The professor snorted with disdain. Her voice took on a nasty tone. "It was just an unlucky guess. I'll have you know, child, that Volari do not take kindly to people casually using the story of our kingdom's founding hero to name their brats."

"He has every right to it!" Ven interrupted. The sudden interjection shocked even herself, but she could not let the professor insult him. She could tell that the professor's words cut into her friend a little. She would not stand for him to be insulted. "His father is a Wanderer from Volar, so it is his heritage, too!"

Instead of backing down, the professor's face contorted into an even more indignant look. "You mean to tell me that a Wanderer, a traitor who abandoned their name and their culture, had the audacity to name their brat after one of our greatest heroes? Such disrespect." Everyone in class remained silent. From his practice position to the side, Prince Lestreus, who was uncaring about what the common people were up to, had a sympathetic look on his face. The professor looked around and realized what a scene she had made.

She cleared her throat before addressing Rune again. "No matter. At least you use a nickname instead. You must have at least some form of propriety. Know that you now have two strikes against you, boy. Now go, place your hand on the Awakening Crystal to find out your class. Everyone else quit your gawking and get back to work! I see several of you shivering, which tells me you aren't working hard enough."

The professor's tone told everyone that she would not take any answer other than compliance, so everyone quickly returned to their practice. Most of the students were still exhausted, so the Pulses of Aura were fewer, as it took longer for each person to manifest their ability. Ven watched Rune instead. She noticed that Brick and Tayven had come over to watch with her.

"Hey, guys!" Ven happily stated. "That's my friend Rune! We only spent a little while together in Hilden. He's acting a little off, but he's a good guy. I should introduce you!"

Brick laughed, and Tayven winced. "We met. Intimately," Tayven said as he clutched his side. "That's the C-Rank that kicked my ass the other day. Though his neck tattoo doesn't seem to be there anymore. That's weird. I thought he had one."

Ven was about to say something, but her jaw had dropped open and showed no signs of complying with her commands to form words. She then felt a chill run through her spine. Tayven and Brick seemed to shudder, and even the professor appeared to be in a minor panic. All of their eyes were glued to the silver-haired boy who had touched the crystal.

The crystal activated, glowing brightly; brighter than anyone had seen before. By the time it caught their attention, the light should have dissipated and forced a reaction from Rune's body to show his class, but it did not. Aura was visibly flowing from the orb into Rune's dominant hand. A moment later, the crystal cracked beneath his palm. The light diminished, but still glowed ever so slightly.

Ven looked up at her friend's face and saw that his eyes had taken on a familiar purple glow. One similar to a Volari. Black lines formed along his neck, forming a spider-like web. They spread downward into his chest and upwards towards his face. Suddenly, the ones moving around the front of his neck and chin overlapped, until they formed the shape of a skeletal hand, the thumb and index finger cupping his jaw. Rune doubled over, exposing the back side of the neck where, Ven could see more black webbing move outward from the tips of the skeletal fingers and down his back.

"Let go!" Professor Lylah shouted. She activated her eyes. Several stones along the ground vibrated, shaking off a loose smattering of snow. It seemed she wanted to launch them at the crystal. She tried to forcibly remove Rune's hand, but it resisted as if glued. Her eyes somehow grew even larger as she realized her ability was not activating. The vibrating stones uselessly dropped to the ground.

Ven's eyes darted around to the other students after hearing several weird complaints. Something strange was happening to them. Pulse shots dissipated moments after being released, Barriers flickered in and out of existence, and Enhancers lost their bursts of speed and strength. Those who had not noticed before, now turned their attention toward the source of the problem and saw Rune doubled over with his hand touching the broken crystal.

"Rune!" a voice suddenly cried out from the entrance to the practice field. A beautiful young woman with purple eyes ran toward Rune and placed a hand on his back while trying to pry his hand off the crystal. A purple mist soon began to emanate from the young man.

"Shit. Overheating. Brick! Get your overgrown ass over here and shatter this crystal before this monster kills us all!" The professor had abandoned all cares for propriety and simply wanted to keep them all from dying. Ven was at a loss for what was happening. Brick was just as confused, stunned momentarily.

In that moment of confusion, Tayven shouted at his friend, "Do it, Brick! He's a Reaver! If he keeps absorbing the Aura from that crystal and overheats, he could go feral and kill us. Crush it now!"

Brick shook himself free from his stupor and ran towards the podium. Rune's head snapped up. From his hands, he released a ball of energy. "Pulse: Rapid Fire." Dozens, then hundreds of small orbs of light shot from the palm of his hand, decimating the target range. The students currently stationed there were thankfully out of the firing line. Those closer to the impact ducked from the showering debris.

"Shield: Area Barrier." A dome of purple energy exploded outward with Rune at its center. As the light came into contact with people, they found themselves pushed back. The only two people who were not were the two closest to Rune, Professor Lylah and the other girl that Ven thought looked familiar.

"Goddess of Fate, guide my hands. Keep at bay the Lord of Death, but should he call me to the shores of the Sea of Chaos, may my end be swift," Lylah prayed before she once again attempted to shatter the crystal with stones.

Her eyes glowed once more. This time, however, Ven and the other students could see as the Aura within the stones, and the string that connected them to Lylah's hands became visible to the naked eye. This was a phenomenon that non-Volari should never have been able to see. Normally, Volari Weaving was invisible to non-Volari. Only when an Awakened human used Aura was it visible to the naked eye. None of that mattered at that moment. Professor Lylah's efforts were in vain as the Aura strings vanished and the stones once more uselessly fell to the ground.

"You idiot! Stop trying to use Aura around him!" the girl who was trying to cradle Rune shouted. "His abilities are special, Area Disruption and Area Drain. I don't know which one is being used right now, but if it's the latter, you'll kill us faster!"

Lylah dropped to her hands and rushed over to the crystal. The barrier was still up, but the boy showed no signs of exhaustion from this intense use of Aura. Lylah pulled out a simple dagger and struck the crystal repeatedly. She tried aiming for the cracks on its surface, but the strength she possessed was not enough to destroy it.

"Rune," The girl stated calmly, "I need you to clear your head, just for a moment. Please. I need you to help us break this crystal."

What happened to you, Rune? Come back to us. Ven watched helplessly from the side while some unknown woman gently ran her fingers through Rune's hair. A sickening, twisting feeling formed in the pit of Ven's stomach. For a split-second, clarity came to the boy's face, which was covered in the webbing that had originated on his neck.

"Enhance: Grip," Every vein in Rune's hand and arm glowed brightly, his muscles instantaneously flexing at once. The force generated by his grip was strong enough to turn the crystal into a fine powder with a single squeeze.

The mist was still falling off him, though considerably less so now, but the Barrier at least had dropped.

"Rune, listen to me." the whispered. Ven had also run up and placed a hand on her friend's back. The professor backed away so quickly that she fell on her posterior. The girl eyed Ven with caution before continuing, "You are overheating. Just like Karl warned. You need to quickly discharge as much Aura as possible as quickly as possible. Can you do that for me? Remember what it felt like to use the Pulser ability. Do that for me. Please."

Rune nodded swiftly and moved to stand up, causing him to nearly fall over. The black webbing had taken over a considerable amount of his body. Ven and the girl caught him together and finished bringing him to his feet. Rune looked at his hands, brought them together, and pointed them at the sky. The veins in his shoulders glowed, hurrying down the length of his arms before concentrating on his palms. "Pulse: Overshot,"

First, an orb the size of the Awakening Crystal materialized between his hands. Rune leaned back while pointing his hands toward the sky. A massive beam of light erupted from the orb and shot into the air. Everyone's jaws hit the ground as the solid beam of light split the clouds, piercing the very heavens above. Pressure created by the massive concentration of Aura rolled outward in waves intense enough to force Ven's body to subconsciously quiver in fear and fight to retain consciousness. The light forced them all to avert their eyes.

Five seconds later, the beam ceased and Rune collapsed to the ground, panting. His consciousness abandoned him. Ven moved to help, but the unknown girl quickly cut between them by pulling Rune's head into her lap. Once again, she was running her hands through his beautiful silver hair.

"Professor, with all due respect, what the fuck was that?" a student asked.

"A near death experience." Lylah answered between gasps.

Chapter Twenty-Six

Fate weaves her threads together, spinning the tapestry of our journeys. She is our beginning and our future, but her husband, Death, is our end. When our time has come, Death receives these gifts from his lover to then pass on from life. Jealous of Fate's artful designs, Chaos pulls at the loose threads he finds and weaves in new pieces unintended by their creator, leaving his own mark on those he finds the most interesting.

- *Path of Volar* as written by Arkrune vys Volar

Lylah

"Professor Lylah vas Mithra," a voice boomed with ferocity. It echoed through the large space that the poor woman found herself in. "What do you have to say for yourself regarding the incident that disturbed the peace of my city?"

Lylah's leg cramped from being crouched on one knee for such a prolonged period. Still, she did not dare shift while in the presence of Lord Jelmoore. He was an elderly man, in his seventies, but looked many decades younger. His stature was still that of a proud warrior who appeared ready to enter the field of battle at a moment's notice. He was known for his domineering personality and commanding voice.

The impact of his booming voice was enhanced by the wide stone walls and high ceilings of the lord's audience chamber, the only decorations being a few tapestries representing the lord's family, the Kingdom of Volar, and the Vanguard. Bold statements of the aging lord's loyalties. Beneath her was a simple red carpet that led straight to Lord Jelmoore's massive oak chair.

"Your lordship," Lylah squeaked, "I assure you that what occurred today at the Vanguard Academy was something wholly unforeseeable. Had we known then—"

"I care not for your excuses, Professor!" the lord shouted, slamming his powerful fist on the arm of his chair, shattering it. "Tell me, what was that light?"

Lylah looked to the left of the chair and saw the master of both the academy and the Vanguard of Jelmoore, Vincent. He nodded his head, as if to give her permission to speak. She nodded in return. The lord noticed this interaction and gave an annoyed snort.

"My lord, the light was an Overshot... well beyond its normal capacity, of course," Lylah cautiously answered.

The lord eyed the woman carefully before calling her out, "Bullshit. No Pulser on this plane can create a prolonged Pulse, let alone one that large. It split the sky, dammit! You expect me to truly believe that a mere Pulser did that?"

"No, no! Lord Jelmoore," Lylah stammered. "The skill used was Pulse: Overshot but the source was not a Pulser. The source is a new entrant to the academy...a Reaver."

Vincent's eyebrow arched out of curiosity. Because of his lack of surprise, the woman believed that he might have had suspicions about Rune's Class prior to admitting him to the academy. After the incident, she had spoken directly with Vincent and learned that Rune had been granted an exemption and enrolled outside the standard timeframe.

"A Reaver, you say?" Lord Jelmoore's tone turned even icier. "And does it live?"

"Yes, my lord, the Reaver lives and keeps his sanity."

"Is that so?" The old man's tone switched to one of surprise. Though not one to be easily shocked, this news was quite the revelation for Lord Jelmoore. "After that display of power, it didn't go feral?"

Lylah winced. To the Volari, there was only one kind of human that was treated any differently from the rest, and that was a Reaver. It was ingrained in their culture that Reavers were scions of the Lord of Death. They were people chosen by him to do his bidding in the world. Hearing the lord refer to Rune as 'it' grated on her, but there was little she could do. She was also still struggling with how she had treated Rune before finding out what he was, as well as calling him a monster. It was in the heat of the moment, but... *I need to talk to him. If I don't fix this, my family will disown me.*

"No, sir, Rune still retains both his humanity and his mind. He is recovering at present within the walls of the academy."

The lord nodded and leaned to the side to discuss something quietly with Vincent. Vincent nodded occasionally before offering statements of his own into the ear of Lord Jelmoore. The two men worked together to maintain the security of the city and were longtime friends, so it was not an uncommon sight for them to casually converse with each other. At some point, Vincent became more animated, clearly frustrated at something. Their conversation was barely more than a whisper, so Lylah was unaware of what was actually being discussed.

"Alright, Professor. As penance for your incompetence and for endangering the city and the lives of the fifth son of Lord Nefera and the fourteenth prince of Faradin, you will execute the creature. Dismissed." The lord waved his hand dismissively and rose from his seat. Vincent had a complicated look on his face.

"My lord, please!" Lylah shouted, coming to a full stand. She had gathered her courage to finally confront the man. She hoped that this expression of bravery would be good enough to show Lord Jelmoore her resolve. Resolve that could save Rune. Old lords like him were strange in that respect. "We cannot just kill him! He's innocent. No one was hurt, but most of all...my lord he's..."

"He's what?" Lord Jelmoore growled. The old man's intense gaze was filled with anger and hatred. It was as though the temperature within the room had dropped by dozens of degrees. That chill shot up Lylah's spine, nearly seizing her breath. Even Vincent shivered slightly.

"He's a Variant. The existence of Variants of the Rare classes has long been theorized. He might be the first ever Variant Reaver. We cannot kill him! Plus, he absorbed enough Aura to wear out an Awakening Crystal. If that amount of power wasn't enough to cause him to go feral, he may have resistance to it! Imagine it, Lord Jelmoore. Reavers immune to overheating; incapable of going feral! We have to keep him alive, if at the very least to learn from him! He could be the answer that keeps future generations safe!"

"A Variant Reaver, you say? How do you know this? One has never been documented before, so how in creation can you know for certain?"

"He has two abilities that Reavers don't. Area Disruption and Area Drain. I cannot fathom any other explanation than he is a Variant."

Vincent's and the lord's eyes opened wide in shock, allowing several seconds of silence to pass through the room. "He has Wraith abilities? Reavers are dangerous enough that they can already use the abilities of the Common classes. Now you are here telling me he can also use two Wraith abilities? First of his kind or not, such power is a risk. You may have to settle for a simple autopsy to satisfy your curiosity."

"Actually, sir...I'm not sure that he can really use the other abilities of the other classes. At least not under normal circumstances. Normally, when a Reaver touches an Awakening Crystal, it creates a rapid flash of each of the other class skills. Based on notes of past Awakenings, we should have seen a tiny flash of the muscles, a quick Barrier, and a tiny Pulse shot. Then it forcibly activates their Drain ability at the end. That did not happen with Rune.

"With him, the Barrier and Pulse shots did not activate until he was already actively overheating, but he showed signs of an enhancement, Area Disruption, and Area Drain. If I were to take a guess, based on notes I received from Master Vincent and Karl from Hilden, the young man might only manifest Shielder and Pulser abilities when he's overheating and on the verge of going feral. It may also be a safety mechanism for him to release massive amounts of Aura at once to prevent the over-accumulation of Aura in his body. If such a thing is possible..."

Vincent eyed the old man closely, as if trying to watch the gears in his head turn. Lord Jelmoore brought his hand to the beard on his chin and stroked it gently while murmuring something to himself.

After a few minutes of pondering, he finally spoke. "Those are a lot of assumptions you are making regarding a creature that could cause widespread destruction to my city...but I will allow you to monitor him. When he comes to consciousness again, if he still has his sanity, then you will confirm if he is indeed incapable of using the abilities of a Pulser and Shielder. He represents a massive threat to our safety, and I need anything and everything I can to lower the risks."

"Thank you, my lord. I will—" Lylah started while bowing deeply, before she was cut off.

"I will also personally be writing a letter to the three heads of the Vanguard. The Commanders at Fort Black, Castle Nyer, and Tri-Spire. They will be informed of this boy."

Lylah gulped. She was terrified of the Commander at Fort Black being told of this. The woman absolutely terrified Lylah. Very few Volari were members of the Vanguard, and even fewer were amongst leadership. If Lylah's sister gained an interest in the boy after reading these reports, then she feared for the boy's future. Regardless of what the future held, she had secured Rune's for the present and was satisfied to leave it at that. Lylah vas Mithra bowed her head yet again and left the room.

That fossil gets more and more terrifying every time I see him... Lylah sighed as she walked past the armored guards outside the audience chambers. *For now, Rune is safe. I will need to apologize to him. Preferably before the house of Mithra finds out about him. If I put my family in a bad light with a Reaver, my mother would kill me. The family head could well banish our branch if angered enough by it.*

Lylah made her way through the streets of Jelmoore, passing by hundreds of people gossiping about a singular topic: the mysterious light from the academy. Most of the common people would have not understood what the source could be, but veteran Vanguard did. While some might feel the pressure emitted by any other Awakened or Volari using their abilities, they could not tell a Pulser from a Volari Stone-Weaver at a distance. That was, unless they had eyes as sensitive as Lylah's.

However, the Aura emitted by a Reaver was unique. A sensation not soon forgotten. Everyone who possessed the ability to use Aura, or who could manipulate it in some capacity, would recognize a Reaver. The pressure they emitted would make those in the surrounding area feel like a hungry animal was staring them down. Lylah could instantly see these veterans amongst the rabble, since they were the only ones who had genuine fear in their eyes.

After a quick walk, Lylah finally made it back inside the walls of the Vanguard Academy. Hopefully, Rune was still in the infirmary, which would make things a lot smoother. *For his sake, I hope I am right. I don't think Lord Jelmoore will let him get away without penalty. If not, I may have to make concessions and contact some friends on Volar.*

Once she was inside, she saw he was the only patient present and his bed was surrounded by people. One was the raven-haired beauty that stood out as one of the more intelligent students in Lylah's classes. With her were the two boys she spent time with, Brick, and Tayven Nefera. The fourth and final person was the Volari that had shown up when the situation had really turned sour.

"Professor!" Venraya called out. The girl moved into a strangely defensive posture. "What are you doing here?"

The other Volari snorted. "Probably here to beg forgiveness from Rune for treating him rudely." Her eyes were full of disdain.

Lylah noticed Venraya was about to interject, but beat her to the punch, "Actually, yes, you are correct. I am here to apologize for my behavior. As well as other things. May I have your name, young lady?"

"Teryn vas Dena. No one important to the Mithras, I assure you."

"Do not sell yourself short. You find yourself in a close relationship with a Reaver. That elevates your position more than you think!" Lylah retorted quickly and excitedly. She hoped that by putting herself in the good graces of the young woman the Reaver fancied she would be forgiven even quicker.

"In a what, now?" Venraya stated coldly while glaring at Teryn.

Teryn sighed and shook her head. "Only the friendly kind. We are not in any other relationship, I assure you. Rune is my best friend, and we've been through a lot the last several months." Teryn gave Venraya a pointed glare. "For now."

"Oh, okay...right," Venraya said quickly and ended with a quick cough. "Wait, what?" Tayven cocked an eyebrow while Brick chuckled.

"Oh, my apologies," Lylah said, interrupting before anything uncomfortable broke out. "I had assumed since you were roomed together, there was something else going on. Regardless..."

"You what?" Venraya shouted. "What do you mean, 'roomed together'? There isn't co-ed rooming at the academy!"

"You're right there isn't. An exception was made for these two, at the request of the Master of the Jelmoore Hall and Master of the Academy, Vincent." Lylah answered.

Teryn gave the professor a look as if to say, 'you aren't helping,' before turning to Venraya. "We roomed together because, like I said earlier, we've been through a lot. You caught Rune on a good day today. And the blue-haired noble next to you caught him on one the other day, too. Most days are not so good. Besides, don't worry so much. He has a girl he is interested in. He's always writing letters to her and his family."

Venraya seemed to notice the same sigh Teryn added in after the last sentence that Lylah had. "Right, Tara. He mentioned her a lot. Okay. What happened to you guys? And how did he get to C-Rank so quickly?"

Before Teryn could say anything—which Lylah had imagined was going to be something rather aggressive—Rune interrupted the conversation with a groan. He slowly tried to sit up, relying on Teryn for assistance as she moved to be his crutch. She gently advised him to take it easy.

Lylah was about to speak when the words caught in her throat. The boy had handsome features, silver hair, and hazel eyes. However, mixed in with the hazel were flecks of purple with a purple ring around the outside of the iris. Teryn and Venraya also gasped at the sight. Based on the two girls' reactions, Lylah could only infer that this was a recent development as of today.

"I take it that's new?"

"Yeah..." Teryn said. "The purple ring has shown up before. When we fought the Wraith. But it went away after. This is the first time it has stayed."

Lylah left the Wraith statement alone for the moment. "Rune, allow me to be serious for a moment. The Lord of Jelmoore wants you dead. But he agreed to leave you alone for the time being. It was on the condition I watch over you and run a few tests. Do you think you are feeling up to it?"

Rune had a thoughtful look on his face before nodding.

"Great. I had a few of these Alderite Cores. I need you to drain them. One at a time. Only move on to the second if you feel fine. The moment you feel full, like you just finished eating a large meal, stop." Lylah gave Rune three cores she had gathered before meeting with the city's leadership.

He took them gently and passed the two of them to Teryn. "Drain" the young man whispered his skill hesitantly, as if afraid to activate it. Not even a moment later, purple light flowed from the core into Rune's body. The purple ring in his eyes flared throughout the process and stopped once the core was drained completely. He gestured for a second one from Teryn and absorbed it as well, though this time, he did so silently. By not verbalizing the skill, it slowed down the process, because it took longer for Rune to finish absorbing the Aura from the core. He put it on the bed before locking eyes with Lylah. The black handprint and webbing from the Overheating were gone, but by the time Rune was finished, they had returned, though they were much fainter.

"Had your fill? Alright. Grab this." Lylah handed him a small tool. It was used for measuring grip strength. "Squeeze it with your normal strength first. Then try to use an Enhancement and squeeze again. If you can, do a silent then verbalized Enhancement."

Rune complied and squeezed the tool. He then concentrated for a moment to activate an Enhancement. The veins in his hand and forearm glowed for a second before he squeezed the tool. Lylah nodded and recorded the difference in strength before gesturing for Rune to continue. "Enhance: Grip." Rune once again squeezed the tool.

Lylah ran Rune through several exercises for Enhancers, Shielders, and Pulsers. She noticed he was more surprised with himself with each successful exercise. He achieved an increase in physical Enhancement by a multiple of three with a silent Enhancement, and by a factor of four with verbalized activation. A normal Enhancer would see a gain in strength starting around five times, but would increase upwards of a factor of ten or more with training.

Rune's attempts at the Pulser and Shielder abilities were pitiful to say the least. The Barrier he made shattered with a flick from Lylah and the Pulse he created fizzled into nothingness about a foot away from his hand. Lylah, with the help of Teryn, also discovered that Rune constantly had his Area Disruption and Area Drain skills running and he seemed incapable of turning them off. Thankfully, the Area Drain only seemed to affect people he viewed as a threat or active manipulations of Aura. Even then, it was only enough to cause a small amount of weakness that could be recovered from with a marginal amount of extra effort.

Upon closer examination of his physical body, she focused on the tattoo-like markings. The handprint was still partially visible to anyone who was within a foot of the boy, but it was only a shade off his normal skin tone rather than inky black. The webbing that had spread across his body and face was completely gone at the moment. Unlike the skeletal handprint, it was impossible to tell where the webbing had once been. There seemed to be a correlation between absorbed Aura and the progression of the marks. Once he had used some of his abilities, the webbing from absorbing the cores vanished.

"Well, that completes that. I'm going to write up a report and present my findings to Lord Jelmoore. I wanted you to know that he is also sending a report to the three commanders of the Vanguard at Castle Nyer, Fort Black, and

Tri-Spire. So, if you had any hopes to remain hidden, I am sad to be the one to inform you that will not happen." Lylah paused. "Not that it would have been an option after a display like that, anyway. I am certain it was seen from miles around."

Rune nodded solemnly. The purple coloration in his eyes glowed every time he activated a skill, similar to when a Volari used their own abilities. Those very eyes were also unfocused, as if he were looking through her and at something a thousand miles away.

"I also wanted to apologize for the way I treated you earlier. I will be honest, being a Reaver grants you a certain level of respect from the Volari, so that is a factor in why I am apologizing. I figure we got off on the wrong foot because of my own behavior. I want to start over, and I cannot do that unless I am completely honest about my intentions."

Rune refocused his eyes, coming a little closer to appearing as though he were actually looking at her. He nodded slowly with a sad expression before he turned to look at Teryn, who regarded him gently. She placed one hand on his head and slowly stroked it as she guided him back down to the bed. It was at this point that Lylah realized Rune did not seem to have a will of his own at the moment. His actions were akin to a puppet dancing along with whatever performance the marionette strings demanded of him.

Teryn had a pathetic look on her face as she continued to stroke the boy's hair, lulling him to sleep. Venraya had a complicated look on her own face and so did the two young men beside her.

"This is the man I fought in the ring the other day?" Tayven said. "He doesn't feel like the same person. His eyes were even more vacant than when we fought. I had assumed it was because he did not view me as a worthy opponent, but now I do not know…"

Teryn shook her head. "That definitely was not it. Even if he believes his opponent is many times weaker than himself, he would never look down on them. He's the type of person who treats everyone equally."

Venraya nodded quickly in agreement. Lylah assumed she had spent little time with Rune, but even she appeared confident in knowing what kind of person he was.

"It seems you both have been through quite a lot. Do you mind sharing?" Brick asked gently. Lylah and Venraya looked at Teryn with genuine curiosity. Venraya clearly wanted to know what had happened to her friend, while Lylah simply wanted to know if it was connected to the Wraith that was casually mentioned earlier.

Teryn's tales of their adversity before coming to the academy felt like something out of a horror story. Lylah had heard a few details from Vincent, but he left out most of the gory aspects. From what Lylah could tell, it was no wonder the boy was in such a state. Watching his two friends die such horrible deaths and without dignity would scar anyone. She had a sudden respect welling up in her heart at the girl, Teryn, for going through the same thing, but retaining her sanity. Perhaps she simply hoped to help Rune, or perhaps she was simply that strong. Either way, it was commendable.

Venraya had gathered tears in her eyes at hearing what they had gone through, while Brick and Tayven looked at Rune in an entirely new light. Lylah noticed an interesting look in the young man's eyes that spoke of resolve. She had no idea what it was, but he seemed to have a new goal.

Chapter Twenty-Seven

Rune

A gentle breeze brushed against the face of a young man who slept beneath a tree. Next to him sat a woman who was gently humming a comforting tune, her hands gently stroking the man's silver hair. Rune slowly opened his eyes, which once again took in the sights of an endless grassland. The only sounds being that of the wind and the gentle humming from the woman cradling his head. Strangely, he could see the branches of the tree growing, sprouting new leaves with each breath he took.

The woman looked down at Rune with a kind smile. Granted, Rune could not really see said smile, but somehow, he knew it was there.

"I see you've fully Awakened," she said with a gentle voice. "A pity it was under such circumstances."

"You saw what happened? In the heat of the moment, the professor called me a monster. Is that what I am?"

The woman sat for a moment, giving off the feeling she was pondering her answer. With her constantly changing features, he could not truly read her expressions. His assumption was all he had to go on. "That depends on you, I suppose. But if you are asking if being a Reaver inherently makes you a monster...then no, my sweet little Arkrune."

The last part of her sentence sounded as though it came from the lips of his own mother. There was a strange sense of familiarity. For a moment, Rune was angry that this being impersonated his mother, yet he felt a sense of comfort.

He swallowed the lump forming in his throat. "Please don't mimic my mother. It's confusing."

The woman laughed for a few seconds before continuing, "Is that how you saw me? I did not intend to do so. Regardless, I apologize. As far as Lylah vas Mithra, she regrets her actions and words. It is up to you to forgive her. Just like it is up to you to forgive yourself for what happened. I don't mean with the Wraith, either."

Rune's breath caught in his throat. His heart raced.

"I gave you advice the last time you were here, and you chose not to take it. Which saved the life of your friend Teryn, at the cost of Dannon and Jeruul. Do not mistake me, I merely gave advice. I offered a solution to a less painful path. The choice was ultimately yours to make."

Rune gulped heavily before allowing the woman to continue.

"If you had stayed in the bush that Teryn shoved you into, Dannon and Jeruul would have continued running, and the Wraith would have ignored you after feeding on Teryn. By jumping to action, you lit a spark that ignited the fire of bravery in your friends, which ultimately grew into a blaze that consumed their lives in exchange for hers."

Her tone was cheerful and nonchalant despite her discussing the deaths of his friends. She then snapped her fingers. The two of them were suddenly behind her cottage next to the terrifying sea...ocean...river. Again, Rune felt a headache coming on, trying to figure out which one it was.

"Sorry for the sudden change of scenery. I can only step away from the washing for so long!" The woman kneeled by the side of the black and purple 'water'. Next to her was a basket of what seemed to be endless shirts. She grabbed out one that was dyed nearly black and filled with holes and another that was pristine, as though it were freshly washed. "Rune, what do you think about these shirts?"

Rune blinked repeatedly, confused, but the woman simply gestured for an answer. "Um, I think the dirty one has too many holes to be worth washing."

The woman giggled softly. "So it would seem. This shirt has seen a lot. It is dirty, damaged, and undesirable. But if we put a little effort into cleaning off the dirt and work to patch the holes, then we can find the beauty hidden beneath." She *plunged the damaged shirt into the water and when she removed it, she held a clean shirt in perfect condition. "Things are not always what they seem, Rune. The sins of the past can be forgiven and we can keep them from coloring one's future. Remember that."*

"Yes, ma'am."

"If I give you another piece of advice, do you think you will follow it?"

Rune nodded.

"Go back. Not now, necessarily, but soon." The woman snapped her fingers again, making Rune's vision go black.

Rune

Rune gasped suddenly and sat up. Looking around, he realized he was in the clinic at the academy. There was a strange weight on his legs and when he looked down, he saw Teryn laying her head on him, with her hand holding his tightly. He noticed drool pooling on his blanket. Rune smiled and brushed a lock of hair out of her face.

Teryn stirred. Her eyes flitted open. He found himself captivated by the young woman's beautiful purple irises.

"Good morning..." she mumbled.

Before he could stop himself, Rune's hands moved to cup her cheek. "Good morning."

Leonidas

K ing Faradin pinched the bridge of his nose in annoyance. In his hand was a packet of papers, which was a compilation of letters and documents from the kingdom's spy network. Messenger hawks landed in the castle's rookery by the dozens. They usually contained various kinds of information, but every report lately focused on the rising tensions between the northern and southern halves of the kingdom. Despite being a northerner himself, the southern nobles rallied their support and complaints behind Lord Nefera.

As the lord of the largest trade city on the continent, his words held massive political power in the kingdom's high court. Having Erich Nefera as the mouthpiece for the southern nobles was a highly inconvenient situation for King Leonidas Faradin. He had hoped that capitulating to Archpriest Henner's request of sending his son Lestreus to the Vanguard Academy at Jelmoore would be enough to ease some tensions and show that the Royal family valued the southern lands just as much as the northern ones, but the effect had not been as grand as he hoped. In fact, it seemed the original worries he shared with Lestreus were turning out to be correct.

He was not blind to the fact that Henner's own goal was likely to increase the influence of the Crucidian Church at the primary port city in the southern lands. By sending Lestreus to the Vanguard Academy, he could send with him anyone he wanted under the pretense of a guide. That was how had he managed to finally send Father Gelroy to the city.

Leonidas knew his son was heavily involved with the church and received most of his education directly from members of the clergy. In fact, it was at the king's wish that the church directly involve itself with Lestreus' education. The deal put royal eyes into the inner-workings of the secretive upper echelons of the church, and in turn provided, the church a mouthpiece of royal blood within the castle. Essentially, he had taken a risky gamble that did not seem to pay off.

Now that Leonidas had seen his efforts to temporarily soothe the nobility were not working out, he could only wait for tensions to rise even more, as his son would no doubt assist Henner in trying to gain a religious foothold on Volar.

Most of the southern populace were Crucidites, but many also followed the Path of Volar. The Crucidites of the southern regions were also more accepting of the Path. In the northern lands, almost every citizen was a staunch Crucidian faithful and did not look favorably on followers of the Path, and in turn, Volari.

It was their family's policy to let such things be. It was how his father and his father's father had always done things. Everything simply worked itself out. The lords ruled themselves, bringing to him complaints and concerns only when necessary and yet...he had tried something different. He had allowed his son to become more involved, and things only seemed to escalate.

I knew we involved ourselves too much by sending Lestreus there.

"My liege, I bring news."

Leonidas was still pinching his nose and groaned, "Go ahead." He waved his hand at the figure that suddenly appeared from the shadows, having used the secret entrance into the king's office.

"My liege, it seems there was an incident at the Vanguard Academy. A massive tower of Aura burst forth from the Academy and split the heavens. The tower of light persisted for several seconds before dissipating."

The king sat forward, suddenly interested and concerned. He gestured for the messenger to continue.

"Our informants intercepted a message from Lord Dethras Jelmoore, dispatched to the three Commanders. It seems the source was from a student who enrolled recently. A Reaver, potentially the first known Variant of that class."

The king's face paled momentarily as he sighed, "A Variant Reaver, you say? I see. I never thought I would live to see a legend come to life. With that amount of energy, I imagine they Overheated and went feral. What were the losses? What of my son?"

"There were no losses, sir. According to the letter, the Reaver did Overheat, but did not go feral. The student remains at the academy and remains sane. Unfortunately, his identity remains yet unknown. It seems that Lord Jelmoore was worried someone might intercept his message to the Vanguard's leaders."

The king had his full attention on the messenger now. A Variant Reaver was one thing, but to have a Reaver survive Overheating and retain its sanity... such a thing was much more concerning. The king shook his head to clear his thoughts and immediately went to writing a letter.

"Copy and distribute this information across our network. I want to know everything about that Reaver. Find out their name, their family, and their friends. I want to know everything about anyone who so much as breathed around it."

"So it shall be, my liege." The messenger took the letter and vanished from the room, leaving the king to his thoughts once more. He knew that finding out the name of the Reaver would be simple. His own son was a student at the academy, so even if it was just through rumors, Lestreus could easily identify the person. However, avoiding the use of his son was something Leonidas wanted to continue for as long as he could. With Lestreus being as close as he was to Henner and Gelroy, it could not be guaranteed he would not assist in handing the Reaver over to them. The church had many secrets and tools. They did not need one more.

The question remains, who will go after it first? Dethras Jelmoore and the Vanguard have the advantage of having him as a student at the Vanguard Academy. But he could be taken by Fort Black... or maybe the church... or maybe Volar?

King Leonidas pinched the bridge of his nose yet again. None of the possibilities were great, but if he had a choice, the Crucidian Church was the best entity to work with regarding the Reaver. He then started writing another series of letters, which included a formal request for an inquiry into the incident in Jelmoore and the answers to several requests by Archpriest Henner. Leonidas re-read a few of the requests. Both with a sigh and heavy heart, he approved all of them.

Among these requests was one asking for renewed negotiations with Volar regarding the admittance of Crucidian missionaries into their territory. Another was for the granting of Castle Guldin—and the ownership of the village for which the castle was named—into the hands of the Crucidian Church.

The last two were the weightiest of all. Upon his approval, one would allow the formal creation of a holy knight order under the command of the church. The other was for the purchase of weaponry from the kingdom by the church.

Leonidas was aware of the trouble this could cause, but given the state of things, this was his only answer. Perhaps by providing such strength to Henner, the southern nobles would back off and the church would back away from the Variant Reaver. Yes, he involved himself yet again. Violating the sacred promise of his ancestors to let the people be, but Lestreus had already forced his hand. What was one more person tipping the scales? The north was flush with devotees, and should war break out, they would no doubt ally with the kingdom, swelling its forces with their number. With a massive increase in strength, some southern houses might be calmed, if only because of fear.

I need something else... Others will need a way out, one that doesn't hurt their pride.

Rune

"You're a Reaver huh?" Venraya asked her friend.

Rune had spent a few days in the clinic after the incident and then a few more locked away in his room to let some things settle down. Given the severity of what happened, he was still gawked at by students and staff alike. No one could blame them for their behavior, though. While it made him uncomfortable, he was found to be a Rare class of Awakened. Add to that the towering beam of pure Aura that some said 'rent the heavens' and Rune became impossible to ignore.

"So it seems, Ven." Rune sighed. Ven, Tayven, and Brick surrounded him. They acted as a barrier, keeping him from being swarmed by other students, but they also kept asking the same questions the other students would have.

"It seems you are rather lucid today as well," Tayven stated matter-of-factly. This comment made Rune and Ven shoot him a sharp glance. Before Ven could say anything, though, a small hand chopped downward onto the boy's head.

"Don't be inconsiderate, Sir Nefera," Teryn requested. She had entered the room just a moment before Tayven had made his rude statement. She squeezed through the crowd that had gathered in order to sit by her friend.

"So," Ven began, "Rune, are you going to be taking our group out on a mission here soon? Since you are a C-Rank, we don't have to wait till we are in our second year to do missions!"

Rune shook his head, "Not until I figure out what missions we can get. You are all E-Rank while Teryn and I are C-Ranks. I would prefer we take on E and D-Rank jobs, but I am concerned that we may not be allowed to. We aren't ready for C-Rank missions."

"What? With your strength and power? Why would you be so concerned about taking C-Rank jobs? Surely you and Miss Teryn could do just fine, especially if we back you up!" Brick argued.

Rune sighed and looked to Teryn for help. She nodded and answered, "We are C-Rank in name. This is true. But remember, we have not been in the Vanguard for long. Besides, our extra bump occurred during our promotion into D. We are D-Rank in terms of experience, both in worldly knowledge and combat."

"With how Rune fights, there's no way he could be inexperienced!" Tayven and Ven said simultaneously.

Teryn shook her head, "You have only seen Rune fight under circumstances that benefit him. He's strong, and he fights well, but he can't always use his normal fighting style. Especially since Jelmoore hosts a large population of Volari and Wanderers."

Ven, Tayven, and Brick looked confused at the girl's statement. If Teryn had not informed him last night, then Rune would have been confused right along with them. She had confronted him finally after everyone left them alone. Before then, either the twins were around or Teryn was 'distracted'. Or, at least that was what she claimed.

Apparently, the combat style that Rune was trained in was something she had seen before. Back home, other people used performed something similar. A special order of knights that served the king of Volar. She had seen this during a festival where some of the royal family's knights participated in a tournament meant to excite the masses.

If any Volari nobility caught wind of a Reaver using these skills, the noble houses of Volar would stop at nothing to bring him to their folds. Professor Lylah had confirmed this with him as well and though a member of a noble house herself, she had sworn to not release this information to her kin or allies. It behooved her to keep the boy here, and she was not so keen on losing such a strong potential ally. Not to mention, an interesting research subject.

Suddenly, several things made sense. The letter from his father warning him about Teryn, and Teryn constantly confronted and stared at him when they first had partied together. This still left Rune with several dozen questions, ones he shared with Lylah vas Mithra and Teryn vas Dena, but all three of them wanted to know one thing: what kind of man was his father?

Chapter Twenty-Eight

Adulmond

Lord Adulmond vos Prent's footsteps echoed through the long halls of the castle that housed the royal family of Volar. On either side of him were two rows of massive columns meticulously carved from white marble, with a long blue rug that ran the length of the hallway. The columns themselves depticted the Volar royal family's history and deeds. Despite the padding, his footsteps still made solid thuds against the ground thanks to his full plate armor. Lord Prent's eyes glowed brightly as he manipulated the sound of his footsteps to amplify their volume.

Members of the staff were cleaning and rushed out of his way. Others kept busy by charging the Aura Lamps lining the halls. Guards snapped to position the moment they heard him. He did not have time to reprimand anyone for shirking duties, so he made sure his presence was known.

Several minutes later, he stopped outside a massive set of double doors, gilded with golden embellishments. Two heavily armored men stood tall beside them. One stepped forward and slowly opened them, and a butler inside announcing his entrance. "Lord Adulmond vos Prent presents himself to Queen Halthra vas Volar, the fifth queen of her name. Lord Prent, you may approach her majesty and kneel."

Adulmond stepped forward, stopping a dozen feet before the steps that rose to the throne. Dozens of nobles were gathered in the hall to prepare for daily court. He looked up at his queen, a woman in her early twenties with pure white hair and deep purple eyes. To her people, and any other that looked upon her, she was the very definition of beauty. Her visage sent even his aged heart into a wild beat.

"My queen, I bring a message from our contacts within the Faradin Embassy," Adulmond began, schooling his expression. His family was made up of diplomats, and thus he was in charge of maintaining the order of and seeing to the needs of the Faradin Embassy on Volar. His duties also included dispatching orders to their own embassy, housed in the capital of Faradin. "We have received a direct request from King Leonidas Faradin."

Adulmond presented a letter to another attendant who stood several steps below the throne. She took the letter and presented it to Queen Halthra with a bow. The queen opened it to read while Adulmond continued, "He requests a delegation to renegotiate our rules on Crucidian missionaries being allowed entry to Volar."

Queen Halthra snorted. "Obviously, that's a no. I don't want those bumbling pigs setting foot on our sacred land. Those who would deny Lady Fate's words and sully the beautiful finality of the Lord of Death have no place here." A murmur of agreement sounded through the chamber. Lining the sides of the room were dozens of nobles who were attending the day's decrees.

"My queen, while I agree, I do wish to advise caution," Adulmond stated, before pausing at the annoyed eyebrow raise the queen gave him. "Intelligence suggests that the king also granted a village, a castle, and the rights to establish a knightly order to the Crucidian Church. We have also received rumors of a large purchase of weaponry from Faradin by the church. Doing things to immediately spark conflict with them may not work to our benefit. I dare not assume the exact state of our military readiness, but losses would be extreme and the stress to the common people nothing less than devastating. While our answer will inevitably be no, I suggest we delay our response for now."

Gasps escaped the lips of several nobles, followed by shouts of indignation and anger. "What do they think they are doing?"

"Do they dare threaten us?"

"A knightly order under command of the church? Dare they plan a crusade against our people?"

Queen Halthra put up a hand to silence the angry crowd. Adulmond could not blame them for their reactions, as his had been much the same when he had first heard the news. Only minutes after he received the formal request from the embassy had one of his intelligence agents provide him with the information regarding the Crucidian Church's weapon purchase and knight order.

King Leonidas was a coward who sat upon his gilded throne, content to watch his territories crumble. Under the excuse of impartiality, he let corruption fester. Yet, now he chooses to take action. That action being to cater to the whims of the very corruption that eats away at his kingdom.

"Have we received word from Dethras or Vincent regarding these matters?"

Adulmond answered with a slight sigh. Queen Halthra was a young leader and exposed too much by not using honorifics with the two men's names. "There is no word on Lord Jelmoore's position relating to these negotiations. The Vanguard representative from Tri-Spire, of course, has already issued their stance on maintaining neutrality in the matter, barring any additional instruction from Castle Nyer."

"I see. It is to be expected."

"However, my queen, we can likely expect Lord Jelmoore to continue his family's long-standing support of us. Because of that, I believe we can also count on most of the southern nobility. Lord Jelmoore also sent word over to us alongside a message to Tri-Spire. It seems another Reaver has been located amongst the Vanguard Academy's students. Quite a unique one as well."

Once again, excited conversation spread throughout the throne room. The queen's attendant cleared their throat loudly to return attention to Queen Halthra. "A Reaver? What do we know of him? Has Dethras shared this information with King Leonidas?"

"I do not believe the old codger has sent anything to his liege. Though we should assume he has learned of the situation through other means. As for the Reaver, he is being considered a Variant and..." Adulmond paused, as if thinking whether he should finish his sentence. Halthra noticed the hesitation and motioned for the room to clear out. After five minutes of confused shuffling, the room was empty of all but the queen, Adulmond, and the queen's two attendants.

"Continue."

"The Reaver is the son of a Wanderer...from Locke."

Queen Halthra's knuckles turned white as she gripped the arms of her throne. Anxiety flashed across her delicate face. This lasted only a moment, easily missed by all but the most observant of people. She was the queen, after all. Fixing her face was second nature. *If only her tongue could be as careful.*

"I see. Send a letter to Dethras. Inform him we will send a team of Shadow-Weavers to monitor the boy and protect him from Faradin, if need be. We will not interfere with his education or missions with the Vanguard. Should he fall in battle during normal duties, so be it, but I will not have him poached or killed by that fool Leonidas or his bedfellow, Archpriest Henner."

"Your will be done, my queen."

Teryn

Brick, Tayven, and Venraya stared blankly at a mission posting that Teryn had placed on the table in front of them. Their party of five had gotten the release to proceed in taking missions since they had not one, but two C-Rankers in their party. This allowed them to bypass the wait until they had become second-years. They could use the winter break to work jobs instead of wasting time in the practice fields sparring. Teryn had selected a D-Rank quest in Tennfeld, a city just north of Jelmoore.

The three were surprised because it had only been a few days since their conversation with Rune about wanting to hold off on taking quests for a bit until he had figured things out, but after some discussions with Vincent, they could bring the three E-Rankers on D-Rank quests. Vincent had also agreed to Rune's request that they not be assigned any C-Rank quests they did not personally elect to take. Vincent understood their reasoning, since it was a fact that the two were C-Rankers in name and not in experience. Teryn was surprised to learn that the Vanguard would assign work to C-Rankers who were still students, even if she knew that warriors of their skill were in a constant need.

Rune certainly had the power to back up his rank, and everyone felt that his battlefield awareness also met the expectation of a C-Ranker. Despite all of that, he insisted his level of experience left a lot to be desired. Vincent had tried to convince him that simply acknowledging that fact and attempting to work within those limitations was proof enough that Rune was a C-Ranker through and through, but he held strong to his beliefs.

"So, we are hunting down a pack of Spined Toads? What are those things?" Venraya asked. Brick and Tayven's faces paled at the mention of the monster's name.

"They are a large toad-monster, about three feet tall, and if stretched out, about six feet, toe to tip," Teryn said simply.

She had watched many parties fight against the monsters. They were not overtly dangerous to humans, but they were pests that liked to munch on goats and calves, so ranchers and farmers despised them. The downside—which was what made the two boys look as though they might lose their lunch—was that they were covered in a layer of slime that made striking with non-piercing weapons tricky. They also smelled extremely foul.

Tennfeld was a city built in a mostly swampy area. Spined Toads were a pest, but easily ignored. They became a problem when their population grew to a point where they left the swamps and moved to the farmland in the plains outside Tennfeld's area of influence. To prevent issues, they would occasionally submit culling quests to the Vanguard.

"Is there not another job we can take? Like Dire Ants, Echo Bears, Shadow Wolves...something?" Brick whined. Tayven rapidly nodded his head in agreement. Venraya remained silent as she did not understand why they did not want to fight a bunch of overgrown amphibians. Since they were not native to where she had grown up, it was more than likely she did not know about how disgusting the things could be. Even Teryn thought they were fairly gross.

Teryn groaned at the sound of her comrades' whining, "Come on and grow a set, would you? Dire Ants don't live around here, and Rune and I are not stepping foot near the Greatwood to hunt any Echo Bears. That really leaves Jilt, Jelmoore, and Tennfeld as areas of work."

The two boys eventually relented to Teryn's logical argument. They did, however, spend the next several minutes informing Venraya of every detail about Spined Toads, which had the opposite effect the boys were hoping for. Instead of her joining them in mutual disgust, she became judgmental towards her friends for their brazen cowardice.

Teryn guided Rune to the table. He was staring at the job board with unfocused eyes. Teryn had already warned them that Rune had settled into one of his off periods. Everyone already knew there was no way to tell how long one of these spells would last.

Rune was positioned between Teryn and Venraya who took turns caring for him. *What even is this girl's relationship with Rune? Yeah, they adventured together for a short while, but still...* Teryn locked her jaw in frustration.

Venraya flagged down a waitress to ask for a sandwich and a glass of water for Rune. The area where students could take jobs was shared with the Vanguard Hall of Jelmoore, so it also doubled as a bar, just like in Hilden. The waitress momentarily eyed the strange boy, who seemed to stare at nothing, before nodding at the order. She returned a little later and deposited the food in front of Rune.

He was once again in a dissociative state. Teryn had finally gotten the clerics to look at him while he was under watch from his Awakening. They had informed her there was nothing physically wrong with him. Professor Lylah stated it was likely a trauma response. When asked how she could help him, Teryn was told that Rune either needed to come out of it on his own, or be forced into a situation in which he had to confront his trauma.

Unfortunately, she did not know how to do the latter. Teryn sighed as she guided Rune's hand towards the plate. He could feed himself and take care of basic needs and the like. He just needed nudges in the right direction to change tasks. Before Rune grabbed the sandwich, he mumbled something.

"What was that?" Venraya asked. She leaned in closer to her friend to catch what it was he said.

"Home."

This time, the statement was loud enough for everyone at the table to hear him. Teryn nodded immediately and grabbed a sack of coins to count out the cancelation fee. Brick and Tayven protested the expense, but a harsh glare from Venraya silenced them.

Neither boy was brave enough to go against Venraya when she was angry, and they were even less inclined to disagree with Teryn when they really thought about it. Like Rune, she claimed she was C-Rank in name only, but they still had not seen her fight. Even if she did not consider herself a C-Rank, she was absolutely a D-Rank, which was still higher than both of them.

Teryn walked back to the table, pocketing her change and holding another mission flyer. "This one is a Rock Goblin nest encroaching on Locke."

"Rock Goblins? Sure, that's fine. I've not fought any of the beasts before," Tayven stated, with Brick nodding along.

"Alone, they are pretty simple, but in groups, they can become overwhelming. They use primarily weapons made of bone and rock. They live in mountainous and hilly areas. They specifically migrate to areas with lots of loose rock. Because of that preference, mines are overrun by them quite often," Venraya explained.

Teryn was not too familiar with them either, since she never moved further north than the outskirts of Dorn. Rock Goblins simply did not cross her path. While trying to imagine exactly what they would look like from some additional details Venraya shared, Teryn noticed Brick shifting oddly.

"If you have something to say, say it."

"Okay, I feel like I have waited long enough, so I'm just going to say it. We need a name." Brick stated.

Teryn shrugged, indicating she did not care too much. Venraya, Tayven, and Brick tossed around several ideas. Some attempted to include references to the members' backgrounds and skills. Teryn and Venraya immediately vetoed any that referenced Rune's class. No one needed to draw any additional attention to their group more than they already had.

"How about the Rite!" Brick offered. He had a huge and proud smile on his face. "You know, like your last rites?"

"Sounds like someone has read too many fantasy novels from the library instead of assigned readings. Next recommendation," Venraya quipped. Her response even elicited an affirmative grunt from Rune. No one provided alternatives. Rather, they sat in awkward silence.

"No one? Then, how about...First Light," Venraya offered.

The group paused for a moment to ponder Venraya's suggestion. "I'm not immediately opposed. What made you suggest that?" Teryn asked.

"It is from an old Zentus belief. The first rays of light in the morning represent hope and dreams. I figure since we all are still young and relatively inexperienced, that it represents our hopes for the future!"

The others around Venraya nodded in affirmation. Even Teryn gave the girl a thumbs up. First Light then celebrated their formation by ordering a round of drinks before going their separate ways. They walked together to the paths between the dorms, when Venraya turned to Teryn.

"We head out tomorrow?" she asked.

"I think that would be best. It will be a long trip, so pack everything you need. A few sets of travel clothes, rations, and anything you need to maintain your weapons and armor."

"I know that much, at least."

Venraya shifted uncomfortably, as if thinking about saying something. Her green eyes settled on Rune for a moment. Against Teryn's expectation, the girl remained quiet and simply parted at the fountain between their dorms. Her eyes remained attached to Rune for several more moments before she finally entered the E-Rank dorms. Teryn guided Rune back to their room so she could prepare their supplies.

Chapter Twenty-Nine

Vincent

The complex, smokey aroma of a luxurious tea filled the air of a fine office. Anna stood near the door to the room and was in a pseudo-relaxed state while remaining ever ready to respond to a threat to her master's life. Next to her was a guard in full plate mail, holding a shield with the crest of the Nefera family on it.

Across the desk from Vincent was Lord Erich Nefera. He was one of the most powerful members of nobility, politically speaking, in the kingdom. A dangerous glint in his eyes belied Erich's true nature, despite his noble visage. There were many reasons Vincent might have to visit an old friend, but Vincent found himself concerned about this one.

Erich was a patient and calculating man, aspects of him that kept him in power in the largest city in Faradin despite being at odds with his regional peers. Even though Nefera was settled within the northern territories, Erich and his family had long been staunch allies with southern nobility and by extension, nobility of Volar. His family's city, Nefera, was the first settlement along the road from Jilt. Jilt being considered the gateway to the southern territory.

Erich was one of the few northern nobles who did not view Volari in a negative light. This was likely because he had separated himself from the hardline views of the Crucidian Church. Such a thing was necessary as the ruler of a city that was a large trade hub. With people of various cultures constantly mingling and trading within its walls, being known as someone opposed to the beliefs of others could hurt the economy of his land. Outside of Jelmoore, Nefera was probably the city with the next highest concentration of Volari and Wanderers amongst its populace. It might also be in part because of his wild youth...

"Well met, Vincent. I hear my son has formed a party with a newly awakened Reaver," Erich stated between sips of tea. "I am glad that he was not harmed when the boy, Rune, Overheated. Choosing to remain by the young man's side is dangerous, but I am also glad Tayven has elected to adventure alongside such a strong comrade."

Vincent smiled wryly. Of course, his friend had all the specific details regarding Rune. "Yes, Erich, I agree. If things had gone poorly, losing Tayven would have been quite a blow to the young generation of Vanguard. You have raised quite the competent swordsman."

Erich sighed and gave Vincent a sideways glance. "You know damn well that I did not train him. How could I? He's my fifth son and born from a different mother than his brothers; out-of-wedlock, mind you."

"Ah yes, my bad. I forgot he was your illicit bastard. Ah, how I miss his mother. She was such a kind woman. A shame what happened."

"Careful Vincent," Erich growled. "We may be old friends, but that does not mean I won't introduce your face to my floorboards."

Vincent quietly chuckled, though it was dry and devoid of humor. "Anyway, Erich, the king and that old bastard Henner are making moves. Granting Guldin and Guldin Castle to the church, setting up an order of knights just north of your territory... It speaks volumes about their intentions. They've had their own forces for years as guards and their Inquisitors, but now, they can remove themselves from the shadows and grow, unchallenged."

Erich gripped his teacup so tight that cracks formed before it shattered in his hands. "That fool Leonidas is a coward. Suddenly choosing to finally pick a side and he jumps into bed with Henner. The idiot is fanning the flames of war even more! I have done all I could to satiate the southerners.

"Many of their worries, wants, and needs were filtered through me and into the royal court, but none of my ramblings were heard. Drowned out by the voices of those with the privilege of safety and proximity to the capital. If anything, my efforts have only served to make my fellows doubt my loyalty to the crown. I'm not so stupid as to not realize I have spent the last two decades digging my grave."

Vincent could only nod solemnly. He knew all too well the situation at hand; things were coming to a head. The royal family had never had a strong spine, always maintaining the status quo rather than risk changing anything for the worse. Yet, things will worsen now that they had begun clinging to the church's robes instead of working to curtail their increasingly aggressive proselytizing. The royals finally chose a side and ended up choosing the wrong one.

That was not all. Other than Jelmoore, the southern nobility suffered financially. They lived healthy lives but relied upon the Vanguard to protect them. They did not possess the standing armies of Faradin. Their roads were filled with monsters and bandits; beings whose only enemy was a mercenary organization. In the north, the kingdom's forces handled all but the most dangerous of monsters. Foreign trade in the south was restricted due to 'safety concerns' save for Jelmoore's trade agreement with Volar and Boros.

A knock at the door interrupted their conversation. Erich seemed unsurprised and waved at his guard to let the guest in. Standing in the doorway was a tall, lithe woman with short, purple hair and purple eyes so deep in hue they were almost black. She wore a black cloak that cascaded down her back, ending just above the knee. Beneath the cloak was a set of studded leather armor and a saber on one hip. She waved at the two men, revealing a strange pair of gloves that covered the back of her hands and left the tips of her fingers and her palms bare.

"Erich! Vincent! How glad I am to see you two bastards spending time together. A strange sight to see after..." The woman laughed.

"Kyndra, good to see you are doing well. As energetic as ever," Vincent interrupted with a smile. Erich's face held a much darker expression.

"Kyndra."

"Oh, Erich, is that the kind of look you give a friend? Such an icy glare," Kyndra stated with a condescending grin that did not seem to reach her eyes. Vincent unconsciously shuddered. Tensions rose for a moment before Kyndra herself shattered it. "Besides! You were the one who invited me!"

The fearsome woman stepped past both Anna and the other guard to sit in a chair next to Vincent. Normally, a Hall Master would have bowed to the Commander of Fort Black, but Kyndra hated formalities, so he kept himself from doing so. She was a loose cannon who normally stayed in the fort, and the only way to keep her from firing off was to cater to her unique proclivities.

"Welcome, Kyndra," Erich stated plainly. He was one of the few people who could get away with behaving and saying anything he wanted around the woman. "We were discussing the Reaver, Rune."

"Ah, yes. Him. My sister is handling him, so I am considering it not my problem. Fort Black is filled with monstrous fighters more impressive than him." Kyndra said while cleaning dirt from beneath her fingers. "I find myself curious, but he needs more time before he completely catches my interest. Variant or no."

Vincent exhaled a relieved sigh, knowing the woman would not attempt to kidnap Rune. He also could not really disagree with her logic especially since she was one of the monsters she mentioned. As a Sound-Weaver, one of the three Commanders of the Vanguard, and an S-Ranker, only the truly strong deserved her interest. Her job was to maintain Fort Black and keep the numbers of monsters in the Forest of Ruin from rising too high and overwhelming the kingdom. Some of the most dangerous and insane warriors of the Vanguard on the continent called the place their home. Among them, Rune would be a copper a dozen even with his natural talent and inherent abilities.

"Besides, I got my hand on a class just as rare... though they aren't a Variant like the boy."

Erich's stone-faced expression finally cracked. "A Shaper? Truly?"

How in the gods' names did she find one?

Kyndra ignored Erich's question. She smiled at Vincent as if she could read his thoughts. She knew he was just as curious as Erich but still declined to provide any answers. "Hey, wanna spar, Vincent? For old time's sake? I'll tell you everything if you win."

"Absolutely not," Vincent answered immediately. "Such information isn't worth my life. Fight with Erich if you need to let off steam."

"Come on, you are no fun. I can't fight Erich. If I kill him by accident, then the other Commanders and the council will cut my pay," she retorted with a pout. Vincent gulped.

He remembered the last time he had witnessed Kyndra fight. Sound-Weavers were terrifyingly deadly because their weapon was the manipulation of sound itself. She could silence any sound around her completely, amplify it, and even manipulate the directionality. The special gloves she wore were designed with her abilities in mind. Once, when Vincent visited the Forest of Ruin with a party from Fort Black, he had watched how a simple snap of her fingers liquified a monster's insides.

"Well, if all you wanted to do was talk about the Reaver brat, then I will take my leave. This was quite the waste of time, Erich. I'm disappointed in you," Kyndra complained.

If only she knew who his father was. Vincent kept that piece of knowledge to himself. To do otherwise would be to dance further into Death's embrace.

"I did not bring you here for the boy. I have a favor to ask," Erich told her. "I wanted you to allow me to shelter my sons in your fort."

"Eh?" Kyndra blinked. "You want me to babysit your brats and the little bastard? I don't think so."

"No, just my oldest four, and you can put them to any kind of work. Latrine duty, cleaning, the kitchens, anything. Please consider this repayment for that favor you owe me."

Kyndra groaned. "Fine! I'll take them in. But they are also going to be joining our daily training. So, if they get hurt during drills, don't cry to me. And why not the youngest one? Don't care if the bastard dies, eh?"

Dies? Vincent looked inquisitively at the lord across the table.

Erich said nothing and slid a document across his desk towards Kyndra. After reading it, she had a confused look on her face. Vincent accepted the document from her after she passed it to him. It was a letter addressed to Tayven informing him of his disinheritance of all titles, land, and coin of the Nefera family, also disbarring him from further referring to himself as Tayven Nefera. Upon receipt of the letter, Tayven was no longer considered a noble.

"Is this really something you want to do?" Vincent questioned. Anger rose in his chest, pouring out through his words. "His mother would turn over in her grave if you go through with this."

Erich nodded. "I already sent a letter to her family. They have been informed of my reasons. This is the best way to protect him. I sent out a similar letter to all the noble houses in Faradin. Once the one bound for the castle arrives, it will be considered formally announced that Tayven is no longer of house Nefera and has no claims now or in the future on our property."

"You expect the kingdom to wipe out your house, huh?" Kyndra asked.

Erich nodded. Vincent continued to breathe slowly to calm the rage, sending his heart wild. They sat together for a while longer. Vincent was not excited to deliver the news to Tayven, but he figured he should have expected it when Erich ordered Tayven's attendant to leave the boy's side. At least he would have time to figure out how to address this news with the boy, since his party had left on a mission to Locke.

"Fine, if that is how you wish this to shake out, then do what you will," Kyndra growled. "I will take your children under my charge for a time. I will take my leave and have your staff bring me to them." Kyndra stood abruptly, the scraping of the chair on the floor grating on Vincent's ears.

Just before she slammed the door closed behind her, she said in a barely audible whisper, "You fool."

Vincent turned to face his friend. The calm expression on Erich's face returned. The man had resigned himself to whatever Fate had in store for him. There was so much that Vincent wanted to say, but the words escaped him.

All he could manage was, "You're really willing to just roll over and die? After everything?"

"I do what I must. I don't need anyone to understand, and I don't need anyone to agree with my methods." Erich turned to face him fully for the first time. An old smile that had long since vanished from Erich after the death of Tayven's mother had suddenly returned. "Death is but a step in one's journey, my friend. No matter how painful, after everything I've done, it is only right. Come what may, all will be right in the end. It is what I've been promised."

Chapter Thirty

Tayven

After almost a week and a half of travel, the newly named First Light approached the outskirts of a small mining village. The first thing they noticed was the smell of soot from the many blacksmiths in the village. Curiously, Tayven had learned that most of the blacksmiths did not actually work on weapons or armor, but refined ore into shippable bars. Also, despite the village's diminutive size, it maintained a steady flow of traffic from various trading caravans.

The small village of Locke was surrounded by little more than a shoulder-high wall of stones in most places. Some spots had fallen into disrepair, with massive gaps in the stone, replaced by simple wooden fencing. For a place with such great importance to the country, Tayven found it strange the town was not more developed.

The guards at the entrance to the village waved the group through after seeing Rune amongst the arrivals and allowed them to skip the entry line. Because of the amount of people attempting to enter the village at once, neither of them could greet Rune, despite looking like they desperately wanted to see what the boy had been up to.

This behavior left Tayven with a fond smile. He did not know his new comrade very well yet, but that so many of the villagers seemed to look upon him kindly improved Tayven's opinion of him. Every rule had an exception, however. A very rotund man wearing fine clothing was moving from stall to stall. He was obviously the wealthiest of the people purchasing goods for the day. While the group moved through the main pathway which the stalls lined, they came face to face with him. The man turned immediately sour at the sight of the group.

"Guess someone's having a bad day," Teryn joked as she stuck her tongue out at the man's back, now turned toward.

"Not everyone is required to be cheery all the time you know," Ven stated sarcastically. "Case in point."

Ven hiked a thumb at a few other people who seemed to be in a foul mood and arguing with a shady-looking merchant in one of the stalls. Teryn responded with a small grunt. This made Tayven shake his head at them. They had traveled all the way from Jelmoore to Locke in one straight go, not even stopping in a town for more than a night's rest out of the cold. The entire way Teryn and Ven had offered each other little jabs. It was impossible to tell if it was in jest or if they genuinely did not like each other.

Thankfully, the behavior did not impact the group's fighting capabilities. In fact, the two girls worked together exceptionally well. Ven had started to really shine with her archery skills in both long and midrange battles, and Teryn kept her safe, operating in the midrange by slowing or stopping enemies in their tracks to let Ven finish them. Rune also showcased more of his sword skills, which made Tayven feel like he was even further behind than when they had sparred.

He had learned that Rune was actually accustomed to using a shortsword with a small buckler fastened to his bracers instead of the longsword he had dueled with when they first met. Because his own specialty lay in the longsword, having lost handily when he really had a modicum of an advantage... it had deflated his ego just a little. Brick also could show off his prowess as a brawler. He had recently adapted to using strength-enhancing techniques at the point of impact, thus conserving his Aura.

Between the three E-Rankers, Brick seemed to have the best control over his abilities. Ven had been practicing as well, but as a Pulser, her abilities overlapped with her focus on the bow. So, she mostly used her abilities as a quick counter if an enemy broke the line and closed in on her. Unlike Brick, Tayven could only use his Enhancements in a sustained manner, so he either had to finish the fight quickly or risk becoming exhausted. Tayven also lacked the skill required to silently activate his abilities, for now. That was not the end of the world, but it limited his versatility in some ways.

"Here we are," Rune stated, bringing Tayven out of his thoughts.

In front of them stood a simple home with smoke rising out of the chimney. Diagonally behind the house was an open-air smithy. Inside it were people hammering away at a weapon. Metallic clangs clearly hid their arrival from the blacksmiths, as neither reacted to their approach. The door to the cottage opened and a comely woman stepped out into the daylight. She was holding a tray with a pitcher of some sort of pale-yellow liquid, which was immediately dropped as she screeched and ran towards the group.

"Arkrune! My baby boy!" she yelped as she almost tackled the poor boy to the ground. "I did not know you were coming! Oh, you should have written to tell me! I could have prepared more lemonade for you all! We just got a crate of preserved ones in from a trader who visited Volar!"

Suddenly, her face took on an embarrassed hue as she turned around and witnessed the shattered pitcher and glasses on the ground behind her. Rune smiled gently at the woman and returned her embrace. While the two hugged, the duo in the forge stepped out to witness the commotion. They both had purple-colored eyes, of which the smaller of the two were glowing. The man had broad shoulders and silver hair like Rune and the girl, who was small, yet toned, shared the hair color of the woman currently squeezing the life out of Rune.

"Brother! You're back! Who are these people? Is this your party? What have you been up to? It's been a while since you last wrote to us! I've given all your letters you wrote for Tara to her!" The girl joined the woman, who was clearly Rune's mother, in hugging the defenseless young man. Her endless stream of questions overwhelming Rune.

"Alright, alright. Lydia, Ulma, release the poor boy," the man said while clapping his hands together. "It's a long way from Jelmoore to Locke. I'm sure he and his friends are tired!" After he finished speaking, his eyes flashed, and he scanned over the entire group. Momentarily, his eyes landed on Teryn who avoided his focused gaze.

"Yes! Please come in! Oh, my! It's so great to have you home!" Rune's mother turned to enter the house.

Everyone quickly gathered inside the common area of the small home while the woman, Lydia, made more lemonade for her guests. Tayven could not keep his eyes off the girl, Ulma. He had had many girls who were interested in him in the past, but something about this one drew his attention. She was pretty and strong. It was the strength and ferocity he saw behind her eyes that attracted him to her. Unfortunately, the man—who Tayven had discovered was Rune's father—caught on to Tayven's glances and placed himself between the noble and his daughter.

Even Rune noticed what had happened, which made him give Tayven a raised eyebrow. Tayven could feel the sweat form and run down his back. *Gods. The first girl that actually seems interesting, and it had to be Rune's sister. And she had to have this man for a father. Gods, Vickar looks terrifying.* He thought as he glanced at Vickar's muscled form. Being a blacksmith guaranteed a powerful physique, but Tayven's instincts screamed that there was a lot more to it than that. If he was the one who taught Rune to fight, what did that say about the man himself?

"Anyway, Arkrune. What brings you home? You haven't said!" Lydia cleared her throat to break the awkward tension that had formed. This made Brick, Ven, and Teryn giggle at Tayven's expense. Lydia seemed to be rather astute.

"I had to. Also, there are some things I haven't shared in my letters. Master Vincent and Professor Lylah vas Mithra asked me not to, in case they were intercepted," Rune said slowly. "I've fully Awakened my class."

Lydia gasped with joy, but that was not shared by the rest of the family. Tayven could not understand why, but Rune's statement left a concerned look on Vickar's and Ulma's faces. To prove his point, Rune stood and drew his special alderite blade. Now that he had Awakened, he could use it without need for an alderite core. He unscrewed the core, then fed Aura into the blade, causing it to glow and hum. He spun it around in a few small arcs, leaving a trail of light behind it as it moved. With a flourish, he returned the sword to its sheathe and screwed the core back onto the hilt.

"And what is your class, son?" Vickar inquired with a carefully measured tone. By this point, even Lydia's excitement had been tempered—if only slightly. She was just as confused as the rest of the people in the room about why her husband and daughter were not excited about Rune's success. Ven's face started turning red in clear indignation at them for seeming so dismissive about their son's breakthrough.

Rune silently refused to answer as he stepped away and walked outside. The house followed him without a word. They continued to walk a few hundred feet from the home when Rune put up a hand to stop everyone. He took a few more steps, clearing away a small area from a light dusting of snow. He turned around and crouched on the ground with one hand touching the grass. The other grabbed the hilt of his alderite sword. "Area Drain."

A circle of grass, about three or four feet in diameter, started to brown and die. In the blink of an eye, the grass within the circle turned from brown to black before disintegrating into dust. Purple Aura, which was normally invisible to non-Volari crystalized in front of everyone and flowed into the boy's hand before traveling up his arm, across his chest, and down into the sword, charging up the alderite core on its pommel.

"Father, I am a Reaver." Rune took a sharp breath. "And, according to my professor, a Variant."

"I see," Vickar stated as though he were completely unsurprised. "I thought as much."

Ven, whose face was still red, could not hold it in any longer. "You thought as much?" she shouted at Vickar. "You mean to tell me you already knew what Rune was and you let him wander on his own to figure it out without giving him some form of hope that he had a class? Do you know how embarrassed he was to be the only Awakened in Hilden who couldn't use his own sword without the help of others?"

Ven spent the next minute yelling and screaming at Vickar, who accepted it without complaint. Even Lydia did not intervene because she too seemed annoyed that her husband could have helped Rune understand his potential situation more.

"Ven. Stop it." Rune said quietly. He glanced around the party, the emptiness in his eyes that Tayven had grown used to slowly disappearing. "I'm going to go see Tara." He turned and headed back into town. Everything about his body language screamed that he did not want anyone to follow him.

"Sir Vickar, if I may, why did you not inform Rune of your suspicions? At least a small hint would have been helpful to him, I imagine," Brick asked calmly. He did not seem to want to add to the fire that was Ven's rage.

"Volari girl," Vickar called towards Teryn. "How strong is your sight? Can you see the details of an Awakened Human's reservoirs, watch how it flows through their body?"

"No, sir, I'm of common birth and my lineage isn't filled with many people with strong capabilities."

"I see." Vickar paused and stared at the group. "How would you propose I go about telling my son that when I saw him the first time after his birth the first thing I witnessed with my eyes was an empty chasm? Bottomless. Hungry. That, as a young boy, the possibility for his future terrified me. How should I go about explaining—"

Ulma placed a hand on Vickar's arm while also monitoring her mother. Her body flinched at Vickar's every word. *She saw it too.* Tayven realized it. Whatever Vickar saw truly terrified him. It terrified Ulma, too.

Vickar swallowed and took a deep breath. He placed a comforting hand on Ulma's before continuing. "Did you know Locke came under attack a handful of years ago? It's okay if you don't. It was because of the attack that I could finally find an excuse to tell Rune he was Awakened, but I could not tell him everything. It would break him. Kind of like how he is now. I know my son. I can see that he's struggling. All of us could tell that something had happened to him from his letters... How about we step inside and talk about why I couldn't bring myself to give Rune all the answers?"

Teryn stood in place for a moment, content to watch Rune disappear into town. Everyone else was invited back into Rune's family home, but Teryn finally declined, saying she was going to go after Rune. Vickar tried to dissuade her, but it was to no avail. Tayven watched as his friend went into town as well. Ven still seemed to have a bone to pick with Vickar, so she stayed behind, intending to follow him back into the house and give him an earful.

Teryn

Teryn walked through the roads of Locke carefully checking faces and trying to find her friend, a lone Volari in a village of humans. She did not know how, but somehow, she had lost sight of the silver-haired young man. Only he and his father had that hair color in town, how he had vanished so easily. *Is he inside a building? Do I just start knocking on random doors?* Unwilling to give up, she activated her eyes to look for any traces of his Aura. She had spoken the truth to Vickar. She could not see the internal wells within an Awakened, but she could differentiate between people and she had long since memorized Rune's presence.

Suddenly, someone bumped into her hard enough to almost knock her to the ground. Teryn looked at the person who either had not seen her or was trying to pick a fight with her. She was about to yell at them when she heard shouting erupt from a few buildings down the road.

"Get out of here, you damned brat! And keep away from my family!" The voice came from a large, round man who was shouting at someone he had tossed out of the building. According to the sign hanging outside the door, the poor person had been tossed out of a general store of some kind. When the person stood up and dusted off their knees, he turned around and locked eyes with Teryn.

"Rune!" she shouted. "By Chaos' name, what did you do to that man?"

"Oh, that…" he mumbled. "That was Tara's father. He does not like me very much. Even less so now, I suppose."

Teryn blinked, not sure she had heard correctly. "That was Tara's father? What did you do to piss him off? Is that why you send Tara's letters to your family instead of to her directly?"

"Yeah." Rune nodded. "Say, do you want to meet her?"

"You think I can? I mean, I've really been wanting to, but it doesn't seem like you will be allowed inside, let alone allowed to introduce a friend, on top of that."

Rune dismissively waved his hand. "Oh, that won't be a problem. Follow me."

Rune turned to walk away from the store, and Teryn quickly followed his lead. She turned around and saw that Tara's father was staring at them through an open window before he slammed the shutter closed. The girl shrugged and continued to follow Rune through the town. After a few minutes, they left the central area and started heading towards the outskirts of town.

Rune approached the town's church, but instead of heading inside, he went around back through a side gate. Through the gate, she saw a beautiful tree at the top of a hill. Teryn followed him and came to a stop when she saw something that made her heart sink. Rune stopped in front of a small headstone. Laying atop it was a satchel of letters tied together with a simple string, the words *To Tara* written atop them in Rune's familiar handwriting.

Chapter Thirty-One

Teryn

Teryn held Rune in her arms as he sobbed. His shoulders quaked as tears rained freely onto her lap. The girl thought back to all the times she had teased him about Tara's existence and immediately regretted every word. The only thing she could do now was to be his emotional support.

"It was me," Rune said after the sobbing subsided.

"That killed her? How?" Teryn's tone was full of concern and incredulity. She could not imagine how Rune could be responsible for his best friend's death. Not if he acted like this.

"There was a raid on the village a few years ago. We had just sent out a large shipment, which pulled several guards away from the town for a few days. A group of bandits struck while our pants were basically down." Rune shared the story with the occasional sob interrupting his words. "They made it past the walls within moments, but it still wasn't as easy as they expected. We are a mining town full of blacksmiths, after all. We are tough and have a lot of weapons just lying around.

"Anyway, Tara and I heard the sounding of bells. We were sitting together just under that very tree over there when we heard them. We didn't know what was happening and raced to her father's shop. We heard the screams before seeing the fighting. When we realized what was happening, we ran to her home even faster. They had a hidden cellar for incidents like that, so we thought we would be safe, but some bandits had already made their way into the building and were ransacking it. Tara's family were running away screaming, so we just ran with them. We tried to run towards my house, where my father was, but we were cut off."

Teryn rubbed Rune's back to comfort him as another round of sobs kept him from continuing. After a minute or two, he swallowed the lump in his throat and started again. Rune's normally strong demeanor was completely gone. Though it had disappeared frequently ever since the incident with the Wraith, it was still shocking to see how small someone like him could make himself in grief.

"There weren't a lot of them, maybe eight or nine at the most. But we were a handful of kids and the two adults were just merchants. The leader of the group also seemed to be some kind of Volari or Wanderer. I found out later he was a Flame-Weaver. His friends had a series of torches that they used to light some carts of hay on fire. The Flame-Weaver used that to surround us in a ring of flame, trapping us within. They turned it into some sort of makeshift fighting pit. They wanted to toy with us.

"I tried to rush the people that entered the ring, just to do anything that would let Tara escape. Father taught us how to fight, but one of the bandits knocked me aside in an instant. My entire world went black for a moment, but I somehow regained consciousness when I hit the ground. Tara rushed up to me, but I heard another person shout at the same time. The assholes had captured my sister and several other villagers as well and when I saw that...I lost my sense of self; consumed by a blinding rage.

"I grabbed Tara and shoved her behind me, to protect her, but she kept hold of my hand. She was shaking so much, Teryn. That was when something weird happened. The Flame-Weaver's fire flickered, threatening to go out. I think it caused him to panic, and he took what was left of the ring, gathered it together into a ball of fire he threw right at Tara and me. I remember the heat, the fear, the anger...then it all went black again. When I woke up, my father and several guards were there. The bandits...and Tara...were dead. Her body was unrecognizable, along with the two bandits who attempted to fight us, as well as the Flame-Weaver."

Teryn cradled one side of Rune's face and rubbed his cheek with her thumb. Rune leaned into her hand and cupped the outside of it with his own. "It wasn't your fault, Rune. The fire was..."

Rune tightened his grip slightly on the girl's wrist. "It wasn't the fire. I know now, I used the Area Disruption ability; most likely Area Drain as well... I don't know if you knew this Teryn, but Reavers... Professor Lylah told me we don't regenerate Aura naturally. We can only refill our reservoirs through our Drain ability. The bodies weren't burned beyond recognition, Teryn. They were husks. Tara was... My best friend, was unrecognizable. When we fought the Wraith, I saw the bodies...when I saw the corpses, I knew.

"Don't get me wrong, losing Dannon and Jeruul, having to kill what was left of them hurt me. But what really broke me was realizing that my best friend, a girl that I loved... I promised her, Teryn! I said I would become strong for her. I said I would come back and we would... I promised. But it..."

Rune stopped to take several deep, shaky breaths. His body fully pressed against hers, only kept up by her own strength. Rune continued, "My father must have convinced the others not to say anything. Maybe they just didn't see. They didn't know. Regardless, since that day, Tara's father has hated me, and rightfully so. He had to bury a corpse that looked nothing like his daughter, and it was all my fault. She clung to me to protect her, and I killed her."

Teryn's own eyes watered as well. She took Rune into her arms and cradled him against her chest, stroking his head gently. Both of them sat on the ground, wordlessly holding each other. Teryn's heart was pounding, but it was a conflicted feeling. It was impossible for her to deny that she had developed feelings for Rune. However, she was worried about the timing. A part of her hated herself for what she was doing, but...

Tara, please forgive me. I don't know how you felt about him, but I promise I will take care of him for you. She stood, pulling Rune with her. The two of them dusted off their knees, Rune wearing an inquisitive look in his eyes.

Teryn grabbed his hand and guided Rune through the town. Instead of heading towards Vickar and Lydia's home, they turned towards the entrance of Locke. Near the diminutive gates to the town was an inn meant for travelers and traders. Inside was warm and comforting. The smell of food wafted from the kitchens as they prepared for dinner. The inn-keeper behind the bar top smiled and greeted the two.

Am I doing this? Really?

"What can I do for you? Oh, if it isn't Rune! Why are you here? Surely your parents didn't kick you out!" The man chuckled.

"One room, please," Teryn requested simply. The innkeeper's smile rose higher before they took on a slight blush. He seemed to mutter something like: "He's an adult now, I suppose." He passed a key to the two and pointed them up the stairs.

Rune maintained his confused expression from the walk, but that did not stop Teryn from guiding him here. It was not until she requested a single room in the inn that even he blushed in realization.

"Teryn, what are—" he began, interrupted by the locking of the door to the room.

"I figure you don't want to go home right now. And there's something that I've been meaning to tell you for a while," Teryn said softly. Her voice became quiet as it took on a gentle tone that was as smooth as silk. Rune gulped in response. She stepped closer to him and grabbed him by the hand, pulling him towards the bed. She sat on the edge.

"Teryn," Rune breathed.

His face was completely flush now, no longer able to hide his intense embarrassment. Seeing that he could actually make such an expression further increased the rapid thumping within her.

"Rune, we've been through a lot," she whispered. "I've been in love with you for some time. Before our date in the Hilden market. Until now, I did nothing. I said nothing. I did not want you to betray the mysterious childhood friend. I kept it to myself, intending to say nothing, but I can't anymore."

"Teryn, I..."

"If you don't feel the same, that's fine. I understand. We can rest, just like we do at the academy. I can bottle these feelings up again, if I need to. But I cannot stand a moment longer letting you keep yourself from moving on because of your perceived sins of the past.

"You had no control over what happened. There was no way for anyone to have predicted it. No one could have known, least of all a young boy and girl. But what I do know, what I am sure of, is that I love you, Rune, and I want you to love me, too. Even if only for a night."

Teryn could almost feel the heat pouring off her own cheeks. All of her existence begged her to run and hide from Rune's calm, kind eyes. She hated and loved that about him. Those beautiful hazel eyes had captivated her well before his Awakening. Well, before they held those strange purple rings. Reaver, Volari, Wanderer, human, it did not matter to Teryn what Rune was. As long as he was hers.

"Wow." Rune said. "I've always been interested in you, Teryn. I had a guess that you might have felt this way. You caught my eye. The night before the Greatwood incident, I almost joined you in the tent, but I held back. Something told me I didn't deserve to...

"You spent so long taking care of me. Protecting me. Staying with me. You could have...should have just abandoned me while I was useless. How could I not have also developed feelings for you? But I would be over the moon if you would have me. I will do my best to match your feelings, Teryn."

Teryn smiled gently. She slowly removed her armor, casting it onto the floor. Rune silently joined her. Once they had laid themselves bare to one another, she laid down and pulled Rune over her. Neither of them made another attempt to talk as Teryn cupped his face and pulled him in for a deep kiss that left them both breathless.

Ven

Ven stormed back to Rune's family home. Frustration, sadness, betrayal; a hoard of painful emotions smacked her all at once. Water gathered in the corner of her eyes, quickly turning into a flood down her cheeks. After Vickar had told them what had happened between Rune and Tara, Ven had immediately figured out where her friend had gone and what made him so empty-looking. She also felt like she had to find him before Teryn did, even though she had a massive head start. Unfortunately, Ven only found her friends as they entered an inn together while holding hands.

She felt a roiling uneasiness in her chest and a pain in her heart. Ven felt as though she had lost something important to her. *Why should I care?* she mentally berated herself. *They can do whatever they want. Besides, she was there for him when I wasn't...but it doesn't feel fair. I got to know him first. I fell for him first, and it's not like I'm Mom. I can't share. I refuse to share.*

These thoughts continued to plague her for the entire walk back, and by the time she went inside, she knew her eyes were puffy and swollen. There was no way to hide her feelings from her friends. Brick was the first to notice.

"Ven!" he shouted. "Are you okay? What happened?"

"Is Arkrune okay? Did you not bring him back?" Lydia asked, worried that something might have happened to her son.

"He is fine. Probably more than fine, I guess." Ven used a monotone voice as she answered Lydia's questions. "He and Teryn won't be back till morning. Ulma, can I stay in your room tonight? We will just meet them at the mines in the morning."

Ulma nodded affirmatively and took Ven to her own room while also showing Brick and Tayven to Rune's room.

After everyone had left the room, Lydia turned to her husband. "Well, Vickar, it seems our boy has grown up more than we thought."

"So, it seems, my love. He is almost a year into adulthood now." Vickar sighed. "Though I don't appreciate the drama he's created. I hope it doesn't endanger their party when they head to the mines in the morning. Such things can get complicated quickly."

Lydia nodded before giggling quietly. "I will say though, both girls are very cute. I don't mind either of them being my daughter-in-law."

Vickar shook his head at his wife's antics. He knew she was trying to make light of the situation, but he was not so blind as to ignore that it held a hint of truth. "I have to admit, I am impressed my son caught the attention of two beauties. I could give him some advice, but I think I'll let him figure this one out on his own. If he wants to make adult decisions, he's going to have to learn some of them have consequences."

Ven stepped back into the hallway and observed their conversation, but decided not to say anything. She simply turned and followed Ulma to her room, hoping things would be better tomorrow. Rune would wake up in the arms of some other woman, but it would just be business as usual... *right?*

Henner

Archpriest Henner walked through the halls of the royal palace with a confident look on his face. The guards and servants he passed each took a moment from their duties to bow, which only fanned his feelings of superiority. Two weeks had passed since ownership of Guldin and Guldin Castle had been granted to the church, and by extension, him. As the head of the Crucidian Church, he already held a position of great power in the north, but land rights granted on top it legitimized the church's strength in the eyes of the people.

Of course, the church already had control over both areas and had been taking advantage of it. The bloodlines of the residents of Guldin were important to them and presented a useful tool in future endeavors. One particular individual had emerged a handful of years ago that presented an exceptional opportunity. They were the reason Father Gelroy had conducted a cleansing of the castle near Guldin.

Even though Henner's request to build a holy order of knights had only just been granted, it was a poorly kept secret that they had been laying the groundwork for years under the guise of training guards to protect the church's assets. These 'guards' were, in truth, highly trained knights that merely waited for legitimacy. Those same guards would now simply become officers in the newly founded Holy Order.

I imagine some of the southerners will regret their decision to decline my gracious offers to help in the past. Now, they will receive nothing. Soon, Lestreus will come to the right decision. Then we can move forward. Henner laughed quietly.

Many knightly families in the north were supporters and believers of the Crucidian faith, so they made quick moves to have sons, daughters, and retainers transfered from their existing posts in other knight commands into the Holy Order. In a few short weeks, the Holy Order numbered almost twenty-thousand strong. At least two thousand of them were Awakened and Wanderers, who had rejected the Path of Volar for the church's righteous faith, proving that even the cretins of Volar could be brought to the light.

Henner approached a large set of wooden doors that led to the king's personal library. The guard at the door bowed to the Archpriest and opened the door for him to enter.

"Lord Henner," King Leonidas greeted without looking up from the paperwork on his desk. "To what do I owe the pleasure?"

"My king, I beg your pardon, but I bring news of unfortunate rumors that simply must be addressed." Henner bowed. "I fear that the faithless Lord Erich Nefera is making moves to betray the kingdom."

"I fail to see how his faith matters to me, Lord Henner." Leonidas eyed the fat priest suspiciously. "And what moves is Erich making that warrant such bold claims?"

"My king, you are aware of the disinheritance of his bastard son. This, of course, is understandable. He is far removed from the line of succession. But he also has decided to hide his four heirs in Fort Black with that blasted Kyndra."

"And? What should I care if Erich send his sons to that castle of death?"

"My king," Henner's voice was measured and careful. "It is well known amongst the nobility that Lord Nefera acts as the voice of the southern half of the kingdom. I, and those who attend your daily court, fear that the rumors of his impending betrayal are true. He no doubt has plans to incite rebellion. To secret his heirs away to a place that we do not hold sway... It is a bold and curious move for someone who is innocent. I think it worth it to invite him here to be questioned, or at the very least, reaffirm his loyalty to the crown. If not, other houses may act on their own regarding this information."

"And how would they have found out this information, Lord Henner?" King Leonidas sounded tired, but did his best to maintain his demeanor.

"As the head of the church, I act as the representative of the church's holdings and lands. My subordinates are all over this great nation, including within the walls of the city of Nefera. It is only natural that any information they obtain is forwarded to me. Now that I have a station that places me alongside nobility as a peer—what with ownership of Guldin Castle—I must rely on my new peers regarding how a noble should react to these kinds of things. As such, it is only natural I ask the other nobles for advice before I confront these concerning rumors."

"I see."

Henner eyed the king before speaking. "Your Majesty, as you well know, as we've been approved the resources to expand the church's influence and been providing with the tools to defend our faith, you might know the southern houses have increased in their anger. I believe many to be...too prideful to back off. When considering how he frequently entertains the southerners at his own home...perhaps one might view Lord Nefera as holding all the responsibility. After all, who is to say he hasn't been the one fanning these flames all this time? Has he once invited a northern peer to these dinners? The crown itself, or a representative of yours, my liege?" Henner made sure to particularly stress the implication behind the world 'all.'

Leonidas eyed the priest up and down, as if trying to discern the man's intentions, but Henner's body language gave about as many hints as a stone.

Still, Henner continued, "You are looking for a scapegoat, are you not, my liege? Something to give the southerners a chance to back off? If Lord Nefera is found guilty of treason during his questioning, then his death may well act as a threat to them. They may take his death and charges as the head of this potential 'rebellion' and let the blame be buried along with the man's corpse."

King Leonidas Faradin was similarly unreadable. "They would not just rally behind Lord Nefera. Lord Jelmoore is an equally powerful symbol. They may simply rally behind *him* and we have done nothing other than further fan the flames."

Henner smiled. "Would they? Lord Dethras Jelmoore is a man in his seventies. He has no wife. No living children. No heirs to his lands. Upon his death, it will be up to the crown to install a new lord over the city. Rallying a rebellion behind an elderly man who may not wake tomorrow morning is a risk I highly doubt anyone will take."

"I understand. Then I shall order Lord Erich Nefera to bring himself before me. You are dismissed, Lord Henner. And thank you for your...concern for the kingdom's stability."

Henner bowed deeply to his king, though it was less about respect and more to hide the smile that had formed on his face. He quickly left the room to return to the church. Though he was now the representative of Castle Guldin, his primary responsibility was that of the Archpriest of the Crucidian Church and as such, he kept himself at the temple in the capital. When Henner had finally entered the temple grounds, he spoke to the shadows.

"Let our assets in Jelmoore, Nefera, and Uldera know it is time to make moves. Return Prince Lestreus to the fold. Also, after finding out who that Reaver's father is, I can almost guarantee that bitch Halthra is watching the child, so avoid contacting him."

"It will be done Lord Henner," a series of voices affirmed in unison. A moment later, the priest could tell he was alone again in the courtyard.

Wind gently blew through the leaves above as the man spoke to himself, *Lestreus, I figured you once for a brat not even worth the energy to think of, but, as long as the pieces fall appropriately, the mouthpiece the royal family bestowed upon the church will instead become a figurehead. We can bestow on you our strength, introduce you to the girl. I will proclaim you as our shepherd and our flock will follow. We will create a new empire. One that recognizes the truth of our faith. On top of that...*

Henner pulled his Aura Lamp from his pocket. An example of technology the Volari excelled at, yet refused to share with the wider public. To hide such things away from others was a direct affront to the Goddess of Innovation. Their worship of a permanent death in violation of the truth in the Goddess of Reincarnation... *Heathens, the lot of them.*

Chapter Thirty-Two

One's life may be destined for a certain beginning and a certain end, but how you travel the distance between those two points in time is something Lady Fate allows you to choose for yourself.

- Excerpt of Arkrune vys Volar's speech delivered during the founding ceremony of the Volari Kingdom

Rune

Teryn held tightly to Rune's chest while she released slow, contented breaths. The first time this had happened there had been worry and surprise... and a hangover. They also had not actually done anything. This time, as far as Rune remembered, a number of things had happened and he remembered everything that led to the lovely scene.

Rune was always aware of her beauty, but it was not until last night that he had allowed himself to really view her in any romantic sense. Now those thoughts consumed him. Months of frustration released all at once. He brushed a strand of hair out of the girl's face, waking her. Teryn yawned and looked up at him with her eyes shining slightly.

"Good morning..." she mumbled, blushing all the while. A similar heat rose in his own cheeks as he realized neither of them were clothed.

"Um...yeah. You too," Rune replied with a nervous cough. "Should we talk about..."

"Absolutely not. At least, not yet. We have a job to get to, and I think we might be late."

The pair quickly got out of bed and dressed before heading down to the main floor. The innkeeper had a smirk on his face as he relayed to them that a message was left for them. Their friends were waiting at the mine entrances for them. Now that a bartender knew what happened, soon all of Locke would. It was in that moment the realization his parents would find out hit him like a ton of bricks.

Teryn eyed him impatiently while he slowed to a walk and ruminated on ideas for avoiding an awkward talk with his mother. Teryn yanked Rune by the wrist and darted through the dirt roads of Locke. He verbally guided her along the paths to the specific entrance they were to meet at.

According to the information relayed, the Rock Goblins had moved into the actual mines a few days before the party arrived and chased out the miners. Dozens of different mines were maintained by the village, so losing one did not impact output or daily business by much. However, a wound left open would soon fester. They needed to oust the creatures before their numbers grew and the threat level raised or they started attacking the villagers.

It only took fifteen minutes to get across the village and reach the entry point, the slowest part of the trek being the roughly carved steps leading up to their destination. Tayven, Brick, and Ven were already waiting for them. Ven had a familiar irritated look plastered on her face, her arms crossed and foot tapping. Tayven and Brick looked away from the pair that had just arrived.

Before Rune could speak up, Ven cut him off. "You two are late. Care to explain why?"

"Not particularly," Teryn responded coolly. A staring contest erupted between the two as neither wanted to give ground.

"Whatever. I don't particularly care what actually happened. Why you mysteriously didn't return to Rune's home. Or why you holed up at an inn rather than sleep somewhere for free," Ven explained. Despite her words, Rune had a feeling that Ven did, in fact, care very much. "What I do care about is that you were late. We owe the client our prompt response. One night of rest after travel is acceptable, but you should have arrived first thing in the morning, not need us to come by your stupid inn to leave you a reminder of where to meet and when."

Us? Wait. If they all delivered a message to the inn, then that means they...

Ven intended to keep her lecture going, but was cut off by a hefty cough that came from a burly, bearded man. Rune immediately recognized him as one of the mine foremen. He was always a straightforward man—a necessity, given how many people depended on his leadership.

"Right, well y'all are here now, so s'fine. Hey, kid," the man said. Rune nodded with a smile at the greeting. "So, what we got is an infestation. When we filed the request, the bastards were just goin' after our rubble piles at night but stayed further up the cliffs. The day before y'all arrived though, they moved into the mines. I imagine they wanted a space of their own for protection."

Brick chimed in with a question, "What do they need protection from?"

Rune answered instead of the foreman. "It's Wyvern breeding season. They nest in the deep caves and crevices high in the mountains, but they come out during breeding season. That's probably what pushed the Rock Goblins to come so close to the village in the first place. Believe it or not, we get more issues from the forest than the mountains."

"Do we have to worry about a Wyvern attack?" Tayven asked. Nervousness hovered beneath his tone, which was to be expected since Wyverns were S-Rank monsters. Thankfully, Rune could decisively wave his friend's worries away. Red wyverns—the ones that lived in the Wyverntooth Mountains—were not aggressive by nature. They were protective, territorial, and rarely left the peaks in which they lived. They spent most of their lives on the highest mountaintops, feeding off the various creatures that also lived there, like Shatterhorns, Rock

Goblins, and Yetis. Wyverns were disinterested in humans as a source of food too, because the amount of effort required to hunt them was not worth the energy gained during the feeding. Put simply, most humans were not meaty enough for them.

This news put everyone other than Rune and the foreman at ease because Rune and the foreman had not had any worries to begin with. Rune also explained what the party was going to face.

Rock Goblins had tough skin with random bumps along their bodies that were as tough as studded leather armor. They were bipedal and used weapons made of sticks, stones, and twine. While the weapons were crude and the monsters themselves weak, the creatures could still be deadly. They could see in the dark and used a rudimentary form of communication that consisted of grunts and clicks to coordinate attacks.

Once Rune ran through what they could expect, the foreman gave the party a map of the tunnels. It was a shallow mine, being one of the newest, but having a map made the job much safer.

"Everyone ready?" Tayven asked. As the son of a noble house, he had been the named as First Light's leader. He tried to give the honor to Rune because of the rank difference, but the latter was not in a reliable mental state to take on such responsibilities. After the decision was vetoed, they elected Tayven as the next most capable.

Rune shivered. First Light entered the mines cautiously. It was a welcome reprieve to get out of the biting air. Winter winds higher in the mountains were harsher than below.

Being entirely man-made and only recently dug, there was a single primary shaft with several smaller shafts branching off it. The plan was to travel the main shaft and when they came to a branch, three of the party would head down the shaft to ensure it was clear while two stayed at the entrance of the branch and kept watch to ensure they would not be unpleasantly surprised.

The first branch was only a few hundred feet past the entrance. Rune, Ven, and Brick went down it, leaving Teryn and Tayven behind. The Volari's

Plant-Weaving would not be all that useful inside a mountain, but she was well-practiced in the saber on her hip when necessary.

Brick led the group with his fists up and ready. Rune took the middle and Ven kept up the rear. She had readied twin daggers, with one meant for her primary grip in the left hand and one built for a reverse grip in her right. The twenty minutes it took them to reach the dead-end of the branch was fraught with anxiety, but it ended up being for nothing. They returned to the two guarding the main shaft and moved along to the next.

The group switched up who scouted and who guarded so that everyone practiced various skills. The guard group also served an additional purpose, which was watching to make sure no monsters got past them and entered an already cleared branch. The only light they had was a handful of torches between them. Several lanterns hung along the walls, but they had either been destroyed by the monsters or had burned out their fuel.

"Rune," Brick whispered, "are you sure it was wise to do what you did?"

"What do you mean, Brick?" Rune answered. He continued to scan the surroundings. It appeared clear, but he did not want to let down his guard for even a second. His full concentration was on keeping watch, so he did not fully process what Brick had said.

"You did not return to your home last night. Ven was in tears. And you spent the night alone in an inn near the front gates. I do not believe I need to spell things out... but in the off chance I do, Ven also has feelings for you. I worry about this affecting the party," Brick answered. His voice took on a harsher tone than the large man usually used. "Especially so soon after we formed. She spoke of you often and fondly. I don't want to discount what you and Teryn went through, nor the time you spent together, but I figure it important for you to be aware."

Rune groaned quietly. Now was not exactly the time to have a conversation, but Brick did not seem to be in the mood to let it drop. "It won't impact how I interact with the party. Ven is still a close friend of mine and I trust her, but if she doesn't feel she can work with me...then I will leave. We can discuss it after we finish the job, yes? Sure, it will prevent you from taking jobs again as a group until next year, but that would be preferable to dying from a mistake caused by jealousy."

Brick relented and allowed the topic to drop, for which Rune was grateful. Ven came out of the shaft first with a look on her face far worse than the scowl she had entering. Teryn followed with a similar look. Rune's heart sank, worried they had gotten into a fight. His fears were exacerbated by Tayven who had the same look as the other two.

"Found what they used as a waste pit. Glad we were hired to kill, not clean..." He gagged. The scent of decayed meat and other unspeakable materials followed the group out of the shaft. *Don't know if that's better or worse than the possibility of them getting into an argument.*

Brick and Rune looked apologetically at their friends and continued to the next shafts. Four hours later, the group came to the last branch at the end of the main shaft. They had all found signs of habitation by the Rock Goblins, including a few more waste pits, some signs of nesting, and an area where they appeared to be stockpiling food. It was shocking they had filled the mine with such a large amount of waste and foodstuffs in only a day or so of time.

"This is a small mine?" Ven asked, rolling her shoulder to release some tension.

"Yes. The mountains are massive. Even if someone were to tunnel straight through to the capital, the trip through that tunnel would take several days." Rune answered.

"You could fit most of your village in here if you wanted," Teryn determined.

"The primary one at the base of the mountain could probably fit all of Hilden, buildings included," Rune proclaimed. His statement drew a few wide eyes. "Alright, that's enough. Here we are."

As they approached the final branch, First Light grouped closer together. Without the risk of being approached from behind, it was better for them all to continue. Per the map they had been provided, this last tunnel led to a larger antechamber that was going to serve as a nexus for future expansions. It was decided they would keep the formation of two and three, with two following about twenty feet behind the group of three. Brick, Teryn, and Rune grouped together to form their front, while Tayven and Ven held up the rear.

The group pressed forward for what seemed like another hour. Not that this shaft was so much longer than the rest to increase travel time by that much. Rather, it was the fact that everyone was being exceptionally cautious. Since the rest of the mine was empty, it meant that the monsters had to be in this one. It also meant that the creatures were preparing for an attack and had huddled their forces in one place.

This was not typically the tactic that Rock Goblins would use, which concerned Rune greatly. The only reason he could think that they would combine strength for a single attack was because they were protecting something. A monster with something to protect was much more dangerous depending on how important it was.

Soon, the frontal assault group broke into a large open room that was several hundred feet in diameter. There was no light in the room other than that which came off the small lanterns the group carried on their hips. They had found a few undamaged in one of the earlier shafts and started using them. They were much safer than torches.

Chittering, clicking, and grunts reached their ears from the opposite side of the dark space. Lantern light reflected off dozens of eyes in the darkness.

Rune stowed his normal sword and reached for his altered one instead. He had been planning on conserving energy by using his normal sword without enhancement, but with the number of eyes they saw gathered, it was no longer an option. The atmosphere was dense with the tension between First Light and the Rock Goblins, but no one made moves until two more people approached from behind.

Tayven and Ven closed the twenty-foot gap they had left between their two groups. Tayven winced once he saw glowing eyes in the darkness. Teryn stepped behind the group, near Ven. Her job as a middle guard was to act as a stop-gap for anything that tried to get to their archer. She shoved her hand into a small satchel on her side, then pulled out a metal rod with a copper-like hue to it. It was a Volari invention known as an Aura Lamp and when the ambient Aura in the air was fed into it; it glowed as bright as a dozen torches. Of course, this feeding required someone to actively direct Aura into it, thus occupying one of Teryn's hands and some of her concentration.

When the light rod's illumination reached its apex, the Rock Goblins made their move. Ten of the largest ones charged them. Each creature stood nearly six feet tall. Their limbs were spindly yet surprisingly strong, and they had bulging pot-bellies. Brick, Tayven, and Rune rushed forward to meet them. Ven stepped to Teryn's side and switched to her bow, now that she had ample room in the large space to maneuver the weapon. She provided covering fire for the boys from the back.

Three of the initial ten fell quickly to Ven's arrows, but the other seven continued their attack. Makeshift clubs created by sticking sharp rocks into thick branches were clutched in the clawed fingers of each creature. Brick smashed his fists together, creating a quick flash of purple light where they met. He had silently enhanced his fists and arms to increase his melee power. A second later, a similar light appeared beneath his feet as he momentarily enhanced his legs to propel himself at two of the monsters.

Brick's trajectory would have taken him between the two. However, just before he blew past them, he reached out his arms. The creature's faces were enveloped by his massive hands before he slammed them into the rocky floor. Blood pooled beneath their now cracked and shattered skulls. A third tried to catch him unawares, but before reaching the massive brawler, it found an arrow blooming from its neck.

Tayven took two while Rune took another two. They separated a little from Brick, but Tayven was still within a second's reach of his friend. Rune had carted his two opponents a few dozen feet away so his Area Disruption did not affect his friends. While he had learned to control and turn off his Area Drain ability thanks to his inherent knowledge of a standard Drain, he had yet to master the disruption one. As it stood, Area Disruption remained constantly active.

Thankfully, unless it was actively countering Aura abilities or manipulation, it did not actually use any of his reserves.

Rune's Area Drain also had two forms. If he silently activated the skill, he would constantly drain small amounts of Aura from creatures around him he perceived as enemies. However, if he spoke the skill aloud, it would activate only momentarily and drain Aura from every living thing around him for a few feet regardless if it was friend, foe, or neither. Not that it could kill anyone, but it certainly hurt.

Area Drain activated, increasing the amount of information Rune took in from the environment. His senses heightened and body felt more responsive. While in this state, the Aura he drained from his opponents would gradually weaken them and strengthen himself. He had thought that adrenaline caused his sharpened senses and increased strength in his past fights, but it was this ability that fed on his enemy's strength.

Two Rock Goblins chased after him at first, but after six of their number fell in short order, additional fighters stepped forward. Now Brick was surrounded by five new enemies, while Tayven had gained an additional three. Thankfully, Tayven seemed to have already killed the first two.

Rune was surrounded by five as well, but the increased numbers did not scare him. In fact, more opponents worked in his favor. *More monsters. More power.* An unfamiliar, dark thought flashed through him. Rune activated his alderite sword with a sly smile. Something in him had clicked into place after coming back home. He had accepted himself for who he was and he had friends and family who did the same. The sounds of the rocky floor crunching beneath every step, the gibbering grunts of the goblins, and the sounds of his allies fighting nearby... For the first time in a while, he was feeling excited.

The closest two finally caught up to him. He deftly dodged a swing from one's club and redirected the second one's attack into his comrade with a deft flourish of his sword and a sickening crunch. A garbled scream accompanied a flash of red and white as the impact ripped into the monster's collarbone.

Rune took advantage of the confusion to perform an upward slash at the back of the injured goblin. He carried the momentum into a small spin, turning around and smashing his buckler into the side of the second goblin's face. Neither were dead, but they were momentarily stunned, with one permanently disabled. The other three charged and surrounded the tricky invader. With their modicum of intelligence, they understood that numbers usually equaled advantage.

Rune's smile widened. He leaped behind the goblin and smacked it with his shield. Once he landed, he kicked the stunned goblin in the back and sent him flying towards his friends, breaking their charging momentum. The young man took advantage of the additional confusion to finish the bleeding goblin by removing his head with a quick swing.

Gods, I forget how amazing my father is at making these things, he mused as the blade cut through the goblin's tough hide like a hot knife through butter.

Now only a group of four, the remaining creatures gathered their senses before charging yet again. Rune dashed back to get a bit of distance. When he did so, he caught in his peripheral vision what the monsters were trying to protect, and it was the worst possible option. In the middle of the room, surrounded by three more monsters, was a group of ten much smaller monsters.

"Everyone!" Rune shouted quickly. "They grouped up to protect their young! Ven…" before Rune could finish speaking, the raven-haired girl had already caught sight of what Rune had called out. She released several arrows right as she heard her name.

The shouting of her name made a few shots miss, but at least three of the young goblins were struck dead by the barrage. As a result, the goblins that had seen the incident cried out in a pained rage. Their screams momentarily distracted the twelve fighters facing off against the boys. Brick released a painful grunt as a club glanced off his shoulder.

"Shit…" Ven shouted. "Might as well go all in now!" She unleashed a second barrage, releasing arrow after arrow, not really caring how much she missed. In less than a minute, the remaining young who cowered in the middle had perished. She cursed herself, now aware that Rune had meant to warn her not to target them.

With renewed vigor, the attacking goblins rushed at their targets once more. The three guardians of the young, now with nothing to protect, raged and joined the battle. One went after Rune, bringing his opponents back up to five, while two ran toward Ven and Teryn. Tayven was struggling with his three-on-one fight, barely keeping them from overwhelming him. Brick was also slowing down after reducing his number back down to only three. With them all distracted, no one blocked the two charging Teryn and Ven.

Rune had to quickly make a dangerous decision. He could not help either Brick or Tayven. Teryn and Ven should have been able to handle one each, but he was barely keeping the attention of the five facing him. If any broke off, the closest would be the girls, and since Ven was the one responsible for the death of their young, it was highly likely they would go straight to her, anyway.

Fuck it. I'll have to use it... Just have to be careful, Rune thought before shouting, "Teryn, if you see any signs, do it."

He could not see if Teryn understood his request, but a moment later, the skeletal handprint on his neck changed from its off-color tone to jet black. Rune flexed his left hand and met the goblin charge. He planted his hand firmly on the front of the leader's skull. "Drain."

Black scars stretched along the monster's skin, emanating from where his palm was planted. It howled in pain, giving the other four a momentary pause. The scars grew in size quickly becoming deep crevices in its skin before its body crumbled into a black dust. Power coursed through Rune's body. The world became clearer. His friends' and enemies' movements slowed to a crawl. Faster than they could recover, he wrapped his fingers around the neck of another goblin. After the second monster crumbled to dust, he panted, not from exhaustion, but from an odd hunger. Strangely, the darkness of the room faded away as his world took on a shifting series of colors, all different hues of hues of purples, from nearly white to almost black. The river from his dreams flashed through his mind.

Is this the world as a Volari sees it? Rune pondered as he carelessly severed the head of a third goblin. A desire to continue using Drain itched in the back of his head. It hungered. It wanted more. Death for strength. Rune gritted his teeth as he repressed the urge to devour. Within seconds, he dispatched the fourth and fifth goblins, finding them suddenly as dangerous as children. Ven and Teryn had to enter the melee with the enraged monsters that had made it to them, but Rune's priority was to help the rapidly overwhelmed Brick and Tayven.

"Enhance: Rush!" A wave of light burst from beneath his feet, followed by a cloud of cracked stone and dust. With a single step, he seemed to materialize on the other side of the room with his sword dripping with blood. Brick's jaw threatened to hit the floor as two of the goblins before him lost their heads. Before the skill ended, Rune moved to help Tayven. Unfortunately, Rune had only enhanced his lower body, so the force of the impact turned his arms to jelly and he lost the ability to grip his sword.

The weapon clattered to the ground mid-rush, so Rune improvised and placed his shield in front of him. He bashed directly into two of the goblins facing Tayven. The speed of the attack turned the first one into paste, while the second one was flung in one piece into the wall of the mine. All four limbs and its neck were bent at unnatural angles.

The webbing on Rune's neck, chest, and back vanished, but the skeletal handprint remained. More importantly, the shield bash dislocated his shoulder. Still unused to using these abilities, he was unable to reinforce his upper body once again, even if all he needed was enough to manage the recoil.

With the numbers evened out, the rest of First Light handily finished the creatures. Teryn rushed to collect Rune's sword and then seemed to teleport to his side to check on his condition. Brick and Ven did the same while Tayven stood back awkwardly.

"Um. Thanks for that. I guess I still need to figure out how to balance my Aura skills so I can last longer in a fight," the blue-haired one said shyly.

Rune yelped when Teryn reset his shoulder, and then comforted Tayven. "You were trained as a knight. I know you are excited about using your Aura abilities. Just remember that your training also gave you skills just as, if not more, useful as those given to you by your class. Balance is key, my friend."

"Ha," Ven scoffed. "Good advice, but might I give you some? Try not to overwork yourself. I know you're just as excited as him to use your own powers…"

He winced at his own word pointed back at him. She seemed upset about the risk he took. It was only fair. Rune ended up slightly injured. Ven also gestured to her neck. It seemed they all saw his gift from the Wraith showing up more noticeably. Teryn nodded in agreement with an angry expression, though behind it was one of genuine concern.

"You are right, Ven," Rune said with a wince at rotating his shoulder once Teryn finally let go. "I just saw that a member of my party was in danger, so I moved before I could think. Say… anyone have any ideas about how I explain this thing to my mom?"

Everyone laughed at his expense. Having known Rune's mother for only a short time, they could not claim to know her well, but they all easily realized that the woman babied her son. Ven patted Rune's good shoulder solemnly before shaking her head, confirming that he was indeed on his own.

"Great…"

Chapter Thirty-Three

Erich

Erich Nefera stood in the center of a large, circular room surrounded by men in luxurious chairs. Directly behind him was the entrance he had been escorted through. Before him sat a red-headed man with a flowing cloak and a golden crown. King Leonidas looked down at the man with some form of pity in his eyes. Standing slightly in front of the king was a rotund man that Erich immediately recognized to be Archpriest Henner.

Erich had originally entered the room with his own guards, but they had been escorted away by the king's knights. Another came up and placed iron shackles around Erich's wrists and feet. They rattled as he turned slightly to observe the faces of the hundreds of nobles in the room. Only a handful were landed and possessed any sort of economic power, but as members of the northern nobility, even those who were unlanded still held great political influence by regularly attending the king's court.

Erich thought about the fact that he might have been one of their lot if he actually cared to attend the court's daily proceedings, or even if he simply sent an attendant in his stead. After he glanced about, he realized he knew several of the faces quite well. Many of them were knightly families who resided in the areas around his own city. Several others had frequented his home and dined with his family. Of course, none of the participants of this court were from the southern territories.

Those who lie with snakes should expect to be bitten one day, I suppose. I was aware of this, though, he mused.

"Lord Erich Nefera, son of Lady Jaleah Nefera and Lord Ferond Nefera. You find yourself before the great King Leonidas Faradin, first of his name. Greet his majesty," a high-pitched voice called out. It came from a weasel-looking man who was the personal attendant to the king.

"Your Highness, King Leonidas Faradin, I, Lord Erich Nefera of the city of Nefera, greet you. May the gods provide health and prosperity to your family," Erich responded with a bow accented once more by the chains around his wrist. Several nobles stifled laughter at seeing a powerful man such as him bound helplessly.

"You stand here charged with the crimes of Treason and Incitation of Rebellion Against the Crown. What say you regarding this charge, Lord Erich Nefera?"

Sneers broke out across the room. Despite not being told the reason for his summons to the capital, he had figured that this would be the outcome. Erich scoffed. "I would like to say, these allegations are slanderous lies meant to do nothing but placate the assholes who wish to see me kneel before the headsman. But since I can't say that, I'll instead say: I deny these charges laid against me."

A thunderous roar echoed throughout the chamber as the nobility screamed at Erich's words.

"Traitorous coward!"

"A mongrel not fit to beg before His Majesty!"

"Die a dog's death, you heathen!"

The angry cries did little else other than bring a small smile to Erich's face. While he could not do what he would like to have done, like physically slap the pompous bastards that surrounded him, he could verbally irritate them. The king's attendant put both his hands in the air, demanding silence, but none of the crowd listened to his whiny pleas. Moments later, Henner stepped forward and put a single hand in the air, at which the entire crowd calmed almost immediately.

"Calm, my children and fellows. The God of Honor demands we protect the weak. Lord Nefera is a strong warrior, but while bound in chains, he has all the power of a child." While Henner's words had started out gentle, by the time he finished his speech, they dripped with the venom that suited a viper.

Erich glared at the priest before looking at the king. "I deny these charges," he repeated.

Leonidas showed a pained expression, masked by a forced smile. It was clear he did not wish to hold this farcical trial; however, he lacked the power to prevent it.

No, he does not lack the power. He lacks the spine. Once more, he bows to the whims of those around him. Of course, Erich thought as he declined to return the smile, leaving a frown on Leonidas' face. The attendant cleared his throat before continuing with the trial.

"It is noted that the accused denied these charges. The court will now question the accused on the evidence that has been brought before it. Lord Erich Nefera, you are to answer questions with a 'yes' or 'no' unless otherwise asked. Lord Henner, if you will?"

The priest stepped forward with a smirk on his face that screamed his confidence. Erich instantly knew who to blame for this and silently thanked the gods for the foresight he had in protecting his sons.

"Lord Erich Nefera, some say that you regularly host dinner parties at your castle in Nefera, is that correct?"

"Yes."

"And is it true that at many of these dinners you regularly host the southern nobility?"

"Yes, but I also extend the invitations to—"

"A simple 'yes' is quite enough, Lord Erich, thank you. Now, at these dinners, several members of your staff have informed us that the southern nobles complain to you about the king's policies as it relates to taxes and diplomatic relations with the...Volari."

Erich sighed. "Yes."

"I see. So, you have done nothing to stop these complaints. You let these slanderous statements not only occur, but you condone them."

"No."

"No? Then how is it that we have stacks of reports and copies of these invites to your 'dinners' dating back nearly a decade? Are you saying you do not host these parties?"

"No."

"So again, you do hold these parties, just as you admitted previously?"

"...yes."

"Very good, Lord Nefera. Please do try to be consistent with your answers. To do otherwise questions whatever integrity of yours remains," Henner hissed. The nobles around the room erupted into hateful cries before being settled by Henner's outstretched hands. "Then one might say you instigate treason by providing a stage for which these disrespectful and treasonous words to be shared amongst the nobility? We have it on good understanding that whispers of secession and independence are often shared at your dinner table."

"That is taken out of cont—"

"Erich, yes or no," Leonidas commanded. His sudden intervention in the trial ushered in a series of excited whispers and sneers among the nobles.

"Yes."

My guilt is decided. Everyone here knows this trial is flimsy. Better arguments are found in the mouth of a child caught sneaking food from the larder. There is no proof. I am simply to die. They will share my charges, but not the 'evidence'. But I knew this.

"Did you disinherit your bastard son and hide away your four legitimate heirs to protect your family name from your no doubt lost cause of a civil war?" Henner asked with a smirk.

"No!"

"Oh, but we have here a letter on your stationary announcing your disinheritance of your bastard Tayven. And we also have many accounts of your four heirs being escorted into Fort Black. Might I remind you, Lord Nefera, to tell the truth when answering the court's questions."

The knight acting as the guard keeping Erich in place kicked the back of his leg, dropping him to his knees before he struggled to stand back up. Laughter escaped the lips of several of the nobles, once again creating a loud echo from the high ceilings.

The trial continued on in this fashion for several hours as Henner continued to twist what was occurring to suit his own needs. Instead of acknowledging that Erich was simply trying to offer a place to have their concerns heard, it was instead framed as him trying to take the position the king held. When Erich provided a platform with which to speak, he was "fanning the flames of rebellion" instead of simply listening to people's grievances.

Everything that Erich did to prevent war was instead considered incitement. Nothing he said or did would have changed their minds. All the others wanted was to have the same rights, protections, and trade agreements as the northern territories. They only wanted to be equal and to do so without being shackled to the church as repayment for their "kind offers" made in the past.

"Any final comments to add to the record?" the weasel-faced attendant asked. Henner had returned to his original position near the king, having said his piece.

"I put forward that should the court find me guilty, that I alone take the blame for my actions," Erich said, glaring at the king. Leonidas sighed. Not in resignation, but in relief.

"I, King Leonidas Faradin, hereby proclaim that Lord Erich Nefera is declared guilty of the charges levied against him. He is to be sentenced to death for crimes against the Faradin Kingdom. His sons and family are stripped of nobility with no path to reclamation. Those who attended these 'dinners' are considered victims, swayed by the honeyed words of a rebel, and shall be granted the chance to repent without consequence. Let all in the kingdom know: Erich Nefera's guilt lies with him and dies with him."

The king waved his hand, and the knights escorted Erich out of the room. He thought they would have turned towards the dungeons. Before they could approach the doors it, they instead made another turn and headed outside where a large crowd waited.

The light of the day momentarily blinded Erich, blocking his ability to see how many people were present. From the sheer volume of the boos and cries for blood, he imagined it was quite a lot. After adjusting to the daylight, he saw a large wooden stage with a man wearing a black mask and holding a large axe. Erich had known this was what awaited him, but he had hoped they would have waited a few days at least.

It seems that the decision to kill me was made the moment they penned the letter requesting my presence. And here I thought they would imprison and torture me first.

People continued to yell and throw things at Erich as he was guided up the stairs to the headsman's block. The only dignity he had left was remaining in his formal garb; the proud emblem of his house still plastered on the cloak hanging from his shoulders. The knight kicked the back of his knee once more, forcing Erich to reflexively fall. He was guided downward by the shoulders, toward the groove where his head and neck were to rest. The stone was cold despite sitting in the sun, and it was stained with streaks of crimson and black. Remnants of those who had faced the axe in the past.

Stay safe, my sons. I love you. Erich prayed. An image of Tayven passed through his mind, *Keep him safe, Dethras, you old bastard.*

Erich Nefera felt a strange pinching sensation, but it vanished as quickly as it had appeared. The world seemed to spin momentarily as the crowd in front of him was replaced with birds flying above. The last thing Erich saw of this world was his own body being kicked aside.

Darkness overwhelmed his vision while his ears filled with the sound of a woman humming a beautiful tune alongside the rhythmic thrum of a washing board. A calm voice called out to him, "Hello again, Erich. Don't worry, she's waiting for you."

Kyndra

A group of ten people stood together in a small room with a single woman sitting at the end. She casually flicked, throwing knives at a wooden target across from where she rested. Each one silently impacted the target, although it should have echoed throughout the stone chamber.

"Well, then... you four are Erich's brats, huh?" the woman said sternly. "Don't look like much. But I owe the dumbass a favor, so welcome to Fort Black. The most dangerous place on the continent."

The four young men looked at each other nervously. All of them were rather well-built, having been raised to be knights from a young age. Each was an Enhancer as well, so they could amplify their impressive strength significantly. Yet the fear in their eyes told her they could scarcely imagine a world in which they could defeat her.

"Well? Any complaints?" Kyndra demanded.

All four men gulped and shook their heads no before the eldest spoke up. "Lady Kyndra vas Mithra, thank you for your hospitality, but I don't understand why we are here."

"Ah...wait a minute...Myrvin, right? The eldest?" Kyndra asked and waited for him to answer. After he nodded his head, she continued, "Your father asked me to watch you four. And good thing too, 'cause I just received a letter. He's dead. At that pig-faced Henner's command, too. Well, I imagine the words came from that piss-ant this country calls a king, but we all know who was really behind it."

"What! You lie, you witch!" the youngest of the four yelled. His name was Jarrod, and he was rather devout, so his opinion of the Volari was not very high. The poisonous words of the church had taken root within his immature heart.

"Careful, boy. I warned your father that you will be tasked with jobs here at the fort. Best keep your mouth shut before I send you on supply runs to our caches in the forest."

Jarrod paled and shut up rather quickly. The reason Fort Black was considered so dangerous was that its inhabitants regularly thinned the monster population in the Forest of Ruin beyond it. The weakest monster in the forest was B-Rank, but most were A-Rank. It was also quite common to come across multiple S-Rank beasts throughout the year. Death was all that awaited the young men if they left the fort's walls.

"The king sent a letter announcing Erich's 'betrayal' of the kingdom, preparing to incite civil war...blah, blah, blah, random bullshit," Kyndra droned. "To make a long and sad story short, your dad is dead and the kingdom is attempting to use him as a reason for the southern nobles to bow down by charging him with inciting nobles in rebellion. A show of force to indicate the kingdom's strength in the hopes the disgruntled southerners can throw the blame on a corpse and will back off out of fear. A simple plan, to be sure, but effective."

The four brothers were silent. When the woman explained the details of Erich's death, they understood the politics behind it. Myrvin asked if they could be excused to process the information. Kyndra easily dismissed them and had the room cleared.

Once the door shut completely, she threw one final knife at the target. Her eyes flashed the moment it struck. Unlike her previous throws, this time, the knife made a sound much louder than possible. The vibrations from it shattered the target to pieces, and the knives stuck in it clattered to the ground.

"If it wouldn't put Erich's bastard or my sister in danger, I'd just forget to stop a couple S-Class beasts from entering the kingdom..." She groaned aloud. "Suppose I shouldn't leave the fort for a while."

Kyndra remembered the discussion she had privately had with Erich after Vincent left. She had met back up with her friend before leaving town and he took that time to warn her about this outcome. He also warned her that the southerners would back off should he be executed, but only for a time.

They would gather their strength during the momentary peace his death bought them and instead of rallying behind Erich, they would change their focus to Lord Dethras Jelmoore who had strong ties to the Volari queen. Eric predicted that the civil war would not be for independence but instead, a war of secession, with the southerners putting their strength behind Queen Halthra and defecting from the Faradin Kingdom to become vassals of Volar.

Dethras, being without an heir presents a problem. If he kicks it...it won't stop a rebellion, but it may hold one off for a few more decades.

Lestreus

The fourteenth prince of Faradin, Lestreus Faradin, sat in the personal office of the head priest of Jelmoore's Crucidian Church. During break periods, the prince would pray in the large church in the city's central district. It was here he also wrote and received letters from Archpriest Henner.

Originally, Lestreus could not fathom why it was so important for him to leave the Knight Academy and transfer to a commoner school. However, with time, the prince had realized Henner appreciated the boy's faith and efforts towards education. The archpriest put a lot of effort into providing for his needs in Jelmoore and even sent the prince extra funding and research materials. The library of the Vanguard was expansive, but it lacked the important holy texts Lestreus had been studying since he was a boy. Lord Henner had also fanned the boy's hidden desires for power.

After seeing the raw power that the Reaver possessed, Lestreus desired strength for himself. He knew such power would never be his because of his miniscule talent for Aura manipulation, but if he became king, then what would an individual—even one like that—matter against an army?

The most recent letters had asked for a bunch of information about that Reaver, which I happily provided. Now Lord Henner wishes me to ally myself with him. It will be difficult since he is friends with Lord Nefera's bastard, but I will do what I must. Having such a powerful tool supporting the church will be extremely helpful, he thought, while sipping a cup of tea.

The man in the gray robes had visited him earlier that day and asked the same question he did every week. This week, though, he had had an answer. Seeing the true power of an individual and being supported by Lord Henner, who praised the boy's intellect, he knew he needed to take power. The change he wished to see was to cast aside the fading neutrality his predecessors had kept over the last dozen generations.

Leonidas partnered with the church out of necessity and only on the surface. Truly, the cowardly man had no intention of making any moves on his own. He would simply let the church act as it wished. Not Lestreus. No, the Crucidian Church—Henner—offered a gift, and he would finally seize it. He wasn't his father. Lestreus would finally crush the followers of the Path of Volar and make its blind followers see the truth of the gods.

No more would they worship false gods such as Fate and Death. No, he would show them all the true gods. They would know the comforting embrace of the Goddess of Reincarnation. They would embrace the future and betterment of all of man, as the Goddess of Innovation desired. With the God of Honor's strength and the will of the God of Change, Lestreus would carve this very truth into the souls of the non-believers.

Soon, Lestreus thought to himself, *in just a year's time, two at most, the non-believers will be brought to face the truth, or die upon the blades of my kingdom. I will bring the south to heel, place loyal vassals over its lands, and make Volar mine. All of Vendreya will be under my supreme rule.*

Dethras

Dethras Jelmoore slammed his massive hand down onto his desk, leaving behind a spiderweb of cracks in the wood. Attendants and guards alike recoiled from a combination of surprise and fear. The lord did not notice this reaction for he was too focused on the series of letters that had just reached him. He had spent a few days hunting in the woods outside his city to relieve the stress of reading the missive that Erich Nefera had sent the nobles about his youngest son.

"That foolish, brainless, muscle-headed, good-for-nothing, waste of good air!" Dethras shouted. He did not notice the glances his employees gave each other when he used the word muscle-headed to describe someone other than himself. "Erich, you absolute buffoon. Why would you willingly enter that den of vipers? You should have ignored the king's summon..."

"My lord," the steward stated calmly. He was the lone individual in the room, unaffected by his master's tantrums. "Lord Nefera could not simply ignore a direct request by King Faradin. It would have been tantamount to declaring he is preparing for civil war."

"Bah!" Dethras spat. "Fat lotta good that did him. Idiot practically shouted he was prepared for war and death the moment he disinherited the only son he couldn't hide away in Fort Black. And now he's dead. Should have taken my suggestion and shirked Faradin's rule a decade ago."

"My lord, that is treason. Statements like that are what led to Lord Nefera losing his head. They may take yours next."

"Let them try." Dethras' steely gaze was accented by an odd pressure that quickly faded.

Dethras threw down the letters in his hand that detailed the execution of Lord Erich Nefera on the grounds of sowing discontent amongst the common people and inciting rebellion among the nobility against the crown. The elderly noble had seen this song and dance many times in his life, but it was the first time it had happened to such a high-ranking noble, let alone one of his friends.

He knew that King Leonidas did not have the spine to plan this alone, which meant someone else was pulling the strings.

His first thoughts immediately went to the pudgy priest, Henner. His people had been causing problems in the southern cities for years, and Jelmoore even longer than that. Since Jelmoore was the only city in which the island kingdom of Volar would allow ships back and forth from the Faradin Kingdom, Crucidian missionaries did everything they could to gain access to the island. Lord Jelmoore was good friends with the previous Volari king, so he had spent his entire political career trying to act as a barricade.

Erich was a good friend of Dethras' daughter, Vincent, and the Vanguard Commander, Kyndra. When he had taken power over his family's city, he moved that barrier north, which angered the devout northerners. It seemed they had had enough of being blockaded.

"Get a letter to Erich's boy, Tayven. Send a copy of the missive to the academy, Hilden and Locke. We will catch him somewhere. He deserves to know what happened to his father, and I would prefer it to come from me rather than rumor. Also, let him know I want him to meet me when he returns to the city."

The steward nodded. "You do not wish to write the missive yourself, sir?"

Dethras grunted. "No. I need to go hunting again...Erich... foolish boy."

Chapter Thirty-Four

Rune

First Light collected the signature for completion from the mine foreman after they helped him inspect the shafts. Once they ensured the job was complete, he happily signed off on their quest papers. Exchanging several greetings before leaving, the foreman quickly ran to town to tell the workers that they would start cleanup and resume work within the next few days. Cleanup was not part of their quest duties, so that would be left to the miners. Besides, the extra coin from processing the corpses would give the workers extra incentive to hurry back to work.

The fight was exhausting and the Drain ability had taken a lot out of Rune. His head pounded, but since he had purged a large amount of the siphoned Aura, it was only a mild headache. The mark was still present on his neck and he panicked at the thought of explaining it to his mother. His nerves were also on edge because he needed to have a proper discussion with Ven before they left town.

Soon, the group made it to Rune's childhood home. Outside, his sister and father were working the forge together, something that Rune had never expected from his sister, who had never had an interest in something so tiring and sweat-inducing. It almost felt like she had been blessed by the Goddess of Innovation herself, if the letters his father sent him were to be believed. Rune had a lump in his throat as his mother was outside hanging laundry up on a clothesline. A scene flashed in his mind of a woman next to a black body of water constantly pulling laundry from a never-ending basket. He shook his head clear of the image after he heard a faint giggle from the woman.

Lydia saw the group approaching, but her smile turned to a face of concern and worry when her eyes fell on her son, then the mark on his neck.

"What happened? Are you all okay?" Lydia shouted as she ran towards the party. Her shouts caught the attention of the two smiths who ceased their work to greet their family member and his friends. Lydia grabbed her son by the arms, which forced him to stifle a yelp. Though his arm was already popped into place, the rest of his muscles in his arms were screaming at him from the strain of his attacks without being enhanced.

"That is not from a Rock Goblin, son," Vickar stated plainly. His tone was dangerous, as if warning Rune to tell the truth.

"A few months ago—" Rune started.

Teryn put her hand up and interrupted, "Father, Mother. Rune and I were in a party before this. We, along with Master Vincent and several men, were chased into the Greatwood by a large group of bandits. There we were attacked by a Wraith. Rune received this wound when he saved my life. His injury is my fault."

Rune was left speechless by Teryn's words. Ven coughed, nearly choking in surprise at the Volari's forward speech. Lydia eyed the Volari girl carefully, as if appraising her fully. Vickar, on the other-hand slapped his son upside the head. "You fucking dumbass. You run from a Wraith, not charge it...but good job for surviving."

"Oh, sweetie...why didn't you tell us sooner? Why is the mark here now and not before?" Lydia asked. She had finished her appraisal of the girl who had tried to call her mother, but her face was unreadable at what her decision about it was. The only thing visible was the look of concern she had for her son. She pulled him into a deep hug, running a gentle hand through his hair.

Rune explained what had happened during the battle in the Greatwood, unable to escape his mother's embrace. He detailed what his Awakening had been like at the academy. Professor Lyla had guessed that the more Aura he absorbed, the darker the mark became. He also explained that when he overcharges his reserves and starts getting closer to Overheating, a black web-like marks cover his neck, face, and upper body.

Lydia, Vickar, and Ulma processed the information silently as they listened to Rune's explanation of events. Lydia looked to be on the verge of tears, while Ulma and Vickar maintained stoic expressions. After he finished explaining everything in great detail, Vickar finally spoke. "All of you are getting weapons."

First Light immediately glanced in Vickar's direction in surprise. It was one thing to get a custom forged weapon, but it was quite another to get one forged by a Metal-Weaving master smith. Tayven seemed doubly excited because once he had learned that Rune's father was Vickar. The noble explained that his father, Erich, had had a weapon made for him special by a Metal-Weaver named Vickar, who possessed the rare ability to manipulate alderite. As far as Tayven knew, all three commanders of the Vanguard in the Faradin Kingdom also carried weapons made by this master smith.

"S-s-sir, truly? Will you truly make us weapons?" Tayven stuttered, not even containing his excitement. He had hoped to buy even a failed project from Vickar's reject bin, but this was more than he could have dreamed.

"Yes. Besides. If any of you are going to stand a chance of fighting by my son's side and preventing him from going feral, you'll need the best. And failing that...you'll need something capable of killing what he becomes," Vickar answered solemnly. He cleared his throat. "Now, they will be suited for you, but I won't be going as far for them as I did for Rune. He is my son, after all."

He and Ulma then started collecting information from the group about what weapons they used and their preferred techniques. Teryn used a single-handed saber for quick attacks. Her fighting style relied upon speed and nimble movements while using her Plant-Weaving to trip up her opponents or to bind them.

Tayven used a longsword and shield. His style of fighting was a fairly standard style among the knights and nobility of the kingdom. Ven used a bow at long range and twin daggers up close, so Vickar would provide her with alderite versions of all three. Her current bow could actually be altered without being remade since Vickar had the idea of merely adding an alderite plating to the outside. Since the bow was made of wood, the intricate plating would look decorative when not being used and increase penetrating power and distance by double when she enhanced it. He also intended to give her a special bow string that used an alderite thread that would complete a full circuit through the entire weapon.

"Girl, do not, under any circumstance, let anyone know about this bowstring I will give you. If you need more, have Rune send me a letter," Vickar warned. "This is a secret Volari alloy made of alderite and a few other metals that, when mixed at the right amounts and tempered carefully, create a thread-like product. The kingdom does not know about it. If I find any of you leaked this outside of your party..."

Vickar's words hung in the air as his eyes flashed. Weapons around the smithy floated into the air, looming behind him. Normally, such a massive amount of inorganic material could not be manipulated at once. However, Vickar's Weaving abilities affected alderite itself, meaning he could control a lot more with a lot less effort.

All of First Light gulped simultaneously, including Rune, while nodding their heads. None of them wanted to incite the wrath of this not-so-simple blacksmith. Ulma appeared to have formed stars in her eyes when she saw what her father could do. Since she shared his abilities, a world in which she fought off enemies with a horde of hovering swords obviously flashed through her mind. Rune chuckled nervously, reading her like a book.

Rune already had a top-of-the-line sword from his father, so instead, Vickar opted to improve the shield attached to his son's gauntlet. The plan was to strengthen the bracing then move the buckler a little further back to allow complete movement of Rune's wrist, making it easier for his left hand to activate his Drain easier. This left Brick as the last one with special requirements. Tayven and Teryn would only need swords.

Vickar had a few ideas for the brawler. Most brawlers only settled for normal hand protection or opted for none since they relied on their Enhancer skills to strengthen the body. Vickar figured he could create a complex armored glove with linked finger guards connected by the same bowstring woven between the lightweight chain. He claimed this would allow for Aura to evenly flow through the alderite circuits woven throughout the armor.

"Alright, big guy. This will be the first of its kind...also it relies on a lot of delicate alderite work. Whatever you do never, ever hit something with these on unless you are Enhancing them. Otherwise, they'll shatter," Vickar warned. Brick enthusiastically acknowledged the instructions. He was excited to receive a one-of-a-kind piece of equipment, even if it meant being a bit of a test dummy.

"Alright then. Ulma, let's get to work. This is gonna take a while. Lydia, you come too. We are going to need some refreshments so we don't kick the bucket from heat stroke. Damn snow could at least be useful and cool off the forge a bit, but no..." Vickar eyed Rune carefully and flitted his gaze to Ven and Teryn. Rune nodded in understanding and silently thanked his father for pulling his mother away. Brick also noticed the interaction and pulled Tayven into town for some sightseeing.

Rune asked for the two girls to follow him away from the house to the training area he used as a kid. When the three of them arrived, Rune started the conversation. "Ven, I need to know, is this going to be a problem for the group?"

Ven looked slightly wounded at the way Rune worded it, but kept her temperament calm. "Is what going to be a problem? You screwing another party-member?"

"Ven..."

"Oh, please," Teryn chided. "You are just pissed off it wasn't you."

"Teryn could you not—"

"So what?" Ven said flatly. "Fine. I'll admit it. I wish it was me. So what? Is saying it out loud going to change anything? No, it won't. Don't worry, Rune, we are still friends. And Teryn...I don't hate you either. I don't want either of you to leave the party. Look, you're both strong and I trust you, despite how I feel in other ways."

Rune and Teryn stayed silent. He was honestly shocked she was acting so maturely. She had come a long way since they first met.

Ven continued, "I get it, though. You guys saw some shit. You fought a Wraith, lost your friends, and she got to be there for you after. I only knew Rune for a short while before heading off to the academy while you two spent months together. So, yeah, it hurts a little to lose out on the little crush I had. It's clear to me that Teryn feels strongly about you, Rune. I only ask you don't flaunt it in front of me, okay? Do that, and we are good."

"I promise," Rune responded, "We will do our best."

"Oh, and if we are camping outside the city, please keep it in your pants. I don't want to hear anything while on watch or something." Ven then turned to leave. Before she got too far, she sighed. "Thank you for actually talking with me about it, Rune. You know, instead of letting it fester. I guess I appreciate it."

Rune smiled awkwardly and Teryn huffed slightly. Before completely leaving though, Ven stopped and whispered into Teryn's ear something Rune could barely hear. "Watch yourself, Teryn. If you fuck this up, I'll be right there to pick up where you two left off... after I kill you for hurting him."

Rune

Vickar continued working non-stop, day and night, on the new equipment for his son's friends. Ulma helped most of the time, but Lydia insisted, to the chagrin of both the girl and her father, that she needed more rest for her growing body. Ven bunked with Ulma at night while Brick and Tayven took Rune's old room. Teryn and Rune, however, opted to stay at the inn near the gates instead of in the home. Occasionally, they would spend a few hours in town at the small market or visiting the church where Tara was buried. Every morning, they would arrive at the quaint home to spar and train with one another.

Tayven spent most of his time training with Teryn since she had a lot of practice with the instantaneous activation of her Plant-Weaving. This was something Brick also excelled at, but since he was a natural, he was a god-awful teacher. Brick's attempts to train his friend resulted in both of them having multiple bruises from the lessons turning to arguments, then to all out fist-fights.

Rune and Ven spent a few days hunting with the town's hunters on the outskirts of the Greatwood. Ven used this to practice her Pulser skills on moving targets to learn to control the strength of the shots to either make them large and powerful or small and weaker. Rune used this time to figure out how to turn off his disruption skill. He could not train it with Tayven, since Tayven needed to understand how to use his abilities with all of his power available, not some of it.

Eventually, Tayven managed to attenuate the power level of his Aura usage, which would allow him to fight longer. He was still working on instantaneous activation to conserve even more of his Aura reserves, but he had made a large amount of progress. By the time he had made that breakthrough, Vickar had also completed everyone's upgrades and new equipment.

"Who's ready to spar?" Vickar asked with an evil glint in his eye. Rune subconsciously felt himself sweat as a lump formed in his throat. The look on his father's face was one he had seen frequently as a child when he angered his father before a training session. As much as he wished, he knew there was no getting out of it.

"I'll do it!" Tayven called out excitedly. Rune said a silent prayer for him because the young noble had forgotten what they had seen Vickar do almost two weeks ago.

Tayven stepped up to face the blacksmith. There was a decent amount of snow on the ground, but they cleared out the sparring pit in advance. Vickar eyed the young man's equipment before selecting a quarterstaff with a thin blade on each end. Tayven looked confused because he expected to be fighting someone with the same style as Rune, since Rune had told them all that his father taught him everything he knew.

Rune apologized to his friend in his heart, because he never clarified that Vickar had taught him everything Rune knew, not everything that Vickar knew.

Tayven charged towards Vickar with his new enhanced longsword held in a striking position and his shield held up slightly. Vickar dashed to the side and attempted to circle around his opponent. Not wanting to lose sight of the enemy, Tayven pivoted on his lead foot in the direction Vickar had gone just in time to block the blade at the end of the staff with his shield.

Sparks flew as the blade glanced off the shield multiple times in rapid succession. It was all that Tayven could do to continue blocking while Vickar held him at length. Tayven was well within striking range of the blacksmith, but the constant attacks kept him from reaching Vickar with his longsword.

Having had enough of this game, Tayven shouted out, "Enhance: Power Strike!"

A burst of Aura flashed through the veins in his sword arm as he brought it down against the quarterstaff, smacking it into the ground. This created an opening for Tayven to jump forward at Vickar. Just as he brought down his sword against the smith, Tayven felt weightless. Suddenly, his vision was filled with a blue sky and white, fluffy clouds. Air rushed out of his lungs as he landed on his back in a small snow drift.

"Nice plan to smack my weapon away with force. However, you did not fully disarm me, so I could recover and sweep your legs from under you. You made sure to always pay attention to your enemy's eyes and body, but know where their weapon is at all times as well." Vickar informed Tayven before turning to the rest with the same wicked smile as before. "Now, who's next?"

Chapter Thirty-Five

Rune

Ven stepped forward to take her turn against Vickar in the ring. Rune's father chuckled as his eyes glowed. With a wave of his hand, an archery target floated out of the smithy. Around each of the three legs that made up its base was a band of copper-colored metal. The target hovered past Ven and continued another three hundred yards.

"Shoot," Vickar ordered.

Ven nodded and took aim at the target. She willed Aura to fill the bow by using the contact points built into the grip. Purple light flowed outward along both ends of the bow, like water in a channel. It then moved down the string until it met itself at the girl's drawing hand. Ven's eyes glimmered with excitement.

She slowly exhaled and released the string. The arrow flew toward the target three or four times faster than normal, the only thing visible was a streak of purple left hanging in the air. A loud crack echoed through the air like thunder. Vickar smiled in appreciation of his handiwork. He waved his hand yet again and pulled the target back again. As it approached, a few people let out a low whistle thanks to the smoking hole that used to be the central circle of the target.

"Great. Looks like it works. Take out your daggers, girl," Vickar demanded. He had already donned another set of equipment, this time a sword and shield.

The change-up from his previous weapon threw most of the group for a loop. Only Rune and Ulma were unfazed. Ven worked to clear her mind of the surprise as she drew the daggers. Vickar stood stark still while she advanced towards her opponent. Once she was in position, Vickar walked slowly towards the girl at first, but after he had closed the gap to about ten feet, he quickly charged her with his sword held out to the side.

Ven matched his pace and charged to meet him. She initiated a strike with the weapon in her left hand, but stopped after seeing Vickar initiate a strike as well. She altered the swing of her dagger to a more defensive position, then reinforced it with the second. The force of the blow lifted her slightly off her feet, but she used it to assist in a jump to the side. Before she could land, Vickar was already on top of her, this time with an overhead strike.

Ven immediately crossed her blades above her head, taking the moment to charge them full of Aura to increase their strength. Vickar's blade came down on the spot where the blades crossed. Her arms took the blow well enough, but her legs trembled after Vickar pressed the attack instead of backing off.

"Thanks to your dedication to the bow, your upper body strength can handle a lot. However, your core and your legs leave a lot to be desired. If you want to take blows like this, work on your lower body as well, or use speed to your advantage." Vickar coached. He refused to let up on the force, and Ven's legs threatened to give out. Just as she was about to collapse, Vickar finally relaxed the pressure. Taking advantage of the reprieve, Ven moved to attack, but Vickar brought a foot up and planted it solidly in Ven's gut, sending her tumbling backwards. The girl rolled a few times before coming to a stop.

"Next," Vickar stated calmly. To everyone else, his face was expressionless, but Rune could see the excitement in his father's eyes. He was having fun.

Teryn gulped, but stepped forward while Tayven scratched his head. "Quarterstaff, then a sword and shield...and he supposedly taught Rune. Where did this man learn to fight?" He was thoroughly confused, trying to determine Vickar's origins.

Teryn drew her saber against Vickar, who had replaced his equipment again, this time opting for a saber of his own. Teryn charged her new alderite saber with Aura while Vickar did the same. For a few moments, neither moved, as if assessing each other's stance. Teryn had already seen that Vickar could move in a multitude of different ways, but he had seen none of Teryn's capabilities since he had been away in the forge for the last several days.

The first one to make a move was Vickar. He ran towards his opponent in a wide arc instead of in a straight line. His sword was once again held out to the side, but this time, it was pointed at a forty-five-degree angle, with the blade edge facing Teryn.

In response, Teryn stepped to meet him. Her eyes flashed in concert with a subtle movement of her fingers. Blades of frozen, hibernating grass shook off the frost before they lashed out and wrapped themselves around Vickar's feel. The sudden trap caused him to stumble and fall. Against her expectations, instead of planting into the ground, he tucked into a roll. Four streaks of light flew from Vickar's body towards the girl. The lights pierced her armor above the shoulders and at her waist. Vickar finished the roll, coming back up to a standing position in a single move. Everyone looked on with wide eyes as he walked slowly towards his opponent, who was struggling on the ground against four small knives that had her pinned.

"Don't assume that every enemy will fall for your first ruse. Always have a backup plan in the event of failure. Continuing to use the grass to pull on my neck and lock me to the ground might have worked better." Vickar laughed. "Then again, maybe not."

He waved his hand and the four blades removed themselves from Teryn's clothes before floating gently into the belt around Vickar's waist.

"Also, never assume that an enemy's only weapon is the one you can see," he advised while helping the girl stand. He locked eyes with Brick and motioned for the boy to join him next.

Ven had watched the fight with Teryn closely. She also watched Tayven's fight, and of course, had her own. Some sort of pattern had stitched itself together in her mind. Other than his fight against Tayven, he was using fighting styles that their party also used. It was at that moment, things clicked into place.

"He's teaching us how to fight with our own weapons! This isn't just a test for our equipment, it is also a lesson!"

Rune sighed. "Yeah, he likes to exploit his opponent's weaknesses. Says it helps them learn to fix them."

When Brick stepped into the ring, Vickar pulled out yet another set of weapons, a pair of daggers very similar in design to Ven's. Vickar was very strong thanks to his time in the forge and the time he spent training, but Brick dwarfed him. This was almost like the fight between Vickar and Ven, other than this time, it was Vickar that was the smaller one.

Brick silently Enhanced his fists and gauntlets. Slamming his fists together, he created a flash of sparks and a small pulse of light.

"Alright, Sir Vickar, shall we begin?" he questioned before suddenly dashing at his opponent. Vickar stood still, waiting for the much larger man to approach. Sensing a trick, Brick slowed his approach before coming to a stop just outside of striking range of Vickar.

"Good. At least someone is learning."

Vickar changed tactics and made the first strike in this bout. Brick met the blade with his charged gauntlet. Sparks flew between the two as the blade met armored fist again and again. Neither man relented. After a constant barrage of heavy blows, Vickar began to sweat for the first time. Even he would wear out after so many back-to-back fights. Brick also noticed the fatigue and pressed his advantage. Rune had expected Brick to go all out, but he still held back, rightly assuming that this was a trap.

I bet Father could give Karl a run for his money.

The fight continued, Vickar was truly sweating now and being forced back again. This time, Brick had gained a bit more confidence and put more and more force behind each strike. He was not intending to go for a finisher, but to wear the competition into the ground and outlast him. On the final strike, Vickar let the dagger be forced out of his hand. Since the strike met no resistance, it threw Brick off balance. Vickar twisted and used the momentum of Brick's force behind the blow to increase the impact of his elbow into Brick's lower jaw.

There was a dull *thud* as the towering man fell flat into the dirt, unconscious.

"Well, that is that," Vickar said, wiping the sweat from his brow. "The kid really gave me a run for my coin. All of you would do well to learn from his patience, even in battle. I was sure he would take the bait much sooner. No notes for him, though! Even made me dip into using... well, I won't go into detail. Good work, everyone, truly."

Rune nodded solemnly. He and Teryn knew he was referencing the rare fighting form Rune was taught. Tayven went right up to Vickar, who was now gulping down an entire tankard of ale that his wife had brought him.

"Lord Vickar! How do you know so many fighting styles? That was insane. You showed us four different styles and I know there's a fifth since you taught Rune! Speaking of, why aren't you sparring with him? Surely there's one more fight left in you, Lord Vickar."

Everyone saw the stars practically twinkling in his eyes. Until coming to Locke, Tayven had acted the part of a quiet, well-mannered person of noble birth. Being around someone who he viewed as somewhat of a childhood idol let him cut loose with a bit of his childish side.

"Calm down, boy. Too many questions and most of them I don't feel like answering," Vickar complained. "And why should I fight Rune? I taught him everything I wanted to teach him already."

"You mean you can fight like all that Rune?" Ven asked.

Rune laughed. "Absolutely not. I could make due with daggers or a longsword, but a large shield, a quarterstaff, or a saber...not a chance. As for the bow, I can use it to hunt game, but any monster above E-Rank would be impossible for me. Don't have the talent."

Vickar laughed. It was important to the group's development that Rune so readily admitted to being inept at fighting outside of his specialties. Knowing that would help them avoid any inferiority complexes. Ven was almost doubting her worth on the team with how skilled Rune seemed to be, but knowing that she outclassed him in something helped boost her confidence. The same went for Brick and Teryn.

While First Light was chatting with Vickar and Ulma about their new equipment, a familiar face appeared several hundred yards from the house. As the man approached, Vickar's face darkened. "Vincent."

"Damn, is this guy everywhere or what...?" Rune muttered to Teryn, who giggled.

"Read the room, guys," Brick whispered. It was at that moment that Rune noticed Vincent's face was as unhappy as Vickar's was, but he was not looking at the smith. Tracking his eyes, Rune could tell he was staring at Tayven.

Tayven's relaxed demeanor dissipated in a flash as he returned to an upright stance. His demeanor also changed back and was no longer as carefree looking as he had the last week or so.

"Relax, Vickar, I'm not here for you," Vincent said when he approached. "I need to speak with Tayven."

Tayven visibly flinched. In truth, he scared many people just by being around. The fact Vincent came all this way to specifically speak with someone was even more terrifying.

"Tayven, we might want to have this discussion away from prying eyes and open ears."

"Master Vincent, my party is trustworthy. Whatever you wish to say to me, you may do so in front of them as well."

Tayven nerves were palpable and now was not a good time for him to be alone. His statement also carried risk, as Vincent's message could be something private or knowledge that could put the lives of his friends in danger. He glanced at his party, who all gave him supportive looks.

"So be it. It'll work out that you kept your friends by your side..." Vincent sighed and handed the boy three different letters. "Tayven, I have three different messages for you. The first is that your father has formally disinherited you from the Nefera household. From this moment forth, you are to cease using the Nefera family name when interacting with others. Second, your biological father, Lord Erich Nefera, was summoned to the castle a few days ago and tried for treason."

"Treason?" Tayven shouted. He had remained calm about his disinheritance, as it was something he expected.

Rune had learned that Tayven had never expected to be more than a knight if he stayed on the path of nobility, but he gave that up for a chance at the Vanguard. No longer being a noble was not that big of a deal in the grand scheme of things for the young man. Likely, it would have served as little more than a headache.

"He was convicted that same day and executed by beheading. As per Faradin law, his body and head will be held on display outside the prison as a warning for such behavior," Vincent continued without addressing Tayven's outburst. "Finally, Lord Dethras Jelmoore requests that you visit his estate upon your return to the Academy. He also provided a letter to you that is for your eyes only."

Vincent handed Tayven a letter with House Jelmoore's seal adorning it. The young man took the document, but said nothing. Brick put his hand on one of Tayven's shoulders and Ven put her hand on the other. Rune and Teryn did not know him as well and chose not to do much of anything other than remain present.

"Why was he tried for treason? All my father wanted was peace and to stand up for the southerners and Volari."

"I know, Tayven. Tensions between the south and north have risen too high. The flames of discontent have been fanned too intensely. King Leonidas recently approved the formation of a Holy Knight Order under the leadership of the Crucidian Church. Likely, this was his way of threatening the southern nobles with a new power, separate from the northerners, but it did little to change anything. I, and many others, believe he executed your father, charging him with the crime of inciting noble houses to rebellion, to give the southern houses a chance to...atone without losing status or risking criminal trials.

"The southerners will take that offer of atonement, Tayven, but only temporarily. The core issues have yet to be resolved. Neither does hatred vanish under threat of violence or application of fear, it only grows. Quietly at first, but eventually, it will burst and with it, war will follow. I'm sorry." Vincent bowed. "Listen to me prattling on about politics when you lost your father. I will give you a moment with your friends. Oh, your brothers are safe. So don't worry about them. An old friend is keeping them somewhere the even the kingdom's men dare not go."

Vincent walked away, Vickar reluctantly following him. Once they were out of sight, Tayven turned around to the group.

"What do you want to do?" Brick asked. Ven, Rune, and Teryn all stared at Tayven, whose world had just shattered.

Despite everything, his face was unchanged. He neither quaked nor quivered. With a resolute tone, he spoke. "I will meet with Lord Jelmoore. Then I will train. As much as I wish to avenge my father, he disinherited me for a purpose. He wished to save my life and give me a way to live separate from his world. I will continue to fight as a member of the Vanguard. Will you all do that with me?"

Ven smiled. "Of course. You are the party leader, so we have to go along with what you say."

Brick laughed and answered with a thumbs up. Teryn eyed Rune with an inquisitive look. She had known the whole truth for a while, but it seemed now everyone else did, too. Rune locked eyes with Tayven, his eyes filled with understanding and support.

Tayven spoke. "I know what you have gone through, Rune. Your family told us about your friend. Learning something like that... I don't know how I would handle it. So, please, do whatever you need to do."

Rune paused. Here he was being babied by someone who had just lost everything. Yet Tayven held firm to his beliefs and dreams. He made a choice to move forward despite what happened. Rune thought back to his own journey. When had he stood as firm and resolute as Tayven did now? When had he chosen to move forward despite struggles?

The memories that returned to him felt pathetic. The only choice he had made was to join the Vanguard. After that, he had fought and survived, but that was not enough. There was no way that he could ever rise to the peaks of the Vanguard that way. He needed resolve; action.

"I once made a promise to my friend. I promised I would become stronger; one of the strongest." There, among a gently falling snow, Rune made a new promise. He clenched his fist and took in a sharp breath. Purple light flashed around his body, as if his power acknowledged his new truth. "I haven't done that yet. You have my blade."

Afterword

To the readers,

Thank you so very much for reading my first-ever published book. If you enjoyed this novel and want to know what our lovely cast of warriors are up to next, have no fears. They will return again. Runes adventures are not over and his saga will continue.

Acknowledgements

Thank you, everyone who joined me on this journey. Every alpha and beta reader helped polish this story into something that can be shared. Looking at you: Lee (YG), Freezing, Leah, Faith, Kris, Sam, Conor, and many more.

A special thank you to my lovely friend and editor Nichole Aaron (Dark-Elven6, 'Elfie') who worked closely with me and continually helps me learn to become a better writer. I promise to TRY to get better at ellipses...

Also thank you to the final editor and proofreader Vicky Skinner. Working with you was an absolute pleasure and you are an amazing proofreader.

About the author

Verity Rose grew up in a blink-and-you'll-miss-it Indiana town where the school library doubled as an escape hatch. She wrote her first fantasy scenes at thirteen, lost the thread for a while, wrestling with undiagnosed ADHD and mental-health potholes. She rediscovered her voice after becoming a mom and stumbling into a gaggle of online book nerds who egged her on. Armed with a social-work degree from Ball State and a lifelong conviction that characters are as real as the hands on the keyboard, she now pours that people-first empathy into stories that refuse to stay quiet.

When she isn't tormenting her characters, Verity is probably reverse-engineering a Korean street-food recipe, sourcing single-origin coffee beans from ethical roasters, or hoarding trash in Dragon Age or Skyrim. Her literary inspiration is equal parts Rick Riordan's mythic swagger, Suzanne Collins' high-stakes heart, and John Flanagan's cozy camaraderie.

Verity is raising her family (and her caffeine tolerance) amid Indiana cornfields with the hopes to move to Oregon. Say hi on Instagram @veerozeauthor or on Bluesky @verityroze.bsky.social—she's always down to swap book recs, coffee tips, or preferred RPG builds.